Euphoria

Claire
Highton-Stevenson

Copyright © 2024 Claire Highton-Stevenson
All rights reserved.
ISBN: 9798879844276
Editor-Crystal Wren
Proofreader-Michelle Arnold
Cover Design-May Dawney
This is a work of fiction. Names, characters, businesses, places, events, locales, and incidents are either the products of the author's imagination or used in a fictitious manner. Any resemblance to actual persons, living or dead, or actual events is purely coincidental.

Dedication

To all the staff at Costa Coffee, Havant.

Without whom I would be a very miserable author

Dedication

Acknowledgments

My furry baby, Tumble.

Thanks for not dying when they said you might.

I need all of those snuggles and scratches and the constant meowing for brushes and treats.

approach into the editing process.

Chapter One

The last days of May

There was not much in life that Alexandra Montgomery hadn't experienced in her forty-six years spinning around on this planet, but there was certainly a lot she was missing.

Standing by the graveside between her brothers and her mother, she glanced down the line at their wives and the children behind them. Even her mother had her dad's brother by her side. She wished she had that special someone, too.

That certain someone who would be reaching for her hand right now and squeezing her fingertips. Someone who would lead her away once the coffin was lowered and shield her from the media circus that was gathering, wanting their piece of her.

But she was a fool for even thinking it, wasn't she? Sometimes, she wondered if it was the transaction she'd unknowingly paid. When the tour bus she'd been on all those years ago had crashed and her bandmates either killed or horrifically injured, she'd just walked away unblemished. Physically, at least.

Of course, she knew logically that was because she was the only one of them strapped in and wearing a seatbelt, but still, she wondered sometimes if there was an element of getting away with it, and she'd been forced to suffer in other ways instead. There had been a mental cost, hadn't there? Nobody ever asked about that.

Not that there hadn't been women in her life, there had been plenty over the years, but nobody who had stayed. And she couldn't blame them, not really. The life she'd been leading didn't really fit with most women. Women who wanted to show her off, walk out into the world holding her hand. And she wanted that too, wanted it more than anything, but the trade-off was the intrusion of the press, always wanting their pound of flesh.

Like today, at her father's funeral, there they all were crowding around every available space to snap long lens photos of her in her grief. Well, she wouldn't give them that. No, they could fuck off if they thought she was going to let them print pictures of her falling apart.

Standing there stoically, she kept her head down, face hidden below the over-sized hat and sunglasses.

"Alright?" Her brother Anton nudged her.

"Yes," she agreed, furtively glancing at him. "I just want to be anywhere but under this spotlight."

Their mother hushed them.

"Sorry, Mama," Alexandra said quietly, checking her watch.

Her mother turned to her, the same eyes and cheekbones staring back at her, damp with tears that would fall at any moment. "You have somewhere else to be, Sasha?" she asked, using Alexandra's nickname, her accent still heavy even after all these years away from her homeland.

The former Russian ballerina who defected to the West when she fell in love with an English businessman working in Moscow had never lost her love for her country. All three children bore Russian names and spoke the language perfectly. She wouldn't have had that any other way.

"No, Mama," Alexandra replied quickly. The last thing she wanted to do today was upset her mother. Her mother was fierce at the best of times, loving in her own unique way, but certainly not someone to have upset with you.

"As I thought." Natalia reached out a hand to cup her daughter's cheek, gently wiping away the tear that slowly slid and rested upon her cheek. Then she turned back to hear the priest speaking, and Alex was alone with her thoughts once more.

"Ashes to ashes, dust to dust…"

Alexandra closed her eyes, tried to think of herself anywhere but here. Fragments of images flashed and slipped away: on stage, the lights blinding her from seeing the audience, the music taking her somewhere else. In bed with a beautiful woman. Anywhere but here, but it was impossible.

The soft touch of a hand against her arm brought her back to the world. A world where mourners were moving away, and her mother was shaking hands with the priest. Her brothers and their families lined up behind her, dutifully ready to follow her lead. It was over.

"Ready to go?" the familiar New York accent whispered from behind her. She smiled and turned to find her long-time friend, personal assistant and manager all rolled into one, smiling sombrely at her.

"Yes."

"Then let's go. Before the Tsarina has you playing for the congregation." Francine Carlson winked.

"Heaven forbid." Alex smiled.

Francine linked arms with her and pulled her in as closely as anyone had done for months. "Mike's got the car ready for our escape."

Of course, she had a chauffeur. How else would someone as famous and recognisable as she was get around when she needed to travel? Mike was a safety net, in more ways than one. Ex-military, he often acted like a pseudo bodyguard whenever she needed him, which wasn't often, thankfully. People generally didn't bother her too much; it was the press that invaded her life.

Mike, though, was a godsend. His soft voice, with its Irish lilt, was calming. He had an attention to detail, too, that worked well alongside Francine's whirlwind approach.

But primarily, he drove her anywhere she needed to be, and for that she was grateful. It wasn't like she could just jump on the bus, was it? Not that that would ever be an option.

Not since the accident.

That still haunted her, even now as Mike drove them sedately along the motorway; it was always the motorway where she felt it most. A heightened sense of awareness, the speed, every bump in the road. She breathed deeply and sat back, staring out of the window as her fingers gripped the seatbelt and pulled it tighter, her heart rate already racing faster than it should.

They were almost home, she told herself. Almost home.

Breathe in, breathe out. She remembered the mantra of one of the many therapists she'd paid over the years. Mike took the left, turning at the roundabout, and she felt her heart rate slow, her breathing more stable now they were onto the smaller residential roads that would lead down to the sea, and to where her home was waiting.

Building this house had been a dream come true, even if her neighbours had been opposed at first. The village wasn't used to new houses being built, but the space had opened up when an old building had come up for sale. It was in a sorry state and didn't need much of an argument to take it down and rebuild. But it had still been a battle with the council and the locals: the celebrity moving in on their space and causing chaos.

A glass fortress overlooking the beach was somewhat different to all of the other houses along the way, except for one that had set the precedent that allowed Sasha the in to have what she wanted.

In the summer, it was usually wonderful to open up the huge sliding doors and step outside onto the veranda before stepping onto the hot sand and striding into the sea for a swim. In the winter, it was something very different, and she liked that, she liked it a lot. In the midst of the elements, at one with nature swirling all around her. It felt like that today. Sombre and cold, but it was the middle of May.

"Do you want me to come in?" Francine asked as Mike came to a slow halt.

"No, I'll be fine. You get home to David. I'm just going to have a bath and relax for the rest of the evening." The door opened and she stepped out. "Thank you, Mike. Will you make sure Francine gets home?"

"Of course." He nodded, shifting the short blonde hair just poking out from under his hat.

She watched her driver climb back into the car and drive away, Francine already with her nose in her phone. Work never ended with that woman.

She caught her reflection in the mirror and sighed. She was starting to feel old. She mentally berated herself for how ridiculous that sounded. She was barely forty-six, in her prime according to every woman's magazine she read, so why didn't she feel it?

Her long dark hair had been impeccable this morning beneath the wide-brimmed hat that hid half of her face from the waiting photographers. They couldn't just give her today, could they? Desperately flitting around like irritated moths around a lightbulb. She sighed again and turned away from the world, withdrawing inwards towards the sanctuary of her bedroom.

Undressing, she placed the black suit into the washing bin and reached for her gown. The royal blue silk slid against her skin with ease, soft and caressing, familiar. Tying the belt, she wandered into the bathroom and twisted the tap until steaming hot water flowed downwards, splashing into the bath. She added a generous amount of bubble bath, something expensive but worth every penny, as the scent of rose-infused coconut milk filled the air. She breathed it in, remembering a visit to Kuala Lumpa the previous year. She needed a holiday now, though she wouldn't complain. She was grateful for her life; she really was. It was just…not really what she had expected all those years ago when she'd been dreaming of success, and with every passing day it was not what she wanted anymore.

Pulling her hair up into a band, she noticed the dark rings around her eyes. The blue hue looked almost grey in this light. Make-up had covered the lids earlier, but the tears and constant dabbing with a tissue had made light work of removing it. Thank god for the sunglasses; otherwise she could just imagine the photos in the papers and magazines from now until someone else's life became the talk of the media.

She tested the water and, deeming it a little too hot, she twisted the cold tap into the mix and watched as more bubbles erupted into life. A crash of thunder reverberated, and she counted like she did when she was child. One, two, three, four, a flash of lightning lit up the sky and then subsequently the room through the skylight above the bath.

At night, sometimes she would lie in the warm water with the lights off and just stare up at the stars as she touched herself and thought of one of the many women who had graced her bedsheets at one time or another. They never hung around for long. A few weeks, a few months, but eventually, they all left. And the worst thing was, she couldn't blame them.

She swirled the water again, and this time it was perfect. Shutting off the taps, she slipped from her robe and climbed in, dropping under the warm liquid blanket of foam.

No, she couldn't blame them.

It was hard to be in her life.

Chapter Two

Huge white-crested waves crashed angrily against the shore outside; she could hear them. Raindrops as big as pennies lashed the glass above with such force that she pushed back, just in case the glass shattered into a million tiny particles. Logically, she knew that couldn't happen. Each pane was toughened, able to withstand the elements, even a bullet, but as the wind howled, a little doubt crept in.

Her phone buzzed from the other room. A text or email by the sound of it; she didn't care. Whoever it was could wait. Nothing was more important today than her own well-being.

As her eyes closed and she sank further into the deep bath, her mind wandering back to all those years ago when life had been snatched from so many, and yet, she'd somehow walked away with barely a scratch on her. But she remembered it. Every second of it. She sat up quickly, water pouring over the side as she gasped for breath and tried to calm herself, but it was the noise in her head.

The unbearable screeching that seemed to echo on forever before the tone of it changed into screaming—then the silence. Just for a second, complete silence before the noise thrust back in again, deafening her screams. She'd been twenty-five, and now she was forty-six and feeling every year of it as she fought off yet another panic attack.

Five dead, one in a coma, two more with broken bones, and herself, Sasha Montgomery, walking away as though nothing had happened. Twenty plus years had passed and still it haunted her.

She was reminded more so on days like today.

Her dad dying was expected; he'd been ill for a while, but still, you're never quite ready for death's touch on your life, are you?

The fucking press, always trying to get a picture, and always somehow managing to find a way to print a picture of that bloody bus.

She felt her heart race just thinking about it.

But if the accident had taught her anything, it was that life was for living, and she'd done her best with that over the years. Exploring as much of the world as she could. Meeting people and exploring herself, spiritually and sexually.

Euphoria

Cultivating a new career away from the band she'd once loved performing with, heading behind the scenes and out of the limelight had been what she'd needed then. Writing and producing for some of the biggest-selling artists and keeping well away from prying eyes and newspaper headlines, until her manager Francine had introduced her to her now-agent, Marty Daniels, and a decade later, she'd gone out on her own.

And she'd played the game. Given the press access when needed, but it never stopped them prying and spying, trying to get the inside scoop on the one thing she wanted to remain private: her love life.

She'd had a lot of success in the UK and Europe: number-one albums, and had even had a small role in a couple of films, but acting wasn't for her in the long run. She loved performing her music. Moving away from the pop scene of her youth into classical had been the making of her. Marty had been right about that. She'd scored an opera alongside one of the world's most renowned tenors. Composed film scores and theme tunes, and in five years she had turned herself into one of the most familiar household names in the country, if not the world. So why didn't it feel enough?

Many in the world of show business knew Alexandra Montgomery, but the world knew her as Sasha, the lucky one. Solar Flare's fortunate one. The one who escaped unharmed. And she agreed; she was fortunate. Her career had soared, unlike every other surviving member of the band who had drifted off into obscurity. She was destined for this life. She'd known that since she was a child, pushed by her mother towards greatness. Now though, there were far more moments when she envied them all and their quiet, private lives.

But lucky?

She wasn't so sure.

A lifetime of panic attacks had been her curse. Untimely, unavoidable, and frightening, she'd done her best to keep her condition quiet; she didn't want the sympathy or the intrusion the press would bring, rehashing it all in the papers again.

That was not something she wanted to deal with ever again.

Picking up her phone, she opened it to reveal a text message from a number she didn't recognise.

Unknown Number: Did you get it?

Alexandra rubbed her forehead. *Who was this?* There were only a select few people who had this number. Any press-related problems, work concerns etc. all went via Francine Carlson, a loud American who got things done, didn't bother *Sasha* every two minutes, and was more loyal than a Basset hound. Technically her manager, but pretty much her personal assistant and best friend all rolled into one. Without her, Alex would be lost. She knew that much. There had been many times in her career when she'd have been spiralling out of control without Francine there to hold it all together. So, it wouldn't be a leak from her.

Maybe it was a journalist, who had somehow bribed someone into giving them the number and was now trying to get a reaction from her. Well, she wasn't falling for it. Deleting the texts, she put the phone down and went to make a coffee. More thunder shuddered above the house, making her jump a little, and her eyes were drawn back out through the nearest window to a stormy sea. This was summer on the English south coast, and tomorrow it would be sunshine and heat, but not today.

"Alexa, play something from my soothing playlist," she said aloud for the smart speaker to pick up.

"Alright, playing 'Moonlight Sonata…'" The words drifted away, and soon enough the gentle and arpeggiated movement from Beethoven began to fill all of the rooms. An inbuilt speaker system broadcast music to every corner of her home, or any number of them depending on how she set it up. Only when she had guests staying did she limit it. She closed her eyes and let herself enjoy the soothing melody while the fancy new coffee maker brewed her a drink.

By the time she picked up her phone again, there were several more messages.

Unknown Number: Have I upset you?

Unknown Number: This isn't funny!

Unknown Number: Why aren't you replying, it's worrying me.

"For god's sake," Alex muttered to herself, hitting the reply button. Patience was not a virtue she'd been blessed with, especially with people, but politeness was instilled like a tattoo.

Alex: Sorry, I think you have the wrong number.

She hit send and thought nothing more of it. The message was clear; the other person would realise what they had done, and no more unknown number texts would arrive.

Buzz.

Unknown Number: Oh, very funny. You're just going to bin me off?

Alex: Yes because, I've no idea who you are!

Unknown Number: That is the rudest thing I've ever heard.

Alex: I'm sure it isn't, and yet, it still remains the same response.

She should put the phone down; that was the best solution. Just block the number and forget about it, but she didn't. And she had no idea why; only a deep sense of awareness that she shouldn't. An intuition she had learned to rely on, one that had kept her alive and uninjured when it told her to put her seatbelt on all those years ago.

Unknown Number: Who is this?

Alex: I thought you knew who it was?

Unknown Number: Why are you being like this? I thought we had something meaningful the other night.

Oh, it was a love interest. Well, that put a very different spin on it, didn't it? She suddenly felt sorry for...her. She was positive it was a woman. A man wouldn't be so upset, they'd be obnoxious and probably just call, so she was pretty sure it was a woman, and she felt badly for her.

Hadn't we all been there?

Alex: Look, I don't know who you're trying to connect with, but I assure you, I am not them.

Unknown Number: You're serious? I can't believe it. She gave me someone else's number? You're not Jeri?

A her, hoping for a she. Well, that did sound more interesting. Jesus, how dull was her love life lately that living vicariously via an unknown person and a wrong number was now the highlight of her day?

Alex: I guess so, I'm sorry, but no, I am not Jeri. She sounds like a delight (Not) and you're better off without her.

Unknown Number: I guess it's me that should be sorry, pestering you all afternoon. Just my luck.

Alex: I know the feeling. Don't worry about it. I'm sure someone just as lovely will come along again soon.

What on earth had she said that for, and more's the point, why was she continuing this conversation? She had things to do, like stare out of the window and watch the storm as it raced across the channel. Or get on with composing her next album, or a multitude of other things.

Unknown Number: I'm not so sure she is lovely, now. And I really am getting past the point of hoping I'll ever meet anyone lovely again. Everyone is so selfish now, don't you think?

Alexandra knew that feeling way too much. Her last serious relationship, if you could call it that, had been over a year ago. A woman she'd met at a concert. Alex had been the guest of Hans Von Speltz, a revered and most talented pianist himself. His shows in Amsterdam had been magnificent, and Laurel had been spellbound by him. They'd met up back in London and gone out a few times before Laurel decided that she thought the spark would be there by now, and for her, it wasn't.

If Alex was honest, she had been a little smitten, and a little unsure why Laurel wasn't feeling it because she certainly acted like she was. In fact, Laurel had been quite agreeable to the many things Alex introduced her to, parties and people, especially things in the bedroom, so it was a bit of a letdown to suddenly be single again.

But Alex had taken it on the chin and gotten over it like a grown-up. She didn't want to get involved with anyone who didn't know how they felt about her. There had been plenty of those situationships in her time, and she wasn't looking for that.

Now though, she felt ready for some romance, real romance. The heated, exciting, pulse-racing kind, but romance didn't seem ready for her right now. And in the event that she did meet someone, asking them to be somewhat closeted, to avoid the headlines and keep secrets, wasn't what most out women were looking for, was it?

Alex: I get that, it can be quite difficult. Sometimes all we have is hope, and music, we always have music.

All she had was music, more like.

A musical prodigy as a child, she'd spent all of her youth learning to play the piano. Using her family's nickname, Sasha, she joined Solar Flare, the biggest rebellious thing she could have done to step out on her own and away from her mother's control where her music was concerned. It had been fun to be hanging out with people her age, travelling, and performing and finding themselves in the process.

But the pressure of that, to be seen, to be who the media wanted them to be, had been hard. She could never have been like Lucy, and just done it anyway. Instead, Alex just didn't date. It was easier than pretending to like boys. Chris had been the same. Sometimes they let the press think they were an item, but it was never the case.

It was funny, how Chris was the only one she was still in touch with now, her pseudo-boyfriend from twenty years ago. Lucy had disappeared. Unable to cope with the scars and the loss of Nicky, the last Alex had heard, Lucy had taken herself off to America and got lost in the woods somewhere. Jenna had pretty much done the same, just closed the door on that part of her life, changed her name, changed her number, and moved. Their agent at the time didn't know where she was, but a few years later one of the big music mags had done a five-year anniversary piece. She'd grimaced at that, and refused to take part, but it hadn't stopped them printing photos and stories about where they all were now. All except for Lucy of course, but Jenna was married, a mum to two small kids and living somewhere north of London with her stockbroker husband. The photos they used had clearly been taken surreptitiously and without Jenna's permission, but they at least blanked out the faces of her kids. Sasha was happy for her but didn't try to get in touch.

After the crash, everything changed. She came out to her family, the press got wind and it was exciting headlines for a few weeks before they moved on to someone else's love life. She'd grabbed life by the scruff of its neck and had been like a kid in a sweet shop for a while, but nobody cared anymore about the keyboard player from a group that didn't exist and had been forgotten about.

A change of hairstyle and nobody recognised her, moving from one woman's bed to the next without any hassle. Until finally, she was forced into therapy to deal with the aftermath of the survivor's guilt that she carried and realised that bedhopping had been a way to numb the pain, to release endorphins that made her happy and kept her busy enough that she didn't think about the crash.

That had helped somewhat with lessening the panic attacks. Time and healing had given her tools to deal with them on the whole, but feeling stressed and overwhelmed always gave them the opportunity to rear their ugly head. An upcoming tour would definitely push her limits.

God, did she really want to bring a new lover into her life to deal with this?

Unknown Number: Music certainly helps. God, I can't believe I've been ghosted. Typical of my luck, I guess. Thanks for being so understanding.

Alex: I know what it's like. I'm sorry things didn't work out for you. And it's been no problem actually, it was kind of nice to break up the silence of the day.

Unknown number: Well, you have my number, if you're ever in need of a silence breaker.

Alexandra shook her head and put the phone down, her attention turning to the piano that took centre stage in the living room. She sat on the stool and lifted the lid that covered the keys.

"Alexa, off." The sound system shut down and the room was silent again, bar the noise of the wind rattling outside. Her fingers touched the keys like a lover would touch a cheek, gently and curious, before they began to glide up and down, hitting the notes perfectly as the music gradually increased to an impending crescendo. She felt every part of it seep into her soul and energise her.

Chapter Three

The beginning of July.

For several days, Alex lost herself in the music. Hours on the stool inspired by the summer storms that kept rolling in and passing through, but now, the sunshine had returned. She'd barely eaten, barely slept, but something was missing, and she was frustrated when she couldn't quite put her finger on it and find the solution. Everything just sounded so dreary.

Sultry nights that made sleeping difficult had rolled into hot, humid mornings. The sea was calm, reflective but for where it gently lapped the shore in the distance. The tide was on its way in, and the beach was relatively quiet still; she made a decision.

Stripping down and into her bikini, Alex wandered through the patio doors, across the decking before stepping down onto the sand and pebbles that battled for dominance. She walked until her toes were kissed by cool water and began to sink into the wet sand that had won out on this strip.

These were the moments she loved living here the most, before the tourists made their way down and set up for the day with towels and windbreakers spoiling the view. Only a few eager sunbathers had set up already, and they barely paid her any attention, which was nice. It was one thing being asked for autographs and photos when she was working, but at home, she just wanted that privacy.

The water was cold as it hit her knees and splashed up her bare thighs. She'd yelped and jumped back, laughing at herself when she got deep enough for it to reach her stomach, but once she was settled again, she took the plunge and dropped down into it until all that was visible was her head. Hair piled high on top of her head, she floated like a giant sea sponge.

As her body got used to the temperature, she began to swim, enjoying the movement of the small waves as she rose and fell along with them. It reminded her of the way music moved, each wave rising to a gentle crescendo and then falling away with a diminuendo only to start again in a riff that kept you hooked until it was time to bring in the conclusion in the form of a coda.

She flipped over onto her back and watched the blue sky and the one fluffy white cloud that was passing through. Maybe she should just retire now and enjoy this every day, she mused, because she could quite easily do that. Music would always be important to her, but she didn't really need the money. She could just quietly disappear from the public forum and live out the rest of her life on the beach if everything went to plan.

That would be a life someone might want to join her in, wouldn't it?

Rolling over again, she swam back to shore, standing when her feet touched the sand once more. Francine was coming by, and they had some things to go over before she went on a short tour of English cathedrals. She was looking forward to that in a professional sense. The sound in those buildings would be magical, and an experience she knew would send her senses into a hyper state.

Picking up her towel, she stood on the deck and looked out. More sunseekers had arrived and were setting up for the day. She was just grateful that the roads around here were no parking, and her house was gated on the roadside. It was a nightmare getting in and out of the village at times, which was why she didn't bother, preferring to stay indoors and enjoy her surroundings without the need to venture out and deal with the issues fame brought with it. It was the payoff, of course; fame provided all of the luxuries she enjoyed, and she would pay her dues when needed to.

Sometimes though, the urge to go out and enjoy the world in a different way would win out, and often, she'd pull on a disguise and just wander the streets and bars as invisibly as she could. It always surprised her that barely anyone recognised her if she didn't look the part. Not expecting to meet a celebrity, their brain didn't put it together. Often, she would get, *you remind me of someone* or *you look like that woman who plays piano*. She'd just smile and say, *yeah, I get that a lot.*

When she was dry enough, she wandered back inside and picked up her phone. She hadn't deleted the texts from the stranger, and as she re-read them, she wondered how she was doing.

Was she that lonely that a mystery stranger's love life was so interesting? Probably, she chuckled to herself. Stepping into her bedroom, she peeled away the damp bikini and hung it off the towel heater in the bathroom. Naked, she felt the chill and quickly headed into the shower. Hot water pounding down on her was what she needed as she thought about her day so far.

If she were honest, she'd actually enjoyed the conversation with her unknown friend. The anonymity provided a shield where she could talk about herself without the need to always think about every single word in case it was repeated, or worse, sold to a magazine. She hadn't had that kind of friend since she was a teenager.

Maybe she needed to broaden her horizons where friends were concerned. Go out and meet new people. After all, she was using an anonymous missed call as her newest confidante; that wasn't normal, was it?

By the time Francine arrived, looking like her very own copy of Meryl Streep in *The Devil Wears Prada*, Alex was at least clean and presentable. She sat on the stool to her piano, going over a piece she'd written recently but wasn't satisfied with, while Francine moved around the room, unable to sit still.

"I've organised all of the hotel accommodation. Suites in all but one, although they have said that the moment anything becomes free you will be moved to it. And yes, I was polite about it, but I made it very clear that Sasha Montgomery only stays at the very best hotels." Francine was rambling as she moved around the room, running her hand through her hair occasionally, before she'd stop and stare at Alex to make sure she was paying attention.

By organising, she meant she had dealt with the relevant people who would organise it all for her, but Alex didn't correct her.

Alex wasn't sure that she cared much about the very best hotels. She just wanted some space and for it to be clean. She also wondered if Francine would ever say her stage name without the added R she seemed to always put in it. Sarshar seemed so…she heard her dad's voice in her head. *'It's poncy, why can't she speak like normal people.'*

"Okay," was all she said in response, not that Francine seemed to notice because she was soon off again.

"And Exeter are being a little prissy about how many speakers we can have. I told them, listen, you want Sasha, you need to get with the program." New York born and bred, Francine had a way with words and making you feel like you'd been naughty and were one step away from being made to sit in the corner and face the wall. "You know what he said?"

"No."

"He said, sure, whatever you need. You know why?"

"No."

"Because he knows losing you is gonna hit his little world like a nuclear reactor exploding, that's why." Francine used her hands dramatically to enforce the point.

Alex wasn't sure that was the case, but she wasn't about to disagree and have Francine launch into a diatribe of why she should have more faith in herself. She needed a drink, something sparkling and alcoholic but she couldn't, not right now, not while she was readying for the tour. She needed a clear head at all times, otherwise, Francine really would take over.

Her phone buzzed on the countertop, and she reached for it while Francine took a call. The screen was dark. She tapped it to life, and she groaned internally. Why did she always seem to text whenever Alex had been thinking about her love life? It was like she had some inbuilt sensor that picked up on lonely thoughts and homed in.

Laurel: Hey, how are you?

Alexandra typed as she watched Francine push open the patio doors and step out onto the deck.

Alex: What do you want, Laurel?

Francine looked anything but calm as she animatedly told the person on the other end of the call something that, from this distance, looked like it might get violent. Those hand gesticulations told a story all of their own.

Laurel: Hey, nothing, I was just checking in, haven't spoken to you in a while. You okay?

Alex: There's a reason for that, Laurel.

Heading back in, Francine looked murderous and, for some reason, Alex felt like a naughty kid being caught doing something she shouldn't be. She squeezed her phone into her pocket and felt it vibrate against her hip.

"Cecil had better get his act together," Francine yelled. In England, it was a yell. In New York, Alex wasn't sure it was much more than a whisper, but to her delicate eardrum, it was loud. She dropped her hands to her sides and grimaced. "They want a tour bus."

Just the words "tour" and "bus" were enough to send Alex into a spin of hyperventilation.

"I told him, Cecil, you're a prick, there ain't no way."

Alex felt her throat tighten and the panic that rose through her must have looked bad because it startled Francine and she instantly moved into action.

"Okay, honey, just breathe. What's happening?"

"Don't…know…" Alex gasped, her fist pressing against the pain in her chest. She'd never had chest pain with a panic attack before. "Hurts."

"Okay, no need to panic, we're going to…" She checked around for her bag, one hand grabbing Alexandra's elbow as she dragged her towards the door. "Come on, let's get you checked out."

"No, I'll be…"

Francine gave her that look again, the one that said she was one word away from sitting on the naughty step. "Come on, we need you fit as a fiddle for this tour."

Chapter Four

The urgent treatment centre, thankfully, wasn't too far away. Though with Francine's driving, Alex was sure she was lucky to only be having a heart attack. It was funny how being in a car didn't have the same effect as a bus, any bus. She couldn't use public transport or take a trip if it meant getting into a coach. And no amount of therapy made any difference.

"You alright?" Francine asked, glancing towards her as they neared a hairpin bend. Her face was white as a sheet, and Francine was beginning to panic herself.

"If you'd concentrate, I'd be—shit, Francine!" Alex gasped for breath, clutching her chest again. Why today? When Mike was off.

The car jerked around the bend, skidding its back wheels out. Why hadn't they called Mike? He'd have come in if he could.

"Sorry, I'm just…you look like you're having a heart attack." Francine's face was also white as a sheet, which didn't help quell the panic already bursting from Alex's chest.

"I'm sure it's just a…panic…" Alex grabbed at her chest, her heart pounding in her ears. "Please slow…down."

"It might be a heart attack."

"Not…help-ing."

By the time they finally got there and parked the car, the pain in Alex's chest had subsided, but her heart felt like it would beat a prestissimo right out of her chest. The car door wrenched open, and Francine leaned in, unclipped her seatbelt and all but dragged her from the car and into the small accident and emergency department. A baseball cap was pulled from one of the numerous places they were stashed and shoved onto her head, and not for the first time, Alex was grateful to have a Francine. Alex wasn't incapable. She didn't do anything she didn't want to do. She could put someone in their place if she needed to, but letting Francine take that responsibility on day-to-day things and emergencies was a blessing.

They marched up to the desk where a young woman smiled warmly at them; Alex tried to remain as anonymous as she could, which on the whole was usually okay. People didn't expect to see musicians at their local hospital.

Completely unaware that a celebrity was standing at the desk, the woman said bluntly, "Hold on a minute, I'll be right with—"

"She's having a heart attack," Francine whispered, cutting her off. "But we need a little privacy, you know? Otherwise, word gets out and you'll have all manner of the paparazzi here."

"Not a…heart attack," Alex managed, but it was no good; the wheels were in motion the moment she looked at the woman.

The woman's eyes searched Francine's face before moving across to look at Alex, eyes widening as she finally recognised the face in front of her hidden under the brim of a New York Jets hat.

"Uh, give me…I just need to…hold on." She stood and rushed through a door behind her and out of sight.

"Give me strength," Francine said to the polystyrene tiles above her head.

Barely a moment had gone by when a side door opened and the woman from before popped her head out and beckoned them over. "Follow me."

She led the way, with Francine following, still holding onto Alex for dear life. They rounded a corner and were shown into a small anteroom. There was a bed for the patient and a chair for anyone with them.

"The doctor will be right with you."

"Thank you…" Alex managed, waiting for the girl to say her name.

"It's Liz, I'm a huge fan by the way."

Alex grimaced as much of a smile as she could muster and sat gingerly on the edge of the bed. Francine reached into her bag and pulled out a photo, already signed, and handed it to Liz.

"Here you go, Sasha appreciates her fans." Then she leaned in and said to the woman, "And her privacy."

"Thank you," Liz gushed, staring at the image as Francine herded her out of the room.

It was a surreal moment, one Alex hadn't endured for a long time. She'd avoided hospitals as much as she could over the years. It was the smell that was unique and the first thing she always noticed whenever she set foot in one. It brought with it flashes of memory.

The night that changed everything.

When she had just sat there watching, as everyone she knew was wheeled past, injured, dead, or dying.

Her heart began to pound again, and she gasped for breaths, fingertips clutching at the edge of the bed. Telling herself to relax didn't work. Neither did Francine's worried-looking face.

The door swung open again and a tired-looking woman in her thirties, wearing the expected blue scrubs, calmly walked in. Curly chestnut hair was piled high on her head in a messy bun that looked as though it were trying to escape, and she wore no make-up other than a pale lipstick. She looked serious and busy, very busy, and Alex felt guilty for wasting her time.

"Dr Morgan Kelly. What's the problem today?" she said quickly, glancing at Francine before her attention turned fully towards Alex, who was gulping air and looking as terrified as anyone she had seen that week. "Alright, I see we are having some trouble." She moved quickly and dropped down to her haunches, staring up into Alex's eyes.

"I can't…breathe," Alex managed.

There was something kind about her eyes. They were *captivating*, Alex would remember later. As dark as her hair, brooding, a little sultry. If her heart hadn't already been pounding, Dr Kelly's appearance might have done the trick for Alexandra Montgomery.

"I can see." The smile again was disarming. "So, let's see if we can manage that a little better and find out what the cause is." She adjusted the bed by lifting one end until it locked into place. "Can you swing round and lie back? Concentrate on my voice and focus on the words as much as you can."

Alex nodded, still a little unsure as she swung her legs up, twisting at the hip until she was able to lie back but remain almost sitting up.

"Perfect, you've done that before." Dr Kelly continued to smile down at her. "Okay, I want you to look up, look down, look left and right." She repeated the instruction three times before Alex realised that she was breathing almost normally again. "Now, deep breath in through your nose, and out through the mouth, in…and out."

As her lungs began to function again, Alex focused more on the doctor. She was younger, by a decade or more maybe. She was stunning actually, natural, and just…stunning.

"Better?" Dr Kelly's voice brought Alex back from wherever her mind had just taken her. Somewhere this woman might be part of.

"Yes, thank you." Alex stared, a little in awe at how quickly she'd been put at ease.

"So, can you tell me what triggered this event?"

Francine's voice eased back into her consciousness.

"We were just talking, and she clutched at her chest. Been in real pain the entire way here," Francine explained when Alex remained silent. "I thought she was having a heart attack."

"Alright, let's have a listen then, huh? Just to be sure." Dr Kelly raised her hand to reveal the end of her stethoscope to Alex. "Can you just unbutton your shirt for me?"

Alex felt her body react to the words, something sexual and intimate hitting her harder in the chest than any pain earlier had. Maybe it was just her brain's way of switching focus, away from the panic and onto something more manageable, more interesting. Like the bedhopping scenario of her past, an instant sexual intrusion to remove having to worry about what was actually going on.

"Sure." Slowly, her deft fingers unbuttoned the white cotton shirt all the way down to her navel, not once looking away from those eyes that were definitely having an effect on her, and definitely not looking away either.

There was something knowing in the way Dr Kelly's smile slowly spread across her face once more, but this time, there was a hint of a smirk twisting the corner of one side of her mouth upwards. There was a spark between them, and both recognised it. Slowly, Dr Kelly licked her lips before she asked her next question.

"Can you describe what it was you were talking about or doing just before this event?" She put one end of the stethoscope to her ears and pressed the instrument to Alex's chest. When Alex gasped at the coldness touching her hot skin, Dr Kelly chuckled. "A little cold, I'm sorry."

Alex smiled and closed her eyes. The thought of explaining everything meant her breathing sped up again. "I…the bus…we were organising the tour and—"

"She was in a crash, years ago. Solar Flare?" Francine jumped into explain when it became evident that Alex explaining was making it worse again. "The band?"

Dr Kelly narrowed her eyes. "I'm sorry, I'm not up to date on—"

"It was a long time ago," Alex managed to say, feeling embarrassed. Clearly, it was before Dr Kelly's time, which made her definitely too young for the kind of thoughts Alex was trying not to have.

The doctor pressed the end of the stethoscope to Alex's chest again, the other end hooked back into her ears, and listened once more. "Take a deep breath for me….and exhale…" When she was done, she asked, "Can you show me where the pain was?"

"It was like a stabbing pain," Alex said, poking her chest, "right here." Calmer now, she wondered if it had just run its course or whether this woman really did affect her that easily. "It's gone now."

Francine jumped back in. "That dick Cecil is insisting we use a tour bus, I was explaining, and then this happened." She waved her hand around to indicate Alex.

Morgan placed the stethoscope back around her neck. "You can button up." She pulled a stool over and sat down. "I think what you have had is a severe anxiety attack, but just to be sure, I'm going to organise an ECG of your heart and have a specialist from the Cardiology department in the hospital come down and take a look. It might be a while, though."

"That's great, thanks so much," Francine threw in, but neither woman turned her way, their eyes firmly locked on one another. "And can we keep it off the record?"

Dr Kelly sighed and stood up. "A medical episode needs to be noted, no matter who it is. It could be vital information if there were a next time."

Francine huffed but nodded obediently; she couldn't control everything.

"Thank you," Alex said, enjoying the smile that continued to cause a reaction within. *She's too young*, she reminded herself, *and you're having a panic attack.*

"Any time." Dr Kelly jotted down a few things before she said, "Okay, I'll get that all arranged, you wait here. Good luck."

And then she was gone, and Alex felt the unease creep back in. Those feelings of her life spiralling out of control again.

An unease that was well founded when twenty minutes later, the very person in the entire world that Alexandra would have hoped to avoid, strolled in like Alex owed her a favour for just turning up.

"Alexandra Montgomery," the icy voice said loudly as the body owning it sauntered into the room and the temperature dropped instantly.

Calista Urquhart was the friend of a friend, who had been set up on a blind date with Sasha and hadn't quite clicked with Alex. It hadn't gone well. They'd barely managed two dates before Alex had called time on it.

On the surface, they were very well matched, both accomplished in their field. Calista was beautiful, tall and blonde. She could have been an actress or a model, as she moved through the world so confident and desirable to everyone who didn't dare touch.

They were both high-earning and successful, available with no hang-ups on ex-partners, and on the outside, on paper, she should have been a perfect fit. Despite Alex's inclination towards successful, confident women she could reduce to a whimpering, pleading puddle of submission, she also needed to like and respect them. And witnessing Calista speak to people she considered subordinates left Alex cold and with no desire to continue. Much to Calista's chagrin.

"When they said it was you, I was in half a mind to pass it onto someone else, rather than come down from my important work in the cardio department." Calista's unwavering glare made Alex feel uncomfortable given the circumstances. "However, I am a professional, and we can't have Britain's favourite composer dying on my watch, can we?"

Dying?

"Dying?" Francine voiced Alex's thought.

Calista turned to her and cackled. "Oh, I'm sure she's not. I'm not sure who this Dr Kelly is to be diagnosing anything. But she does at least know her arse from her elbow, and the diagnosis is most likely correct, but we need to be sure of that, don't we?"

Francine dipped her head, turning to Alex, and giving her the *who the fuck is this* look. Alex squirmed a little more under the intensity of both women. God, why was her life never simple?

She spent the best part of the day being put through test after test, most of which she thought were likely unnecessary and just Calista's way of getting back at her.

Eventually, Calista smirked at her as she passed across a pamphlet.

How to avoid a panic attack.

"Read this, rest, try and avoid buses," she said before getting up, turning her back, and leaving the room without a further word.

"You know, in the States, I'd be suing her ass right now," Francine stated.

"For being rude to someone who dumped her?" Alex asked, answering the unasked question.

Francine raised a brow. "Oh, that explains a hell of a lot. When did you date her, and how come I don't know about it?"

"It was last year when you and David took that trip to Hawaii, after Laurel. A friend of Tommy set it up, but it didn't go anywhere and was over by the time you got back, so it wasn't worth mentioning."

"In future, mention it. I would have dealt with this a whole lot differently had I known." Her mouth scrunched up as though she were chewing a wasp and looking to spit it out, keeping the venom for her own special barbed comment at a later date.

"Hm, that might be a good reason not to tell you." Alex grinned, feeling a lot better now than she did earlier. "Come on, I need to get out of here. It's creeping me out."

They left the room and wandered back along the corridor they'd come from hours earlier, only to end up back at A&E but unable to get in and find their way out. Francine was frantically waving, hoping to grab somebody's attention, but to no avail.

"It's no good. We'll have to walk round and find another exit." Alex sighed. She was exhausted with it all and just wanted to climb into her bed and forget all about today. Well, all except for Dr Kelly. She had a feeling that woman would haunt her dreams for a while – in a good way, of course.

Francine turned and was about to launch into something when she smiled over Alex's shoulder. "Dr Morgan…I don't suppose you could help a gal out?" She indicated the door. Alex turned quickly, blushing a little. Did she just have to think about the woman, and she would appear?

If only.

Morgan's eyes moved quickly to Alex and held. "I guess I could." She flashed a quick smile and reached for the ID card on her belt. Pulling it up, she held it against the keypad. "Don't tell anyone," she whispered a little conspiratorially.

"We wouldn't want to get you into trouble," Alex replied, matching her smile. She was cute. Far too young, but cute, far too cute. "And thank you again."

"You're welcome, just doing my job."

She pushed the heavy door open and walked them through the emergency ward and back out into reception where Francine left them to go and fetch the car.

"You look much better, by the way," Dr Kelly said as her eyes studied Alex's face.

"Yes, I feel good now. You were right, just a panic attack."

"There's no *just* about it. They can be really scary in the moment." Her palm wrapped around Alex's bicep and squeezed. "I'm just glad we could help."

Once more, Alex felt comforted by the touch. "You did, very much so."

The palm moved away, but Dr Kelly stepped forward just enough to say quietly, "Well, anytime I can help…you know where I am."

Alex hadn't blushed like that in a long time, but the young doctor's beautiful eyes staring at her were intoxicating. "I…"

Morgan fumbled in her pocket, pulling out a dog-eared wad of cards and plucked one from the bottom. Holding it out for Alex to take, she said, "Gimme a call if you feel panicked again." Her eyes held Alex's attention as she continued confidently, "Or just gimme a call."

"That's very kind." Alex took the card and their fingertips met fleetingly. She felt it, that little jolt of excitement that ran through her any time she met somebody who started to tick boxes. How frustrating that it should happen now. Alex laughed at herself, because she would what? Ask this young woman out? Maybe under other circumstances, but not right now.

"Dr Kelly, you're wanted in triage," a woman on reception called out, breaking the spell. This was followed by a loud car horn being blasted from outside by Francine.

"I'd better go." Morgan smiled.

"Again, thank you."

"Don't mention it," Morgan called over her shoulder.

As she turned the corner, she bumped into a colleague. Pascal grinned. "Who was that?"

"Someone who needed our help," she said, still thinking about Alex Montgomery.

"Uh huh, someone you liked."

Morgan smiled. "Yeah, someone I'd like to know better." She shrugged. "But I doubt I'll meet her again."

"You never know." He winked. "We've got a head gash in Bay Two."

"Great, let's stitch then."

The car journey home was quiet, and Francine took it much slower, allowing Alex to gather her thoughts. She hated being the centre of that kind of attention, and being in hospitals. It all creeped her out and triggered things she didn't want to think about, but she was already in a state when she got there, so none of that really mattered. Dr Kelly, on the other hand…she hadn't expected her, or the feelings she would evoke.

So, lost in thought, she barely noticed when Francine pulled the car into the drive and came to a halt.

"Right, let's get you inside."

"I'll be fine," Alex said, stepping out of the car quickly. The last thing she wanted right now was to be stuck in the house with Francine for hours. She loved the woman, couldn't be without her careerwise, and if she was honest, she was her best friend, but at home, she'd just fuss around her and drive her demented.

"I don't like it. I think I should stay."

"Franny, I love you, but no. I'll be fine. You can call me in the morning. I'm alright. I just want to chill on the decking, watch the sunset and then go to bed. Go spend some time with David; god knows that man barely sees you as it is."

Francine huffed, and for a moment, Alex wondered what a full-on Francine tantrum might look like, not that she would ever witness such a thing. Francine got things done. She didn't throw a strop over things not going her way; just deviated until she found the right path.

"Fine, I'll call in the morning."

Alex watched as she got back into the car, took eight turns to finally spin it around and drove off. Sand from the beach that had blown in and covered the road blew up in a dusty cloud. She stood there for a moment, the red lights of the car getting brighter in the distance as Francine applied the brakes to take the left turn, and then she was gone. Alexandra's world fell silent once more, except for the occasional squawking *ha ha ha* from the seagulls as they searched for morsels of food left behind by visitors.

By the time she'd showered off the stench of hospitals, gotten changed and brewed a cup of chamomile tea, she remembered that she hadn't had her phone with her all day. Searching the house, she found it by her bed and carried it out onto the deck, taking a seat in her favourite spot.

The swing chair was like a giant bubble of softness that she could sit in and float above the world, the gentle sway often lulling her into slumber. She watched as the sun dropped lower in the sky and spewed hues of orange, pink and red out like layers in a cake. Picking up the phone, she pressed the button that lit up the screen and saw she had a message.

Laurel: So, miss me?

Alex sighed. Wasn't this day bad enough already without her ex still bothering her?

Alex: No, and I'm not going to respond anymore, okay? You ended things a long time ago, and I'm okay with that. You don't get to just waltz back into my life when it suits you.

The reply came back almost immediately.

Laurel: Okay, but I just wanted to say that I'm sorry and I miss you. If you ever want to talk again, I'm here.

Chapter Five

July comes to an end.

Francine would be arriving any minute, and Alex wasn't really in the mood this morning, but needs must. She had said Francine could come over and check on her, hadn't she? Check on what though? It had been almost a month since the hospital visit, she couldn't still be worried about that? *But you're still worried*, a small voice in the back of her head said.

Maybe they needed a conversation on what Francine really meant.

Alex had finally managed to fall asleep around five, but the alarm going off at eight had cut short any opportunity to feel refreshed. She needed to be dressed, ready and focused. And not still be thinking about Morgan Kelly. The very reason she would need a nap later, the exact reason why she had lain awake half the night with thoughts one should definitely not be having about someone they only met once.

Gimme a call, she heard replaying in her head, and she had to admit, she was tempted to do just that, but then common sense had swept in and reminded her that it wouldn't work. Apart from being way too old for her, their lives were so far apart, it could never work. But she couldn't shake the idea completely. She'd felt so calm and relaxed around her; that was rare.

It was another beautiful day though, and Alex decided to focus on that. The sun was still warming up and had just caught the edge of the decking. Over the next eight hours, it would slowly move around until it was directly overhead, beating down its heat onto the wooden planks and anyone sitting out enjoying it. Slowly, she sipped her morning tea and watched as the early day trippers began to arrive and set up their tents and towels. Since when had sunbathing become such a production? She smiled as one of her neighbours waved at her, out on his morning constitutional.

There was a small boat bobbing about a little further out. They were out early, she mused. Maybe fishing, or diving. She couldn't see anyone in the boat.

"Hey, where the hell are you?" Francine called from inside the house. Sometimes, Alex wondered what had possessed her to give

Francine the codes and access to her home, but she smiled when the gregarious woman marched out onto the decking. "Oh, there you are, I should know by now, but hey, one day you'll surprise me." She flopped into one of the chairs that were still in the shade.

"Good morning to you, too," Alex said before lifting the cup to hide the smile on her face.

"Yeah, well, I've been awake for hours. It doesn't feel like morning anymore and I need coffee; you want another tea?" She stood up again, ready to march back inside and complain about the lack of decent coffee in the kitchen.

"No, thank you, I'm good."

"You know, I think I'm just going to buy some good coffee and hide it in your cupboard for when I'm here," Francine was saying as she sauntered onto the decking and nestled back down in the chair she had previously vacated. Alex smiled to herself at the predictable comment.

Placing her book down on the table, Alex watched a seagull swoop down and flap its wings at some smaller birds before stealing whatever it was they'd all been happily pecking at.

Sometimes, she felt like the smaller birds.

"I don't know why you complain. I spent a fortune on that machine, just for you, and all of those whatever-they-are that coffee is in these days, not to mention that I have to keep them all so I can recycle them."

Francine chuckled. "You treat me good with those pods, that I cannot deny, which is why I always go the extra mile. Cecil has given in. He's happy with Mike and hotel rooms, no fucking bus in sight, the cheapskate. I told him, Cecil, quit whining and just get it done. You know what he said?"

She leaned forward and poked the table with a perfectly manicured hand.

"Not a clue, but I think you're going to tell me."

Francine grinned. "Damn right I'm gonna tell you. He said, and I quote, 'Okay Franny, you got it, whatever Sasha wants, Sasha gets,' and I said, 'thataboy Cecil, see how easy it is when you just do what Franny asks ya?'" She sat back and lifted her cup, twisting her head to look out at sea. "Yeah, he didn't like that, but fuck him, right? Am I right?"

"Absolutely, 100% right," Alex agreed with the tiniest smirk on her lips. Francine took no prisoners, and Alex paid her handsomely for it, though she wasn't sure Eton-educated Cecil had said it quite so dramatically. She couldn't imagine having to deal with everyone the way Francine did for her. Without her P.A. life would be a series of people-pleasing events that Alex did not want to endure, or more likely, she would end up a hermit, never going anywhere.

She wasn't sure which was worse.

"So, we're starting in Winchester on the second, then we make our way west to Salisbury, then it's Exeter."

Alex placed her mug down. "So, how's this going to work?"

The tour had been planned for a year now; these were all finalising matters. Dates for shows that were sold out had been set in stone, and all Alex needed to know was how they navigated it all. Twenty-four nights away with twelve shows throughout October, which would lead nicely into the one-off Christmas TV show they would be recording in November for a Christmas Eve slot.

"It's a two-night stay at each venue. Arrive in Winchester late morning. You'll have press, sound checks, rehearsal, and the evening to relax before the following day's evening performance, and the following day, we'll be off to Salisbury. Rinse and repeat for all twelve destinations. Travel times are between two and four hours, press will be mainly local journos wanting a soundbite for a local gazette, nothing difficult. Nancy and Gert are available the entire tour. Jessie is running the crew again," Francine explained, before adding, "Twelve performances, and a cool one and a half million banked."

Alex sighed. She hated talking about money and the obscene amounts she could earn, but she didn't complain either, knowing that in the end, it was what paid for this lavish lifestyle, the houses, the car, Francine.

It was a means to an end, a way to pay the bills and never have to worry financially, and all it would take was twenty-four days and nights of her life.

"It all sounds very tiring," Alex commented.

"Of course, you're gonna need a vacation after." Francine laughed. "As glorious as this is," her hand swept from left to right across the view of the beach, "you need to actually get away somewhere. Take a break."

"I know, I just—" What did she just? Didn't want to go on holiday on her own? She turned away from the boat she was watching, her attention was back on Francine.

Mindreading, Francine said, "You don't like doing things on your own, I get it, but some of these resorts are great places to meet people. You'd never feel alone."

"Maybe. I'll think about it. Right now, I just want to relax and get ready for this tour." She sagged back in her seat.

"Great, that's my girl." Francine stood up. "Hey, you think we should get that doctor to come on the tour with us?"

Alex turned her head and stared up at her. The mere mention of Morgan Kelly had sent a jolt of something through her. Something very sexual.

"Why?" she said quickly, too quickly.

Francine shrugged. "I dunno, just seems like a good idea, you know, in case you have another panic attack or something, or someone else is injured?"

"You think that's likely?" An image of those eyes smiling at her sent her heart racing, but it was definitely not in panic.

"Probably not, but it's always best to be prepared, and you know how much I like to cross those T's and dot those I's."

"Yes, you do, and that's one of the reasons I keep you around." She smirked at her friend.

Francine grinned back at her. "True, so you got her number, right? Still got it?"

"She did, yes." Francine stared at her as though it were obvious. Alex exhaled, because it was such a hardship, wasn't it, calling up a beautiful woman? "I'll call her then. But I doubt she can just take off from her job."

"Make it worth her while, and I bet she can." Francine winked.

Oh, she could make it worth her while alright, but somehow, she didn't think that was what Francine had in mind, was it?

Chapter Six

August gets the ball rolling.

Dr Morgan Kelly had been only too happy to hear from her.

"Oh, hi," Morgan said cheerily, trying to sound casual and unbothered by a celebrity calling her up. Because it was the last thing she had expected, despite being brazen enough to give the woman her card and number. Working the way she did meant her social life was practically zilch. Handing out her number now and then at least made her feel like she was attempting to live a little.

She quickly followed up with, "How are you?"

"I'm much better, thank you," Alex said, trying to remain as cool and calm as she spoke into the earpiece.

"So...what can I do for you then?" Morgan asked, with just a hint of flirty. She couldn't help it; Alex was the kind of woman who brought that side out of her, and she enjoyed the way Alex's breath hitched a little before she replied.

"Actually, I was wondering if maybe we could meet up. There's something I wanted to ask you, to run by you, and I'd much prefer doing it face to face."

"Sounds very intriguing, okay. When were you thinking?"

"I'm pretty flexible, I can fit in with—"

"How about this morning? I'm working but I could arrive early and meet you. There's a staff bar that's open twenty-four hours, it will be pretty empty."

"A bar?"

Morgan chuckled. "They do coffee and tea."

"Oh, well that sounds perfect, what time?" Alex asked.

"Can you make 10.15? I start my shift at 11 a.m." There was a flutter of butterflies, the excitement of possibilities rippling through Morgan. This was crazy, wasn't it?

"Yes, sure, I'll be there," Alex confirmed before she disconnected the call and replayed the conversation over in her head. Morgan's voice was soothing, and she couldn't deny how she liked the flirtatious nature the doctor had about her. Opening her wardrobe, she considered what she would wear, and asked herself, why did it feel like a date? Alex laughed at herself. Wishful thinking? Possibly. It didn't matter, because this was a business proposition, she told herself.

Now though, as Alex drove into the car park, she was sure that it was ridiculous. It wasn't often she drove anywhere nowadays, but she kept the car anyway for local trips. A gift to herself when Solar Flare's first number-one album meant they actually started to earn some money.

She pulled her little sports car into a space in the corner and watched as a crying woman supported by a friend got into a car in front. That ominous feeling began to sink in again. Why had she agreed to meet at the hospital? She should just leave, reverse back out, message Morgan and arrange a different place to meet.

Twisting the key in the ignition, firing up the engine, prepared to reverse out and forget all about this silly idea of Francine's, something stopped her. Not something, someone. Someone very attractive and looking at her with a mix of confusion and concern.

The figure in the rear-view mirror moved closer, right behind her, blocking her escape and staring with big eyes that then squinted as she tried to make out if she was seeing what she thought she was seeing.

"Bugger," Alex muttered to herself. Turning the engine off, she climbed from the car and turned to find a smile aimed in her direction before the voice and face turned very serious.

"Is everything alright? You're not having another panic attack, are you?"

God, the way those eyes stared at her made Alex feel weak and aroused in an instant. She couldn't remember that happening with anyone else, not as intense as this. She shook it off. Now was not the time to start anything with anyone. She needed to focus.

"No," Alex said slowly, taking in the full view of Dr Kelly in front of her: blue jeans and a white shirt, simple and classy. A raised heart rate had nothing to do with panic. "No, I'm fine actually, I just—" She slammed the door closed and stepped towards Morgan, feeling herself pulled like a magnet. "I just—" God this was awkward. "The thing is...I was going to leave," she admitted. "Hospitals are difficult for me, but I wanted to see you—to speak to you, so..."

The smile returned, along with a little something else...something sexy and alluring, Alex thought. She wasn't sure if it was on purpose or just part of her personality: disarming and yet, enticing.

"Well, I am eager to discover why you wanted to meet me."

No, it was flirty. The doctor was definitely flirting, which probably made sense given the situation they were currently in. *Gimme a call*, she had said, and Alex had done just that, hadn't she? Invited her to meet for coffee, of course, Morgan would be flirty.

"A proposal of sorts." Alex felt herself blush. How did this woman do that so easily? Alexandra Montgomery was not someone who melted under someone's gaze. If anything it would be the other way around, always. And she liked it that way, especially with women she was attracted to, and she couldn't deny that Dr Kelly was someone in that bracket right now.

Morgan checked out their surroundings before she stepped closer, seemingly unaware of the reaction Alex was having to her. "Do you want to get that coffee then? I've got about forty minutes before I'm due on shift."

Alex acquiesced. "Yes, that would probably make sense." She held a finger up. "Hang on." Opening the car door, she reached inside and found one of the baseball caps that Francine had bought in bulk. She had them everywhere: in her bags, cars, luggage when she travelled, always available to hide beneath should the need arise. With it firmly pulled down, she turned back to Morgan, who stood there assessing her with one brow raised and a comical expression on her face. "Okay, lead the way."

Dr Kelly was already a few steps ahead of her, and Alex couldn't ignore the way her eyes scanned that tight arse, hugged in those blue jeans. For a split second, she wondered what Dr Kelly's cute backside would look like bent over her knees, or her bed.

She sped up and shook that image away, walking beside the doctor as they entered a shabby-looking building and pushed through some double doors with flaky blue paint into what she supposed was the staff bar.

"Grab a seat. I'll get us some drinks? Coffee, tea?" Morgan asked, as Alex glanced around the darkened room. There were windows, but with the towering building above them and the tree-lined walkway outside, very little natural daylight would come in.

"Tea, please. Thank you, and honey, if they have it."

Morgan smirked. "I'll certainly ask, but don't hold your breath." She walked towards the bar, and once more Alex found her line of sight drawn to Morgan's backside. She forced her eyes away and took a look at her surroundings, a room that could do with a makeover if ever she'd seen one. At least there wasn't a sticky carpet to contend with. Linoleum covered the surface, but not like the light blue style of a hospital that you might expect. There was a man half asleep on one hand with a pint of orange juice in front of him, and two women sat giggling in the corner. Nobody had taken any notice of her.

A large woman, tall and broad, with a warm smile greeted Morgan from behind the bar and they spoke quickly. Unable to hear the conversation, Alex imagined it was the banal ordering of drinks and how are yous, and then Dr Kelly turned and sashayed back towards her. Grinning.

"She'll bring them over, no honey though I'm afraid." Morgan shrugged as she took the seat next to Alex.

"Oh, well that's okay, I'll live."

Morgan leaned forward, elbows on the table, her hands supporting her chin. "So, what did you want to talk about?"

Those eyes penetrated somewhere deep inside that hadn't been touched for years.

Alex could barely think.

It was intoxicating, and yet, she wouldn't call it intimidating. Alex rarely felt that with anyone, but it was something about the way

Morgan looked at her with such an expectation. Did she feel it too, or was this just her usual state of being? If it was, Alex pitied any woman, or man, she set her sights on, because it was intense.

"Ms Montgomery?" Morgan spoke gently.

"Sorry."

Morgan smiled. "You wanted to speak to me about something?"

"Yes, well, the thing is. I'm going on a short tour in a few weeks. Around the UK, and, well, Francine thought it might be wise in the light of my attack if we…maybe, considered the possibility of taking a more experienced medic with us."

Morgan's head lifted, and her hands turned together, rubbing palm to palm slowly as she considered the question. "A medic?"

Nodding, Alex smirked a little. "Yes, in case of—"

Brown eyes narrowed and darkened as they focused on her inquisitively before turning a little disappointed.

"Are you offering me a job?" Morgan said. Her voice had lost the playful flirtiness, and Alex felt that disappointment too.

"It would appear so, yes." Alex tried to smile, not enjoying for one moment how it felt to disappoint Dr Morgan Kelly.

Maybe this wasn't a good idea. If Dr Kelly made her feel like this now, what would it be like on the road, forced to spend time together day after day? This was madness, wasn't it?

Alex looked away, ready to make an escape, but the sight of the woman from behind the bar walking towards them, carrying a tray ladened with pots and cups, put paid to that idea.

"Here you go." She smiled down at them both as she slid the tray onto the table before turning and leaving them to it without a further word.

"You know, your GP could just prescribe a simple anti-depressant. Sertraline works well for—"

"I've tried them, and they do help, but the side effects meant I was constantly sleepy, and I had headaches. My mind couldn't focus properly on anything creative, and my work suffered as a result. So, I won't take them now. I'd rather get through it, but that last one was different. It frightened me, if I'm honest. I'd feel better knowing I had someone there who could help."

"Why me?" Morgan asked as she passed the empty cup and saucer across the table. "I mean, I assumed a tour would have a medic on staff already."

"Yes, we do usually have someone, but this is more personal. I'd want someone I could—" Alex reached for the pot. "I like you." She caught the smirk that reappeared on Morgan's face and added, "What I mean is that I feel comfortable with you, and you managed my situation quite adeptly, and Francine feels—"

"Is she your girlfriend?" Morgan asked out of nowhere.

"Francine isn't my girlfriend." Alex chuckled. "Seriously?"

"She isn't?" Morgan asked in astonishment. "She acted like it."

"Yes, she has a habit of being a little too…intimate when it comes to my safety, but she's straight. Married actually, and there is absolutely nothing between us in that way," she said resolutely, before adding, "She isn't my type." *Why did she feel the need to be quite so adamant about that?*

"Oh, and who is your type?"

The playful smile was back, and Alex clenched her thigh muscles to control the ache.

"I—can we stick to the matter at hand?" Alex asked, internally pleading with herself not to spurt out, *you, you're my type.*

"Right." Morgan sat back and considered things. "I have to admit that this all feels a little surreal. It's not every day one meets Sasha, and gets a job offer from them, and obviously I am very flattered that someone like you would—" Morgan started to gush until Alex reached out a hand and placed it on top of hers.

"I'm just a person, nobody special or different to anyone else you meet. In fact, I would argue that you, a doctor, might be more important than me."

"Oh, I don't know about that." Morgan blushed, and it might have been the cutest thing Alex had seen in a long while. "But thank you, it means a lot to be appreciated."

Alex sipped her tea some more and then placed the cup gently back onto the saucer. "So, what do you think? Is it something you'd be interested in?"

"Yes, who wouldn't be interested? I'm not sure I'd get the time off, but I guess it wouldn't hurt to ask. Do you know the dates you'd need me?"

Alex smiled and pulled out her notebook, jotting down the dates she would require Morgan to be available. She ripped the paper from the pad and handed it to her.

Morgan studied it while Alex spoke. "You'd travel with me and Francine. Accommodation would be supplied, of course, and you'd be paid substantially for your time, and you would need to be discreet. If the press got wind that I was still suffering anxiety attacks, the photos of that accident would be all over the front pages again and I can't—" She smiled sadly. Too much was at stake to throw her off her game. "I want to avoid that, at all costs. You saw for yourself what it triggers for me."

Morgan nodded; it certainly had been a severe reaction.

"I will think about it for sure. I mean, it would be an experience. I'm just not sure I'd be able to take the time off without explaining it. It would be unusual for any doctor to get that many days annual leave all at once."

Alex watched her for a moment. There was a hint of genuine interest, but also, a sadness hiding behind the smile. Because she wouldn't be able to take up the offer, or because it was only a work offer?

She couldn't quite tell.

This was business, she reminded herself, despite her growing interest in Dr Morgan Kelly. There was no denying she was beautiful. And now that she'd seen her out of the scrubs and in everyday clothing, she could appreciate the look even more.

Under very different circumstance, despite the age difference, she might have considered making it personal and asking her to have dinner with her, maybe more, but there was a lot at stake, and right now, Alex couldn't let anything get in the way of what she needed to do.

"Yes, I suppose you're right. I hadn't really considered that. Honestly, I thought you'd just turn me down and I could go back to Francine with an 'I told you so.'" She chuckled at that idea. "With your permission, I can have Francine contact your employers and speak with them. She can be very persuasive."

"Somehow, I can believe that. Yes, I think that would probably make more sense. They'd at least be more inclined to believe her than me." Morgan smiled.

"Alright." Alex glanced at her watch. Morgan needed to go. "Well, thank you for your time, and I'll have Francine call you to get further details." Alex stood and held out a hand. When Morgan took it, she felt something ease inside of her. She enjoyed the touch. Maybe a little too much as she kept talking and holding. "Oh, and…it's Alex." When Morgan looked confused, she added, "My name. Sasha is my stage name, well, a nickname. My mother calls me that, but I'm Alexandra."

There was a slowness to the smile Morgan gave her that said a lot more than the words that followed. "Well, it's been nice talking to you, Alex, Alexandra."

Morgan forced herself to release her grip and stepped back, reached down for her bag, and smiled.

"I should get going," Morgan said. "Duty calls."

"Yes, of course." Alex watched as Morgan Kelly walked away from her. At the door, she turned and looked back over her shoulder, gave a little wave. Alex waved back, and then Dr Morgan Kelly was gone.

Alex pulled out her phone.

Alex: Hey, did you ever meet someone and just want them?

The answer came back quickly.

Unknown number: All the time. Who did you meet?

Alex: Someone definitely not allowed.

Unknown number: Well, now I am intrigued. Why not?

Alex: She's far too young, and brilliant, and, goodness, I feel like a lovesick teenager.

Unknown number: Sounds promising. How too young are we talking?

Alex: I don't know, 10, maybe 15 years.

Unknown number: If you're both older than 30, I'd say age differences don't count as much. Is she cute?

Alex: Very…

Chapter Seven

Sitting on the balcony of her tiny flat at the marina, Morgan sipped a glass of Ribena from a wine glass. Anyone watching would assume she had a decent Shiraz or Merlot in there, but the truth was, she didn't much like wine. She just liked the feeling of being an adult with a wine glass like everyone else used, and blackcurrant was the perfect fruity thirst quencher in her opinion.

Tonight, she was by herself again, like most evenings. Watching the sun start to drop in the sky above the masts of all the boats in the near distance bobbing up and down was as romantic as her life got nowadays. On a windy night, she could hear them all clanging as ropes and pulleys hit metal on metal like giant wind chimes.

Her flat was nice and quite spacious considering. She loved living here. It would have been nicer of course, had she been able to afford something nearer the actual harbour and not one of the blocks further back, but she wouldn't complain. She still had a view of the marina and the sea.

She had great neighbours like Zoe, which was something you couldn't always rely on nowadays. Zoe and Ken were always happy to pop in and check on Nightingale, a ginger cat she'd rescued as a kitten. She wasn't sure he liked his name, but she hadn't known at the time that he was a boy and not a girl. She'd shortened it at some point to Knight, and he seemed much more attentive, so she assumed he felt more seen now.

Maybe once she was a consultant, or a GP, she'd be able to live that dream of living right on the harbour overlooking the water and the bars. For now though, at thirty-three, this was as perfect as it would get. She just had to get through the next couple of years and then things wouldn't be such a struggle financially, because honestly, she was only just scraping by as it was, what with her mortgage, student loans and all the other bills that came with being an adult. Not to mention, she was exhausted and bordering burnout.

Living the dream would have to wait.

It was still warm out. Just a slight breeze to remind you it was evening. She had three more days off now to relax and enjoy herself before she went onto a week of nights that would be stressful and exhausting.

In the background, she had Sasha playing on the speaker. Her mind went back to their meeting a couple of days ago and the offer of a job. Admittedly, that had been a disappointing turn of events. She'd hoped the phone call had meant Alex had felt it too, that natural pull towards someone that made you wonder if the universe really did work in mysterious ways. But really, who was she kidding, imagining a superstar would fall for her? She needed to stop thinking her life was a Hollywood Christmas romcom, and her soulmate would just fall into her lap.

It wasn't even December.

She picked up her phone and Googled *Sasha*. That was all she needed: one word. One name, and a plethora of pages of information and photos and videos appeared on her screen.

Clicking on the first, she started to read.

"Forty-six?" Somehow, she hadn't worked that out from the information Alex had given at the hospital, but then why would she? She was there to make sure she wasn't having a heart attack and then pass her onto the relevant department, not check out her vital statistics and age. She also had to admit that Sasha, or Alex as she needed to get used to thinking of her, didn't look forty-six. Morgan would have put her in her late thirties, maximum.

"I guess money does keep you young." She chuckled to herself, imagining the pampered lifestyle someone like Alex must enjoy.

She'd never dated anyone older than herself before. Stopping that thought in its tracks, Morgan laughed. "You're not dating her."

Nightingale wandered out and looked up at her, sniffing the air as he inspected the balcony, like he expected to find someone else there who she must be talking to. When he didn't, he turned his back on her and wandered inside, tail in the air.

Opening the next page on her phone, she found a gallery of photos. She scrolled through and found one of a young Sasha, on stage behind an electric keyboard with her band, Solar Flare.

She was cute. A little bit punk, but still cute.

There was a brief description and Morgan read it.

Sasha's leap from child prodigy to superstar began when she joined up with Solar Flare. The band took off as one of the UK's brightest musical talents of the decade. With hits such as "Don't Leave," "I've Got to Dance," and "Pick Me." Solar Flare was on a massive high. A tour of the US beckoned, and superstardom was just around the corner when tragedy struck. The tour bus the band was travelling on crashed at high speed on the motorway. Sasha was the only member of the band wearing a seatbelt that night and walked away unscathed, unlike…

Morgan stopped reading; it felt macabre to be delving into it all, but she could understand why the woman still suffered from panic attacks when the next image she flicked to was a photo of the mangled bus lying on its side in the darkness of a wet night. Jagged metal and crushed glass sparkled under the flashing lights from the emergency services.

It looked like hell on earth.

The following image of the crash showed the coach in the daylight, and it didn't look any better. Her trained eye could see the tell-tale signs of blood and emergency services debris scattered and left behind while paramedics had rushed to get the wounded to hospital.

She'd dealt with hundreds of car accidents in A&E over the last year. It was never an easy sight when the worst of them came rushing through the doors with paramedics shouting instructions and information at her.

And somehow, Alex had made it out of that physically unscathed.

"Jesus," she whispered in disbelief.

There were images of the other bandmates, some covered with blankets on the tarmac, Lucy Owens strapped to a bed and being wheeled towards an ambulance with parts of the photo blurred to save the viewer from seeing such awful injuries. A photo of the band smiling on the cover of a teen magazine bore the headline,

Tragedy strikes Solar Flare.

The next images were much later, at least a decade after Sasha's time in the band. Opening night to a film Sasha had a small part in. Sasha, standing hand in hand with a woman in front of the press. Sasha wearing a black tailored suit, heels and a red tie loosely worn around her neck. Sasha craning her neck back and laughing at something someone behind her had said. Sasha drinking coffee, unaware of the photographer. Sasha on stage, lit up next to a huge piano.

She looked hot.

"Blimey," Morgan whispered, zooming in and out of the photo at Sasha's smiling face. She moved across to the woman beside her and examined the kind of woman Alex Montgomery went for. Femme, gorgeous, model, was her conclusion. Not a bedraggled, knackered, barely able to comb her hair junior doctor.

She took a long swig of her drink, almost draining the glass, when she noticed a neighbour along the balconies staring at her. Their eyes widening at the young woman downing a glass of what they supposed was wine.

"Long day." Morgan smiled and raised the glass, getting a look of disgust in return. She chuckled to herself and got up to go inside, closing the sliding door behind her, and the world outside disappeared behind the curtains.

She sat on the couch with her feet up and slid down until she was comfortable, flicking through image after image of *Sasha* on stage, out shopping, having dinner, interviews. The more she looked, the more interested she became.

Could she really get to travel with a world-famous musician like Sasha? Morgan wondered what kind of world Alex lived in. Was it really like the movies, all glitz and glamour? How did someone like Morgan fit into that?

Mentally she slapped herself. "You don't. You would be the hired help, that's all. Just another member of her team," she said, stroking Nightingale when he jumped up. "Right boy?"

Nightingale had no opinion either way as he kneaded his paws against her thighs before curling up on her lap.

Regardless, she wanted to do it. An opportunity like this didn't knock twice, and if there was one trait Morgan was most proud of, it was her sense of adventure. Persuading her bosses at the NHS, however, would be the issue, but she considered Alex's personal assistant, Francine. With her on-side, it had to be possible, didn't it?

Chapter Eight

The Seeds are sown...

"Absolutely not," Alex said into the phone before Francine had even finished speaking.

She was watching the sunset over the sea and feeling quite relaxed before Francine's name had flashed up on her phone's screen.

"She hasn't even agreed to come on the tour yet, and if she does, we are not putting her into that situation. And she's far too young for that to even be a consideration," Alex said, shaking off the irritability the suggestion had incurred.

"Look, I don't like it either," Francine sighed, "but the publicists are questioning why we need a doctor on staff. If the media gets wind of that, you can kiss your quiet life goodbye. They'll be hounding till they find out about the panic attacks, and then they will bring up the bus crash again, and the legal team is suggesting it's going to impact the insurance, so that is why it makes more sense to let the world think she's..." She hesitated to say it again. "Your girlfriend."

"No, that is just...it's a lie for a start, and I don't even know her. How the hell would we pull that off? I really don't want a reputation for being a cougar." Alex stood up and walked to the edge of the decking, her toes moving in the sand that had settled during the day, ignoring the hearty laughter coming from the other end of the speaker.

"She's a hot young doctor; what's not to like, Alex?" Francine chuckled. "I'm sure you can find a way to enjoy looking at her. And you're a celebrity, having a younger partner is barely noticed."

That was the point, wasn't it? Dr Morgan Kelly was attractive, very attractive. And having to pretend to be her lover would mean having to get close, intimate on a certain level to make it realistic, and she wasn't so sure she could do that and not actually want to be intimate.

She knew what she was like after a show. Someone like Morgan Kelly in the room would potentially be explosive.

Would that really be a bad thing?

Alex tsked. "You're as bad as every inappropriate man I've ever had the misfortune to encounter. I'd notice!" Hadn't she already noticed? You couldn't not notice a woman like Dr Morgan Kelly.

Francine laughed again. "Look, I'm not saying you fuck her for gods' sake, but how difficult is it to stand beside her and smile once in a while, and if asked, dodge the question like you would in any other situation when you're asked about your private life. And I don't think she's as young as you think she is. What's a decade?"

Alex wrapped her free arm around herself. "I don't like it," she said quickly and bit her lip, hearing the lie that just passed her lips, because she did like it, didn't she?

Close proximity to Dr Morgan Kelly would be dangerous, very dangerous, she warned herself again, *but isn't that part of the excitement? Isn't that what you've been looking for, asking the universe for, something to put some oomph back into the life you're barely living? Now it's on offer and you're what, going to say no?* Her brain threw out questions with no time for answers.

"You don't have to like it; you just have to act like you do," Francine said in that no-nonsense way that meant she wasn't taking no for an answer.

Alex sighed. Why couldn't her life ever just be simple? Pretending to like someone as beautiful as Dr Morgan Kelly really wasn't that difficult. Francine was right about that. The problem was, someone like Dr Morgan Kelly was exactly who Alex could lose all focus over.

"She'll say no anyway."

Francine chuckled. "Not by the time I'm done with her, she won't."

"And just what are you going to do to persuade her?"

"That's not for you to worry about. It's legal. Have I ever failed you?"

"No, you haven't," Alex had to admit.

"Then trust me now. This is the best solution."

Euphoria

Morgan put her phone down on top of the wireless charger and stood up, ready to start the process of going to bed. She needed a hot shower. Her knotted muscles would enjoy the pounding of hot water pulsing from the newly installed fancy shower she'd over-indulged with.

Her phone ringing this late didn't bode well. She wasn't on call, but any kind of major incident could change that in a moment. Many an evening had been ruined: a gas leak explosion on a residential street, multi-car pileups in the fog; a cruise ship had come into the harbour with forty-four cases of food poisoning once. Morgan knew that literally anything could spoil her night.

Her friends didn't usually call without texting first, knowing her hours and sleep pattern was all over the place, and not wanting to disturb her. So, she picked it up hesitantly and was intrigued when an unknown number lit up the screen.

"Hello?"

"Francine Carlson speaking, is this Dr Morgan Kelly?" The voice was abrupt, completely to the point and very American. Even without the introduction, Morgan would have known who it was.

"Yes, hello."

"I was wondering, can we meet tomorrow? I need to run something by you before we go and speak to your human resources department."

"Uh, okay, I'm off for a few days but I can come into the hosp—"

"That's fine, I'll come to you. Text me your address. I can be there around ten. Don't you worry about a thing; this is what I do."

"Right, and what does that actually mean?"

"It means that I get what needs to be done, done, so that my client, in this case, Sasha, can have everything she needs at her disposal."

Morgan frowned. "Kind of sounds like I'm a commodity."

"Don't take it personally. For her, you're what she needs: a doctor, a confidante. For me, this is business and a negotiation. So, I'll see you tomorrow at ten."

She ended the call before Morgan could agree or disagree.

"I guess so then," she said to herself while texting her address and adding Francine Carlson to her phone's contact list under *Ice Queen*.

Chapter Nine

Hospital administration and human resources were not offices where any staff member felt totally comfortable. You weren't meant to. They were places where you got sent. They were the office where punishments were handed out; rarely were they the place where a pat on the back occurred.

Waking up that morning to a message on her phone from the head of HR had been alarming for Morgan.

A meeting was scheduled for early afternoon. Today! And she was invited to attend. Invited, such an odd word to use when summoned was a much better alternative. Dr M Kelly had her orders.

As she waited for Francine to arrive, she wondered just how Francine had pulled this off with such short notice. It was nigh on impossible to get an appointment with one HR staff member, let alone a meeting like the one that had been set up.

The woman was a walking, talking bulldozer, and Morgan had to admire that, even if it was a little intimidating.

Had she made a mistake even contemplating this?

Morgan thought about it. What was the worst that could happen?

They'd talk, attend the meeting and Francine would either persuade them to release her or not. Either way, in two days she'd be back on shift as usual, dealing with the public and all number of illness and injury.

She almost jumped out of her skin when the intercom buzzed. Pressing the button that opened the door downstairs, she calmed herself and opened the inner door, listening down the hall for the tell-tale sign of the lift arriving.

"Hi," she said as brightly as she could muster when Francine came into view, moving aside to allow Francine into her home. "Found me okay, then?"

The American woman smiled at her quickly before getting straight to the point.

"So, let's get down to business."

Not that Morgan expected any other approach. Ms Carlson didn't sound like the kind of woman who did small talk when there was something to get done.

"Sure, take a seat. Can I get you a coffee?" Morgan asked. "How is Ms Montgomery doing? Any more anxiety attacks?"

"She's fine, but you know how it is, gotta keep it that way." Francine grinned like a shark. All teeth and ready for the kill. "I'm fine for coffee."

"So, what do—"

Dropping her bag onto the table, Francine kicked out a chair and sat down.

"Look, what I'm about to ask you is a little delicate, okay? And you can't go spilling ya guts to all and sundry about it, whatever decision you make, so I need you to sign an NDA." She reached into the bag and pulled out an envelope and slid it across the table.

"I'm already bound by patient confidentiality," Morgan said, taking a seat and sliding the envelope back.

"That may well be, but you're not her doctor, and this isn't a hospital, and we're talking about you having access to a part of Sasha's world that even her doctors don't get to see, so we can argue about this, or you can sign the document."

Morgan considered it. She reached out a finger and pulled the envelope back towards her and picked it up. Opening it, she withdrew a single sheet of paper and began to read.

She had no idea what she thought an NDA looked like, but if she'd had to imagine it, this wouldn't have been it. A simple declaration that all topics discussed today – it was dated today – would be held in confidence and subject to litigation should she – her name was written in – break the confidence and trust of Sasha.

"Is this it?"

Francine sat back and inclined her head. "If you were to accept the terms I'm about to lay out, then we'll move on to a more robust document, but for the purposes of right now that will suffice." She leaned forward. "But mark my words, any breach of confidence about today, with anyone, will see our lawyers take action."

Morgan had no interest in talking about Alex with anyone, but still, it rankled that she was being asked to sign this. Then she considered, why wouldn't they ask this? It was probably the norm with any kind of working relationship that involved a celebrity. And really, what did Alex know about her? There was no relationship of trust between them.

Holding out her hand, she waited for Francine to root through her bag and produce a pen. With a flourish, Morgan signed her name along the dotted line and handed it back, along with the pen.

"Okay, so what did you want to discuss?"

Francine took the document, checked it once and then pushed it back into the envelope and then into her bag.

"Firstly, I need to know what you're hiding?"

Morgan frowned. "What I'm hiding? What do you mean?"

"In your past, your now, what are the skeletons in the closet? I don't care, I'm not here to judge but I need to know. I can't protect what I don't know."

"None, I don't have anything."

"You sure about that? No exes with a grudge, no estranged family members who'd want to earn a quick buck?"

"No, not that I'm aware of."

"Alright."

"Is that it?" Morgan sat back and folded her arms. Something was off. A doctor on staff wouldn't be something anyone else cared about. "What's this all about?"

Francine puffed out her cheeks. "We got a small PR issue. Alex is a very private person, her life is her own and the press usually leave her to it. However, there is one subject they just love to talk about: the coach crash."

"Okay, and what does that have to do with me?" Morgan questioned.

"If we take a personal doctor with us on tour, questions will arise. They'll wanna know why? What's wrong with her? And if they discover it's panic attacks, they'll have a picture of that mangled bus on the front page of every newspaper and glossy magazine you can think of. I won't allow that to happen. She's been traumatised enough by this. It's my job to keep her public image intact as well as to make sure her private life is kept that way: private."

"Right, I get that. So, what does that mean for me?"

"Simple, I need you to be there as something other than her doctor."

Morgan frowned. "I don't understand. What will I be other than her doctor?"

The corner of Francine's mouth lifted. "If anyone asks, you'd be her lover."

If she'd been drinking in that moment, she'd have just spat it all over the woman sitting across the table from her. "Are you serious?"

"As a heartbeat," Francine replied. "It makes sense; she's travelled with partners before. And she doesn't flaunt it."

Morgan leaned forward and in a low, quiet voice, she asked, "You want me to go on tour with Alex and pretend to be her girlfriend. You think that's less of a headline maker than the real story?"

Francine nodded slowly. "Sure. If, and it's a big if, anyone were to poke around and ask questions…" Francine smiled. "Look, we're not against headlines, Dr Kelly, just the right ones. They'll publish a photo or two, they'll speculate and then you'll be forgotten once the break-up occurs and it's back to business as usual."

"The break-up?" She snorted. Francine had it all planned out.

"Sure, we'll just put out a statement—"

"Hold on." Morgan raised her hand, palm out. "So, let me get this right. You want me to take time off of work, go on tour around the UK with Alex for weeks, potentially have my face plastered over any and every news outlet. I'll have to lie to everyone who asks about it, including my family and friends, colleagues et cetera, and then there will be an imaginary break-up, where I assume I'm painted as the bad guy and what—I just go back to my life?" She held her palms out and stared wide-eyed at the ludicrous idea.

Francine sighed. "We won't paint anyone as the bad guy. It will just be a case of work differences and in a few weeks nobody will remember you." She grabbed her bag. "So, I'll see you this afternoon at the meeting to discuss everything?"

Morgan said nothing but walked her to the door. Turning quickly, Francine smiled.

"Oh, I almost forgot. You'll earn £100,000. For the inconvenience."

Chapter Ten

One hundred thousand pounds for less than a month's work, and it wasn't even work, not really, not when Morgan considered how hard she worked at the hospital every shift. Staying in luxury hotels, she didn't even have to pay for her own meals. It wasn't exactly a difficult proposal, was it?

But pretending to be interested in someone she was actually interested in, while knowing they weren't interested but were also pretending. That was a mind fuck, wasn't it? That had the potential to emotionally drain her, didn't it? And yet, it was still appealing.

"One hundred thousand pounds," she muttered under her breath. Saying it aloud made it feel even crazier.

She could pay off what was left of her student loan, pay her mortgage for another year, or more, without worrying. Maybe even buy a better car than the little Fiat that was one fix away from being written off.

All she had to do was travel the country, and be on call should Alex, or anyone else, require medical aid, and if needed, be seen in public with Sasha and let the press think they were more than friends.

How difficult could it be?

She'd earn more in those few weeks than she'd earn in a year as a GP when she was finally ready to take that step, and that was at least three years away still, if she even made it. She was already feeling the effects of burnout and considering her life choices most weeks.

It didn't feel real.

Even as she'd sat back and watched Francine sell the idea to the head of HR – a man Morgan had never met before, but who would have the final say on whether this worked out for her or not – she couldn't believe it wasn't a dream.

George Eustace had clearly never met a woman like Francine Carlson before either. She went into that office with an intention, and she wasn't leaving until she got what she wanted, at any cost. The cut of her very expensive suit should have given him a clue. She was on a mission, at all costs, and she took no prisoners.

"I noticed on the way in that the hospital is holding a fundraiser in order to buy a new MRI machine, am I correct?" she asked, holding his gaze. "One hundred thousand required, and you've raised what? Forty-five?" That was what the red-painted line said they were up to.

A woman sitting beside George leaned forward and smiled proudly. "Forty-six, actually."

"Well, my client is willing to add what you need, a cool fifty-four thousand, as a gesture of goodwill and recompense for borrowing Dr Kelly."

The woman, a Grace Moncerath, straightened up and gulped.

"Why this doctor?" George asked, nodding towards Dr Kelly. "Not that there is any reason not to ask for Dr Kelly, of course, all of our doctors here are very good, and we're proud to have them on staff, but we have far more experienced doctors who could—"

"My client has been through some very traumatic events. She requires her team to consist of people she's comfortable with, can trust, you know? Dr Kelly fits that criterion. We don't need a brain surgeon. We need someone capable, someone calm, someone who knows their shit." She sat dead still, but her eyes moved from one face to another on the panel before adding, "Look, it's one month. You'll get your scanner, and then Dr Kelly will back and raring to go."

There was silence for a moment before George rubbed his chin and spoke again.

"Obviously, if we were to agree to this, there would be certain conditions that would have to be met."

Francine smiled. "Sure, shoot."

"For one, we'd have to keep the hospital out of the press. It wouldn't do for us to be having to admit to lending out our staff, and it wouldn't do to have that attached to the scanner. The word bribery bandied around would not be helpful to anybody's career." He glanced at Morgan.

"Bribery? Who said anything about bribery? Listen fella, I'm offering a deal here that works for all concerned. We work with NDAs, and I'm happy to sign one for you if that's what it takes because I'm not leaving this room without Dr Kelly's signature on this contract." She flopped down a small stack of papers she'd pulled from her bag onto the desk. "So, you want that scanner or not?"

"We'd need to work out how Dr Kelly can be away from work for such a period without there being any bias. Setting a precedent for an entire month's leave, unless under a dire situation such as a death of a close family member, would be frowned upon and could potentially create issues among the ranks."

"I could take unpaid leave," Morgan suggested. "That way, I can't be accused of wasting taxpayers' money. If anyone were to question it, we could vaguely explain that Ms Montgomery and I are close friends and I've taken a mix of annual and unpaid leave in order to spend time with her during a difficult period."

"Good point. Any whiff of a financial scandal and the board would be under pressure." He sighed and leant back in his chair. "Tell me why you wish to do this?"

"I think it would be an experience for me personally. I think it would be a learning curve, and I think that regardless of Ms Montgomery's status and wealth, everyone deserves to feel safe, and I think that I can provide that assurance." She glanced at Francine before adding, "And if my taking a few weeks out can also provide the hospital with a much-needed piece of equipment too, then I can't see any reason not to accept the offer."

"I'm sure that the financial recompense is equally as dazzling for you too, Dr Kelly," the other woman on the panel said.

"I—" Morgan went to speak but was stopped by a firm hand on her thigh squeezing.

Francine smiled. "I'm gonna cut right in. Ms Montgomery's financial package on the table for you is the only one we will be discussing. As part of the NDA Dr Kelly has signed, she isn't able to discuss those matters with anyone."

"I find that a little preposterous," continued the woman.

"Sure, and I find my time is really starting to come to an end, so, do we have a deal?" Francine stood up, prompting Morgan to follow, and then one by one the panel also rose from their seats.

"If we were to agree, and allow a valued member of staff to take an unprecedented amount of time off, would Ms Montgomery be available to attend the charity event we have coming up?" George asked Francine.

"What kind of event?"

The woman jumped in again. "It's the fundraiser; members of the local community will be attending a charity gala to raise as much money as possible...for the scanner."

"Money Ms Montgomery is giving you," Francine responded, face hard as stone.

"Yes, but obviously, we can't cancel the gala now. It's all been planned and paid for. We're sold out on tickets, so we may as well go ahead and anything more we raise could go towards the sensory room we want to add that will help children with—"

"When?"

"The end of the month?"

"I'll need to check Ms Montgomery's diary and get back to you, but I guess, if there's nothing stopping her, she would love to attend." She turned to George. "So, do we have a deal?"

George eyed the mouthy American before he finally agreed, "We have a deal. "I'll have our legal team put together our paperwork and we can reconvene in three days to sign and seal."

"Sounds like a plan there, Stan." Francine reached out her hand.

"It's George."

"I know, it's a…" She grabbed his hand and shook vigorously, "Never mind, I'll see you soon." She turned to Morgan. "Sign on the dotted line."

Morgan glanced down at the contract on the table. "I'll need to read this."

"Sure, three days." And with that, Francine Carlson swept out of the room with every set of eyes staring after her.

Chapter Eleven

Charity starts with chemistry.

Sitting in the back of the car, Alex fiddled with the hem of her designer dress. A charity gala was not something she had planned any time soon. It was not that she didn't want to support a good cause, but it was a lot easier to just make a donation than actually take time out of her life to turn up and schmooze a bunch of people she had no real interest in getting to know.

"Stop fussing. You look great, doesn't she, Mike?" Francine said.

Mike looked back through the rear-view mirror and grinned. "She sure does."

"It's not gone amiss that I pay both of you to be nice to me." Alex smiled back.

"You pay me too much to lie to your face," Francine joked and settled back in her seat. "So, we get there, we go in, you mingle for thirty minutes and then we skedaddle, alright?"

"Barely worth the effort," Alex bemoaned. Her hair and make-up were done, she'd gotten a new dress, she was wearing heels again after a summer of flats. "Not that Nancy minded the extra days' work."

Turning to her, Francine grinned. "We can always stay longer if you want to."

Someone at the hospital had obviously tipped the press, because the expected local news brigade was very much swamped by national papers and magazine paps all jostling for position when the car pulled up.

"Don't sweat it, just smile and keep walking," Francine said when Mike stepped out and opened the door.

Putting on her public persona, Sasha emerged from the car, leaving Alex in the background. She waved and stood still for a moment and let them get their photos.

Moving on, she was greeted by several reporters, all intent on asking her questions. She stopped and listened.

"Sasha, how excited are you to be supporting such a local event?" one asked, holding out a tape recorder.

"Of course, it's always a wonderful opportunity to show support on a local level."

"Who designed your dress?"

That was a question she always hated; would they ask about attire if she were Hans Von Speltz? She ignored the question and turned towards Francine, an unspoken *get me out of here.*

Stepping inside the building, she was quickly met by two women, the same two Francine recognised from the HR meeting.

"Ms Montgomery, it's really an honour to meet you and have you attending the gala," one said, before the other stepped forward.

"Absolutely, you wouldn't believe the buzz your attending has created. I really think it will make all the difference in how much we raise tonight."

"Thank you for the invitation. I'm looking forward to a wonderful evening," Alex replied, not believing a word of what she'd just said. There was a sensation of eyes on her, and she turned just slightly to her left. The image caught her breath in her throat as her eyes landed upon Dr Kelly. Maybe it wouldn't be as bad an evening as she had thought. "If you'll excuse me." Turning to Francine, she said, "Can you get some drinks? I'm just going to say hello to Dr Kelly."

Francine raised a brow and pursed her lips into an amused smirk. "Sure, probably an opportunity to start up a few rumours, huh?"

"Oh, stop it." Alex slapped her arm gently. When Francine chuckled and walked away, Alex breathed deeply before turning and walking confidently towards the woman watching her every move.

Dressed in a simple black cocktail dress, hair piled up on her head, barely there make-up, Dr Morgan Kelly looked stunning.

"So, you made it through the throng," she said, smiling at Alex when she was within earshot.

Alex glanced back over her shoulder at the two women watching her like a hawk. "Hm, I did. I even managed to slip my chaperone."

"Is that what we're calling Francine now?" Morgan laughed, but then said, "Do you need a chaperone?"

Now, it was Alex's turn to laugh. "Possibly, I don't get out much. I can be easily led astray."

"Really, well, that sounds like a job for me." Morgan shimmied her shoulders.

Alex raised an amused brow. "You think you're up to the task?"

"Of entertaining you for an hour before you scuttle off back to the safety of wherever superstar pianists hide from the limelight these days?" Morgan leaned closer. "I think I can manage."

Alex felt it hit her like a brick wall. Arousal. If they were in the confines of somewhere private right now, she wasn't sure she'd be held responsible for what she might do with Morgan Kelly if allowed.

"I see, well, lead the way… I'm in your hands."

Morgan touched Alex's elbow before slipping her arm through and linking them closely together as she led the way into the hall. "So, are you planning to stay through dinner, or escape at the earliest opportunity?"

Alex smiled at people as they moved through, between the tables already filling up with guests, with Morgan's hand now trailing across her lower back.

"I haven't decided," she answered, shaking hands with a man Morgan recognised from the physiotherapy department. "I wasn't sure what to expect," she turned to face Morgan, "or who might entertain me."

"I guess you'll be here till I leave then." Morgan grinned, before moving away and leaving Alex speechless.

Before Alex could follow, she felt another arm slip through and link her to them. Francine whispered, "So, I've shmoozed with George, and he's asked if you might draw the winning ticket in the raffle?"

Alex groaned. "Really?" She looked up and found herself being studied, those brown eyes just as dangerous from a distance. "I thought it might be a good idea to get to know Morgan a little better before we subject her to being my lover."

Francine pursed her lips. "I think you'll have plenty of time for that too." She reached out and took two glasses of champagne from a passing waitress carrying a tray. "Here."

Taking the glass from her, Alex immediately took a sip and glanced over the rim of the glass. Those eyes were still staring at her. "Fine, I'll do the raffle."

"Great, go mingle. I'll organise it all."

There was no time to argue. Francine was already moving away. Alex swigged the champagne and drained the glass. To her left, she could see a figure moving towards her with purpose. She was about to head towards Morgan and escape when she realised the doctor had moved. Alex scanned the area and couldn't see her anywhere.

"Alexandra."

Sucking down the disappointment, Alex turned to find a familiar face not quite smiling at her.

"Hello, Calista."

The other woman studied Alex for a moment before she said, "So, the big question is, what did you do that means you've had to attend this annoyance like me?"

"I'm sure you could have found something else to do instead," Alex replied without answering the question.

"Nope, all heads of department are expected to attend functions, especially fundraising ones." She sipped the champagne and grimaced. "So, I take it you're feeling better now?"

"Yes, much, thank you."

"Hm, I should probably apologise for being quite so—" Calista smiled. One hand held a glass, the other rested against her stomach. "My ego took a hit when you decided not to continue our…"

"I—"

"And I suppose, I can understand why, it must be quite intimidating to be around someone so capable and—"

"Ms Montgomery, sorry to interrupt." Alex turned away from Calista and found herself potentially saved, with warm brown eyes and the sweetest smile she'd ever seen aimed right at her.

"Dr Kelly," Alex said, a hint of hope in her tone. "You know Dr Urquhart?"

"Of course, well, we all know of Dr Urquhart." Morgan smiled at the ice glare coming her way, before thrusting out her hand. "Morgan Kelly, Doctor."

"Very James Bond." Calista sneered, limply taking her hand as though it were diseased. "You're the one who diagnosed Alexandra's anx—"

"Yes, I was the doctor on call." Morgan cut her off from announcing loudly to anyone listening what Alex's diagnosis was. "I'm just glad that we got it all sorted for her."

"Ladies and gentlemen, if I can have your attention."

The three of them turned toward the MC. Everyone else around them began to move and take their seats.

"I guess we should sit down," Alex said, looking around, wondering whether they had allocated seating.

"It was nice to meet you," Morgan said to Calista with a smile that almost looked sincere. "We're on the front table," she said, leaning into Alex before offering her elbow.

They walked away, leaving Calista to find her own seat, not quite at the back but far enough that she wouldn't be bothering anyone.

"She doesn't like you, does she?" Morgan stated as they moved between chairs, and *Sasha* smiled at those they passed. "What did you do to piss her off? Not that it requires much from what I've heard."

Alex sniggered. "I guess Dr Urquhart and I didn't see eye to eye on our…dates."

"Oh, you dated. Wow, okay." Morgan smirked. "I guess that's a story for another day." She pulled a chair out and acknowledged the other people sitting at the table, including Francine. "Looks like you're next to me."

"Looks like I am." Alex smiled, sliding into the seat.

"So…" Morgan leaned in. "Tell me why someone as accomplished and attractive as you is still single?"

Alex chuckled. "I think that might be a question with a complicated answer."

"Really? I like complicated. Like a puzzle?" She sat back and let her eyes move over Alex for a moment. "You're an enigma, aren't you?"

"Only when the cameras are looking." Alex's eyes sparkled as they both turned to find a photographer ready to take their picture.

Morgan moved effortlessly between the tables as she made her way towards the bathroom. Three glasses of champagne were her limit, and the soda and lime she'd been drinking since had had a definite effect on her bladder.

She pushed the door open just as it was pulled from the other side, and Calista Urquhart swayed. *Clearly, more than three glasses*, Morgan thought as she smiled and stepped aside.

"You know, she'll just dump you when she's done with you," the icy doctor slurred, bumping against the doorframe.

"Sorry, what?" Morgan smiled.

"I said." Calista stood in front of her and poked her bony finger into her chest. "She won't want you forever."

"Who?" She knew who Calista was referring to, of course she did, but she wasn't about to give her the satisfaction of knowing she'd just poked a nerve.

Smirking, Calista slid a cold palm over Morgan's warm cheek. "Don't play coy. You know who I'm talking about. You're just her type." Her head tilted, and the smirk widened into a smile. "Mine too…if you were looking for a little no-strings fun and a guiding hand through promotions."

"Are you propositioning me?"

"I'm just giving you options. Like I said, she'll drop you the moment—"

"Morgan, I thought you'd gotten lost," Francine said from behind Calista's back. A cold stare slowly turned around. "Dr Urquhart, how are you?"

"I'm fine, thank you…" Urquhart narrowed her eyes as though trying to remember where she knew the face from.

"Francine Carlson, Sasha's PA. We met at the hospital."

Calista removed her hand from Morgan's shoulder and closed her eyes as she got her alcohol-hazed thoughts together. "Oh yes, I remember, the brash American sticky beak."

Morgan's eyes widened at the outright rudeness.

Francine just grinned. She loved this kind of animosity; it fanned her fire.

"I'm so pleased I made such an impact. You may go now." She closed in on Morgan as they both watched Calista stalk away, grabbing the backs of chairs to hold herself up as she drunkenly swayed. "What a bitch."

"That's one word for it." Morgan laughed.

Chapter Twelve

The morning after...

"What?" Alex said without looking up, after a full minute of Francine staring at her across the table, with a smirk on her face that didn't go unnoticed.

Francine reached forward and picked up her coffee mug. Slowly bringing it to her lips, she sipped. "I don't know what you mean," she finally answered, placing the cup back onto the tabletop.

"You've been staring at me like that for—"

"Like what?" Francine tilted her head and narrowed her eyes.

Alex sighed and decided not to play the game. "Why are you here this early anyway?"

"Just checking in. Last night was—" Her lip curled on one side. "Interesting."

"Was it? How so?" She knew how so, but she wasn't going to give Francine the satisfaction.

"Oh, come on, you didn't enjoy it just a teeny-weeny little bit?"

"That would make me a terrible person, wouldn't it?" Alex said, managing to keep a straight face as she picked up her cup of tea.

"Yeah, well, I'm all good with being a terrible person. Karma is a beautiful thing."

Finally, Alex cracked, smiling over the rim of her cup. "I guess it is."

"I mean, it couldn't happen to a nicer person. Maybe she will think twice before necking that amount of alcohol next time."

"The entire cake though, I mean, that was a waste. I wanted some of that cake," Alex whined playfully.

They both burst into laughter.

"All I'm going to say is that woman, she pissed off a lot of people in that room, judging by the reaction afterwards. I mean, I knew it that day at the hospital, how she spoke to you. Wow, what a bitch."

"I'm sure she has some good qualities," Alex offered, pondering for a moment. "She's a good kisser."

Francine scoffed before changing subjects just slightly. "So, you and the doc are hitting it off."

"Unlike Calista, Morgan is a very likeable person."

"And is she a good kisser?" Francine winked.

Alex blushed a little at that. "I wouldn't know. I thought it best to keep things on a professional level."

"Hm, yes, probably a good idea. No distractions, right?"

"No distractions," Alex agreed.

"Did you know Calista propositioned Morgan?" Francine said with a curious eyebrow raised.

That gave Alex pause for thought. The little jolt of jealousy that rippled through her in that moment didn't go unnoticed and felt very unnerving. She had no hold on Morgan, did she? And hadn't Morgan flirted with her all night, not Calista? She smiled to herself. No, she had no competition from Dr Calista Urquhart, should she want to enter any race for Morgan Kelly's attention.

"Calista is a very—"

"Difficult, rude, an ungrateful individual?"

"All of that, yes." Alex placed her cup down. It was a beautiful day, the sun glistening on a glasslike sea. There was that little boat again, just floating, nobody in sight. "I wonder what's out there."

"Huh?"

Alex jutted her chin out towards the boat. "Out there, that little boat. It's been out there a few times over the last few weeks. I can never see anyone onboard, so I'm guessing they're diving, but I didn't realise there was anything interesting out there."

"Fish? People like fish, I mean, I like to eat 'em, but some people like to look at them."

"I suppose so. It's not something I've ever wanted to do, you know? Go under water. I like to breathe air." Alex chuckled. "Lots of fresh air. I don't think I'd be very good with a dive suit and apparatus. Maybe there's an old wreck."

"Well," Francine said, standing up, "you don't have to ever worry about that, but you do have to start packing. I know what you're like. Do you need help?"

"No, I'm all good. I'm going to go through my wardrobe tomorrow. I'll be ready on time. Six suits and shirts and some casual wear for off time, I'll manage."

"Good, because you've only got two more weeks and then we're off."

"It's Winchester. It's literally an hour up the road."

"Uh huh, an hour and twenty actually, and that's only in good traffic, and once we leave, we're not popping back for things you've forgotten."

"Okay, consider me told."

"So, you're going away for how long?" Morgan's mother asked as she buttered bread and slathered it with French mustard, ready for slices of ham and cheese.

"Just a few weeks, I'll be home in time for Dad's birthday."

"And what is it exactly you're doing?"

Morgan blew out her cheeks. "I told you I've been requested to go on tour with a musician; I can't tell you any more than that."

"It all sounds a little fishy. The hospital's just letting you go?" She cut the first sandwich corner to corner and pushed the plate across towards Morgan.

"Yep." She picked up one half and bit into the crusty edge. "They're very happy with the deal."

"The deal?"

"Ma, I know it all sounds..." She sighed. "I've signed papers, it's all legal and above board but there are privacy issues I'm not allowed to discuss. Where is Dad anyway? I was hoping to see him."

Mrs Kelly finished her own sandwich and wiped her hands on her apron. "He popped out to the bookies, you know he likes his bet on Saturdays."

Morgan nodded hesitantly, because she knew full well that her dad wasn't at the bookies. He was more likely down the pub with Gary and Rob, watching the football that her mother hated.

"Seen Mason lately?"

Her brother had a habit of popping in with his washing, despite the fact that he hadn't lived at home for three years.

"He's taking Alison to London to see a show she's been wanting to see."

"Mason?" Morgan almost laughed. Her brother and culture didn't go hand in hand at all; he was more likely to be with her dad down the pub.

Her mum chuckled. "I know. I think that Alison is a good influence on him."

"Well, it will be nice to meet her...eventually. Is he still refusing to bring her home?" She took another bite of her sandwich.

Pursed lips told her the answer to that, but her mother answered anyway.

"Yep, you'd think he was ashamed of us or something."

"Hardly, your daughter's a doctor." She smirked.

"And very proud of you we are too."

"I know you are," Morgan mumbled.

Her mum studied her for a moment. "Do you? Cos we are. Sometimes, I think you doubt that. The day you went to medical school was the proudest day of my life."

Morgan shrugged. Shouldn't it have been the proudest day of her own life too?

"It's not that I doubt it, I just…" Her thoughts went to her brother Mason again, always in trouble as a kid, in and out of the police station for minor things, while Morgan stayed in, diligently finishing her studies and working hard. "There were times when Mason took up a lot of your and dad's attention and maybe, if I'm honest, I felt a bit ignored."

Her mum stared at her for a moment, before she inclined her head. "I can understand that. It was never intentional. I suppose you never gave us any reason to worry and so that allowed us to deal with Mason's issues."

"I never gave you any cause to worry, cos I knew we were all at breaking point." Morgan stood up and took her empty plate to the sink. "Mason needs to learn to stand on his own two feet and stop thinking the world still owes him something."

"What your brother went through…"

"I'm not unsympathetic, Mum." She dunked the plate into the hot water in the bowl. "No child should ever have to deal with that happening to them, but…he can't keep using it as the excuse to screw up. He needs more counselling, and you and dad have to stop bailing him out every time he messes up with another cockamamie idea." She put the dripping plate into the rack and turned back to face her mum while she dried her hands on the tea towel.

"He's trying, Morgan, and I really think this time he might be on to something. This Alison, I told you, she seems good for him. He listens to her, and this new venture sounds like it has some legs to it."

"I hope you're right. I want to see him succeed, just not at you and Dad's demise. Has he paid you back for the last fiasco?"

Her mother breathed deeply and exhaled loudly. "Most of it, yes."

Morgan stared at her in disbelief. "So, that's a no then."

"It isn't that simple, darling, is it? He's got Christie to pay for, too."

Morgan's heart sank at the mention of her niece, a child she'd only met once. Her brother's drinking and clubbing had led to a baby with a one-night stand called Leanne, a girl who now lived with another man on the other side of the country and refused to allow Mason any more contact than was absolutely necessary.

"Has he seen her lately?"

"He went down last month and stayed for the weekend." She picked up her phone and opened the picture app. A little dark-haired girl with a big cheesy grin stared into the camera, cheek-to-cheek with Mason. They looked happy. "Leanne is coming up at Christmas to visit her parents and said we can all see Christie then."

"All of us?" Her heart leapt at the idea.

Smiling, her mum, close to tears, said, "Mason said, they talked while he was down there, and Leanne said that Christie asks about us a lot now she'd old enough to understand who we all are. He and Leanne have agreed to try and be a little more flexible around Christie and to let her decide who she wants to spend time with."

"Wow, that's—"

"A miracle, I know. I think Leanne just wanted to see Mason grow up. He's done a lot of that in the four years since Christie came along. He wants to be her dad."

"Well, I for one, am happy about that. I want to be a proper aunt, too."

"I'll keep you in the loop for everything."

Morgan caught the time on the microwave clock. "I'd best be off, got a lot to do before we head off."

"Alright, have a nice time and fill me in when you can."

Chapter Thirteen

The night before...

"How long will you be gone?" Zoe asked again. Morgan's neighbour and best friend since moving here stood in the kitchen, hip leaning against the counter, with her arms folded across her waist.

Morgan poured hot water into the cups. "Sixteen nights," she answered. It had been a weird last couple of weeks, and she hadn't heard from Alex at all. Which had both calmed and unnerved her all at the same time.

Francine had only called to confirm dates and pickup times and make sure she understood this was a job, and not a jolly. She'd been given an itinerary and told to make sure that any medical bag she carried would *blend in*.

"That's a long time. Where are you going?" Zoe asked for the second time.

Standing tall, Morgan looked her friend in the eye. "I told you, I can't give any details."

"Very mysterious. Come on Morgan, it's me."

Handing her a cup, Morgan smiled. "I know, but I've had to sign an NDA. All I can say is that I'm not leaving the country, I'm getting paid, and I'll be back in a few weeks. It's just a work thing."

Zoe narrowed her eyes. "Well, I'm not sure I like it, but of course I'll look after Knight. He can move in with me till you're back. That way he has company instead of someone just feeding him."

"Thanks, Zo. I knew I could count on you."

"Of course you can, which is why it's a little frustrating that you won't—"

"Can't," Morgan cut in.

This time Zoe rolled her eyes. "Whatever, I'm your friend, and you should always have someone who knows where you are in case anything happens."

"I'm still available and have my phone. You can call anytime. I imagine most of the time I'll be bored to death. It's a work thing, okay? It's a precaution and it's sensitive."

"Fine, but you'll tell me when you get back, right?"

Morgan chuckled. "Probably, assuming I don't have to sign another NDA."

Zoe scoffed. "NDAs, only rich posh gits and celebrities use those—is that it? It's someone famous?" Morgan remained silent. "It is. It's a famous person, why else would the NHS allow you to take time off and go swanning around as a *precaution*."

"Look, I'm neither confirming or denying, but if you watch the news, and see something, just remember that not everything you see is true."

Zoe's face beamed with anticipation. "Oh my god, I mean, cryptic but, oh my god." She bounced around enthusiastically. "When do you leave?"

"In the morning. I have to be ready by ten."

"Dammit, I'll be working. I wanted to see you off."

Morgan laughed. "Snoop, more like."

"This is the most exciting thing to happen since Harry from the fourth floor hooked up with that model from Only Fans."

"You need to get out more."

Morgan sat on her bed cross-legged, picking at a loose fray on her jeans while she considered the empty case beside her. She should probably have done this a couple of days ago, but she'd been full-on working every hour lately, working extra shifts so her colleagues could get a day off before she disappeared from the roster for four weeks, a long time in A&E shift patterns. Exhaustion was setting in, and she was looking forward to this being a bit of a break.

She blew out her cheeks and got to her feet.

"Might as well start with the obvious," she said to herself, opening the top drawer and rifling through her underwear. There had to be a laundry service at one of the hotels, surely, she thought. She counted out seven sets of what she called work underwear, plain and comfortable. Tossing them into the suitcase, she followed it up with two sets of her nicer options. The lacy, black, sexy stuff that made her feel desirable when she wore it. Which hadn't been often lately. She hadn't even had a date for over a year. Who wanted to date a doctor who was working the hours she did?

Sighing, she turned back to her wardrobe.

The difficulty she had was trying to find things that were practical and yet still looked as though she were someone different to who she was. Jeans and t-shirts were the main items she chose, adding in some light-weight jumpers and a few pairs of cotton slacks. Flicking through the coat hangers, she stopped at some dresses zipped up into dustproof bags, because that was how often they got an airing. Minus the one she'd worn to the gala; that was still in the washing basket waiting to go to the dry cleaners. She had a couple of nice cocktail dresses and an evening gown, but would she need those?

She opened her email to read the itinerary Francine had sent and noticed a new mail from her with the word "update" in the heading. She clicked on it and the original itinerary appeared. Narrowing her eyes, she re-read it and tried to decipher what the update was. And then she noticed it.

Picking up her phone, she found Francine's number and called the Ice Queen.

"Morgan, what's the issue?"

"Hi, Francine, I'm just packing and going through the itinerary, and I noticed there's quite a big difference in—"

"We scrapped the original plan and extended our stay at each hotel. Issues with the crew and set-up, is there a problem?"

"No, I guess not. I just…it would have been nice to be consulted."

"I negotiated with your bosses to have you available for four weeks. I considered that consulted."

"I see. I didn't realise, last time we spoke it was—"

"Is there a problem?" Francine asked again with a firmness that was quite intimidating.

"Well, no, I guess not." It was polite to at least ask, wasn't it? "So, now you need me for twenty-four nights?"

"Yes, again, is there a problem?"

Morgan sighed. "No, I just have things I need to organise, like my cat sitter thinking I'll be back in sixteen nights."

There was a commotion in the background of wherever Francine was. "Listen, I'm sure you can get it organised, right? It's no big deal." Her voice went muffled as she covered the phone and spoke to someone else. "Anything else?"

"Yes. Am I expected to go everywhere with Alex? Dinner, sightseeing?"

Francine laughed loudly. "My dear, there won't be time for sightseeing."

Morgan puffed out her cheeks. "So, just casual stuff then?"

"I'm coming," Francine shouted at whoever was trying to gain her attention. "Pack something nice. We eat in the suite most nights but sometimes…pack something sexy. Oh, and I need a photo for your ID. Email me one, please. I gotta go."

And with that she hung up.

Morgan pulled the dresses out of her wardrobe and laid them down on the bed.

Where they sexy enough?

And then another thought struck her: Shoes. She couldn't wear any of these dresses with the trainers and brogues she planned to take. Delving down into the bottom of the wardrobe, she found the pair of black heels that would work. Black went with everything, didn't it? Into the case those went too. Make-up bag, washbag, couple of books to read, phone charger. By the time she was finished and the case zipped up, she could barely lift it; thank goodness it had wheels.

Chapter Fourteen

The day that changed it all…

Ten o'clock on the dot the following morning, Morgan's doorbell rang. She answered the intercom and heard a man's voice. It was soft with just a hint of an accent. Irish, she thought.

"Car pickup for Dr Kelly."

"I'll be right down, thank you."

She took one last look at herself in the mirror. She'd gone with smart casual, pulling on a pair of grey slacks with a white blouse that billowed somewhat, but she liked it. She'd kept her hair simple, tying it back into a ponytail, but nothing would control the escaping tendrils that wisped out here and there. Her make-up was light, but slightly more than usual when she was at real work. She figured she could get away with a little more while on tour with Sasha.

She took one last look around to make sure she had everything she would need. Everything was switched off, and it felt eerily silent.

Zoe had picked up Knight an hour ago, and after one last attempt to find out who she would be working for, she'd given up and sulked her way back to her flat for a teams meeting that was planned, and she needed to prepare for. Knight glared at her from under Zoe's arm. How dare she go off and leave him to be pampered by his other favourite person?

Pulling her leather jacket on, she dragged the heavy case on its wheels behind her along the corridor, down in the lift and out into the world to start this new adventure.

"Dr Kelly, I'm Mike. I'll be your driver this morning." The same voice from the call up. A smart-looking man in a suit stepped up and took her case from her.

"Hi Mike, thank you."

He smiled and took several steps towards the large vehicle with its blacked-out windows and opened the door for her.

Morgan glanced up at her flat above before she got in and settled herself on the white leather seats. It wasn't a limousine like the one she'd been in for a friend's birthday years ago, but it was just as flash with extending legroom and a small cupboard to the side.

"Please help yourself to anything in the fridge," Mike said, as if he'd just read her mind.

She laughed to herself. This was wild, wasn't it? She could just imagine Zoe's face if she was here. She snapped a pic on her phone and sent it to her friend.

The sound of the boot closing was quickly followed by the driver's door opening and then the dark window between them slid down. Mike smiled at her, his hat now off his head to reveal a receding hairline.

"Make yourself comfortable. If you need anything, there's a button to your left, just press that and you can speak to me. Otherwise, sit back and enjoy the drive."

"Thank you, Mike."

She sat back as instructed and relaxed into the comfortable seat, barely noticing when the car pulled away from the kerb. The cabinet was interesting. A small fridge filled with mini bottles of champagne and water, some small tins of Coke and tonic water. Beside that was a cupboard with bottles of vodka, gin, and rum. Four crystal glasses, as well as packets of fancy crisps and nuts. She closed the door on it all and sat back again, letting her eyes shut. The drive wouldn't be that long, up the motorway to Winchester where she assumed Alex would be arriving along with Francine and whoever else her team consisted of.

She woke with a jolt and checked her watch. Was she really that exhausted? They'd been driving for less than twenty minutes. They couldn't have arrived already, could they? Looking out of the window she could see a large house, lots of glass that reflected the morning sunshine. She didn't recognise it, and she had Googled every place they were planning to stay in.

The car door on the opposite side opened and Morgan glanced over, ready to ask Mike where they were, when a familiar face appeared.

"Good morning," Alex said with a smile. She looked refreshed and glamourous in her black suit and heels. Morgan knew instantly that there would be a red sole on those beauties.

"Hi," Morgan finally managed, confusion etched across her features. Alex stepped into the car and took the seat beside Morgan, instantly pulling her seatbelt across herself and locking it into place.

"I assume Francine didn't update you on the travel information. We're trying to keep my carbon footprint as small as possible."

Morgan shook her head, beginning to understand that details changed often with these two. "No. I mean, maybe, I haven't checked my email this morning."

Alex breathed deeply. "I'm sorry, I just assumed... Are you okay with all of this? I know how persuasive Francine can be."

She thought about her P.A. Francine had insisted it was all under control and that Dr Kelly was more than happy to jump on board, but Francine had a way of spinning the truth to fit any narrative. After all, wasn't that why she employed her in the first place?

Morgan finally smiled. "Yes, sure. I mean, it all seems simple enough, right? We can get to know each other a little more."

"Right. as long as you're comfortable, I don't want—"

Morgan reached out, her palm gently landing on Alex's arm. "Right now, I should be coming off a night shift, having dealt with accidents, stitching up wounds from drunken punch-ups and dodging vomit. I think sharing a car, a few nights in a fancy hotel, listening to you play your music and hanging around just in case, is something I can handle."

Alex smiled. "Quite."

They both settled back in their seats and waited while Mike loaded up Alex's personal luggage, several more bags than the solitary case Morgan had brought with her.

"Nice house," Morgan said by way of small talk, though she did mean it. It was an amazing-looking home with its multitude of windows and white plastered walls.

Alex turned to look at it. "Yes, I'm very happy here."

"I live at the marina," Morgan announced when it seemed as though silence might take over, and she didn't want that. Alex was someone she wanted to keep talking to, to know all about.

"Lovely, do you sail?"

Morgan laughed. "Oh, no, I'm not that lucky. I just liked the set-up. Everything is kind of on my doorstep: restaurants and bars, there's a gym and coffee shop. It's nice when I come off of a long shift and just want to relax for an hour before I climb into bed again."

The vehicle rocked a little when Mike climbed back in and closed his door, the car moving slowly away a moment later.

"You work hard. I mean the NHS in general, it's such a vocation, isn't it?" Alex said, half-turning so she could look at Morgan more comfortably.

"I guess so, it's certainly not for the faint-hearted. Long hours, stress and responsibility, death and illness, and you can forget about a social life." Morgan chuckled. "I have no clue why we do it."

"I can say categorically that the rest of us are glad you do."

Chapter Fifteen

Winchester

The hotel was on the outskirts of Winchester, a huge building that looked more like Downton Abbey than any hotel Morgan had ever stayed at, and she had stayed at some nice ones in her time when she'd had a girlfriend to whisk away and enjoy it with, or just fancied a little spa break.

Mike opened the door, and Alex stepped out first, waiting at the door for Morgan to join her. They'd barely moved before Francine's dulcet tones could be heard.

"You're here," she bellowed as she walked briskly towards them. "I checked you both in already." She turned to the young man following behind pulling a gold trolley. "Make sure these all get taken up."

"Yes, no problem," he said, taking the £20 note she shoved into his hand. "Thank you."

"So, all set?" she asked Alex, greeting her with a stiff hug.

"I'm as ready as I'll ever be."

"Great, well you've got a couple of hours to rest before we go to the cathedral for a sound check." Francine now turned her attention to Morgan. "Where she goes, you go."

"For goodness' sake, Fran, I'm fine," Alex admonished with a quiet hiss.

"Good, let's keep it that way, huh?" Francine said, turning back to Morgan. "Like I said—"

"Where she goes, I go. Got it." Morgan saluted, and out of the corner of her eye, she caught Alex smirking.

"Right, let's go."

Francine marched off, leaving Mike and the kid to deal with the luggage, and Alex and Morgan to do as they were told and follow behind. Which they did, keeping a small distance between them and Francine.

"Does she ever chill out?" Morgan leaned in and asked quietly.

"Not so far," Alex replied with another grin.

If Morgan had thought the outside of the hotel was grand, she was even more impressed when they entered through the huge double doors and into a marble foyer that wouldn't look out of place in New York.

"Wow," she said in awe as her eyes swept around the room. "It's magnificent."

Alex studied her for a moment and was transfixed by the way Morgan looked with curious wonderment at the place they would be staying for the next two nights. She was so used to just rocking up somewhere, sleeping and moving on that she hadn't realised just how much she was missing. The architecture and the history of somewhere like this should have been as captivating to her as it was to Morgan, and she wondered when that had stopped being the case. When had she stopped enjoying these moments?

"It's breathtaking, isn't it?" She stared at the grand ceiling, though she wasn't sure she wasn't talking about the doctor herself.

Morgan was silent a beat before she said, "Yes. Makes you think about who else has stayed here over the years."

When Francine reappeared beside a smartly dressed woman with impeccable hair and make-up, Alex moved into professional mode and became the celebrity they were all expecting: *Sasha*.

"Sasha, may I say what a pleasure it is to have you staying here at the Albany. Anything you need, anything at all, you just let us know and we can arrange that for you," the woman said in an accent that wasn't from around here, but Alex recognised instantly as Russian, if Alex had to guess by the way her vowels moved with the R sound. It was almost made melodic by the excitement in her voice.

"Thank you." She quickly read the name badge. Nadia, Duty Manager, and had to stop herself from replying in her mother's native tongue. "Nadia. I think right now we'd just like to get settled in our rooms."

"Of course, you have the beautiful Mayflower suite. I highly recommend it. The views are just stunning. And of course, you have access 24/7 to our concierge."

"Wonderful, is it this way?" Alex pointed towards a bank of lifts in the far corner, wanting to move them along as swiftly as possible, and away from the potential glare of the public.

Nadia beamed. "Yes, of course, I will show you myself, please, follow me."

There were two lifts, one was already on its way down. Nadia inserted a small key into a lock, sending the other lift on its way too. With only a couple of floors to travel, both arrived almost simultaneously, and as the doors opened, a surprised voice spoke out loud.

"Isn't that—" the woman stepping out was saying to her husband as he ushered her away.

"I dunno, but they don't need us gawping at them," he said hurriedly, and Morgan smiled at the interaction.

"Please, after you." Nadia's permanent smile radiated warmth as she held the door open with her key. Morgan stepped towards the back and was joined by Alex, while Francine took up position in front of Alex. The all stared out into the foyer as the doors slid closed and the gawping faces disappeared.

"I guess you get that a lot?" Morgan whispered, chin jutting towards the now invisible audience.

Alex twisted around. "Yes, I'm used to it. Most people mean well, and don't actually recognise me right away. They just have this vague notion of knowing my face." She chuckled. "That's when I can usually make my getaway."

When the lift stopped and they stepped into the hallway, Nadia explained, "There are only four floors to the hotel. The fourth floor is entirely made up of suites. The lift will not come to the fourth floor without the correct keycard." Francine held their three in her hand in the air like a prize awarded for best listener. "And each suite has its own spacious living area and balcony to enjoy at your pleasure." Nadia withdrew her key card from her pocket when they came to a door marked 404. She opened the door with a flourish and stepped back to allow Sasha to enter, followed by Francine.

Morgan hesitated, not wanting to intrude in Alex's private space. She assumed she would be on another floor altogether.

"You can go in." Nadia smiled, and hesitated to move before Morgan did.

"Oh, it's fine, I'll just wait here until you can show me—"

Francine appeared at the door and glared at her. When Morgan still didn't move, she grabbed Morgan by the elbow and dragged her inside.

"This is your room too." She smiled at Nadia's confused look, before lowering her voice. "If we need the rumour of you sleeping together, you need to actually be in here with her."

Morgan's eyes went wide, and she hissed back, "I didn't realise we'd actually have to sleep together."

"Because that would be such a hardship, right?" Francine threw at her.

She couldn't answer that, so she turned her attention back to Nadia, who was speaking again.

"As you can see, the room has everything you need, but please, don't hesitate to ask. I'll leave you to settle in. Room service will bring some champagne, yes? On the house." Nadia glided across the room, closing the doors behind her as she left them to it.

"What do you mean, this is my room?" Morgan demanded to know. The deal had been to provide a room, food, and anything else she needed. They hadn't discussed sharing a bed. There was no way that could happen. Just being around Alex was having too much of an effect. She couldn't imagine how that would ramp up if they were in the same bed.

Alex turned quickly, just as agitated. "I thought you'd already explained everything to Morgan."

"I did. I sent an email this morning giving details." Francine huffed and threw her hands up in the air.

"This morning?" Morgan asked. "This morning when I was a tad busy getting ready. And how is it that only this morning I'm hearing about this? Shouldn't sharing a bed have been something we talked about?"

"For god's sake. You have your own room, your own bed," Francine insisted, moving across the room to another door that Morgan hadn't noticed till now. She flung it open, revealing a bedroom. "But to the outside world, if anyone asked who you were, then hotel gossip would only be able to say that you're sharing a suite. If people put two and two together and come up with fifty-three, so be it." Her face lit up with a satisfied smile.

"Morgan, if this isn't something you want, we can organise another room. Or you can stay here, and I'll move," Alex offered, removing her jacket and hanging it over the back of a chair.

"The hell you will," Francine said with a raised brow and a firm stare in Alexandra's direction. "This is the deal, the back-up plan, and it needs to be in place."

Looking around the room, Morgan considered things. Was it really that awful to have to sleep in this fancy suite? There was a piano for god's sake, and Nadia was right, the views across the hills was spectacular. And she had her own room, and bed, and champagne was coming.

"It's fine. I'll…we'll be fine. I was just caught unawares, that's all, and I'd appreciate updates when things change so dramatically."

"Great." Francine grinned like a cat that got the cream and ignored the update part of it. Saved by the quick rap of knuckles on the door. "Come in."

The door opened and a luggage trolley entered, being pushed by a young man. "Which room would you like me to leave it?"

"Um—" Morgan looked to Alex, who in turn turned to Francine.

"I gotta do everything round here, huh?"

Chapter Sixteen

With the porter gone, Morgan dragged her case back from Alex's room and into her own. It was impressive. The large bed that took up the space looked comfortable, and there were a lot of pillows, something she always complained about at cheaper hotels. Pillows made up for the lack of another person sleeping beside her. Pillows where huggable.

Laura Ashley walls and matching bedding made it feel more homely than a hotel room. Just inside the doorway was a space to put her case next to the wardrobe.

Unzipping the case, she laid it flat on the floor and began the process of hanging what needed to hang and refolding what needed a drawer. Everything else she placed onto the small desk, except for her wash stuff that went straight into her very own bathroom.

When she was finished, she sat on the edge of the bed and sighed. Maybe she should have brought more books to read. Glancing around quickly she noted the small TV. If she got really bored, that would come in handy.

The sound of a piano playing filtered into her thoughts, and she stood up, hovering at the door, deciding whether she would be welcomed to listen to Alex playing. But then she supposed that if she were expected to share this suite, then Alex would expect her to move around as much as she wanted to, so she opened the door.

Standing in the doorway, Morgan watched Alex. Shirt sleeves rolled up to her elbows, her fingers gliding across the keys playing some kind of sad lament that evoked emotions. Her eyes were closed, body moving in rhythm. It was fascinating.

"She does that a lot," Francine said, noticing Morgan. "Just starts playing and disappears somewhere the rest of us aren't allowed to go."

"It's magical," Morgan said in awe.

"Yeah, it is." Her palm flattened against Morgan's arm. "Enjoy it, I'll be downstairs organising lunch. You eat everything, right?"

"Yes, I'm not vegetarian or anything."

Francine took one last glance across the room at Alex, and then she left, leaving Morgan with a decision to make. She could step back and quietly close the door, give Alex the privacy to enjoy her music. It would still be audible in her room, but she didn't really want to spend the day stuck in her room or standing in the doorway either.

As though reading her mind, Alex spoke. "You can sit down." Her eyes fluttered open, and she smiled up at Morgan, inviting her into the room with a sweep of her hand before she reached up for a sheet of paper and a pencil. She jotted something down and, with her right hand, played several keys quickly, before jotting something else down.

Morgan moved towards the settee, but said, "I don't want to disturb you."

"So, just listen then," Alex said and waited for her to sit. Then she turned back to the keys and began to play again. The music began with a gentle roll into something busier and uplifting, and Morgan sat back in the seat and let her shoulders relax and her eyes close. "My mother always said, when you have nothing to say, listen."

"She sounds very wise."

"Oh, that she is, and very Russian." Alex chuckled and began to play again.

It was only in that moment that it occurred to Morgan that she was being paid for this, to sit in a fancy hotel room, on a comfortable sofa, and just listen while a world-famous musician wrote a song. Music nobody else had heard.

How many people could say they'd experienced this?

The music stopped again, and this time when Morgan opened her eyes, she found them met with a warm stare from across the room.

"I'm sending you to sleep?"

Morgan laughed lightly. "No, I—it's just relaxing, that's all. I think that's a good thing, and I'm still coming down from a hectic set of shifts. I'll catch up sooner or later. Is that something new you're playing?"

"It is. I'm working on my next album, it's called *Serenade*. At least for now, it will probably change."

"You don't like the name?"

Alex twisted around on the stool until she faced Morgan. "I rarely like the titles. They always seem so…lacking, as if a few words can describe the emotion of the music?" She scoffed. "Sorry, that sounded very prima donna, didn't it?"

Morgan smiled at her. "I think you've earned the right to be a little bit prima donna here and there."

The conversation was halted when a loud ringing sound came from the phone in the corner of the room. Morgan got up. "I'll get it." Bounding over, she picked the handset up on the fifth ring. "Hello."

"Good afternoon, this is the front desk, Ms Carlson asked us to call and let you know that lunch is being served in the restaurant, if you wanted to join her."

"Oh, thank you, I'll let Ms Montgomery know." She replaced the handset. "Francine would like you to join her for lunch."

Slowly, reverently, Alex closed the piano lid down over the keys, her hands smoothing over the polished wood like a lover would do to someone's cheek. She tidied her notes and placed them into a folder.

"I guess we should do as we're told before Francine sends security up to find us." She chuckled. "And believe me, she would."

Morgan hesitated. "So, how does this work?" she asked before Alex reached the door.

The dark hair whipped around. "What do you mean?"

"I mean—we're going to just do things together and let people come to their own conclusions, or do you want me to act like I'm your girlfriend? Do you want me to join you for lunch?"

"Well, you have to eat, don't you?"

Chuckling, Morgan walked towards Alex, holding her gaze with an intensity that Alex both loved and feared.

"Yes, I just don't think Francine has really thought this through. Her plan is that I stay out of the way and only if asked do we suggest I'm your lover."

"Right."

"And yet, I am instructed, where you go, I go."

"Ah." Alex's brow raised.

"So, how do I stay out of the way, while being wherever you are?" Morgan questioned.

"Yes, I see how that could be confusing." She stared at Morgan, wanted to move closer and solve the issue by just kissing her, but that would be inappropriate, wouldn't it? "How about for now, I decide when I think you should be wherever I am, and when you should keep in the shadows?"

Morgan chuckled at that. "Makes me sound like Batman."

"Well, I'm sure you have your very own superpowers," Alex said. *That stare for one*, she thought.

Grinning, Morgan nodded slowly. "I hope I do." The stare continued. "So, lunch?"

Alex shook herself out of it. "Yes, I'd very much like it if you joined me for lunch, and as for pretending to be my lover, we should probably play that by ear. Maybe have a signal."

"A signal? Like…"

"I don't know, I suppose I could…maybe if I reach for you, touch you in some way? That would indicate to you that..." Had she moved? She suddenly felt very close to Morgan, and hot, very hot. "Your knee…that's…it's an intimate thing to do, right? I…"

"Sure, okay." Morgan smiled slowly. "My knee works if we're sitting down."

"Yes, Oh, that's…" Alex laughed nervously. "That would be weird, wouldn't it, if we were standing and I reached for your knee." She pulled at her earlobe and looked away, "Okay, your hand, maybe that…maybe that works better?"

Morgan reached for the door handle and smirked. "Sure. I'm good with either."

Chapter Seventeen

It was quiet as they rode the lift down, and Alex considered the conversation they'd just had. There was something about Morgan Kelly that set Alexandra Montgomery on fire. She needed to be careful about that. Even though she was sure the feeling was mutual, it wasn't the time. Not now, not when she needed to be focused and on top of her game. But still, penetrating every thought lately had been those eyes, that smile, and the way Morgan Kelly took flirty playfulness to another level.

She was so lost in her thoughts that she didn't notice the doors to the lift opening until she heard the gasp and then the voice following it up.

"Oh, it's you?" the woman said, grinning and pointing at Sasha. "You were on my TV last week."

It took mere seconds for her smiling persona to kick in and say a friendly, "Hello." Not stopping to chat, she casually walked past with Morgan following. The woman wanted to say something else, but Alex had already moved on.

A couple of people pulled their phones out and began to film or take photos, which Morgan thought was incredibly rude, but par for the course, she assumed. She understood right there that she needed to make sure she too always looked her best if she was going to pop up in the background of photos that could essentially be online forever and ever amen.

"Could I get a photo, Sasha?"

The woman had caught up with them, determined to get her moment with a celebrity. Morgan wondered why Alex didn't have, for want of a better word, a bodyguard. Not that the woman was particularly scary, with her twinset and pearls and her iPhone at the ready, but still, Alex was an easy target for a nutjob with an obsession.

Alex stopped and allowed the woman to move in closer, her hand stretched out holding the phone as they both smiled at it. It clicked three or four times before Alex tried in vain to move away.

"Just one more?" the woman said, holding onto Alex's arm like they were old buddies catching up. The smile on Alex's face waned, and Morgan moved in.

"Sorry, but I really do need to steal her away. We have lunch plans and we're already late." Morgan smiled, taking Alex by the hand, and gently peeled away the woman's grip.

Alex smiled up at Morgan, grateful, before turning to the woman, and the other fans who had gathered. "I really do have to get going."

As they moved away, instead of releasing her hold, Alex squeezed more tightly, and Morgan just kept walking.

"Thank you," Alex said, still keeping her head down. "It's not that I don't like meeting fans, I just…I'm not good in those situations when I'm not prepared for them. I can feel my heart racing—"

"Do you want to go back to the room, so I can check you out?" Morgan asked quickly once they were out of earshot of anyone else.

That was an offer that Alex was finding more enticing by the minute, and she had to stop herself from answering with a firm *yes,* followed up with *get me naked* and *check me out*.

Finally, Alex looked up at her. "No, I'm fine. I just…once we get to the dining room and I can get a glass of water, I'll be fine." Releasing Morgan's hand, she slid her arm through the crook of her elbow instead and leaned against her, breathing in that sweet citrus and berry aroma of her perfume. "I just need to sit down."

When they reached the entrance to the dining room, Morgan extracted herself and smiled at the waiter to get his attention.

"We're meeting—"

"Hey, over here!" Francine all but bellowed across the room.

Morgan smiled in that way English people did so well when they felt somewhat embarrassed by another's behaviour. "And there they are."

The waiter smiled back, an equally British response that said, *I understand.* He led them over to the table and seated them alongside Francine and a man Morgan didn't know.

"Your waiter will be over soon to take any orders," he said before backing away and leaving them all to it.

Morgan instantly reached for the jug of water and poured Alex a glass, passing it to her before she'd even taken a seat. Alex smiled gratefully and mouthed a silent *thank you.*

"Cecil, I didn't know you'd be joining us today," Alex said once she'd finished drinking. She pulled the napkin into her lap and spread it out.

"Alexandra, darling." His accent belied his physical image. He certainly did not look like a posh boy from Oxford or Cambridge. "It was a last-minute change of plans, thought I'd pop in and see how things were going. Francine tells me we're all on track." His line of sight moved beyond Alex to land on Morgan, watching her intently as she took a seat finally. "And you are?" His grin turned lascivious.

Morgan turned her attention to him. His dyed black hair receding at the front and grown longer around the back and side did nothing to counteract the fact he was aging. He half stood and grinned with crooked, stained teeth, and Morgan instantly thought of the child catcher in *Chitty Chitty Bang Bang.*

"This is Dr Morgan Kelly," Alex explained, quickly dampening any ideas he might have had. "She's my…companion." With that, Alex moved her hand under the table to land firmly upon Morgan's knee.

Morgan got the distinct impression that Alex was making a very loud point with this man, rather than any real pretence of romance for her own benefit. He gave Morgan the creeps. The stereotypical music Lothario, she thought to herself as she leaned in closer and played along with Alex, her arm slinking around the back of the chair Alex sat in.

Francine looked back and forth between the pair with a knowing look on her face.

"A companion, huh?" His grin grew wider as he imagined what that might entail. "And a doctor? Smart and pretty."

"That's right," Alex agreed, turning slightly to smile lovingly at her *partner*, not realising quite how face to face they now were. "She is incredibly smart, and beautiful." Their gaze held and she began to drown in those eyes. "And very much off limits."

"Noted," Cecil said, picking up his glass and sipping. "Francine tells me you're working on something new."

Euphoria

Something new that she was struggling to find motivation for.

Alex finally turned away from Morgan to give Cecil her attention, but her hand remained in place, slowly caressing the firm thigh beneath it.

"I am, yes. It's very early days though, so don't go getting excited," Alex said to him.

It took everything in Morgan to keep her breathing steady and focus on the conversation. She imagined the palm moving higher still, her thighs parting and creating the space for Alex to let her fingers slide against her aching need.

Where had that come from?

She needed to get a grip of herself. Staring at Cecil, she listened intently as he spoke. Forced herself to focus on him rather than the wanton need building inside of her to just grab Alex's hand and pull it closer.

"Well, make sure to keep me in the loop. Us promotors like to be in the know with these kinds of things. I can guarantee another sellout tour with a new album." He winked, and Morgan felt like she needed a shower, it was so slimy.

Francine leaned forward. "You know we will absolutely do that, when the time comes. Right now though we need to get through this tour, right? Right?" She laughed and held her drink up. "Cheers to that."

"Shall we eat?" Cecil said once they'd all raised their glasses.

"Yes, let's do that," Alex replied. She finally moved her palm from Morgan's leg.

Morgan was unsure what she wanted more: to grab the hand and put it back, or breathe a sigh of relief that she could focus again. She was grateful when Alex offered her a menu to look at, something tangible to focus on.

"Thank you," she whispered, and Alex leaned closer, a move that would look intimate should anyone be paying attention.

"Order anything you want, alright?"

"Sure." Morgan smiled. Catching Cecil eyeing them both, she reached her own hand up and gently stroked Alex's cheek. "Thank you."

For a moment, Alex looked perplexed, conflicted, as though she might actually lean forward and kiss her. And then she glanced behind her and understood. She sat back and picked up her menu, and Morgan realised that this was not going to be as easy as she thought it would.

Alex Montgomery was making her feel things.

"Enjoy the hotel and what it has to offer," Alex said as she was about to climb into the car after Francine. "I hear the hot stone massage is a dream."

"You don't want me to come with you?" Morgan asked, puzzled.

Alex licked her lips as her real thoughts ran through her mind. Thoughts that involved Morgan coming with her, but not in the way of travel. She needed some space from her, that was for sure.

"No, I think I'll be fine, and if I'm not, I can send Mike back for you. It's only up the road."

Morgan sighed dramatically. "Alright, I guess I can force myself to enjoy a pampering." She grinned, and Alex laughed at the playfulness.

"I know you can." Alex's eyes lit up at the affirmation. "I'm not sure how long we'll be, but I'll see you when I return. Just…" She looked up at the grandeur of the hotel. "I want you to enjoy yourself, relax a little. It's going to be a long few weeks."

"Hey, are you coming or what?" Francine shouted from inside the car. "We've got sound checks and people greeting, so let's skedaddle, okay?"

Alex raised her brows. Morgan pressed her lips together to stop the giggle that threatened to erupt. "I've had my orders. See you later."

She finally climbed into the car and turned to look back at Morgan as Mike drove them away, wishing she could shout "stop" and run back to her like a movie scene.

"Why isn't Morgan coming with us? She's supposed to be wherever you are," Francine questioned once they were settled and halfway down the hotel drive.

With Morgan out of sight, Alex turned to Francine. "Because it's going to be a long few weeks, and I think it will do her some good to relax and actually enjoy this experience. She works hard in her proper job; she deserves to get pampered." What she didn't say was that she was finding it difficult to keep herself in check where the delightful Dr Kelly was concerned.

"Uh huh, just so long as she's ready to go the moment—"

Alex looked away and out of the window. "I'm hoping she's going to get paid for doing absolutely nothing."

Francine cracked a smile. "Yeah, I guess so."

Thinking back to what Morgan had said earlier about Francine not thinking this through, Alex sighed. Maybe she should have thought harder about it too.

Back in her room, Morgan flopped down on the bed.

Lunch usually meant a limp sandwich and a large coffee. She hadn't eaten that much mid-afternoon since…she blew out her cheeks. She couldn't remember. It had been delicious though in more ways than just the awesome food, and the very nice wine she'd allowed herself one glass of.

The way Alex had used their 'signal' not for her own needs, but to create some kind of boundary between Morgan and this Cecil guy. A shudder ran through her at the thought of him. He creeped her out. But Alex had made it clear, Morgan was not available.

Off limits, that was what Alex had said. But it wasn't the words that had had the impact, it was the way Alex had looked at her and not him when she'd said it. Along with the firm, warm palm on her knee that hadn't remained there. She could still feel the caress as it moved up and down her thigh. Reminded how turned on she'd been imagining more, she let her hand move lower, sliding beneath the band of her slacks and underwear.

Finding herself wet, her hips moved involuntarily, needing her touch. She closed her eyes and conjured up the image of Alex staring at her, the words off-limit playing on a loop. Her fingers splayed herself open, digitus medius pressing against her clit, making her moan out loud.

Her free hand squeezed and caressed her breast as she headed towards an orgasm. "Alex," she whispered into the air, gasping as she sped up her movements, ligaments tightening as she fell over the edge. She pulled her hand away in shock. Breathing heavily, she considered what it all meant, and the answer was something very, very dangerous.

She sat up quickly, readjusted her clothes, and tried to clear her mind. She needed something to focus on, to go and do something instead of hanging around here. Maybe Alex was right; maybe she needed to relax and let some of this tension go.

There was a phone beside the bed, and she picked up the handset, dialling one for main reception. It barely rang twice before it was answered by an eager-sounding man.

"Hello, The Albany, Mathew speaking, how may I help?"

"Hi Mathew, this is—" She held the phone under her chin and stood up.

"Ms Montgomery's suite," he said brightly.

"Yes, that's right, I wondered if I could book in at the spa this afternoon."

"Of course, let me just transfer you."

Soft music came on for less than a minute before the phone was answered again. "Good afternoon, Serenity Haven. Caroline speaking, how can I assist you today?"

Morgan went through the options and was booked in; it was that simple. Anything for Ms Montgomery's friends.

Putting the phone down, Morgan considered things. Her hand ran down her shin and felt the short prickle of hair. That was not something she was turning up to the spa with.

She hadn't really taken it in when she'd popped her wash bag in earlier, but her bathroom was a thing of opulence. A claw-legged bath with a free-standing tap gave her all kinds of ideas for later.

Unzipping the wash bag in the silence, she stopped, noticing all of the small bottles of fancy shampoos and shower gels. She shook her head at her naivety. Of course, everything would be provided. She took the razor and put her bag to one side, and stepped up to the shower, turning it on to heat up. A huge rainfall showerhead lit up, and she studied the panel that controlled the water. A musical note caught her eye, and she pressed it and waited. Gentle music began to play through hidden speakers.

She blew out her cheeks and imagined whether Alex had a shower like this in that big old beach house of hers. Of course, she did. A house like that had everything and more, didn't it? A house Morgan could easily see herself living in.

"Stop being ridiculous." She laughed at herself. "This really is another world."

Chapter Eighteen

Winchester Cathedral, built over 900 years ago, really was the most perfect place to hold an event like this. As with all buildings of this magnitude, it was built to enjoy sound. Stone surfaces carried the acoustics perfectly in its reflection of the music to the audience, and Alex loved it. That tiny spark of something entered her nervous system and she felt it ignite the tiniest flicker of a flame.

The crew had been working since the early morning, installing a sound system and lighting rig, as well as the small stage area that her Steinway Model B grand piano had been wheeled onto, and she would finally get to sit down and do a sound check ready for the following night's performance. She nodded hello to them as she passed by.

Looking around now, she could see why the crew would need more than a 12-hour turnaround. It was a massive undertaking just to set it all up, and they'd be working through the night to take it all down again.

Just walking into the impressive building had given her goosebumps.

Her phone buzzed.

Unknown number: So, how's it going?

Alex: I'm okay at the moment, but later might be different.

Unknown number: Really? Why? What's happening?

Alex: I've just got something going on that will mean I'm in the mood, if you know what I mean.

Unknown number: In that kind of mood, huh? Damn, maybe we should meet, I could use a woman in that kind of mood.

Alex: I'm sure you could but I actually like having this unknown quantity to bounce things off of.

Unknown number: I guess, I've actually got a bit of a crush on someone myself. Someone at work, who is so out of my league, but it's nice to fantasise, right?

Yes, it was, Alex thought to herself with an image of Morgan floating into her mind. She was about to reply when she heard her name being shouted like a foghorn.

Francine called her stage name, and it echoed in the chamber. Alex managed to avoid rolling her eyes when she saw Francine beckoning her over to meet yet another human being she could probably have avoided, but should probably be polite to.

She smiled and waved back, and after one final look around, she headed over to meet whoever it was that Francine deemed important, mentally slapping herself for feeling so uncharitable. It was nice that people wanted to meet her, she reminded herself.

"Ms Montgomery, it's so lovely to meet you." The woman extended her hand from beneath the red cassock she wore so pristinely. "We're all so very excited about the performance this evening. It's a sellout I believe."

It was indeed a sellout, her shows usually were, but she simply answered, "Thank you…"

"Oh, so sorry." The woman laughed. "Cassandra Ogilvy, I'm the reverend dean here at Winchester."

Alex continued to smile as though she had any clue what that actually meant. "Well, this is such a beautiful building. I'm about to do a sound check if you'd like to listen."

"That would be wonderful. Do you mind an audience? I know some of the staff would love to enjoy your music too."

"Of course, why not?" She turned to Francine. "I'll just be—" She pointed to the piano in the middle of the hall.

"Sure, sure." Francine shooed her off. "You go get started."

As she approached the small stage and the grand piano, Alex felt the first tingling of excitement. Her fingers twitched, eager to reach out and touch the ivory keys and play something, anything, it didn't matter. All that mattered was the sound, and her chance to escape this world for just a moment. It was the only time lately that she felt alive. Really alive.

There was a small step for her to use to move seamlessly onto the podium, the comfortable stool on its marker. Reaching out, she dragged her forefinger along the polished edge as she circled the instrument and allowed herself to enjoy its presence.

She breathed in the smell of the lacquer, freshly done before every tour. She found a comfort in it. Like a new car or the smell of a newborn baby, it was as distinctive to her.

When she finally took a seat, she noticed a small group of people quietly walking in to take seats at the back, trying not to be noticed. It wouldn't bother her now though, not now that the keys were in reach, shining under the lights.

Raising her hands, she flexed her fingers and went through the motions of moving her fingers one by one against invisible air keys, and then, when she was ready, she pressed down and ran the scale.

Starting at A and ending on G, up and down, she let her fingers loosen up and then just like that, she was playing without thought. Her mind closed to everything and everyone else around her as she listened and focused on the acoustics.

Without speakers and microphones, just the power of the piano and the thick medieval walls around them, sound bounced and weaved and echoed perfectly. She felt the shiver run down her spine and lifted her head, eyes shut, and revelled in it.

This was what she was born to do, wasn't it?

Morgan hadn't even bothered to get dressed following her afternoon at the spa. She'd just wrapped the huge, soft, robe that she'd found in the room around herself and walked barefoot through the lobby and back up to the suite.

She hadn't felt this relaxed in years, and she revelled in it, and considered how she could manage now, with the whopping payment she was getting for this, to be able to treat herself more often.

Another sensation was lying just below the surface though, something equally relaxing, and one she would need to take care of later: arousal.

Lying face down on the bed being massaged, she'd considered just how she was going to deal with this situation. She needed a plan if she was going to deal with this constant sexual attraction to Alex. Otherwise, it was going to be a very long three weeks or more.

She opened the door, walked inside the suite, and kicked the door closed, flopping down unconcerned onto the sofa. Stretching out, it was so comfortable. She didn't stand a chance, and promptly fell asleep.

When she woke, the room was almost dark. The sun set earlier this time of year, but also, the curtains were closed. A small desk lamp lighting the other side of the room was the only illumination in the room. She had no recollection of turning that on.

Morgan stretched her legs out and groaned at the quiet ache in her hip from lying in the same position too long, and almost jumped out of her skin when she realised that she was no longer alone.

"You're awake? I didn't want to disturb you." Alex's voice was quiet, soft, and yet, it sent a shiver down Morgan's spine as she sat up. How long had Alex been sitting there, watching her? Her arousal spiked again.

"God, I'm sorry, I just sat down for a moment and…" She shrugged and laughed nervously. "The spa was very relaxing."

Alex smirked. "I can see." She twirled a glass in her hand, the ice clinking gently against the side. She held it up for Morgan to see. "Can I interest you in one?"

"Uh, sure, why not?" Glancing down at herself, she blushed when she realised the gown had split open, revealing her very bare thigh. "I should get changed."

"Don't on my account." Alex smiled over at her as she poured a drink before catching herself. "That was— My apologies if that made you feel uncomfortable." She poured a second. "That was inappropriate."

There was something different about her, Morgan thought. She couldn't quite put her finger on what it was, but it was stirring something all the same. Something about the way Alex kept glancing at her made Morgan feel a little…unnerved, but not in an intimidating way. No, it was very much wanted.

"It's fine, honestly." But she tightened the belt anyway.

She glanced up as she felt Alex's presence in front of her. A glass was dangling from fingers for Morgan to take, and there was an intensity in the eyes that stared down at her.

"Thank you," Morgan said, taking a sip of what she assumed was very expensive scotch. It warmed her tongue and throat as it slid down like velvet, and she wondered what it would taste like on Alex's tongue. Alex continued to stare, and for a brief moment, Morgan questioned whether she could mind read.

"Did it all go well?" Morgan asked, needing to say something to break the silence. "The rehearsal?"

Alex stepped away. "Yes, thank you. It's going to be a wonderful place to play." She sat down again in the chair she'd previously been sitting in. Relaxed, assured as she sank back into it and raised a leg to rest her ankle on her thigh.

"I can imagine." Morgan sipped the drink, wondering if dropping to her knees between those legs would be welcomed. "I'm looking forward to it, assuming I'm invited."

Sitting forward in her seat, Alex scanned Morgan's face, searching for something, before she finally said, "I'll make sure you have a front-row seat."

The energy in the room had shifted and amplified. There was nothing obviously flirtatious, and yet, it felt charged, as though something was building between them that at any moment might explode into something more.

Into something Morgan was sure she wouldn't stop from happening.

She couldn't keep trying to deny it to herself anymore. Alex Montgomery had something about her that was hot, and under any other circumstances, Morgan would make it very obvious she was interested, but this was dangerous, wasn't it? She was working. She wasn't being paid to fraternise, was she? But then, she had been asked to pretend to be a lover.

God, it was all so frustrating. She had no idea how any of this was going to work.

The tension was like a hot sheet between them, that if dropped would leave them both bare and naked with one another. Heat emanating from both—too hot to touch, and yet, the risk of getting burned made it all the more exciting.

As though reading her thoughts, Alex stood up and downed the last of her drink. Placing the crystal glass onto the side table, she held onto it for a second, twisting it back and forth, deciding something, before she let go.

"I should go to bed before I say or do something—"

"It's not just me, right? You feel it, too," Morgan said quickly, standing to join her but keeping an appropriate distance between them that felt safe enough, for now at least.

Alex said nothing, and when Morgan stepped towards her, she didn't retreat.

"Dilated pupils, increased breathing. I don't need to be a doctor to know when someone is aroused around me. You feel it too, don't you?"

Alex smiled. "I felt it the first time I met you, but I appreciate that right now, what I'm feeling is—I'm euphoric. I'm feeling things that in the morning will have subsided. When I play, it makes me feel powerful and very sexual, that's what I'm sure you're picking up on."

"Is that all it is?"

Closing the gap between them, Alex smiled when Morgan's tongue slid out and wet her lip. Slowly, Alex raised a hand. Her finger extended and gently followed, deftly gliding along the soft bottom lip.

Alex stared deeply at her. "No, that's not all, but I don't think what I need right now," she swallowed, "is in your job description." Alex forced herself to step back. Back and away from this temptation, but she didn't get far, stopped by Morgan's fingers gripping her sleeve.

"Tell me what you need?"

Alex glanced down at the fingers resting on her arm, and then she looked up and into the warmest eyes she'd ever known.

"I need to be in control, Morgan. I need to focus on…" She let her words trail off before she glanced away. "…someone else's needs and let the adrenaline work itself out of my system."

She waited a moment for that to register with Morgan. And when nothing more was forthcoming, she finally moved away.

"And if I want that?" Morgan said confidently, her words stopping Alex in her tracks. "If I wanted to provide the focus for your need?"

Alex said nothing.

Morgan continued, moving closer as she spoke. "You're failing to take something very important into account."

Alex turned back to face her. "What's that?" Her blue eyes flashed an intensity that struck Morgan deep within.

Morgan waited, and then very slowly, her hands deftly untied the belt on her robe. "That I have a mind of my own."

Watching her, Alex let her eyes scan slowly downward as the bare skin between Morgan's breasts was exposed, her stomach, and then lower to the shaven area between her thighs.

"What does your mind think it wants?" Alex asked, her voice an octave lower, husky and sultry. Wanting her more than she'd wanted anyone in a long time.

Morgan stepped towards her.

Alex held her ground, she didn't want to back off, not now it was being offered. Permission granted. How could she deny it any longer?

"I want you to play me the way you play that piano," Morgan whispered. "Touch me the way you play."

"Are you sure about that?" A perfectly arched brow raised as Alex spoke. "You think you can handle that?"

Morgan nodded slowly, pulling her bottom lip between her teeth, as she closed the space between them. "I want to find out."

Chapter Nineteen

Taking her hand, Alex led the way, guiding Morgan into the bedroom. Her bedroom, not Morgan's. When they were inside, she closed the door and locked it. Alone, confined, together. Alex leant back against the door and watched as Morgan scanned the room, still half naked, confident in her skin. She liked that.

Taking her time, Alex silently unbuttoned the cuffs on her shirt as she moved closer. Waiting when she was just a step away, she considered what she wanted to do first. So many possibilities, but she didn't want to do anything too intense, not yet, not until she was sure Morgan could and would want it. When she'd made up her mind, she took the final step and with her lips almost touching Morgan's ear, she instructed, "Take this off."

Morgan smirked.

Her nipples hardening instantly. The shiver of excitement that rolled under her skin created a pathway of goosebumps that culminated right between her thighs.

She did as she was told.

With shaky fingers, she shimmied until the robe slipped from her shoulders. Slowly, it slid downwards to reveal the bare, pale skin of her back, buttocks, and legs.

Alex caught the garment before it landed on the floor and pulled the belt from its loops, tossing the rest of it to the side, not caring where it landed. She couldn't take her eyes off Morgan's naked form. She'd imagined it. Of course she had. Many nights since meeting Dr Morgan Kelly, Alex had satisfied herself with images and thoughts about what she would do if she had the opportunity to explore the real option.

The submissiveness was just enough.

She trailed a finger across flawless skin, riding the bumps of Morgan's spine until she came to the path that parted her buttocks. Divine, she thought to herself, a guttural groan emanating from her when Morgan twitched at the ticklish movement.

"Are you sure you want this?" Alex asked once more. mot because she was unsure herself. This was a question born of confidence that she knew entirely what she wanted to do next, and would do it, if given permission.

Morgan nodded.

The thrill she had felt from that one fingertip alone had been enough to make her wet. But that was nothing compared with what she felt when Alex reached for her hand and wound one end of the belt from her robe around her wrist. She moved around Morgan to stand in front of her, their eyes locked as Alex reached for her other hand and tied the wrists together. "Sure?"

"Yes," Morgan managed to gasp out before she was yanked forward towards the bed, a huge four-poster frame without the curtains. Her arms were lifted, and the end of the belt looped over the frame and tied. She was thankful that she was tall enough to wrap her hands around the metal edge, her feet planted to the carpeted floor, toes scrunching in the thick pile.

"If you want me to stop at any time, you say Caesura." Alex spoke softly, her breath husking against the shell of Morgan's ear, making Morgan whimper. "Do you understand?"

Morgan nodded.

The sharp upward slap of a palm against her buttocks made her yelp.

"Do you understand?" Alex asked again, a little more dominantly this time.

Breathing deeply, Morgan uttered a single, "Yes." She felt an overwhelming urge to push her backside out and into the warm palm that stroked the spot that still tingled.

"You'll answer me with words," Alex instructed.

"I will."

Morgan closed her eyes, let herself feel the movement of the hand lovingly caressing her bottom. She'd experienced something similar before, with other lovers, but never quite so…thoroughly, so reverently.

"Have you ever been spanked before, Morgan?"

She went to shake her head but then remembered.

"No, never." Her clit throbbed between her legs, and she squeezed her thighs together to try and stave off the pulsing ache. But her mind was thrown when once again the upward strike of flesh upon flesh smarted, and the vibration rocketed between her legs.

She cried out, squeezing her thighs together more tightly until she felt a booted foot push between her feet and gently urge her to open her stance.

"I decide when you will find relief. Do you understand that, Morgan?" Alex unbuttoned her own shirt slowly, enjoying the feeling of each tiny button between her fingers, imagining Morgan's nipples later.

Moaning when she felt the same soft palm rub over the area that moments ago had smarted, Morgan whimpered a desperate, "Yes."

Relaxing into the touch, Morgan almost forgot the sting of the spank, wanting to enjoy this moment for as long as it lasted, which was never long enough. Jolted once again.

She felt the cold air first, and the sting that came seconds after the loud crack sound hit her ears.

Her cheek burned, her clit ached, and Morgan had never felt more turned on in her life.

She breathed deeply, until she finally felt it, the comforting, gentle rub and caress that seemed to connect with her throat and eject another moan of approval.

"You like that?" Alex asked, softly rubbing the red mark that was starting to show.

"Yes."

Alex chuckled, as she unzipped her trousers and let them fall to the floor, kicking them away as she stepped forward. "I knew it, the moment we met. I had this feeling that you were quite the naughty one." She ended on a whisper against Morgan's ear. Her tongue slicked around the shell, and Morgan's knees almost gave way.

"Are you wet, Doctor?"

The use of her professional title threw her for a moment, but the next strike quickly brought her to her senses. "Yes, yes, I'm—" She gulped and tried to think, but her mind was quiet. She couldn't focus on anything, nor did she want to. There was a calmness she was sinking into.

"Say it." Another smack of her flesh almost made her come, or was it the way in which Alex was speaking, taking charge, demanding of her?

"I'm wet," she forced out, gripping harder on the bedframe.

"Wet for who?" Alex asked. Her underwear, already soaked, joined the rest of her clothing on the floor.

Morgan's head dropped as one more smack against her backside caught her off guard.

"You," she whispered.

A naked arm slid around her waist from behind, and she felt the warm, nakedness of hard nipples pressed against her back, a knee thrust in between her legs, snuggly pressing against her backside. Alex rested her chin on Morgan's shoulder.

"I want you to come. I want that for you, but only when I allow it, alright? If you come before I say so, there will be a punishment." Alex's breath quickened along with Morgan's.

"I won't, I won't…until…"

The arm around her waist tightened, and she mewled with the words "Good girl" whispered in her ear.

"Such a good girl," Alex repeated as her other hand moved around and teased Morgan's folds. Stroking her, spreading her wetness for so long that Morgan thought she'd never be allowed to come.

Her head fell back against Alex's shoulder when Alex dragged a finger along her slit. Cool air hit her clit when Alex finally parted her and delved between. A feeling of complete ecstasy when the intruding digit moved and began to manipulate her clitoris with expert handling. Pinching and rubbing indiscriminately, until finally, the fog of almost delirious pleasure cleared enough for Morgan to understand that there was a rhythm, her climax building and falling, building and falling.

Euphoria

Her body was an instrument, and Alex was playing her.

Morgan's fingers turned white, her hips pressing to meet the touch. Uncontrollable whimpers escaped her mouth before she could even think.

"You can't, not yet," Alex said, as though reading her mind again. "Ritardando," she whispered, decreasing her speed before bringing her touch to a virtual stop. "Lento."

"Please," Morgan pleaded unabashedly. Where had that come from, an urge to beg and plead? She'd never felt anything like this. They hadn't even kissed and yet, Alex was knuckle deep inside of her, dictating if and when she could come.

"I like that." Alex smiled and rewarded her. "Andante." Her fingers began to move again, the tempo increasing to hold Morgan in a sense of more but not enough.

Pressing her hips forward, her legs feeling weaker, arms aching as every sinew stretched and tired, she begged, "Please, Alex, I need—"

"Accelerando."

The word whispered that way was erotic, but the gradual increase of pressure and speed that accompanied it felt out of this world.

The pressure between Morgan's legs intensified, her clit swelling with every movement as Alex's palm hit against it. "Please, I just want to— Please."

Alex's arm that had at some point eased around her waist, tightened again, holding Morgan against her nakedness, fingers speeding up.

"Allegro. Allegro," Alex said before she whispered once more, and Morgan finally understood the random Italian words. "Now, crescendo."

Morgan had never lost control of herself like that, her bones liquifying, muscles collapsing, her nerve endings on fire as everything she'd been fighting for and had been held back from achieving, surged. All of it, all at once, pulsing through her until all that was holding her up was Alex's arm around her waist. It took a moment to realise that Alex had loosened the belt, and Morgan's arms dropped by her side. Her body collapsed, spent.

When she came to, she found herself on the bed. Rolling to one side, she acknowledged the nakedness beside her against her skin, and she enjoyed the comfort of it. Fingers dragged through her hair slowly, reverently. She was being held, embraced, and it felt wonderful.

"You didn't even kiss me," she said quietly, still trying to make sense of what had just happened.

Alex chuckled. "Is that so?"

"Hm, I've never come without kissing before." Morgan smiled and levered herself up onto her elbow. "Don't you like kissing?"

Reaching up to touch her cheek, Alex answered, "I love kissing."

"So, why didn't you kiss me?"

"That wasn't what I needed." She lifted herself until their mouths were almost touching. "Now, I'd like it." Her lips ghosted Morgan's, faintly brushing, moving away every time Morgan tried to capture them.

"I want to kiss you."

"What's stopping you?" Alex breathed against her. "What stops you doing what you want?"

Morgan thought for a moment. "Permission."

Alex smiled.

She hadn't been wrong.

"Kiss me."

It wasn't an invitation. It was a demand, to take what she wanted. Morgan wasn't used to being in this kind of dynamic, and yet, she fit like a glove with it. Slowly, her hand reached up and threaded her fingers into Alex's hair, her eyes locked on Alex's mouth.

"Now," Alex encouraged.

Tightening her grip, this time when she pressed forward, Alex couldn't move out of the way. Morgan captured her lips and forced her tongue between them, revelling in the groan of satisfaction that rumbled from Alex's throat.

Morgan pressed her body forward and constrained Alex into the mattress, all of her weight on top of her. Only when she was trapped beneath her did Morgan stop kissing.

"You liked that, didn't you?" Alex grinned and opened her legs wider. An invitation. Permission granted silently.

"I want to kiss you elsewhere." Alex's raised brow made her rethink her wording. Alex might be up for switching, but she was still very much in control right now.

Morgan considered. "May I kiss you elsewhere?"

"Put your mouth here." Alex pointed between her legs.

Rearing up onto her knees, Morgan thought for a moment, coming to a decision. Alex watched in amusement as Morgan got off the bed. Slightly confused, she internally shrugged and relaxed back against the pillows, her arms lazily moving to stretch out behind her head.

Just as she got comfortable, she felt her ankles grabbed, and she was dragged down the bed.

She gasped when she looked down to find Morgan grinning up at her, already dropping to her knees.

"Full of surprises, aren't you?" Alex sighed and relaxed into the first touch of lips against her skin.

Chapter Twenty

The morning came quicker than Morgan had hoped. She stretched out and smiled as she remembered the hours earlier. Her body ached in that delicious way that reminded her of every touch of her body.

She closed her eyes and tried to shake herself of the instant arousal that sent her clit into overdrive again. "Fuck," she muttered as her hand moved towards the pulsing need.

It wouldn't take long, she thought to herself. Her fingertips worked in tight circles, while her mind replayed the sound of Alex instructing her, demanding of her, encouraging her.

She pressed harder, moved faster and was just about to fall over the edge.

There was a sharp rap of knuckles on the door, followed by, "Doctor, are you awake?"

"Shit." Morgan whipped her hand away and pulled the sheet higher to cover herself in case Francine took it upon herself to just waltz in.

"Yes, I'm up."

"Okay, good, we need to be at the venue in an hour," Francine said.

Morgan groaned and reached for her watch on the bedside cabinet. Almost eleven. She threw the cover back and swung her legs out of bed. Grabbing the dressing gown, she pulled it on and tied it tightly before opening the door and stepping out.

There was no sign of Alex.

"If you want breakfast, you'll have to be quick," Francine said. "I told Alex to wake you, and she insisted you should decide when you want to wake up, but we're on a schedule so…" She shrugged.

"Where is Alex?"

"She's gone for a walk in the grounds."

Morgan picked up the jug of orange juice and poured a tall glassful. She picked it up and sipped as she wandered to the window and looked out. There was no sign of Alex.

"I'll be ready in thirty minutes," she said, turning to Francine. "I just need a shower."

"Alright, I'll be downstairs."

"Sure, I'll be down ASAP." She didn't wait for anything further. Leaving Francine behind, she went back to her room, closed the door behind her and swigged the orange juice down.

She tried to shake off the disappointment, understanding that her expectation of what this morning would look like wasn't the version of events she was experiencing. But that was okay, wasn't it? She wasn't a needy lover.

Sighing deeply, she allowed the disappointment to leave her body, untied the robe and strode naked into the bathroom and the shower.

Hair piled up to avoid getting wet, she scrubbed herself clean and stepped out. Pulling a towel around herself, she walked back into the bedroom and opened the wardrobe. Her suitcase was at the bottom, and she yanked it out onto the bed, opening it.

While her body dried, she opened drawers and took out underwear and a neatly folded t-shirt. She left it all on the bed and wandered back into the bathroom to brush her teeth. When she returned, there was another knock on the door, this time lighter.

"Yes," she called out, turning to face the door as it began to open.

Alex appeared. "Hey, I just wanted to—" She bit her lip before taking the final step inside the room and closing the door behind her, leaning against it, her hand still wrapped around the knob. "Hi, I just…can we talk?"

Morgan felt a prickle of disappointment wash over her again, and she pulled the towel tighter around herself. "Sure, what's up?" she said as brightly as she could manage.

Pushing off from the door, Alex stepped towards her, but kept a safe distance away. "The thing is I…" She paused to think before smiling sadly. "Last night was—"

"A one-off?" Morgan gave her the out.

"It's not that I didn't enjoy it, I very much did, and under different circumstances—" Alex looked away from the intensity of that stare. "I like you a lot, Morgan, and last night was—"

"Magical?"

"Yes." Alex nodded quickly. "Yes, it was exactly that, and that's why we can't do that again."

Now it was Morgan's turn to nod, but this time, slowly, methodically, an understanding setting in. "Alright." The thin-lipped smile was anything but happy, but she wouldn't make this into any bigger deal than it needed to be.

"I'm sorry, I just—"

"Please don't apologise. We had sex, I was a willing partner. I don't want to feel like it was a mistake that you're sorry for—"

"Oh god, no, that's not…" Alex rubbed her face. "No, I didn't mean it like that at all. I'm sorry that I can't continue this, I'm sad about it if I'm honest, but right now, it's such an important time and I need to be focused. I need to—"

Morgan sat down on the edge of the bed. "You don't need to explain. I'm a big girl. We had fun and I really enjoyed it and would be open to it happening again, but I can accept that's not the same for you."

"That makes it sound as though you cared, and I didn't and that's not a fair representation of what happened between us." She dared to step closer. "I took a walk in the gardens and thought it all through and I just can't get into something right now."

"Okay," Morgan said gently.

"So, are we alright? Can we go back to a working relationship?"

"Where we just pretend that we're fucking?" Morgan's head tilted to the right as she continued to stare at Alex.

Alex didn't have an answer. "I'll understand if this isn't something you can do anymore," she said before backing away.

"I'll be ready in ten minutes."

Alex considered something. "Why don't you stay here, and if I need you, I'll send Mike to get you." She tried to smile. "I'm only going to be doing interviews and preparing for the recital. It will be very boring, and you can enjoy the hotel."

"Won't Francine have something to say about that?"

"I'm sure she will, but at the end of the day I make the decisions, and for now, I think I'll be fine."

"Okay then." Morgan smiled and watched as Alex opened the door and left her to get dressed.

Chapter Twenty-One

And nothing more was said...

When Alex returned from the show, it was late, and Morgan was nowhere to be seen, her bedroom door firmly closed.

Pouring herself a drink, Alex swigged it down quickly, trying to douse the impact of euphoria that raced through her system again. She'd gone to the after-show party, something she didn't usually do for more than a few minutes to say hello and network as required with the few celebrity faces she liked, while the crew got stuck into taking things apart and ready for moving them on the following day.

This time, she'd tried to dance it out for a while, but every sinew in her body ached for the one thing she couldn't allow herself to have – not that it stopped her mind from wandering and her body from punishing her with its insistent pounding between her legs to be attended to.

She sank another shot and slammed the glass down, stalking quickly across the room, her clenched fist raised and ready to knock on Morgan's door and plead to be allowed to worship her once again, but she stopped herself. That kind of mixed message was not going to be helpful to anyone.

Her arm dropped to her side, and she rested her forehead against the door.

"I wish this was different," she whispered. "I wish I could just—" She sighed and straightened up, turning to face her own room and the lonely bed that awaited.

There was too much at stake.

From her bed, Morgan lay on her side, curled up with her hands under her cheek, facing the door and staring intently at the light under the door and the shadow of someone. She assumed, and hoped, it was Alex standing on the other side.

She willed her to open the door and for Alex to step inside, ready to make a plea to be allowed to climb onto the bed and under the covers beside her. Wanting Alex to touch her again, like she did the previous night.

It didn't happen. Moments later, the light switched off, and Morgan fell back against the mattress, staring up into the darkness of the room until her eyes adjusted again.

She'd spent all night waiting. Hoping for a call, not because Alex was unwell, she didn't wish that at all, but somewhere deep inside, her romantic nature wanted to be called upon. Imagining Alex introducing her to all of her famous friends.

"This is my girlfriend, Dr Morgan Kelly," she'd heard in her head over and over as she imagined different scenarios in a world where Alex wanted her. It was ridiculous, she knew that, but still, it had helped ease off the sexual tension she'd been edging all day.

She rolled back onto her side and thumped the pillow.

"Why can't it just be simple," she whispered into the darkness. She reached out for her phone, squinting at the screen when it lit up to reveal the time and a message that had come through while it had been set to silent.

Zoe: Just checking in. Knight is fine. How's things with you?

"Pretty crappy, Zo, but I can't tell you that right now, so…" She quickly typed a reply.

Morgan: Hey, all good thanks. Glad Knight is enjoying his holiday!

Surprisingly, the message ticks turned blue before she'd put the phone down. Zoe's typing flashed at the top of the screen.

Zoe: Ooo you're still awake. Been out partying?

Morgan: No, early night actually. I just woke up and checked the time and saw you'd messaged.

Zoe: Ah, shame. I was hoping you'd be drunk, and I'd get it out of you who you're working for. ☐

Morgan: Bad Luck, Duck. ☐ Right, I need to get to sleep.

Zoe: Okay, but you're alright, yeah? Not missing us even a teeny bit?

Morgan sighed. How easy it would be to spill it all and tell her friend about the situation she had found herself in?

Morgan: Of course I miss you. I'll be home before you know it.

Zoe: That's alright then. Okay, go to sleep.

Morgan: Night x

She closed the phone and placed it back on the nightstand, rolling on to her back for a second time to stare into the darkness before she fell into a fitful night's sleep.

Alex stripped and headed for the shower. She closed her eyes and let the water beat down on her, soaking her muscles and warming her skin with a beat, fast and constant.

She pressed her left hand against the wall and bent her neck forward as the water cascaded over her. There was no way she was going to sleep anytime soon.

On any other tour, she would stay up all night playing the piano, working on her new pieces. She couldn't do that and not wake Morgan, but she could go down to the bar and play theirs.

The bar was empty. No staff on duty, closed to the public and guests unless ordered via room service. Alex wandered in, wet hair tied up and wrapped into a messy bun. She looked anything but a classical composer with her baggy sweatpants and matching hoody, not to mention the bare feet.

In the corner was an upright Steinhoven SU. The kind of piano you found in school halls and old-fashioned pubs. Ideal for taking up little room and giving a nice sound in a room like this.

Euphoria

She lifted the lid and pressed a key. Its soft tinkle sounded louder in the empty room. Her fingers moved along the keys and then she pulled the stool out and sat down.

The big clock on the wall said 3 a.m. She looked away and back down at the keys before deciding on a version of Interstellar. She was almost halfway through when a man appeared. Night staff, she assumed as he nodded a hello and backed out of the room with a smile as she continued to play.

Maybe this was all she needed, she thought, just the music. Her eyes closed as she got swept away in it and then the inevitable happened: Morgan, naked, writhing in time with the music. She kept playing, one piece into another, into another.

"You been down here all night?" a familiar voice asked. Alex smiled and turned on the stool to find Francine standing there, a room full of staff working around her to clean and organise. She'd been so lost in her thoughts that she hadn't heard a thing.

"Couldn't sleep."

Francine nodded slowly. "Maybe the doc can give you a pill or something, or I can you know, organise something."

Alex knew what "organise something" meant: someone, not something. A paid for, discreet, someone.

"No, I'll be fine." She looked up at the clock, almost six. "I should go up and try to get a few hours. What time are we leaving?"

"Eleven," Francine said quietly. "I'll have breakfast and packing sent up at ten. It's going to be a long drive."

Alex stood up, wrapping her palm around her friend's thin arm. "Thank you."

Francine watched her leave, closed the piano lid and pushed the stool back into place. "It's going to be a long day." She smiled to herself.

Chapter Twenty-Two

Salisbury

The journey to Salisbury was quiet. Alex slept, Francine was answering emails and taking phone calls, and so Morgan stared out of the window as the car flew down the motorway, past fields and trees and spectacular views of the English countryside. Her mind, however, wasn't registering any of it. All she could think about was how she was going to make it through the next three weeks.

She didn't regret her night with Alex, that wasn't it at all, but she wished it hadn't happened. It was one of those moments where you knew what you were missing. Before, it would have just stayed a fantasy in her head; no substance, nothing 3D, no soundtrack. She wouldn't have the intoxicating scent of them, and the bed, all mixed together into a stimulating memory that surged her thoughts at any quiet moment. And there were going to be many quiet moments over the next three weeks, weren't there?

Morgan picked up her phone and Googled the cathedral. Built in the twelve hundreds. It was definitely old then, she mused as she skipped through images of the building. She wondered if she'd get to see it or be kept at the hotel again.

"Francine?"

"Hm?" she replied without looking up from her tablet.

"I was wondering if it would be okay to go to the cathedral with you all, rather than just sitting around at the hotel?"

Francine looked up at her, the three-second stare as she contemplated her response. "Well, I'd prefer it. It makes sense for you to be within shouting distance."

"Good, and would it be alright if I wandered around and did the touristy thing?" Morgan asked, holding up her phone to show an image of the sun shining through the stained glass windows. "I'd really like to check it out."

Francine was already back into whatever she was doing. "Sure, why not."

Morgan settled back into her seat, smiling to herself. She could find ways to keep herself busy. The Magna Carta was there, that would be interesting.

It should have only been a ninety-minute journey from Winchester, but roadworks had caused a diversion, and it was nearer two hours by the time they pulled up in front of another version of Downton.

"Are all the hotels like this?" Morgan asked curiously as she stared up at the beautiful brickwork and façade covered in ivy.

"I guess." Francine shrugged. "Give her a poke, will ya?"

"Why's she so sleepy anyway?" Morgan asked, unbuckling her seatbelt and turning towards Alex.

"Up all night," Francine answered. "She's worrying about something, that much I do know. Found her in the bar this morning playing the piano all by herself, well, and a bunch of cleaners and the early shift arriving."

Morgan said nothing, instead, she leaned forward and gently shook Alex by the arm. "Hey, time to wake up. We're here."

Slowly, Alex's eyes prised open, and she squinted against the bright light until everything came into focus and she found that intense, concerned stare aimed in her direction.

"Hi," Alex said, still half asleep and not wanting to turn away.

"Hey," Morgan said gently. "We're here."

Finally, Alex turned to look out of the window. "That was quick."

Francine rolled her eyes and smirked at Morgan. "Maybe for you, sleepyhead. We had to sit through traffic and diversions."

Alex stretched.

"Sorry, that must have been a bore without me here to entertain you."

A grin stretched across Francine's face, just as Mike opened the door. "You'll never know just how much you're wrong," she said before climbing out. "Thank you, Michael."

Alex chuckled, before her attention moved back to Morgan, who waited patiently because she couldn't get out without clambering all over Alex and invading her personal space. "I hope it wasn't too long a journey with Francine ignoring you."

One shoulder shrugged. "I can deal with it." Morgan smiled and held her gaze for as long as Alex could deal with it.

"Okay, let's get inside then, and you can enjoy the spa and—"

"I'm going to the cathedral," Morgan interjected. "I think it makes more sense, and I'd like to see the buildings. I enjoy the history and architecture. Francine said it was okay."

"Oh, right, okay, that's a plan then." Alex smiled quickly before she turned and got out. "Shall we go in?" She didn't wait for an answer as she sped towards the entrance and a waiting Francine, alongside someone who she suspected was the manager.

Morgan watched her go before she, too, got out of the car. "Thanks, Mike."

"Any time. Go on, I'll arrange for bags to be taken up." He smiled sincerely at her, and she returned it, before she took a deep breath and walked towards the disappearing group already entering the building.

The grand suite was in fact, just like the name suggested: grand. The manager smiled as everyone filed into the room. Morgan didn't wait for pleasantries this time; it was obvious which room would be hers, and she opened the door to it and stepped inside, closing the door behind her.

Another four-poster bed, this time with huge curtains hanging on all corners and huge pillows stacked up against the headboard. It looked comfortable and huge. There was a small walk-in closet for clothes and a shower room to one side. The large window looked over rolling hills and the tennis court.

"I guess this is home for now," she said to herself, swinging with one hand around the closest bed pole.

Inspection over, she re-entered the living room and found Francine and Alex going over details for that afternoon. More interviews, sound checks, rehearsal. Nothing Morgan needed to be concerned about.

"What time are we leaving?" she asked.

Francine looked at her watch. "In about forty minutes."

"Okay, great, I'm going to go for a walk. Is that alright?" She looked to Francine and then Alex and waited for one of them to answer.

It was Alex who spoke up. "Of course, you're not a prisoner."

"I know, but I am aware that I am being paid to do a job and swanning off whenever I like would seem a little inappropriate."

"Quite right," Francine chipped in, but raised a brow when she saw the glare Alex gave her. "Of course, as long as you're to hand and reachable by phone, it shouldn't be a problem."

"Okay, that sounds fair." Morgan reached into her pocket and checked the battery life and service on her phone. "I'll log onto the hotel wi-fi and then there shouldn't be a problem."

Alex smiled, unable to look away. "See you soon then."

"Yes," Morgan answered, holding the stare. "Won't be long, just need to stretch my legs." It was only when Alex looked away that Morgan turned and left the suite, leaving Francine staring at Alex.

"Have you two had a fight?"

"What? No, of course not, what makes you think that?" Alex said, a little too defensively.

"I dunno, just feels…" She left it unsaid when her phone started to ring. She looked at the screen. "It's David, get ready." She turned away. "Hi darling, yes, we've arrived." She was still talking as she left the room.

Alex turned full circle and suddenly felt the loneliness of her life suffocate her. The silence, louder than anything she could produce on the piano. A silent echo of a life she could have had but had chosen against. Sometimes, it made no sense to her at all, and then she would be on stage and the world she lived all fell into place. Enough, at least, to keep her on the path. Transactions at every marker.

Her love life was always the payment for everything she achieved.

She sighed and crossed the room to the window, looking out over the huge garden and further afield, to the hills. As her eyes were drawn back, she saw the image of Morgan, walking slowly between flower beds. Pensive, tired, sad. Alex knew it was her fault, that she'd given into the temptation, taken a forbidden bite of the apple, and then run from it, not because she was a coward, but because she needed to focus on something else. Something she hoped, one day, would mean no more transactions. No more trading love and the likes of Dr Morgan Kelly.

Turning away, she wrapped her arms around herself and breathed deeply. She had work to do, and that was all there was to it.

Chapter Twenty-Three

Morgan could hear the music as she wandered the building. It didn't matter where she went, the echo of the piano would follow. It was beautiful, and added another dimension to the tour she was giving herself. It had stopped for now, but no doubt it would begin again when Alex decided what changes where needed.

When Morgan had first arrived with Alex and Francine, she had watched from the seating area, Francine giving instructions and Alex discussing something quietly with a man. He was tall, broad, and hairy. One of the roadies, she assumed. After a few minutes, Alex had sat on her stool, and their eyes had met. Morgan was sure that Alex had searched for her, scanning the area until finally they stopped looking and settled on just her. It was a little unnerving if she were honest. Not that she didn't want the attention from Alex, of course she did, but she had no idea what it meant. All these little moments that added up to what? A night of fantastic sex and then…nothing.

Alex finally looked away, down at the piano and lifted the lid. She began to play, and Morgan got up and left her to it.

She'd never been in a building like this by herself before, without the public jostling around her. Her phone was in her hand constantly as she stopped to take photos here and there. It really was something to be admired.

Rounding the last corner before she re-entered the main building, she was panicked a little by the sound of footsteps running at speed. She froze on the spot when a man appeared, out of breath and waving at her.

"Doctor Kelly?" he rasped once he'd come to a stop in front of her.

"Yes," she replied with a confidence she wasn't feeling right this moment. "What's wrong?"

"You have to come quickly. It's Sasha. She's hurt."

The surge of adrenaline that rushed through Morgan in that moment was unlike anything she'd felt since a multicar pile-up on a motorway had brought fifteen patients in all at once.

"Where is she?" she asked urgently.

He looked around them, and then pointed to the nearest door. "We can get through there. She's by the stage." He took off as though it were his life that depended on it.

It was mere minutes when Morgan rushed down the aisle, boots stomping loudly against the stone floor. She could see a small group of people standing around in a circle, all peering down at what she assumed was Alex.

"Let me through," she said, and several heads peered up and turned her way, bodies instantly moving back to open a path. She could see Alex sitting on the steps that led up to the stage.

"I'm fine, honestly," she was saying in a tone that suggested she'd already said it several times. But she gave up protesting when she caught sight of Morgan closing the space between them, worry etching her features.

"What happened?" she asked Alex, adding a penetrating stare into the mix that forced a reaction.

"I just slipped, that's all. Landed with a thump and everyone panicked."

Francine stepped forward. "It was a crack, you screamed, and then you couldn't get up after, so let's stop being brave and let the good doctor do what she's paid to do." She turned to everyone else and shooed them all away with a silent waving of her fingers.

"Okay. Do you feel any pain now?" Morgan asked, lowering onto her knees so they were on a similar level.

Now that everyone else had gone, Alex winced. "I guess I do feel a little bruised and foolish."

"Foolish won't be a problem, bruised however... I'll need to check you over properly, but I can't do that here. So, did you bang your head?"

Alex shook her head. "No, my ankle turned and then I landed on my arse." She blushed before admitting, "The ankle did really hurt."

Morgan smiled. "Can you move all of your toes?"

"Yes."

"And fingers, any pain in your back?" Morgan leaned in close and reached around, prodding here and there.

"No, nothing."

Sitting back on her heels, Morgan stared up at Alex. "And you had trouble standing?"

Alex nodded.

Gently, Morgan rolled the trouser leg up to the knee. And then carefully, she took hold of Alex's calf and raised it a little in order to remove her shoe and take a better look. When she pulled the sock off, she could already see some bruising appearing around the ankle bone.

"Can you move your foot up and down?" The foot moved gingerly, and a hissing sound emitted from Alex with the movement. "Side to side?"

This time, the sound from Alex was much more painful, but her foot did move.

"Is it broken?" Alex asked.

"No, I don't think so. But I'm going to strap it up so we can get you back to the hotel." She pulled the sock back on as she spoke. "And I can do a proper examination and get you some pain meds set up." She looked at Alex then. "You'll need to rest it."

"God, I have to—"

"There's nothing that can't be done tomorrow," Francine interrupted. "If the doc says you're to rest, then that is what you'll do."

Morgan said nothing, but she raised an eyebrow and smiled at that.

"I just need my bag," Morgan was saying as Francine swooped down and swung it in her direction.

"Already got it."

Chapter Twenty-Four

With her foot up, Alex huffed and pulled open the next page in the magazine Francine had gone and got her. This wasn't how she had expected the rest of her day to look.

Dinner had been ordered and would be brought to the suite. Francine had left and gone to her own room to continue working, and Morgan was locked away in her room, avoiding Alex.

At least, that was how it felt to Alex.

Morgan would pop out every thirty minutes or so and check to see if she needed anything, and when Alex smiled and said, "No, I'm fine, but thank you," she would retreat back into her room again.

She slammed the magazine down on her lap and huffed again. Her watch said Morgan would be out again any minute, so she waited, staring at the door and urging it to open.

When it did, she picked up the magazine again quickly and pretended to be interested in the wedding of the year, two minor celebrities from a reality show whose wedding was being featured in an 8-page spread. It was horrendous, Alex thought.

"Everything alright?" Morgan asked.

Alex looked up at her, standing just outside of the door, arms folded around her waist. All of those brown curls were hanging messily around her face as though she'd been lying down and the hair band had loosened.

"Actually, I'm bored." Alex decided honesty was the best policy right now. "I'm hungry, bored and frustrated."

Morgan took a couple of steps forward, her arms falling limply by her side.

"Do you want me to put the TV on? There might be a film worth watching. I can order room service." She found the menu, picked up the remote and handed them to Alex. "Just let me know what you want and—"

"I want you to stop avoiding me," Alex said. "Or at least go and do something, instead of locking yourself away in your room."

Morgan said nothing, but moved across the room to an armchair, where she sat down and thought.

"I don't know what else to do," she finally said.

"I don't want you to feel like a pariah, exiling yourself to a room whenever it's just you and me."

"That's not—"

"Yes, it is. You're keeping out of my way, and I get it. I'm feeling the same difficulties around you, but it's going to be a long three weeks if we can't even spend time in the same room together."

"I don't understand you." Morgan leaned forward, elbows on her knees, hands clasped together. "From the moment we met, there's been this crackling electricity between us. I know you're attracted to me, I'm not blind, and I've made it very clear how I feel and so when we—" She closed her eyes and let the image of a naked Alex hovering above her disperse. "When we spent the night together, I just—it made sense, and now, you want me to just switch off my feelings, my desires and ignore the chemistry that is still there."

"I know, and I'm sorry, I really am. I take full responsibility. I should have kept my libido in check and not ruined—"

"Ruined? Nothing was ruined, it was exhilarating and fun, and I want more of it, but if I can't then I need to create space between us, and remain completely professional and not interact with you, because all that will do is confuse the message you've given." She waited for Alex to say something, to argue with her or debate the way forward, but when nothing came, she said, "So, shall I order dinner?"

"Would you at least eat with me?" Alex asked when the porter left, and the entire room filled with the scent of hot food.

Morgan considered the offer and nodded. "Sure, do you want it on your lap or—"

"I'd like to sit at the table if that's okay, and you don't mind helping me up?" She gave a small, vulnerable smile in Morgan's direction and watched hopefully when Morgan moved closer. "Thank you."

"It's in my job description," Morgan said a little pithily, reminded of the same words Alex had said in Winchester.

"Touché." Alex swung herself around and into a sitting position. When Morgan reached under her arm, she pushed herself up and placed all of her weight onto her good ankle. Morgan then slid her arm around her waist, Alex's arm easing around Morgan's shoulder as they shuffled together the few feet to the table.

With Alex situated at the end, Morgan dragged another of the chairs closer and raised Alex's leg up before she found a cushion and squeezed it under her ankle. The bag of ice from earlier had worked well, and the swelling was minimal, but the bruising was a nice shade of blue and red, maybe even a hint of purple.

"Is that necessary?" Alex asked.

"Are you suggesting that I'd make you do it for fun, or as some form of sadistic punishment?" Morgan retorted.

Alex shook her head. "No, of course not, I just… It isn't very comfortable, and dinner isn't going to take much more than half an hour—"

"Do you want to walk on stage tomorrow, or hobble with a cane?"

Alex nodded. "Fair enough."

Satisfied with her position, Morgan set about lifting the lids off of the plates and bowls, passing Alex her plate and offering to add accompanying side dishes.

"Yes, thank you. A little of each would be lovely." When both plates were full and Morgan had taken her seat again, Alex said, "I'm not used to people making me feel better and doing things for me. I'm sorry if I come off abrasive or ungrateful."

The comment surprised Morgan. "I thought with the way Francine is, your entire life was about people doing things for you and making you feel good."

Cutting into a lamb chop, Alex said, "Yes, I guess in some areas of my life that's true. Francine manages all of the practical things, the logistics, I suppose, but I don't have anyone who just makes me feel better or helps in a more emotional way."

Morgan was already chewing a piece of salmon, so she just nodded an acknowledgement.

"We come from very different worlds—" Alex was saying but stopped with the clanking sound of steel against China. She looked up and found Morgan and that stare, swallowing the mouthful she'd been chewing.

"You have more money, that's all. Being alone is no different to me than it is to you. I work, I go home and the only living thing to greet me is my cat. I spend my limited time off with friends if my shifts fit with them, and then I go home, alone, to a flat that I clean. I cook myself dinner and I eat alone, and if I'm unwell, I get on with it. More money just means you can employ a Francine to make sure bills are paid and your life is running smoothly. You can pay Mike to drive you around and make sure that you get everywhere on time. You don't have to worry about the car being so old it might actually fall apart when you're driving, and if it did, you'd just buy another one. I've no doubt you have a cleaner too, and when you work, it's for three weeks lounging around in fancy hotels being waited on, and your bank balance inflates to the point you don't ever have to worry about it…"

Morgan ran her tongue around her teeth before she picked up her knife and fork again, frustrated with herself for letting anyone get under her skin like this.

"I'm sorry, that was uncalled for."

Alex pondered it all for a moment. "No, I think it was a fair assessment." She pushed a chip onto the fork. "And I am aware of how lucky I am to have been born with a talent for something that really took no effort on my part. I am grateful for everything that I have, but money doesn't buy everything, and for me there is always a transaction to be paid."

Morgan said nothing.

"That's all I meant."

Chapter Twenty-Five

Painkillers, excellent strapping, ice, and plenty of rest meant that Alex climbed up on stage the following night with barely anyone noticing the slight discomfort she was feeling. Not just physically, but the emotion pulling at her too. Several times, she glanced out into the audience, hoping to catch a glimpse of Morgan, and every time she was left disappointed when she couldn't see her.

So, she did what she did best and focused on the music. She played her set and brought the audience to their feet for an encore of "Rhapsody in Blue," her most famous and most recognised piece of music. And when it was over, she took her bow and descended the stage to greet the people she needed to speak with. It was exhausting, and she was relieved when Francine hooked her elbow and led her away, away from it all, straight into the car, heading back to the hotel.

"How's the ankle?" Morgan asked from her seat in the car. She looked concerned.

Alex sat back against the seat and smiled. She must have been there. "The meds are wearing off." She grimaced. "But it held up, so thank you."

"Just doing my job," Morgan said, rifling through her bag for more painkillers. Francine took a small bottle of water from the fridge and passed it over. "Here take these. Two will help with any pain. I can give you a light sedative to help you sleep later, too."

"I'm not sure I—"

"It might do you good. You didn't get a wink the other night and last night mustn't have been too great with the injury," Francine encouraged. "The last thing you need right now is to be tired and unfocused. A good night's sleep will do you the power of good."

Alex looked back and forth between them both. Two very different women, each trying to care for her in their own way.

Morgan was already doing something else and paying no attention, but Francine was watching her.

"Fine." Alex sighed, swallowing the painkillers. "If I can't sleep later, I'll take one."

"The show went well," Francine said, changing the subject.

"Thankfully." Alex breathed out a sigh of relief. "The pedals were harder obviously, but I just about managed it. Did you watch?" she asked hopefully.

Morgan was looking down at the ankle, just about visible where Alex's trousers had ridden up with sitting down. When nobody else spoke, she glanced up and found Alex waiting for an answer. "Yes," she said quickly before changing the conversation back to medical-related topics. "As soon as we're back into the hotel room, I want that foot elevated and another ice pack on it before you go to bed."

Alex saluted. "Yes, boss."

As much as she tried, Morgan couldn't resist smiling; it was returned equally, and in that moment, everything felt a little lighter between them both.

"Should we hire a wheelchair for moving around generally?" Francine questioned.

Morgan shook her head, her eyes still set on Alex. "No, some weight-bearing exercise will be okay. With rest and icepacks, and anti-inflammatory meds, she should be up and about and 100% by the end of the tour at the latest, but I'm hopeful of a week?"

"A week?" Alex grinned. "I thought I was done for."

"It's a relatively minor strain," Morgan explained. "It looks nastier than it is, but you've got to do as your doctor says, alright?"

Alex continued to grin. "Yes, whatever you say."

"It's not even midnight yet," Alex moaned when Morgan stood beside the bed and pulled the duvet back.

"And your point is?" She plumped the pillows and piled them up so that Alex could sit up for a while. "I'm not saying you have to go to sleep, although that would certainly help."

"I'm too wired for that." Alex's eyes widened as though Morgan should understand. Which of course, she did.

"Alex, you're a grown-arsed woman who is perfectly capable of not acting on her impulses. Now, if that isn't the case, my professional opinion would be more therapy to address it, but this heightened state of being you feel will wear off if you relax and allow it to."

"Oh, I like her," Francine said from the doorway, overhearing the conversation.

"Shut up. I don't pay you to like her." Alex laughed, and turned to Morgan. "You're right, I guess I can try and find another outlet."

"I'll order a hot chocolate to be sent up; you need to rest," Morgan asserted. She glanced around to make sure Francine was out of earshot. "You're not the only one who can take control of a situation. Now, pyjamas and bed." She turned and walked out of the room, leaving an open-mouthed composer wide-eyed and a little more turned on than she had been.

In the lounge, Francine was pouring a drink. "If she does as she's told, I'll eat my hat."

"Challenge accepted."

"She told you about the euphoria then, did she?" Francine swung around with two glasses in her hands and held one out for Morgan.

She took it. "Thanks, she mentioned it." Morgan turned before the blush could give her away. "I think it's probably a normal reaction for most people in her situation. The adrenaline pumps and a heightened sense of joy can build and at some point, it needs to be released."

Diplomatically, Francine said nothing more, and Morgan wasn't going to let slip just how well she understood Alex and her blissful reaction. Francine swallowed down her drink.

"Right, I'll head off then. Call if you need anything."

"I won't, but thank you. I'll give her the sedative in a few minutes and then head to bed myself."

She saw Francine to the door, holding it open as she watched her make her way down the corridor, and then she closed the door.

"Morgan?" Alex called from her room.

"Yes?" Morgan answered, walking back into her room. She was sitting up, hands clasped together on top of the bedding.

"Will you sit with me for a while?"

"I think that would be difficult," Morgan answered honestly. She wet her lips and looked away. "Unless there's a medical issue, I should probably go to my own room."

Alex nodded slowly. "I see. Yes, I guess that's…"

"I think it's for the best, for now, don't you?" Morgan said, now staring at her intensely. Daring her to say otherwise. When nothing further came, she turned and walked slowly back towards the door.

"I can't give you what you want," Alex said, and Morgan stopped but didn't turn around. "I wish things were different, but I have to…focus. I made three mistakes tonight. Thankfully, most won't notice but I can't do that if I want—" She cut herself off from saying anything further about what she wanted. She couldn't jinx it or mess it up. "I just have to focus right now."

"Goodnight, Alex."

Morgan closed the door behind her. Her eyes closed and she fought back the tears that threatened, letting out a shuddery breath before she headed back to her room and the sanctuary of her bed.

Chapter Twenty-Six

Exeter

The following morning, Morgan was ready to leave and headed down to the car. A long journey awaited with the next stop, Exeter. She had a little bit of mischief in mind and figured why not. It would be fun to get one over on Francine, and she needed something to lift her spirit right now.

Mike already had the boot open, ready for the luggage. She spotted what she needed and grabbed it, climbed into the car, and tossed it onto Francine's seat.

She giggled to herself when barely a few minutes had passed, and she could hear Francine's loud voice shouting instructions to Mike. When the door opened, Morgan was almost surprised that it was Alex who poked her head through the space first.

"You're eager," she said with a sad smile as she stepped inside and sat in her usual spot. "Sleep well?"

Morgan nodded and picked up her Kindle, pretending to read. "Like a baby, you?"

"Eventually," Alex confirmed. "I watched some TV and then I must have switched it off and fallen asleep."

Morgan dropped her Kindle into her lap and turned to Alex. "I came in to check on you. You were sound asleep within the hour, so I turned the TV off."

"Was I?" Her eyes widened at Morgan. "I haven't done that since…well, it's been a long time."

Shrugging, Morgan picked up her Kindle again. "What can I say?"

When the door opened again, Francine had one foot in before she noticed her seat and the hat that stared up at her from it. Her gaze fell on Morgan, eyes narrowed. "Well, played, Doctor. Well, played."

Morgan smiled and continued to read but said nothing.

"What? What did I miss?" Alex said, bemused by the pair of them.

Now, Morgan looked up at Francine, still saying nothing, ready to take her cue from the American.

"The Doctor and I had a small wager last night, and it seems as though I lost and need to eat my hat."

Alex frowned. "Really? What was the bet?"

"You," she replied, sinking her teeth into the rim of the hat theatrically.

"Me? How so?"

Morgan placed her Kindle down. "Francine didn't have any faith in you doing as you were told, and I proved her wrong."

"The cheek of it." Alex chuckled. "Next time, I want in on these wagers."

A two-hour drive took Alex, Morgan, and Francine from Salisbury to Exeter, the furthest point west on the trip. Mike kept to a reasonable 70 MPH for the most part, and the journey was barely noticed as Morgan continued to read and the other two discussed the day's events.

"We can do the interviews right before the sound check and then straight back to the hotel. It worked well in Salisbury, I don't see the need to alter it," Alex said. "That way, I can spend a few hours with my leg up at the hotel before I need to leave and then rest again all evening."

Francine glanced again at Morgan, who just read her book, smiling.

"Who are you?" Francine asked. "What have you done with the pain in my ass?"

"I don't know what you're talking about." Alex sniggered and looked away out of the window. She caught Morgan's face reflected in the glass every time they passed something big enough to cut off the sun shining against the window and forced herself not to turn and look.

"Uh huh, well, I am not complaining. You keep this up. It's much easier to deal with than the other version." She glanced at Morgan again. "I guess this is your doing?"

Morgan held her hands up. "I just administer medical advice. I have no sway on anything else."

"Uh huh," Francine repeated before settling back into her seat. "So, I got nothing else to do all day then, once I organise the interview time changes."

"Well, you can hang around. I do like you hanging around," Alex said.

"Or go and enjoy the spa," Morgan offered. "I really enjoyed it."

The face Francine pulled made them both burst out laughing. The idea that workaholic Francine would take an afternoon off to pamper herself was hilarious.

"Oh, laugh it up the pair of you," she said, trying to hold a straight face before succumbing to the laughter. "I've got plenty of work I can do to keep me busy."

Before anyone noticed, Mike pulled off the motorway and the scenes outside changed from open fields to a more built-up landscape, more cars, and then more people. The fourth leg of this journey was about to commence.

The hotel room was, yet again, out of this world. Morgan moved around the room just looking at everything while the manager gushed about how excited they were to have someone so prominent and talented as Sasha staying at their establishment.

Eventually, Francine guided her away and left Morgan to deal with Alex and the leg rest.

"Like it?" Alex asked, already taking her seat on the couch with her leg up.

"It's just..." Morgan twirled around. "It certainly beats triage and the emergency room at work." She smiled before taking the space at the other end of the couch and reaching for Alex's foot.

Gently, she removed the shoe and the sock and unwound the strapping bandage. She examined the bruised area, moving the joint around. She watched Alex's face for any sign that it was painful. There was only a small wince when she turned the ankle inwards. This was the angle at which it had overstretched when it was sprained.

"There is definitely more movement."

"That's good," Alex answered, but her focus was on Morgan and not the injury.

"Stop looking at me like that," Morgan said, as she re-strapped the bandage. She hadn't looked up at all, she dared not, but she could see out of her periphery that Alex was staring at her.

"Sorry, I—"

Morgan finished what she was doing and finally looked up, holding the now somewhat embarrassed gaze. "Make up your mind, Alex. Do you want me or not?"

"That's an unfair—"

"No," Morgan interrupted. "No, it isn't unfair. We had sex, and then you said it couldn't happen again, and I'll respect that, but if that's the case, then you have to stop looking at me like you want to devour me."

"I know." Alex hung her head.

"Or tell me you made a mistake," Morgan said confidently. "Tell me you fucked up and you want to do this, but you can't have an in-between mixed message of flirtatious glances. That's not fair." She stood up. "You let me know what it's to be, but once you decide, that's it. No going back."

Alex only looked up again when she heard the sound of the bedroom door closing with a soft click. "Well, that told you, didn't it?"

Chapter Twenty-Seven

Rehearsals had gone well, and Alex had done everything she was asked and rested the moment they returned. Between getting back and now, Morgan had gone for a swim and left Francine to take charge of making sure Alex behaved.

She'd needed the break.

Since her little outburst earlier, Alex had barely spoken to her. Not in a punishing, silent treatment kind of way, but that she was just quiet, as though lost in her thoughts. And Morgan was okay with that. What was happening between them needed to be acknowledged and dealt with, one way or the other.

When she returned, Francine was speaking to a member of staff who'd brought dinner up on a huge trolley and decanted it all onto the table.

There was more food than anyone could possibly eat. It was like Christmas. Francine stood to the side, opening a bottle of champagne, while Morgan felt herself being observed by Alex on the couch.

"We didn't know what you wanted, so…" Alex shrugged and smiled. "Francine said order everything."

"You didn't?" Morgan said, a little overwhelmed.

"No, I thought back to what you've ordered previously and kind of took a gamble that you'd enjoy the pork."

Morgan smiled. "Thank you for being so considerate."

"The hotel has sent a bottle of very nice sparkling wine," Francine said as she poured into the first glass. "Are you partaking, Morgan?"

"I guess one glass won't hurt." She turned her smile on Francine and tried to ignore the intensity with which she was being viewed by Alex, as though something was being sized up. She wished now that she'd dried her hair and at least attempted to control the curls before she'd thrown on her leisure wear and come back up. "I'm just going to change into something more…appropriate for dinner."

Francine's eyebrows raised. "It's just dinner with us. The world isn't going to judge your attire."

"You look fine, Morgan, be comfortable." Alex pushed herself up and limped across to the table. "I'm starving," she said, quickly averting her gaze.

Morgan looked more than fine, and that was the problem, wasn't it?

"Okay," Morgan said, taking a seat at the table.

With dinner over, Morgan had excused herself and left the two women with their glasses of scotch, and a lengthy list of things to discuss for the following day. Which was fine by her. She was in need of a long shower to finally get the last remnants of chlorine off of her. It was faint, she had of course showered at the pool, but still, it wasn't her favourite scent, and it rankled every time she moved and it wafted up to her sensitive nose.

"I'll just be—" She pointed over her shoulder, and if she wasn't mistaken, a look of disappointment flashed across Alex's face.

She left them to it.

Stripped off again, she walked into the shower and stayed there for what felt like an eternity as the heat seeped into her muscles, breathing deeply, inhaling the steam, and exhaling her tension. Her mind flashed back to when she was naked and cavorting, yes, actually cavorting in Alex's bed. Her clit ached to be touched, but she wouldn't. Not while Alex and Francine were both in the other room. It didn't sit right.

Finally done, she wrapped her hair in a towel and sauntered back to her bedroom, intent on drying her mane of curls and tying them up before climbing into that comfortable-looking bed to read for a while, and then she'd finally check on Alex, make sure she was comfortable for the night and hit the sack herself.

It was a plan.

What could possibly go wrong?

At chapter seventeen, she closed the Kindle down and set it on the nightstand. Voices had quieted a while ago and she wondered if Alex had actually fallen asleep on the sofa.

She got up and crept to the door, opening it slowly to peek out. She found Alex alone.

Waiting for her?

She wasn't sure, but it felt that way when her every move was watched as she stepped further into the room.

Drink in hand, swirling the ice slowly as though contemplating something still, Alex continued to stare at her. One leg was raised onto a stool, her body twisted towards Morgan. She looked in control, and Morgan felt herself weaken at the sight. God, was she that needy for this woman's attention?

"Come here," Alex demanded confidently, moving her leg down to place her foot back on the floor, leaning forward on her elbows.

Morgan found herself moving.

Just two words, and she was pulled towards her like a magnet that couldn't push away.

When she was standing in front of her, Alex placed the glass down on the table beside where she was sitting. Her hands raised to rest against Morgan's hips, her forehead falling against Morgan's midriff.

"I made a mistake," Alex said firmly.

"Go on." Morgan waited for more.

Alex sat back, stared up at her and admitted, "I fucked up."

"Okay."

"I want more." Without breaking eye contact, her fingertips pinched the material to Morgan's pyjama bottoms, and they slid down Morgan's thighs until they dropped by their own volition, exposing Morgan once more. "I want more with you."

Innately, Morgan knew not to move. To stand very still and wait, allow Alex to explore these feelings, to explore her too.

"I don't know how we do this, and I don't know if it will even work, but I can't keep looking at you and not be allowed to touch," Alex continued. "It's more than that."

"I'm listening."

"It's more than the euphoric feeling I get. I don't want you to feel like that's all it is... I want more, but I don't know how to navigate that and focus on what I need to do at the same time."

"What is it that requires so much of your focus?" Morgan asked.

Alex stared up at her, her head tilting to one side. "I can't say right now, I don't want to jinx it, but there's a plan in place that Francine and I are working on. It's important, and I can't fail, not now."

Morgan thought for a moment before she asked, "Have you been focused these past two days?"

Alex glanced at her injured foot, remembered the mistakes on stage where her mind was elsewhere, seeking out Morgan and becoming distracted when she couldn't find her. "No."

"So, your focus isn't lost because you want me. It's lost because you won't allow yourself to be with me."

"I guess that's an accurate description, yes."

"So, is this your apology?" Morgan asked, bringing her finger under Alex's chin and lifting just enough that they were looking at one another again. "Because I think I deserve one, don't you?"

Smiling, Alex said, "See, this is what scares me. I've never been with anyone who can do that."

"Do what? Demand respect? Expect accountability?"

Alex shook her head. "No, I can do that, always, that's not...you have this ability to turn the tables on me. I'm not in control of this, even when I think I am. You have this way of letting me think I've got the upper hand but really, the entire time...it's you."

Morgan smiled knowingly.

"It's why you stand out. You're calm and quietly confident, self-aware. It's disarming, and attractive, and..."

"Alex, just say you're sorry."

Alex exhaled and settled herself again.

"I'm sorry, Morgan. I'm sorry that I pushed you away. I'm sorry that I've been lying to myself and creating this space between us that has ultimately only made things worse, and I'm sorry that you bore the brunt of that rejection. I like you, Morgan. There's something there between us, I know it, and I want it, I just don't know how…"

"To navigate it, yes, you've said that, and the thing is Alex, nobody does know. It's a guessing game for everyone. There are no rule books and explanations you can study. This isn't something you can control, and as for perfection that you insist on in every other aspect of your life, you're not going to get it in a relationship. Especially a relationship with me. So, just breathe and enjoy it for what it is. Can you do that?"

Alex took a deep breath in and exhaled slowly, nodding. "Yes."

"Good, now, what do you plan to do to make up for it? Because I think that should be your punishment." Morgan smiled slowly.

"I guess that's only fair." Alex returned the smile.

Reaching for her drink again, Morgan watched Alex intently, intrigued with what it was that she had planned for her now.

"I find myself immersed in thoughts of you, of what I want to do to you, but more than that, what I am prepared to let you do with me."

Instead of picking up the glass, Alex dipped her fingers into it and fished out the perfectly round ball of ice. It was large enough to almost fill the glass and fit perfectly into Alex's hand.

"I've never met anyone like you, Morgan. It scares me," she reiterated.

"I'm not asking you to marry me, Alex. I'm asking for consistency." Morgan reached out, stroking the bowed head in front of her.

Alex looked up at the touch, and the words. "Okay."

With Morgan's attention acutely on her, she licked the ice and removed any trace of the scotch it had been swimming in, rolling it around in her fingers until she'd covered every inch of it with the heat of her skin, leaving it wet and shiny.

"Do you want me to stop?" Alex asked before she took things way past the point of no return.

"No, I don't want you to stop. I want you to do all manner of indecent things to me, that I'd never considered before, and then I want to do it all again tomorrow, and the next day."

"I want that too."

"Then you'd best make up your mind what you're doing with that ice before it melts completely."

Alex smirked, enjoying the way that Morgan stood her ground with her.

"Open wider."

Alex smiled when Morgan silently sidestepped, and then gasped as the ice made contact with her hot skin.

"Just how indecent do you want me to be?" Alex asked, keeping eye contact as the ice ball rolled, water melting and running down Alex's arm and Morgan's thighs.

"Very." Morgan managed before heat replaced the ice. Alex's mouth kissing, her tongue licking. There was a clink sound when Alex dropped the ice back into the glass and pulled Morgan closer. "Really indecent," Morgan said before her senses left her.

Chapter Twenty-Eight

This bed was like a dream, Morgan thought as she rolled over and let her face squish against the soft pillows. She had no idea of the time. The room was dark with the curtains pulled closed, something she should consider buying for her flat, for when she got home from a night shift and the sunlight kept her awake for too long.

It had been late when she'd finally left Alex's bed and climbed into her own. There was a part of her that had wished she could have stayed, but she'd been told quite firmly that no, that wouldn't be happening.

"*The last thing I need is to wake up with you. I'll want you, and then I'll be unfocused all day.*" Alex had laughed at the pouting.

Morgan stretched out weary bones and aching muscles, grinning to herself. There was nothing quite like that ache one felt after a long night of sexual activity. Alex Montgomery knew exactly how to play her body, she thought, reaching between her legs to satisfy that knowing ache that was starting to pulse again. The sound of muffled voices outside got louder, putting her off her stroke, and she was pretty sure that Francine had arrived, which was a real dampener on any attempt to get off quickly.

Growling, she got up and grabbed her robe. When she opened the door, both women stopped talking and turned to her.

"Everything alright?" Morgan asked nervously.

Alex scratched the back of her head before running her palm through her hair, over and down her face, trying to smile. "Nothing for you to worry about."

Francine stalked across the room and slapped a folded newspaper against Morgan's folded arms. Opening it, she read the headline in bold type across the front page of a national tabloid.

SICK SASHA'S HEART BREAK!

As she began to read, her eyes widened.

British composer and musician Sasha was reportedly seen at her local hospital recently, where sources say she was treated for a suspected heart attack.

"They think you had an actual heart attack?" Morgan almost laughed at the idea as she folded the paper again and handed it back to Francine. Someone at the hospital had to have blabbed, but why?

"Yeah, and now we got a ton of pap downstairs, and Cecil's going apoplectic thinking she's going to drop dead on stage. God dammit," Francine blasted.

"She's not going to drop dead," Morgan answered.

"I know that. She knows that, and you know that," Francine said, turning from one face to the other and pointing with a bony finger, "but this...says different." Francine waved the paper before tossing it across the room. Its pages separated and fluttered, like albatross wings, landing on the carpet. She turned to Morgan, all steely-eyed and ready to rip someone a new one. "If I find out that Urquhart women is behind this, I'll—"

"All publicity is good publicity though, right?" Morgan offered hopefully, but that only seemed to incense Francine more. So, she ducked her head and headed for the mess of paper on the floor. Grabbing each sheet, she tried to put it back together in some semblance of order but gave up and just dumped it all in a pile on the table.

"Not when your promotor is having an aneurism at the idea of having to cancel shows because the backers and insurance companies are having a meltdown about their star potentially dropping dead on stage." Francine breathed deeply, turning to Morgan and then Alex. "Get dressed, both of you. We need to give them a story."

Alex held up her hand. "Just wait a minute; let's all stay calm. What are you suggesting?"

"It's simple, you go downstairs and the pair of you let the pap know you're together. Make a statement, give them something else to focus on that shows your need for a doctor wasn't health-related."

Shaking her head, Alex said, "I'm not doing that. It's one thing them putting two and two together and coming up with five, but I'm not making an announcement. If need be, we can tell Cecil that Morgan and I are more than friends and that I was visiting her at work. My heart is perfectly fine."

Francine considered that idea. "Alright, I guess I can swing that past him and shut down the panic. But what are you going to do to give an impression of something more happening?" Francine asked Alex, completely ignoring the fact that Morgan was in the room. "The quicker we head this off with something else, the easier this health issue will be to brush over."

"I'll answer questions during the press meet later." Alex's thin lips pressed together, frustrated with the situation. "We'll arrive at the concert in Gloucester together." Alex looked at Morgan for agreement. "Do you think you can manage that?"

Morgan shrugged. "It's the story we decided on, isn't it?" She couldn't not agree to it. She'd already accepted the deal and the money, and this was always on the cards, wasn't it? Now they really were kind of together, so it should be simple enough, shouldn't it?

"Yes, it is, but I'm not sure any of us thought we'd have to use it. You don't have—" Alex was saying before Francine jumped in.

"The hell she doesn't, listen up. We're paying you a shit ton of money—"

"I'm paying her a shit ton of money," Alex interrupted and glared at her manager. "I'm paying her to be my doctor. I will not force her into telling the world she's just my lover, when she's so much more than that."

Morgan's brow raised at the defence of her reputation.

"Alex, it's fine. I'll do it."

"Alright," Francine said exuberantly. "Get dressed, something nice, sexy just in case there are photographers."

"For god's sake." Alex cut her eyes at her manager. "This isn't the 1950s, we're not pandering to men. Wear whatever you're comfortable in."

Morgan stood and examined the clothes hanging in her wardrobe. What did she wear for this? Facing the press, having her photo plastered all over the globe, her name talked about in magazines and on TV wearing last summer's dress from Next. It could be worse, she supposed.

A sudden thought hit her. She should warn her mum, shouldn't she? Her family would not be impressed to read about it in the paper. Did they even read papers anymore? It didn't matter; they needed a heads up.

Grabbing her phone, she was stopped in her tracks by a gentle knock on the door.

"Come in."

The door opened and Alex stepped in. "Just thought I'd see how you were doing?"

Morgan sighed. "I was just thinking about what I should wear and warning my family."

"Hm, what does one wear to announce they're in love with someone they're not in love with." Alex smiled and moved closer, slipping her arms around Morgan's waist, and resting her chin on her shoulder. "You don't have to do this. I'm a big girl, I can deal with it if I have to."

"But you shouldn't have to. Nobody should have to keep having their past dredged up and splashed all over the newspapers. It's traumatic."

Alex released her hold and took a seat on the bed. "Thank you for saying that. It is, but I don't want to make this traumatic for you either."

"Honestly, I'm more concerned with letting you down." Morgan turned away. "I don't have a wardrobe full of red carpet event clothes. I kind of assumed, at best, I'd just be in the background and people would speculate. I didn't expect to be up front and centre."

"You're right. I should have thought of that." She jumped up excitedly. "Come on, get dressed, we're going out."

"Out?" Morgan's brow creased. "Where are we going?"

"Shopping." She was already marching towards the door. "I'll get the car."

"But…do we have time for that? Francine—"

"We'll make time. I'll handle Francine. Come on."

Chapter Twenty-Nine

Clothes shopping was a very different experience for Morgan in her reality to what it was when she walked in on the arm of Sasha. Alex had phoned ahead, and Morgan felt a little like Julia Roberts's character in Pretty Woman. Except Julia Roberts's character, Vivianne, didn't have the paparazzi following them on a moped and now camped outside the shop, hopeful of a quick photo of Sasha.

"For god's sake." Alex was a little annoyed with the intrusion. "What is so interesting about two women going shopping?"

"I think it's—" Alex's glare told her quickly that there was no excuse going to cut it. "So, what are we doing here?"

"We're taking advantage of my name," Alex said, softening. It wasn't Morgan's fault her life was like this. She didn't have to live her life like this, did she? This was a choice she made, and she needed to quit complaining about it.

The boutique was only too happy to close to the public once Alex had explained who she was and what she wanted. Inside, the staff came back and forth to the dressing area with everything from everyday wear to cocktail dresses.

"Are you just going to sit there and watch?" Morgan asked Alex when they were alone for a moment. The musician had found a comfortable chair and moved it to the back wall where she sat, one leg crossed over the other, observing.

Not that Morgan didn't enjoy it. Because she did, she absolutely did. Having Alex's eyes on her as she dressed and undressed made her feel excited. There was something almost feral about it and how it made her feel, to have Alex just sit back and observe everything silently.

She knew Alex had the urge to get up and move closer, but she didn't. Wanting to touch, but unable to, yes, that was a huge turn-on.

"You're in your underwear, so, yes, I am going to sit here and watch." Alex smirked instead.

They both stopped talking when they heard footsteps approaching, and three women almost crashed through the doors to bring another set of clothes. The manager stepped forwards holding a stylish black dress draped over her other arm.

"I think this would work perfectly," she announced with a smile.

Morgan took it from her, held it up and caught sight of the price tag.

"Oh, no this is not in my price—" She was handing it back when Alex stood up.

"Can we have the room, please, ladies?"

The manager smiled again. "Of course. And all three of them backed out like they were in the presence of royalty. When they were alone, Alex fingered the material of the dress until she too found the price tag.

£2300.

"It's too much, Alex."

"Put it on," she said, staring into Morgan's eyes. "Take off your bra and put the dress on."

Morgan gulped and felt the sensation of arousal hit harder. How did this woman turn her on so much with just a few words?

When she hesitated, Alex moved behind her. Fingers slid under her bra to unhook the two little metal clasps. "Put the dress on," she whispered firmly when her hands slipped further under and around to cup now naked breasts.

Head falling back, body pressing into the touch, Morgan moaned a little when her nipples were squeezed and rolled between deft fingers.

"I want you." Alex's voice was low and sultry. "I want you right now, but I won't because that's a headline I don't need." She chuckled. "But, when we're alone again…later." She stepped back and withdrew her hands, leaving the last part of the sentence hanging in the air between them.

Steadily walking back to the chair, Alex sat down again and continued to observe while Morgan stepped into the dress, wriggling the tight material up over taut thighs and then the roundness of her backside.

"It's a bit figure-hugging," Morgan said as it rested around her waist. "I'm used to wearing baggy scrubs all day." She joked away the insecurity.

Alex's eyes scanned the length of her body, enjoying the curves. "You have a figure worth hugging."

Rolling her eyes, but smiling at the compliment, Morgan slid one arm and then the other into the loops that would bring the front of the dress up to cover her breasts. Her back and arms were completely exposed. In bare feet, she twirled one way and then the other, looking at herself in the mirror.

"What do you think?" she asked Alex, but she wasn't blind. She looked a million dollars.

As though reading her mind, Alex stood and moved in behind her again. "Do I need to even answer that?"

There was a quiet knock on the door, and Alex jumped away just as the manager poked her head around.

"Everything alright?" She caught sight of Morgan as she stepped inside. "Oh, my goodness, that does look amazing on you."

"It does, doesn't it?" Alex answered. "We'll take it, and she's going to need a couple of others, some everyday wear and shoes to match." Assistants scattered, off to find everything they could that might triple their sales bonuses this month.

Morgan twisted around on the balls of her feet. "Alex, that's too much."

"It's not enough." She touched Morgan's cheek. "Let me do this. I want to spoil you."

Chapter Thirty

"Where the hell have you two been?" Francine ranted the moment Alex and Morgan got back to the hotel.

Morgan stepped back and hovered out of the way, unsure if she was supposed to respond or just be quiet. She opted with the latter.

Slowly, Alex removed her designer sunglasses. "We got held up, but I'm here now. What's the big to-do?" She dumped the bags onto the floor by the couch and checked her watch, barely eleven o'clock.

"Oh, I dunno, the fact you have a concert to prepare for. Last-minute sound checks, more interviews with local press, you know, those kinds of to-dos. Not to mention you've got guests after this show."

The way she said guests made Morgan take notice, like it was something more important than usual.

"It's not late. Tell the boys I'll be ready to sound check at five. What time are the press expecting me?"

"I've already set that back till four, but we need to leave," she reiterated. "I don't know how you expect me to fit it all in when you're swanning around somewhere with—" Francine all but pushed her client and friend out of the room. "*Horse and Hound* are first, and you know how they can be, then it's onto half a dozen gazettes and news shoppers and god knows what else. Sound check, and then you'll have two hours to relax and compose yourself before the show. If you can avoid more gallivanting."

"I think it might be you that needs to relax," Alex said sharply. "We just did some shopping."

"Shopping?"

"Yes, if we're going to continue with this *charade* that I have a lover cover story, then my *lover* needs appropriate clothing to be photographed and seen in."

"Well, yes, but…"

Alex didn't wait around for her to finish. "I'll be in the car, should you need to continue worrying."

"Great," Francine said out loud when Alex closed the door on her.

Raising her hand and giving a gentle cough for attention, Morgan asked, "Um, where should I go?"

Francine threw up her hands. "Apparently, anywhere you like." She sighed. "Sorry, it's been a busy day, and it doesn't help when she's being so obstreperous."

"Is she usually so—"

"Disorganised? Unbothered? Wandering off? Yes, sometimes, which is why I run a tight ship. Order is what she needs at times like this. Order and focus."

Morgan nodded.

"She seems pretty relaxed to me," Morgan offered, reiterating, "In my medical opinion, of course. That's what we want, right? Less stress, less chance of a panic attack." *And I intend to do everything I can to make sure she stays relaxed*, thought Morgan with a wry smile. She wondered what Francine would do if she knew the truth, if she knew that the moment they were alone they'd be naked and in each other's arms. That she would do anything Alex demanded of her.

"You're right. Let's hope it stays that way."

Knocking on the dressing room door, Morgan waited until she was told to come in. The door swung open and a young woman's smiling face greeted her. "Hello, you must be Morgan."

"Hi, yes." She stepped inside, the room much smaller than she expected it would be. At the far end, which was only ten feet away, was a vanity station. A large mirror, like in the movies, with bulbs lining the edge and lighting up Alex's face. Make-up cases lay open on and around it, and Sasha sat in a chair with a napkin around her neck, smiling at her through the mirror while another woman twirled a curling iron through her mane. "I can go and wait somewhere else."

"Don't be silly. Here, grab a chair," the woman who'd opened the door said with another smile as she moved some boxes off of a small chair. "I'm Nancy, by the way. This is Gert."

Gert looked up briefly, nodded, and went back to work, uninterested at the newcomer's appearance in the room. The two women couldn't be more different. Gert was all blonde hair and curls, a light make-up style and wearing practical jeans and shirt combo. Nancy was dark, short-cropped hair close to her scalp with a full-on face of make-up, false lashes and what Morgan imagined might have been a touch of Botox.

Morgan held out her hand and Nancy shook it, giggling.

"Gawd, she's formal, init." She continued to laugh. Alex smiled but said nothing. "I'm just kidding, so, what do you do around here? I'm make-up, as you can see, Gert's hair."

"I'm—"

"Dr Morgan Kelly is here at my invitation," Alex said, with a wink, for good effect.

"Oh, say no more." Nancy zipped her lips. "What happens in dressing, stays in dressing, ain't that right, Gert?"

"Ya," Gert said quickly, still focused on what she was doing.

"Jobs like this are hard to come by, know what I mean? We can be trusted with anything, so long as it's legal." She winked again, and Morgan warmed to her instantly. She seemed fun, and easy going, and most of all, loyal.

"Good to hear." Morgan returned the smile. It was hard not to when the atmosphere felt so light.

"Right, I am done," Gert said, her hands still running through Alex's hair until she was happy with the way it moved and fell into place. "I'm going to get something to eat. You can manage by yourself," she asked Nancy.

"Yep, off ya trot. I'm good."

"I'll be back before you go on tonight, Alex." Gert gave another satisfied nod and grabbed her bag. And then she was gone.

"She seems cheerful," Morgan imparted. The woman was definitely a more serious character than Nancy.

"Dutch," Nancy said, as though that explained everything. "I thought she was German. Gawd, did I get a telling off."

"I can imagine." Morgan grinned at the happy-go-lucky girl. Catching Alex watching her through the mirror, she suddenly felt a little exposed, as though she were being mentally undressed.

"Nancy, would you do me a favour and see if Francine can delay the first interview, and then give me ten minutes?" Alex asked through the mirror.

"Of course." Nancy looked from Alex to Morgan, before whispering, "What happens in dressing, stays in dressing."

When the door closed behind her, Alex swivelled around on her chair, curling her finger to beckon her new lover closer. Morgan understood, and with a sway of her hips, she crossed the room and straddled the lap on offer. Warm hands slipped around her waist and underneath the thin t-shirt she was wearing.

"Francine thinks you're on the verge of some kind of breakdown." Morgan chuckled. "I considered telling her you were fine, and just on the verge of orgasmic release…but I figured that might have sent her into overload, and then I'd have to actually do something I'm being paid for."

"You make me smile." Alex lifted the plastic card holder resting between Morgan's breasts and admired the photo. "Cute." She leaned up. "Kiss me."

"I'm not sure this is in my job description." Morgan smirked, taking the ID badge from her, before pressing their lips together.

"Of course it is. I'm relaxed, aren't I?"

Morgan grinned. "Give me ten minutes and I guarantee I can have you more relaxed."

"You think so, ten minutes?"

Morgan slid from her lap and quickly crossed the room, locking the door. "Well, let's find out."

Alex watched as Morgan returned and climbed back into her lap, straddling thighs as her hands slipped over shoulders, hands clasping around the nape of her neck. The kiss was slow, and deliberate. Firmly pressing lips nipped, and nudged until Alex could stand it no longer and opened her mouth to receive Morgan's tongue.

"Mm." She moaned into it, enjoying the way Morgan felt pressed against her, her weight holding her down. Alex's hands moved effortlessly under the cotton of Morgan's shirt, flat against her soft bare skin. "I want you," she mumbled when the kiss slowed.

Morgan checked her watch. "We've got seven more minutes."

"I can do it in six." Alex laughed, already unbuttoning Morgan's shirt.

A thump on the door made them both jump.

"Hey, why's the door locked?"

"It's Francine," Morgan whispered, clambering off of Alex's lap and hurriedly rebuttoning.

"Morgan's just checking my ankle," Alex shouted back. Then she stood up, kissed Morgan quickly and grinned. "Later." She readjusted herself and checked in the mirror that she was presentable. "Okay, let her in."

Opening the door, Morgan stepped aside. "It's all fine. I'll be back with your medication, but I'm going to lower the dose now there isn't as much pain."

"Great, thank you." Alex smiled as Morgan left the room.

"What ya lock the door for?" Francine enquired, already dumping her bag onto the spare chair.

"I had to drop my trousers. They're too tight to just pull up."

Francine glanced down suspiciously. "Okay, let's get this done."

Chapter Thirty-One

Gloucester

The reporter sitting opposite Alex looked as though she'd just left school, and Alex wondered how many more of these she could sit through between now and the end of the tour. It was so repetitive. She studied the young woman sitting opposite, smiling easily as she waited for her to settle into her seat and pull out her recording device.

"Ms Montgomery, Clara Swift, *Gloucester News Chronicle*." She smiled as though butter wouldn't melt. "Is it true that your recent health scare put this tour in jeopardy?"

So, straight to the point, not as wet behind the ears as she appeared then, Alex thought. Francine stepped forward, prepared to step in and redirect. Subtly, Alex shook her head and the rottweiler attack was put on hold, for now.

"My recent health scare?" *Sasha* threw back at her. "You'll have to expand on that."

Clara continued to smile, holding her Dictaphone out towards *Sasha*. "Yes, national news sources reported that you recently visited a local hospital and spent the day having several tests for potential heart issues. Are you okay now?"

Interesting that none of them had asked about her fall, or the state of her ankle, which meant they didn't know, Alex thought. She had a good team around her. Loyal people who didn't go running to the press.

"As you can see, I'm fine. As I was then. It's true, I did visit a local hospital but not because I was having a heart attack, it was more of a..." She paused for effect. "A personal visit and a charitable event."

"A personal visit?" Clara took the bait. "That sounds much better. I'm sure your fans would love to hear that you're well, and dare we ask...are the rumours true of a new romance?"

Alex sat back, picked at an imaginary loose thread on the arm of the chair and tried not to move her ankle too much, but sitting still was causing it to stiffen.

"What would make you think that?" She swatted back the question again, intrigued at how quickly a rumour could start if you fanned the right flames.

"Sources say that you and a close friend spent several hours yesterday morning at a local boutique, where you bought said young lady a substantial amount of clothing."

"Well, if sources say so, it must be true, right?"

"I think that will be all, Ms Swift. Thanks for coming, and we hope to see you tonight at the concert," Francine said with just a hint of boredom to her voice.

"Sure, it was great to meet you. My mum's a huge fan."

Refusing to rise to the barbed comment that insinuated her music was for older people, Alex continued to smile. When the door closed, Francine seethed. "God, I hate these brats with their smarmy-assed faces and leading questions."

"She's just doing her job," Alex argued calmly. "And didn't you want them to shift focus?"

Francine glared at her. "Could you at least placate my shitty mood?" They both stared at one another until laughter bubbled up between them.

"Oh god, how many more?" Alex asked, already done with the hassle of it all.

"Another three, and then I need a drink, and you need to take the good doctor back to the hotel and rest that ankle before the big night."

It was a whirlwind of activity, and Morgan found herself getting in the way of everyone. So, she'd taken herself for a wander around the building while Alex worked through the last of her interviews. It was impressive. She'd been before on a school trip years ago, but hadn't really taken much interest then, other than grabbing Stacey Jones by the hand and heading off to explore without the teachers noticing them missing.

Several of the crew had smiled and nodded as she'd passed them by. Not once did anyone stop her and ask to look at the credentials that swung around her neck on a rainbow-coloured lanyard. She smiled to herself when she remembered Alex's reaction to the photo.

Was she being ridiculous getting involved with someone like Alex Montgomery? Maybe she needed to view it as she would a holiday romance. Go all in for a limited time, knowing full well that it would come to an end, and they'd fizzle out once they both went back to their normal lives.

"Excuse me," a man's voice said, and she turned to find out if he was talking to her or not. He was a bear of a man, and he grinned at her through a huge bushy beard. "Sorry, I've been sent to round everyone up. You're on the crew, the doctor, right?"

"Uh, yes, I guess I am." She smiled back and flashed the ID card.

"Yeah, so, Ms Carlson has called a meeting, everyone is to attend."

"Right now?"

"Yep. Don't worry, its normal. I've worked on a Sasha concert before, and Francine always does impromptu stuff." He turned and started to walk, and she had to speed up. "So, what do you do then?"

"I'm Sasha's—"

"There you are." Francine appeared out of nowhere and for once, Morgan couldn't have been more thankful. This was a lot more stressful than any of them had first thought it would be, having to second guess every answer to every question. "I need you to head back to the hotel with *Sasha*, while I finish up here. Can you manage that?"

"I can dissect a frog with a scalpel. I think I can get Her Highness into a car, driven by a chauffeur, back to her 5-star rated hotel room, yes," she replied, feeling a little put out. She was a doctor, not a first aider out of their depth.

The man bear choked back a giggle.

Francine ignored her.

Turning to Man Bear, she said, "Jessie, I'll be right there."

Shoulders bouncing as he chuckled and walked away, Morgan couldn't stop herself from smiling, until Francine turned back to face her. Now there was something different about Francine, and Morgan had to admit, she was intimidating. A steely look had replaced her usual wasp-chewing face.

"Let me be clear. You're here to do a job, and that job entails not being an asshole when the crew are around. That's my job. I'm the asshole." She pointed a bony finger at herself.

"And I'd appreciate it if you didn't speak to me like I am a child or the hired help." Morgan stood her ground.

Francine took one step forward. "You," the bony finger now poked her arm, "are the hired help. That is exactly what you are. Hired to help make Alex's life less stressful."

Morgan said nothing. Francine was right; just because she was sleeping with the boss behind everyone else's back didn't elevate her above her station.

"Nobody is asking much of you. So, if you could please make yourself available to take *Her Highness* back to the hotel and keep her company until curtain time, and then," Francine leaned in closer and hissed, "make it fucking obvious to the press that you're the reason she was visiting the hospital, I'd be grateful."

Morgan nodded. She was used to people like Francine, throwing their weight about, shouting to make a point. It was something she tolerated at work most days. But what made it even more frustrating, was Francine was a pro at this.

"And Morgan?" Francine called after her, waiting until she turned around and gave her her full attention.

"Yes."

"Don't ever let me hear you call her *Her Highness* again. That woman deserves respect. Got it?"

"It was just a joke."

"Well, it's not a funny one." Francine walked away, leaving Morgan with her tail between her legs.

Chapter Thirty-Two

"You're very quiet." Alex said. Morgan sat beside her in the back of the car, staring out of the window. She hadn't said a word since they'd climbed in and Mike had set off.

"Hm?" Morgan replied, not really paying attention. Her mind was still on what Francine had said: *don't call her Her Highness.*

"I said, you're very quiet. Is everything alright?" Their little fingers touched on the seat between them, and Alex hooked hers over the top of Morgan's, linking them together.

Morgan turned her face towards her. "I said something earlier that I'm not proud of."

"Oh, do you want to talk about it?"

Morgan sighed, before admitting, "I called you Her Highness, and Francine took me to task."

Alex chuckled. "I can imagine how that went."

"Yes, and the thing is, she's right and I feel pretty churlish about it right now, and embarrassed."

"I wouldn't worry about it." Alex reached out and covered Morgan's hand with her own on the seat. "I've been called worse."

"You're not upset about it?"

"No." Alex turned, smiling. "Honestly, it probably helps. If Francine thinks that you think I'm a bit of a princess, she won't be thinking that we're…" She smirked and leaned closer, whispering even though Mike couldn't hear them. "…enjoying each other the moment the door closes on the world."

Morgan smiled. "True."

"Why did you call me that, anyway?"

Morgan sighed again, feeling like a very immature child as she explained, "Because Francine rubbed me up the wrong way, and I just said something flippant in response and then she ripped me a new one." Before Alex could respond, Morgan continued, "She's just so condescending. 'Can you manage that?'" she said trying to sound like

Francine. "Like I'm some kind of incompetent with a Brownies first aid badge, who needs everything spelled out for her."

The car pulled up outside of the hotel, a small group of fans congregating around the door, waiting to catch a glimpse, or get an autograph from Alex.

Alex's eyes narrowed at her. "I want you to go straight to my room, get undressed and wait for me."

"What?"

"You heard me." Before Mike opened the door, Alex touched her cheek. "You need some quiet time, and then I'll relax you."

"Oh." Morgan grinned. "Yes, I probably would enjoy that, but I'm supposed to be relaxing you."

"That will relax me."

The door opened and *Sasha* stepped out. Waving to her small group of fans who had congregated, hoping to catch a glimpse of the celebrity, she smiled and said, "Hi, thank you so much for coming. I hope you haven't been waiting long."

From her periphery, she could see Morgan sneaking past quietly, nobody really noticing her. Taking a pen that was offered, *Sasha* began signing everything that was held out to her until finally, Mike intervened and made her excuses for her.

"Thanks, Mike," she said graciously as they headed inside and straight into the manager. "Get something to eat, Mike. I'll be down as soon as I'm ready."

"Yes, Ms Montgomery," he said, saluting comically before walking towards the restaurant.

There were too many people waiting at the lift. Several people invited her to go first, but she just smiled and said, "I'm in no rush. You go ahead." It wouldn't do Morgan any harm to have to wait just a little longer. Alex enjoyed the idea of her lover getting herself all worked up with Francine and needing an outlet for her frustrations.

Morgan was just the right amount of submissive to match her own slightly dominant streak, but not too submissive that she couldn't make decisions and take the lead where necessary. This was something

Alex realised she'd been missing in every other relationship" someone who challenged her. It was something she was relishing.

Opening the door to the apartment, Alex could hear classical music playing. She recognised the song as one by Einaudi and liked its soothing melody. It was a good choice, she thought.

Kicking off her shoes, she unbuttoned her shirt as she walked towards the bedroom. She couldn't deny that Morgan's presence in her life right now was a godsend.

The sound of the door swishing against the carpet as she opened it was forgotten in a moment, as soon as she laid eyes on the bed and the naked form lying on her side, head resting on a palm at the end of a bent elbow.

"You took forever," Morgan complained with a smile as she rolled onto her back, arms raising above her head to stretch out her torso, breasts pushing higher as her back arched and her legs fell apart, an invitation.

Alex raised an interested brow.

"Maybe next time, I'll take longer."

Shrugging her shirt off of her shoulders, Alex slowly unbuttoned her trousers, enjoying the way Morgan watched, fidgeting around a little on the bed as her need to be dealt with grew.

In just her underwear, Alex climbed onto the bed to join her lover.

"I'm sorry Francine has been hard on you." She settled on her knees at the bottom of the bed and raised one of Morgan's feet, massaging the sole with her fingers. "And I know that right now, you really want me to put my mouth on you."

Morgan sagged and groaned. "No buts about it…"

"But…" Alex grinned down at her and swapped feet. "Well, firstly, we don't have time for me to do that justice. Nancy and Gert will be here in twenty minutes for hair and make-up, but more importantly…" She placed the foot down and crawled up the lithe body, skin against skin, until they were face to face, lips barely an inch apart as she said, "I want you to remain in this state. Needy, and wanting." Her lips brushed Morgan's and elicited a groan. Her hips tried to rise up and press against Alex. "Because when I come off that stage tonight, and we get back here with you wearing that dress. I am going to spend the entire night doing all manner of things to this body until you plead with me to stop."

"Damn it," Morgan complained. "But you said you were going to relax me now."

The whine was somewhat cute, Alex thought, but wouldn't admit it out loud.

"I am, turn over," she said, raising up to make room for Morgan to turn.

Knitted brows and pursed lips made Alex finally chuckle. But Morgan did as she was told and shuffled herself over until she was prone on the bed, and Alex straddled her backside, warm palms against her shoulder blades.

"What about your fingers?" Morgan suddenly realised a massage was coming. "You can't overwork them."

Leaning down, speaking against her ear, Alex whispered, "Consider it a warm-up."

Chapter Thirty-Three

When Morgan finally looked in the mirror, she was stunned into silence. Not to be vain, but she knew she was an attractive enough woman by society's standards; however, she'd never quite mastered the art of make-up, past slapping some basic eyeshadow and mascara on.

This vision of herself in the mirror was something otherworldly, like she was looking at someone else completely.

Nancy stood behind her grinning, understanding the look she'd seen on many a face over the years when someone was stunned into silence.

Having wheeled the vanity station in not more than thirty minutes ago, Morgan was amazed at the transformation as her fingers deftly touched her face to check if it was real, or just a mask that would slip the moment she stepped in front of the cameras.

"Don't worry, it's all you. Like it?" Nancy asked, pressing her lips together and tapping her foot in anticipation. She'd never had a client yet tell her to do it again, so she was pretty confident.

"Nancy, it's…" Morgan leaned forward towards the mirror again, turning her face from side to side. "It's really me?"

"Yep." Nancy glanced through the mirror over their shoulders to the door that was opening, and they both watched as Alex came out of her room, adjusting the cuffs of her shirt. They were a crisp white and ironed perfectly. Gert stood in the doorway with the hairdryer in her hand, like a female James Bond with a gun.

When Alex looked up and saw the image of Morgan in front of her, she stopped in her tracks, head tilting slowly to the side as she studied her.

"What do you think?" Morgan asked. Standing up, she turned, still wearing her robe with her hair wrapped in a towel.

"I think that I'm going to be headline news tomorrow for all the right reasons." Alex smiled. "You look phenomenal. Not that I doubted you would, because you are already a beautiful woman."

Morgan blushed at the compliment. Her day job was scrubs, filth, blood. Hair scraped out of the way, no make-up unless you counted her pigmented lip balm. She hadn't dressed up to go out for months, but even then, it was nothing like this. She felt like a princess.

"I need to do your hair," Gert said firmly, breaking up the adoration. "We have just under half of an hour." She shook her head, not impressed with the time limitations. "And this is a lot to work with," she said, eyeing up the curls.

Spell broken, Morgan bowed her head. "Thank you, Nancy."

"You're welcome." She turned to Alex. "Now, shall we touch you up?"

Alex's eyes followed Morgan out of the room. "If we must," she finally answered, sitting down on the chair.

Nancy went to work.

Twenty minutes later and Alex was sitting on the couch, eyes closed as she went through a calming routine she'd started years ago. It consisted of breathing techniques, mantras and thoughts that allowed her mind to calm and clear. She heard the sound of the door opening, but by the time she opened her eyes to see, all she caught of Morgan was a blur of blue robe as she slipped into her room.

Nancy and Gert finished packing up their things and waved a quick goodbye and a "good luck" shouted over their shoulders as they left the suite, and Alex enjoyed the silence.

Opening her eyes at the "click" sound of the door moments later, Alex had to remind herself to breathe. The vision that stood in the doorway was just spectacular. She pushed herself up from her seat and took a step forward, stopping herself in order to stare at Morgan again.

She'd seen the dress earlier, even seen Morgan in it, but this, this was different. Her hair piled high up on her head, the long neck, bare shoulders.

Stunning.

Add to that the make-up, the shoes, and it all became like a fairytale, but mostly there was a confidence. Morgan looked taller; chin up, eyes sparkling as she smiled and laughed nervously.

"You look like you've never seen me before."

"I haven't, not this version anyway," Alex answered. "And I'm a little annoyed, if I'm honest." She smiled when Morgan looked confused. "Because I have to attend a concert when I'd much rather be taking you somewhere deserving of the effort."

Morgan blushed. "Oh…Well, I think I'm quite happy to be attending the concert on the arm of a world-famous pianist who's about to perform."

"Turn around, let me see all of you."

Morgan laughed. "Really?"

Alex just twirled her fingers. So, Morgan did as she was asked, stopping when she had her back to Alex and glanced over her shoulder at her. "Do I pass?"

"You're incredible," Alex said, stepping forward, a finger trailing the line of the shoulder blade.

"If you keep touching me like that, I won't be in any fit state to attend anything with you tonight."

The apartment door opened, and in came the whirlwind that was Francine. Which, Alex considered, was probably a good thing, because she was sorely tempted to just ignore the show. She stepped back and away from the temptation.

"Come on, let's go—" Francine clapped her hands excitedly before she stopped in her tracks and stared at Morgan. "Okay, that's more than…wow." She shook herself and checked her watch. "I need you both downstairs in the car in one minute, and then I need to prepare for the headlines this…" she waved her hand around to acknowledge Morgan, "is going to cause."

"Headlines?" Morgan asked. That was the second time it had been mentioned.

"Honey, if you think you're turning up to an event on the arm of Sasha looking like that and the pap ain't gonna print your picture and want to know everything about you, well, I don't know what to say to you."

She hadn't considered that the press would be interested in her. Naïve of course, but she'd assumed they'd write about Alex.

"It'll be fine. I'll deal with it." Francine turned to Alex before Morgan could get a word in. "Ready?"

"Just give me a minute," Alex said.

Francine stood there a moment before realising she was supposed to leave.

"Of course, pep talk time, right!"

Alex just smiled and let her think whatever she needed to.

With Francine out of the way, Alex closed the distance between herself and Morgan, holding her at arm's length.

"You don't have to do this. You can back out right now. I get it. This wasn't what you signed up for, and each step forward takes you deeper into it and I don't want you to do anything you don't feel—"

"Are you attracted to me?"

The question somewhat threw Alex. "What? Of course, I am, that's not the—"

"If I didn't go tonight, would you still want to be with me? Would I still have a job on this tour?"

Alex stepped back and gave them both space, but she answered with a clear, "Yes, of course."

"And when the press come for me, you'll protect me? You'll make sure that Francine doesn't throw me under the bus in the big break-up?"

"I promise that won't happen."

Morgan picked up her purse, something very expensive and not what she was used to carrying her things in, not that she had anything much to carry in it. It was all part of the look, the woman at the boutique had said, along with the designer heels she wore that meant she was at least two inches taller than Alex now.

"Okay then. Let's go."

Chapter Thirty-Four

She didn't know what to expect when Mike pulled the limo up outside of the cathedral doors, but the bright flashbulbs that went off sporadically, along with a lot of cheering and shouting from those patiently waiting for *Sasha* to arrive, took Morgan by surprise.

"I had no idea that you were the Beyoncé of the piano world," Morgan said, staring out through the blacked-out windows with wide eyes taking it all in.

Alex scoffed. "Hardly. But you'd be surprised at just how popular classical music is and how interested people are when it comes to the love life of a celebrity."

"So, how do we do this?"

Taking her hand, Alex squeezed it. "All you have to do is smile. Are you happy to hold my hand, touch me?"

"Yes. You know I am."

Alex smirked. "That's in private, this is very different. Everything will be amplified here."

"I'll think of it as a practice run, for when we do this for real."

"Okay then. And if it gets too much, just walk past and into the venue." Morgan nodded nervously. "It will be fine," Alex reassured before she pressed the button to speak to Mike. "We're ready."

The crowd cheered when Mike opened his door and climbed out. Their long-awaited moment was finally here. Sasha had arrived.

"Here we go," Alex said, ready to step out the moment the door opened.

The noise was louder the instant that happened, and Alex was gone and out before Morgan could take another breath. Looking through the opening, she smiled when she saw Alex staring back at her, waiting with her hand out, jacket slung over her shoulder and held by one finger of her other hand. She looked casual, as though this were just any other day. Which for her, it was.

Morgan took her hand and stepped out to the sound of more cheering and excitable noise from the crowd. Alex nodded, and smiled, holding her hand just tightly enough that it soothed the nerves that were building.

Morgan barely had a moment to take it all in. The flash of photographers and the *click, click* sound of their cameras became all-absorbing. Almost blinding. Morgan needed to look down, away from it for a second, to compose herself before Alex had them walking and moving on. That was the moment she noticed it. The red carpet beneath her feet.

She was walking a red carpet, on the arm of a celebrity, while feeling like a million dollars, pretty sure she was going to wake up any moment and find out that it was all just a dream.

"Alright?" she heard Alex say when they stopped to allow fans to take photos. Morgan turned slightly to find blue eyes smiling at her, with just a hint of concern.

"Yes, I'm fine. You do your thing."

"Okay, let's walk then," Alex said. Her palm landing deftly against the small of Morgan's back felt comforting and warm as they moved, one step at a time.

At the end of the carpet was a huge wall of advertiser's names. They came to a halt in front of it, and Morgan stepped in closer to Alex, still holding hands as the press continued to snap away, calling out at them to turn this way, face that way. It was all Morgan could manage to just keep smiling and not pull a face that would end up haunting her forever in gossip magazines.

"Sasha, it's so good to see you. Are you looking forward to tonight's concert?" one of the TV reporters asked.

It was only then that Alex let go of Morgan's hand as she took a step towards the reporter to speak to them. "I am. I really can't wait. The acoustics in a building like this are…you can imagine." She grinned.

Along the line they moved, each reporter asking one question, Sasha answering and Morgan in the background, smiling and doing her best not to look like a deer in the headlights.

They were almost at the end of the line and about to enter the building when someone threw out the question they'd both hoped to avoid.

"Who's your new girlfriend then, Sasha?"

Taking Morgan's hand again, Alex turned slightly, smiled at the crowd again and then led them inside. The question went unanswered.

"That was a bit terrifying," Morgan admitted once they were away from prying eyes and ears. "But exhilarating." She giggled. "It's starting to feel like a whirlwind. I can barely keep up with where we are and what you're doing, and now this." She laughed. "It's crazy."

"You did great, and hopefully that will be the end of it," Alex reassured her, holding her gaze and wanting to move closer.

"That was great." Francine's loud voice barged into the conversation as she appeared in the doorway. "They're all talking about you." She flashed a grin at Morgan. "So, no more heart attack or bus panic headlines. Great job."

"I guess we will have to wait and see what they have to say about it?" Morgan said before opening her clutch to check her phone was on silent. "God." There were already three texts waiting. Her mum, Zoe, and another from her mum.

"Everything okay?"

"It's my mum." She opened the text and read it.

Mum: Is that you on the TV with that pianist?

Morgan: It's on the news, already?

Mum: It's live on the news Morgan, did you not think to tell me you had a new girlfriend?

She went to run her hand over her face and then remembered her make-up.

Morgan: Yes, mum, it is me. I'm just her date for the night, that's all. x

She didn't read Zoe's text, but she could imagine the squeal of excitement it had all caused. Replying could wait till later when she'd had time to think about it. Because the cat was well and truly out of the bag with her now, wasn't it?

"Okay, let's get this show on the road," Francine interrupted. "Morgan, you come with me while Alex gets ready to go on." Francine was already walking away, and Morgan hesitated just long enough.

Alex stepped forward. "I want to kiss you right now, but—"

Morgan's tongue licked slowly along her bottom lip as she inched closer. "I think this is the one time you could do it. It might even be expected."

"Don't tempt me. I need to be focused and if I kiss you now—" She shook her head and laughed. "I won't stop with just a kiss."

Biting her lip, Morgan swallowed, the thought of that doing nothing to quell her own arousal right now. She was wired after the red carpet and the massage earlier. Maybe she did understand the euphoria after all.

"Alright, I guess I'll just have to keep waiting till later." Morgan glanced over her shoulder quickly, expecting Francine to sternly shout at her, but she was already out of sight. "All the best, and I'll see you afterwards."

Turning on her heel, she hurried to catch up with Francine, but just before she turned the corner, she looked back. Alex was still watching as she blew a kiss, and then disappeared from view. Her footsteps tapped a beat with every step on the worn flagstones.

Walking into the nave, it was easy enough to spot Francine. Lines of chairs filled the space, and people were slowly filing into the building and finding their seats. A hushed chit-chat sound echoed around the huge space, and her eyes landed on the piano up on the makeshift stage.

"Morgan." Francine waved. "Over here."

All eyes seemed to land on her as she waved hesitantly back and began to move towards the loud American. Some people smiled, others whispered, but they all looked in her direction as she eased by them. *This must be how Alex feels*, she thought.

It was only when she got much closer that she realised who else she was sitting with. She gulped, felt her eyes widen, and her mouth dry as she took in the familiar faces.

Every seat in the first two rows, at least, was filled with TV personalities, other musicians, singers, and their dates. All were dressed to the nines and chatting amiably to one another.

Morgan felt her mouth dry. She was really not prepared for it all.

"This is Dr Morgan Kelly," she heard Francine say from behind her.

She spun around and came face to face with the woman who had been the UK's top morning TV host for the last two decades.

"Angela Sparrow," Morgan gushed, reaching out a hand. She'd never been so excited and nervous in her life. "So lovely to meet you."

"Likewise." Angela's subtle Irish lilt made the word feel like they were friends already. "I'm so excited for the show, are you?"

So, she asked stupid questions in real life too, Morgan thought and felt her nerves dissipate a little.

"Yes, I am. It's so different listening to her here than at the hotel."

Angela's eyes wided and flashed excitedly at the snippet of information. "So, you and Sasha are—"

"You know, I need to introduce you to Cecil," Francine was saying, half pulling Morgan away from the nosy TV interviewer.

When they were far enough away, Morgan said, "I've already met Cecil."

"I know. I needed a ruse." Francine leaned in. "You're green kid, these people will pick you apart for any information and as much as the plan is to keep the press away from the real issue, and use you as a little distraction, any more of that 'listening to her at the hotel' malarky and we will have a bigger issue on our hands."

"I thought you wanted people assuming… You're worried they'll write about me, aren't you?" Morgan sagged.

"Yeah, so…try and keep details minimal. I know it's exciting meeting all these people, and I should probably have thought about it all a little more, but I really didn't think we'd be doing this and if we had more time, we could have coached you through it, but…" She shrugged. "It is what it is."

"Ladies and gentlemen, the performance will begin in five minutes. Please make your way back to your seats. The performance will begin in five minutes."

Chapter Thirty-Five

Every note moved through Morgan in a way that music had never done before. Whether it was because the fingers playing it were ones that she knew so intimately or something more out of body she hadn't known before, she wasn't sure, but she felt herself move emotionally with every strike of a key.

Rapt and enamoured with Alex's talent, she understood just how seductive it was to be allowed into this woman's interpretation of music. She felt proud to be sitting here in front of the world flaunted as *Sasha's* partner, knowing that behind closed doors, there was a truth to it that nobody else understood but them.

The music rose and built, telling a story until finally, it crashed down into the crescendo. *Sasha's* arms rose high into the air, and the watching audience jumped to their feet clapping with an enthusiasm Morgan had never experienced in her life before.

Morgan found herself swept up in it, her excitement bubbling under the surface, wanting to erupt. Arousal brewed when her eyes met with Alex's, and she somewhat understood the way euphoria could whip you up into a frenzy.

Up on stage, taking a well-earned bow and enjoying the recognition, Alex took the applause. Morgan could see it, the euphoria. The intensity of it was already pulsing between them.

Arcing like electricity.

Invisible to everyone else in the room.

"What do we do now?" Morgan asked Francine. "Can we go backstage?"

"Sure, you head through. I have to speak to a few more people."

Alex was still on stage, but Morgan felt the eyes on her as she made her way along the front row and off to the side where she could access the hallway that would lead to Alex's dressing room and away from prying eyes.

Standing ovations were not going to be over any time soon, though.

As she approached the door, a member of staff stood guard and stopped her entry. "Sorry Miss, can't go in there."

Morgan smiled and pulled the ID card from her clutch. "Yes, I can, and I'd appreciate you not allowing anyone else in except for Ms Montgomery." She winked and moved past him, opening the door with enthusiasm and closing it gently behind her. She leaned back on it and surveyed the room.

The vanity station was still lit up, and the day bed to the side was made and covered in the clothes Alex had arrived in.

Picking them up, Morgan held her shirt to her nose and inhaled Alex's scent before folding it all neatly and placing it on the stool. She switched the main light off and then debated what to do next: get naked and lounge on the day bed in a 'paint me like one of those French women' pose, or just wait and allow Alex to undress her. Just imagining either scenario was enough to get her hot and fidgety.

"I want to take this off you later," reverberated in her ears and she considered just how that would go down. Yes, the dress would stay on, but she kicked off the heels and paced, frustrated not to be wearing a watch.

"What's taking so long?" she muttered and tried to shake out some of the energy building.

Just when she was about to open the door and go in search of Alex, the door swung open and was slammed shut. Alex stood there, just staring at her, eyes wild with a fire that Morgan had never felt before, and she found she liked it. The intensity of it all pulsed towards her like a radar searching deep water, but more than that, it pulsed from her, too.

There were no words said. Everything was conveyed between them in milliseconds and in silence. Each took steps forward until they all but crashed into one another. Mouths suctioned to one another in a battle between tongues.

The material of the dress inching up Morgan's thighs felt like sandpaper to her nerves. She wanted to rip it off, but she was otherwise engaged with the buttons on Alex's shirt.

"Wider," Alex managed, kicking her foot between Morgan's feet. She smiled into the kiss when one foot moved, and she had the access she'd demanded.

Morgan's underwear shifted to the side as fingers plunged into her. She was so wet that she'd barely felt the intrusion before the incessant thrusting began, and she found herself shuffling backwards until her back hit something hard and her clit throbbed with a need that would have been considered unfathomable before she'd met Alexandra Montgomery.

Reaching her arms around Alex's neck, she clung to her, one leg rising that was instantly grabbed and held against Alex's side. Harder, faster, harder, faster. Morgan cried out with her mouth pressed tightly against Alex's shoulder to avoid the impending noise that would alert anyone passing by to what they were doing. Breathing deeply, she opened her eyes to find Alex staring into her soul, burrowing inside of her literally and figuratively.

"Say my name," Alex urged.

"Al—" Morgan could barely breathe. "Alex," she finally got out. "Fuck, yes."

How she was still standing, she didn't know how, but Alex was relentless, pushing her to the edge and pulling her back again, over and over until she was begging.

"Please, I want…"

"Wait," Alex would say, kissing her again, stilling her fingers to the point that Morgan thought she might cry. The thumb pressing against her clit in painfully slow circles was all she could focus on.

"I need…please…Cresh—"

"Say it." Alex buried her face in Morgan's neck and listened as the word was whispered against her ear.

"Crescendo."

That was all it took.

One word.

And Morgan was being thrust back up towards the tip of the orgasmic hill that Alex had been holding her hostage on, thrusting and thrusting until finally, when Morgan cried out again, this time muffled against the crook of Alex's neck. Her standing leg gave way and she trembled against Alex's chest.

Strong arms wrapped around her, holding her up, until she'd recovered enough to finally feel grounded again. Alex redressed her, grinning at what they'd just done.

"I need to go and network," Alex said, stroking down her cheek. "You can wait here for me, or I can get Mike to run you back to the hotel."

"How long will you be?" Morgan asked with shaky breath.

Alex shrugged. "I don't know." She pressed her lips together. "You could join me, but I want to keep you out of the firing line as much as possible."

Morgan nodded, appreciating that. "I'll go back to the hotel." She leaned in and kissed Sasha's cheek gently. "I'll wait up."

"I hope so."

"Don't be long, or I might have to take matters into my own hands again."

Alex stepped forward. "Don't you dare. I'll be back as soon as I can."

Chapter Thirty-Six

Alex stepped out into the nave of the building to another round of applause. The selected group of friends and supporters, celebrities and members of the press moved around, jostling to get closer to her and grab their five minutes with the musical genius that was Sasha.

"Darling, well done," Cecil said, moving in before anyone else could get close. "A wonderful performance." He glanced around behind her. "And where is that delightful…friend of yours? She was here earlier."

Alex rolled her eyes. "Thank you, yes, it felt like a good performance." She ignored the question about Morgan, and he didn't push it. "We can expect a great tour, don't you think?"

"Absolutely. Never doubted that we would." He raised a brow at her. "Have you seen Marty's here?"

Alex smiled. "Well, I would hope so. He is my agent after all."

Francine pulled her elbow. "I need you to come and meet Goran."

"What's he doing here?" Alex asked, alarmed. "Excuse me, Cecil."

They walked away together, Francine leaning in closely. "I invited him. You need this."

"I do not. You should have told me he was here."

Francine scoffed. "And have you freak out? Not a chance. I dunno what got into you tonight, but you just put in the performance of a lifetime." She squeezed Alex's arm as they approached a grey-haired man in a silver suit, happily chatting to a couple of singers Alex recognised but couldn't name. "Goran, here she is, the woman of the hour."

Goran turned, still grinning, arms out to hug her. "Alexandra, what a performance. My god, you put your heart into every note, don't you?"

He released his grip on her, and she smiled, a little embarrassed. "Thank you, I think music without emotion isn't really hitting the right notes, so to speak." And a woman like Morgan to inspire her was definitely a godsend.

"Yes, yes, I was just telling these wonderful people how we might be working together next year."

When she didn't speak immediately, Francine nudged her.

"I am looking forward to that opportunity," Alex finally managed.

"Me too, me too. Come, let's drink and talk." He guided her to one side, and she smiled an apology at the others for not stopping to speak with them. "I want to hear what you really think about the potential of the project."

Alex stumbled into the hotel suite – not because she was drunk, far from it, but her ankle was throbbing a little. She'd stuck to sparking mineral water in her champagne flute, but she was exhausted. The euphoria from earlier had dissipated over the time she'd been stuck at the cathedral and paraded around.

She'd cursed Francine several times over the last three hours, but what else could she do? Goran was there, and their plan was coming to fruition. A few more months and she would be free. It was starting to feel real now, starting to become less of a dream and more of a reality, but she couldn't rest on her laurels. A lot could change in the coming weeks, and she needed to focus and be ready.

Right now though, she just wanted to fall into bed with Morgan. If she could find her.

The room was silent. A small lamp in the corner was on and illuminated the room enough for her to recognise that Morgan hadn't fallen asleep on the couch at least. Moving quietly, Alex opened the door to Morgan's room and found that bed empty. She smiled to herself as she tossed her jacket onto the back of a chair and made her way to her own room.

Empty.

"Where the hell is she?" She ran a hand through her hair and listened. It was silent.

She was about to turn and leave when she noticed it: the thin bar of light that shone out from under the bathroom door. Opening the door, she grinned lazily at the sight of Morgan under the water, which was almost up to her chin. Foamy bubbles covered her chest, with only her head exposed. Her eyes remained closed as she spoke.

"Well, if you thought I was going to stay in that dress waiting, you were sadly mistaken."

Alex leaned against the door frame. "I'm sorry about that. I couldn't get away."

Those eyes opened, slowly, trained on Alex with that intensity that always managed to weaken her. "And now I suppose you think you can just waltz in here and what? I'll fawn over you?"

There was something a little bit sexy about a riled-up Morgan Kelly, Alex considered.

"I'm exhausted, actually," Alex admitted, looking away and feeling somewhat guilty.

It was the sound of the water sploshing over the edge of the bath that made her look up again. Morgan stood, naked in all her glory, dripping wet.

"Oh, I do not think so," she said, stepping out of the bath. "I've waited patiently for nearly three hours. I'm getting what I want." She stared at Alex, daring her to argue. "Get those clothes off and get into that bath. I'm going to make us some drinks." She stepped towards the door, still naked, stopping directly in front of Alex. "I want to be begging you to stop, understand me?"

Slowly, Alex swallowed and nodded, fingers already unbuttoning the shirt she was wearing.

"Good. I'll be right back." Morgan smiled before she left the room, wet footprints marking every step she took, and Alex found her second wind.

The water was still hot. She pulled the plug and let some water out; otherwise there would be a flood with the pair of them in it.

Euphoria

There was no time to really contemplate what exactly Morgan had planned as she climbed in and sank down into the warmth, before Morgan was back, clutching two glasses, filled with ice and the amber liquid that Alex knew would be scotch.

Without a word, Morgan stepped back into the bath. Her feet on either side of Alex's thighs, she lowered down to straddle her lap. One of the glasses, she placed onto the corner of the bath; the other she held to Alex's lips and tipped until Alex took a sip.

"I've spent all day, waiting. All night, waiting, and do you know what I discovered?" Morgan asked Alex, allowing her another sip of the rather nice scotch.

Alex shook her head side to side slowly, enraptured by this awe-inspiring creature before her. Something was changing between them, something better, more intimate, and equal. And she liked it.

"I discovered that being on your arm, listening to you play with everyone around me in awe of you, gave me my own sense of euphoria, and a quickie in your dressing room did little to alleviate it. I was beyond aroused. Far beyond anything I've ever felt before with anyone, and yet, I was still prepared to wait." She took a sip herself. "For you. And I did wait, and now, I don't want to hear excuses or how exhausted you are. I want to feel your hands all over me. I want to feel you inside of me. I want to feel your tongue against my skin and in my mouth, licking and sucking me until I beg you to stop, and I don't want you to stop. I want you to ruin me until I am nothing more than a quivering wreck, and then when you're done, I want you to comfort me, and soothe me." She reached into the water and found Alex's hand, sliding it between the gap of her thighs. "Adagio."

Chapter Thirty-Seven

Morgan did not enjoy the morning wake-up call or understand why it needed to be before ten in the morning, seeing as she hadn't gotten any sleep before four, but alas, it wasn't her decision.

"Hell," Alex said quickly, jumping from the bed and pulling her robe on. "Morgan, quickly, you need to go to your room."

"Ugh, seriously, can you just tell her not to wake you?" Morgan sat up and rubbed her face before she stood, naked, and walked out of the room.

Alex grinned at the sight of the bare backside, still a little red from earlier.

The banging continued, and Alex followed Morgan out, finding her already disappeared into the safety of her own room. Alex opened the door.

"What requires my attention this early and this loudly in the morning?" Alex said, holding the door open for Francine to stroll inside. She was clutching a pile of newspapers to her chest and grinning.

"So, someone is a little popular this morning." Francine dropped the pile onto the table and fanned them out.

"What's with the noise?" Morgan asked, yawning for good effect.

Newspapers were strewn across the coffee table. And from what Morgan could see, at least four had gone with an image of *Sasha* arriving at the concert, and of those, they all mentioned her date. Which was good news, according to Francine.

SASHA'S MEDICINE and HEARTSTOPPER FOR SASHA

The photos of them both looked intimate, casual, and hot. Morgan couldn't deny that the ruse had worked, or that she didn't wish she could have copies of the photos.

"I can keep on top of these, feed them enough without giving any real information," Francine said smugly, flicking the pages of the red tops. "There's a lot more talk online, but again, nothing we need to worry about for now. Just a little intrigue and a little excitement about the hot woman on your arm." Francine enjoyed the way Morgan blushed. "Never fails to shift some more sales and keep the headlines positive."

"And what about—" Alex said, as though Francine would know exactly what she was talking about.

"All in hand, I'll keep in contact with him."

Alex picked up the paper nearest to her and scanned the copy. "They don't know Morgan's name. But it won't take long for someone to blab."

Grabbing her phone, Morgan sat on the couch in her dressing gown, surrounded by bouquets of flowers that had been sent to Alex, and began to go through the myriad of texts and missed calls since the night before.

"I'll live if they do," Morgan said dryly. "My mother, on the other hand..." She held up the phone to indicate the many text messages she'd received overnight as people she knew caught wind of the story.

Her mother wanted to know if it was serious and should she expect a visit soon. She needed warning to make sure the house was tidy, and that Mason behaved. Zoe wanted all of the details, details that Morgan absolutely wouldn't be sharing with her mother, or Zoe for that matter, and she was quickly kicked into touch with that idea.

She was more surprised to see Mason had messaged.

Mason: Hey sis, any chance your new gf can get some tickets to Swifts concert? Alison really wants to go.

Seriously, it was too early for this. She put the phone down just as breakfast was wheeled in. Coffee, four kinds of juice, cereals, yoghurts, and a heated section with the full English on offer.

"I am starving," Morgan said. "I seem to have worked up an appetite with being your girlfriend." She chuckled and winked when Francine was dealing with the porter and handing over a £20 note.

Alex smirked. "Eat, enjoy."

It was a little unnerving, if she were honest, at just how much she thought she could get used to this lifestyle. Perusing the offerings, she watched in amusement and horror as two women arrived, each one entering a bedroom.

"Uh, who are they? And why is she in my room?"

Francine rolled her eyes. "They're packing. We need to vacate and be on the move."

"But I can do that."

"Yes, you can, but I don't have time to wait for you to do that. So, you can enjoy breakfast and then get showered, dressed, and go without worrying about it."

Swigging down her juice and pulling the corner from her toast, Morgan stood up and went to her bedroom. Her case was already laid out and opened, her evening shoes already packed.

"Hi, it's okay, I can do that," Morgan said, smiling at the woman who, until now, hadn't acknowledged her. She didn't care what Francine wanted. There was no way she was allowing someone to pack for her.

The woman turned to her and all but saluted. "It's alright, there isn't much, I can do this while you—" The woman's smile was warm, and she edged closer. "You're not used to people running around after you, are you?"

Chuckling, Morgan said, "Is it that obvious?"

"How about you pick out the clothes you want to wear today, and I finish off while you relax and enjoy the experience. If it helps, I'm being paid twice what I'd usually earn, and I'm good with that."

For a moment, Morgan considered arguing, but in all honesty, it made sense, even if she did feel guilty about enjoying someone else doing all of her mundane chores for a while.

She supposed though that like a holiday, after a while you missed the normality of the life you lived, but for today, why not?

"Okay, thank you." Morgan shrugged graciously. She pulled a pair of jeans and a teal-coloured turtleneck thin jumper out and laid them on the bed, tossing underwear to join them. "I'll wear those," she said, pointing to the trainers the woman was about to pack. The woman smiled as she handed them over. "Do you do this for everyone that uses these suites?"

"Only those we like." She winked. "Go on, enjoy that breakfast before it all gets cold."

"Thank you," Morgan repeated before backing out of the room and into the lounge area. She picked up a plate and casually moved around the table, picking out a croissant and a slice of sourdough toast. She smiled when Alex passed her a glass of orange juice.

Obliviously interrupting the moment, Francine said, "Happy now?" When Morgan nodded, she continued, "So, we'll be leaving here in the next hour. Once everything is packed, Mike's ready to go. The drive shouldn't take more than an hour."

"I've never been to Chester," Morgan said, looking around the room. "What about the flowers?" There hadn't been this many at the other venues. She hadn't thought about it then, but it seemed an awful waste.

"We leave the flowers for the staff here at the hotel to enjoy," Alex answered.

Morgan shrugged. It didn't matter to her. What mattered right now was the aching limbs and the need for a short nap. Being Alex Montgomery's lover was far more exhausting than being her doctor could ever be.

Not that she was complaining.

She grinned to herself, recalling the night before.

When she glanced up, she found Alex staring at her across the table, that knowing look and the smirk aimed in her direction as she mouthed a silent, "Stop it."

Chomping down the last mouthful of toast, Morgan stood up, her robe falling open and revealing long legs and a barely there t-shirt. "I'm going to grab a shower." She continued to grin at the way Alex appraised her subtly.

"Great, one hour, remember!" Francine chipped in.

"I'll try not to be too long in the shower." Her line of sight flicked back to Alex to witness the narrowing eyes that knew exactly how she would be spending that time in the shower.

"Nobody is keeping watch on the time, Morgan," Alex said, still smirking at her. She stood up and moved gracefully around the table, and as she passed Morgan, she whispered, "Enjoy your shower."

Morgan remained still, the implication that Alex liked what she planned to do in the shower hitting her arousal like a rocket, again. Francine's dulcet tones brought her back to the room.

"I am." Francine tapped her watch. "Move it. I wanna be there before lunch. You've got a lot to do, and I do not want any more swanning off on shopping trips. It's a tight ship, this one."

Alex sat back in her seat, relaxed and at ease, just watching as Morgan turned and quietly shimmied off towards her bedroom, stopping at the doorway to turn and glance just once over her shoulder before she was gone from sight.

Francine slowly turned from the sashaying backside leaving the room to the quiet pianist on the sofa. "You like her, don't you?"

"I like a lot of things, Fran."

"Hm." She sat down and stared at the closed door to Morgan's room. "Just keep it in your pants until the tour is over. Then you can do whatever the hell you want with her. But I need you focused."

"I am focused," Alex answered.

By the time Morgan was dressed and ready to leave, her bags had already been taken down to the car, and the only person left in the room was Alex.

"Ready to go?" Morgan asked, nonchalantly.

Walking towards her, Alex kept her eyes fixed on Morgan, a stare she was practising now she understood just what the effect was on herself when Morgan used it. "I am very ready." Her hand reached up and around Morgan's neck, pulling her closer and into a searing kiss. "I've never wanted someone in the way that I want you."

Morgan stared. "How do you want me?"

Euphoria

"Like this, without the hassle of everything else getting in the way." On cue, her phone rang, and she looked at the screen. "It's Francine," she sighed. "We'd best get down there." She answered the call. "Yes, we're on our way down now."

Before Alex opened the door, Morgan grabbed her arm and swung her around. "Just to be clear, I know that this is all way too fast, and the situation is unlike anything I've ever experienced before, but—" Her eyes searched Alex's face. "I've never felt like this either."

Alex cupped her hand and touched Morgan's face. "I'm open to eternity."

"Good, because my mother is going to have so many questions." Morgan laughed.

"Did you find time to speak with her earlier?"

"Yes, although, of course, my brother is already taking liberties." Morgan shook her head, laughing as they walked towards the lifts.

"Oh, how so?"

"He wanted to know if I could get him tickets for Taylor Swift now that I have a famous girlfriend." She laughed again.

They made it as far as the lobby before Alex needed to morph into Sasha, and Morgan retreated into the background. Nadia, the duty manager, and some of the staff had gathered to wish her well. It interested Morgan at how proud she felt, standing there, watching these people fawn over Alex. She deserved it; her musical talent was outstanding. But it was more than that; she was humble and kind and decent with it. Even though she wanted a quiet life, she understood the transaction of fame and what that entailed and always had time for people, even when it inconvenienced her.

Morgan smiled at her as she stood between Nadia and other staff members, having her photo taken, signing autographs. For a moment, Morgan thought about the future with Alex. Was she crazy to want all of this? To invite this into her world? Did it matter, if Alex was who she was meant to meet, meant to be with? Did Alex really mean eternity?

Her thoughts were interrupted.

"Mike is waiting. You might as well get in the car," Francine said as she sidled up beside Morgan.

"Alright," Morgan answered, taking one last longing look before she moved around the growing crowd.

"Morgan?" Alex's voice rang out and Morgan stopped in her tracks, turning towards it. Alex excused herself from the throng of people. "Apparently there are photographers out there."

"It's okay."

"No, it's not. Mike can drive around the back and get you, then come back around and I'll run the gauntlet with Francine."

Francine appeared. "What's the problem?"

"I don't want Morgan having to deal with the press or being plastered all over the tabloid and magazines any more than she already will be."

Francine wasted no time in beckoning the manager over. "Nadia, could you help a gal out? We don't want our friend here to have to deal with the press. Can she exit through the back somewhere?"

"Sure, sure, follow me," Nadia said to Morgan with a big smile on her face. "Whatever we can do to help."

Morgan turned without a word, and Alex grew concerned with the way her face dropped. She looked upset.

Pulling her phone out, Francine called Mike and gave him the new instructions, then she said, "You know that was an opportunity to sell the story a little more, right?"

"Yes, but I don't want her to become the story. She doesn't need that, and I don't think any of us, her included, have actually considered just how much she could be affected by this. In fact," she turned to Francine fully, "I don't want her used like this again."

"You want me to hide her away?"

"Yes. Mike can bring her back and forth without me in tow."

"The horse has already bolted; the press knows about her," Francine argued. "She agreed to this."

Stepping closer, Alex said firmly, "I don't care what she agreed to. She had no idea what that would mean, and we didn't think we'd need to use the idea. I will not take advantage of her naivety a moment longer. You will not ruin that woman's life, to save mine."

"Fine. I'll do my best. We'll keep her out of sight as much as possible."

"Good, thank you."

"But I don't think they're going to buy it," Francine said, meaning the press.

Alex pressed her lips together before she said, "I don't care. Make it go away."

Francine's phone beeped. Mike was back out front. "Ready to go?"

Chapter Thirty-Eight

Chester

Francine was out of the car the moment it stopped, greeting the hotel staff and organising luggage with Mike and porters, but Alex stayed put.

"Is everything alright?" Morgan asked when a moment of silence began to feel uncomfortable, and the situation felt awkward. She had no idea what was happening. "Francine seems a bit frosty, well more than usual." She chuckled.

"Sorry, yes, it's all fine." Alex glanced out of the window, checking that nobody was watching before she reached for Morgan's hands. "I spoke with Francine about keeping you out of the public eye as much as possible. I know what we all agreed, but..." She smiled at Morgan. "I'm not happy with throwing you into the lion's den like that."

"Okay," Morgan said slowly, taking it all in. "So, what does that mean?"

"That from now on, I'll travel to and from the venues alone. You'll be taken before or after and meet me there. We will limit the opportunities for the press to take your photo or ask questions about you."

"You don't want anyone to know about me, about us?"

Alex squeezed her hands. "I am trying to protect you. I choose to live this life. I chose to allow the invasion of my privacy. You didn't. Your life is yours and I want it to stay that way as much as possible."

Morgan looked out of the car window at the new hotel. Another 5-star monument to the rich and famous. It looked like a stately home. Maybe she should be dropped off at the tradesmen's entrance, she thought dejectedly.

She nodded, silently, logically understanding, and yet, a feeling of rejection fell across her and triggered a fear she'd long since thought she'd dealt with.

"Morgan?" Alex reached for her chin and brought her face back around so they could look at one another. "Have I done something wrong?"

"No, of course not. I just—I guess I'd let myself think it would be okay."

Alex frowned. "What does that mean?"

Morgan grabbed the door handle. "I don't want to be treated like I'm just the hired help."

"That's not—" Alex scrambled out after her, hurrying to catch up and not caring at all what anyone thought of the pair of them. "Morgan, stop right there."

Instantly, Morgan came to a stop, fighting the urge to ignore her, feeling utterly ridiculous, while simultaneously feeling turned on by the commanding tone.

When Alex was as close as she dared, given they were in the public eye, she hissed, "Don't do that."

"Do what?" Morgan rebuffed. "Know my place?"

"When we get upstairs, I will show you where your place is if that's what you need. Until then, act like a grown-up. I'm trying to protect you."

"Everything okay here?" Francine asked as she neared, eyeing them both suspiciously.

Morgan averted her eyes, and Alex nodded for them both. "Yes, everything is fine. Do you have the keys to our room? I'm feeling quite tired and would like to go to bed for an hour or two."

The awkward silence reverberated around the room as they both stood on either side of the couch waiting for the porter to finish unloading their bags. The room wasn't as big as the last one, but it was still as beautiful. Huge floor-to-ceiling windows with heavy drapes and nets allowed a huge amount of light to come in but would offer privacy as the night drew in.

Francine hovered, following the young man in his red uniform from bedroom to bedroom, organising where each case or bag should go.

When he was finally done, she fished out a £20 note and handed it to him.

"Thank you," she said, ushering him from the room. When he was gone, she closed the door quietly and then turned to look at the pair of them. "Anything going on that I should know about?"

Morgan sucked her lower lip into her mouth before slowly shaking her head.

Alex said simply, "No."

Looking from one to the other, it was pretty clear to Francine that something was up, and she would get to the bottom of it eventually. "Alright, I'll be around if you need me." One last glance at them, a hesitation to see if either of them spoke, but nothing. "Three hours, and then we need to go." She opened the door and left them to it.

"Sit down," Alex all but demanded, taking a seat herself. She watched intently as Morgan's decision-making process kicked in, ultimately deciding that doing as she was asked was going to be the best option, given the fact that she was behaving like a petulant child.

She sat on the couch opposite Alex and waited. Hands in her lap, fingers fidgeting, like a child did when they were being reprimanded.

"I'm sorry, I was out of line," Morgan said quickly.

"Do you want to tell me what's going on?" Alex asked when Morgan finally looked at her.

"I don't know," Morgan admitted honestly. "I just felt…rejected?"

"In what sense?" Alex sat forward, listening ears open.

Taking a deep breath, Morgan let it out. "You're not the only one who has been in therapy." She smiled sadly. "I've done my fair share, and I worked out that my childhood was…" Morgan looked up at Alex, her eyes glistening. "I'm still working on it, clearly." She laughed at herself and flicked her hair out of her face.

"Do you want to tell me about it?" Alex asked gently, kindness and concern etched upon her features.

"Yes, I guess so. You need to understand me as much as I need to understand you."

"Very true, and I very much want to understand you, Morgan."

Sitting back, Morgan started to relax, physically at least. Her shoulders lowered, her fingers stopped fidgeting, as she looked across at Alex.

"When I was a kid, everything was great, until it wasn't. We went from being this normal family who loved each other and spent time together, to this dysfunctional setup where everything became a battle."

Alex said nothing, keeping her attention firmly on Morgan, even when her phone beeped a text message had arrived.

"You can answer it," Morgan said, jutting her chin towards the device on the table.

"I know I can, but I want to listen to you."

Morgan clasped her hands together, rubbing her thumbs vigorously over her skin, but she smiled at that. She was important; she knew that.

"Okay." She breathed in and exhaled slowly, trying to remain relaxed, but the tension was creeping back in again. "So, Mason, he's my brother. I was six when he was born. My mum and dad had tried for years to have another child and it hadn't happened, but just when they'd given up, he came along. He was like my little doll. I helped Mum get him dressed, bathe him, feed him, it was great." She looked away sadly.

"You don't have—"

"I do, I want to. It's just hard." Morgan stood up quickly. "Drink?"

Alex shook her head. "No, I'm fine. But you help yourself."

There was a thought process going on in Morgan's brain again as Alex observed her. Ultimately, logic won out and she sat back down again.

"I don't need a drink, I just…I guess finding where to start is the difficulty. Things didn't change overnight, it was gradual. But when Mason was six, he started to play football for a local team. He wasn't going to be the next Maradona, but he enjoyed it, so Mum and Dad took him, dropped him off and then took me to whatever interest I was involved in at eleven years of age. They'd do the weekly shopping while we were busy and then pick me up, and then Mason. His coach never minded if we were delayed. He'd always wait with him."

Something sinister made its way over Alex as she considered where she thought this story was heading.

"Mason started acting up. He went from being this funny, happy little kid, to a defiant ball of trouble. Mum and Dad didn't know what was up with him, but it meant their time was taken up with dealing with him. I realise now that this was the period where I began to feel rejected, not part of things anymore. Abandoned to my own devices, I guess. It was always Mum and Dad dealing with Mason. By the time I was fifteen I was pretty self-sufficient in many ways, but I needed validation, and the only place I got it was at school. I was a swot, I played up to teachers so that I became the teacher's darling, because it was the only attention I got from adults." She looked away, embarrassed. "As I got older and things with Mason came to a head when he turned ten, my need for validation changed into guilt and shame."

"Why?" Alex couldn't stop herself from asking.

"Because Mason was—" She felt the tears begin to roll down her cheeks. "His coach, the man my parents thought was looking out for him, the man they trusted, had been…he'd been—"

"I understand."

"For four years, Alex. Four years and none of us knew. We all just blamed him for being such a little shit, and he was, he was awful, but now we knew why, and the guilt ate at us all. My parents became over-protective. I went from being virtually ignored to being suffocated, and it took having to leave and go to university and then med school for me to find the therapy I needed to work through all of that."

"That must have been a very difficult period."

Morgan nodded. "The thing is, as you know, therapy doesn't cure things, it just makes us more aware so we can deal with it differently. I still find myself needing validation at times, and I can struggle with feelings of rejection, of being left out, and I'm working on it, but sometimes it's going to be triggered."

"Like today?"

"Yes, like today," she agreed. "I knew it was ridiculous, but I couldn't shake it."

"Come here."

Without another thought, Morgan stood up and crossed the rug to sit beside her, letting her hand be taken and soothed.

"The reason I am keeping you at arm's-length in front of the press is not because I am rejecting you, far from it. As I said earlier, this attraction is real for me also, but you were right. This is a situation out of the norm, and neither of us would usually meet someone under such circumstances." Edging closer, Alex reached for Morgan's cheek, her fingertips lightly brushing. "I live my life in the public glare, but there are some things I want just for me. Things I'd prefer to keep private."

"Like me."

"Like us," she reiterated. "Whatever 'us' is, whatever 'us' becomes. I don't want to see you picked apart in the press because of me. Because if at the end of this you decide to walk away, I want you to be able to go back to your life without the damage being with me might cause you."

Morgan considered that. "And if I decide not to walk away?"

Alex smiled. "Let's get this tour done and then see where we're at." She patted Morgan's knee. "I'm not rejecting you. Behind closed doors I don't want you at arm's-length."

"Okay."

"So, are you alright now? Do you need anything, to talk more or—"

"I don't want to travel in a car being hidden. I know what I signed up for."

"Alright. Maybe we can compromise on that."

For a moment, silence descended between them in a comfortable, easy way that allowed them to finally relax and unwind from the journey.

"You said downstairs you were going to show me where my place is…" Morgan smirked.

"I did, yes." Alex sat back again, opening her arms wider. "How about right where you are now?"

"Perfect."

Morgan snuggled in, and for a moment, they sat together in silence before Alex spoke again. "You know, you're right about therapy. It doesn't cure anything."

Now, it was Morgan's turn to stay quiet and just listen.

"I live with survivor's guilt," Alex admitted. "People think that I was the lucky one. That's how they always describe me in the papers. It's the part I hate most, even more than the images of the coach. They think that because I wasn't physically injured that somehow, I escaped unhurt, but they forget that I might have been strapped in, but I was awake. I felt the jolt when the car we hit put the coach into a skid. I was awake when the coach began to tilt and turn onto its side, and everything moved into slow motion. I was awake to watch as my friends were tossed around like a tumble dryer. I watched as Sarah hit her head off the cabinet. I saw Mikey's arm virtually ripped from him." Her voice choked and Morgan squeezed tighter, fighting the urge not to cry herself. "I'll never not hear the sound of the coach as it screeched along the road on its side, glass shattering, the screams, and then the silence. Just for a second, as though everything had come to a halt along with the bus."

"Alex…" Morgan whispered with empathy.

"When I'm triggered, all I see is Nicky's lifeless eyes staring at me, and I can't move, I can't get to her, help her. I hear Lucy screaming, the sirens, it all floods back." She kissed Morgan's head. "I used to see that every time I closed my eyes, every time I tried to sleep, that's what therapy helped with. It gave me back my life, enough to enjoy it again. So that it only affects me when I'm triggered."

"I understand how images in a newspaper or on TV might impact that significantly with panic attacks."

Alex nodded. "Yes, some times are better than others. Most of the time I don't tell anyone, and I just get through it, but that last one scared me."

Euphoria

"Maybe we can help each other then."

"I'd like that."

Chapter Thirty-Nine

Carlisle

"So, let me get this straight," Morgan asked as Alex lazily drew musical notes with her finger across her new lover's bare stomach the morning after the latest show. "We're pretending we're not sleeping together, while pretending we are, but keeping both of those ideas off the radar?"

"That pretty much sums it up," Alex replied, stretching her neck side to side to ease out a kink, upon which Morgan reached for the spot and used practiced fingers to ease out the knot.

"Mm, that's good." Alex moaned, before checking the time. They still had an hour before Francine would be appearing and they'd have to jump apart.

"Because it's not part of my job description?" Morgan smiled to herself, enjoying the shared touch, and the playfulness of post-coital lounging.

"Because that's how it needs to be for now." Alex smiled at her. "Francine wouldn't like…I can lose focus when I'm interested in someone."

"Do you think you've lost focus now?" Morgan rolled over to face her, more intrigued than ever. "Because I don't want to be the cause—"

Alex considered it. "No, I think I've been very focused. And very relaxed." She laughed and placed a quick kiss on Morgan's lips. "I've never started something while actually on tour though, so this is all new to me in more ways than what we've already discussed. Usually, if I have a lover with me, it's because it's been someone I've already got a relationship of sorts with who has come on the tour with me."

"Francine doesn't like that?"

"Francine doesn't like a lot of the things I do. But in the past, they could be a distraction, and Francine has a lot to do already without the added hassle of trying to actually keep a real relationship out of the press."

"And this is a real relationship?" Morgan asked tentatively. "Is that how you see it, honestly? You can tell me otherwise if you don't."

Alex stopped drawing on her and sat up. "I want it to be. How are you feeling about it?"

"Honestly? A little bit terrified. It's all been so...quick. We're halfway through the tour and yet, I feel like I've been in this for much longer," Morgan admitted sheepishly. "Despite the stereotypical lesbian jokes, I've never gotten this seriously involved with anyone this quickly. But I'm intrigued to find out."

"That's how I feel." Alex wriggled closer. "Meeting you feels..." Her eyes searched the room for the word, before landing back on Morgan's face. "...universal, like it was meant to be, that I was being shown something and everything else has kind of fallen into place to allow us this time to explore and experience a possibility."

"I'm on board for that." Morgan craned her neck to reach Alex's mouth and kiss her gently. "But won't Francine be annoyed if she finds out?"

"Probably, but I'm entitled to a private life, even from her."

"And if necessary, you want the press to think you might have a lover?"

Alex sighed and rolled onto her back.

"What I want is to be anonymous and live my life in solitude, but this life is a transaction. I give them enough, and they leave me alone. So, yes, I'll let them think I have a lover if I have to."

"Do I get a say in the matter?"

Twisting her neck to face Morgan, Alex frowned. "Of course. You can be with me in private like we're doing, or you can stop. I won't force you to stay in my bed."

"Yes, I'm aware of my choices, but ultimately, I signed up to pretend I might be a lover, now I actually am. Doesn't that change the dynamics a bit?"

"Right now, none of that matters. It's just you and me, here, in this bed...unless you'd rather be in your own room."

"You're right," Morgan answered, pulling Alex down on top of her. "I'm happy to sleep with you, for now."

"For now." Alex smirked. "Because you have so many women out there who can turn you on like I can."

Morgan laughed at the confidence, because the statement was true, not arrogant.

"I might have a couple—"

"Liar." Alex grinned and stroked the back of her fingers down Morgan's cheek. "Anyway, are you allowed to sleep with your patients? Isn't there some kind of oath about that?"

"Yes, but you're not my patient." She let herself be kissed. "Francine insisted I be listed as assistant on anything official."

"Oh, well that is good," Alex said, continuing to pepper her lips with small pecks and nips.

"Though I suppose technically I was your doctor for all of five minutes, but then I passed you off to Urquhart, and now I'm just assisting you." She smiled into the next kiss. "It's turned out pretty well."

Alex brushed her lips against Morgan's hair. "I don't want to be alone anymore. I'm ready to let someone in—but I should warn you, relationships don't last for me, I know that—"

Morgan took her face in her hands. "I'm not going anywhere."

Alex pulled herself upright, still straddled across Morgan's hips. "You might, when all of this is no longer so new and appealing, when the age gap starts to show, and you feel trapped by the lunacy of it all. Even the money won't keep you here, not if you have any sense."

Morgan stared hard at her, pushing herself upright too. "I don't even notice an age difference. I think we're quite alike actually, regardless of the fact you're older than me. I think my life experience with what I deal with at work means I'm much more of a grown-up than people assume."

"I guess that's a fair conclusion."

"And I'm not doing this because you have money to pay for fancy hotels, you know that, right? I could pay for this myself, you know."

Alex pressed her lips together and tried not to laugh at that idea. "No." Her head shook slowly. "You couldn't."

"Of course I could."

Alex reached for a grape from the bowl by the side of her bed, and bit into it. "How much do you think one night here costs?"

Morgan shrugged. "I would guess, four, five hundred pounds."

"And could you afford that?" She plucked another juicy grape and fed it to Morgan.

"I mean, okay, I'd have to save for a couple of months, but I could probably manage it."

Alex kissed her. "You're very cute."

"That's true," Morgan agreed.

"It's eight hundred," Alex whispered against her ear.

"Holy hell. Per night?" Morgan gasped. Alex laughed at her and nodded. "Fine, I'm fucking you for the money too." She laughed as she closed the space between them and kissed her. "Oh, one question."

"Go on."

"So, that euphoria thing never goes away. It's always going to occur after a performance?"

Nodding slowly, Alex continued to chuckle. "I'm afraid it does. Can you handle me?"

"I think so." Morgan blushed. "Tell me more about it."

Alex thought for a moment. She'd never had this conversation with anyone. Most, if not all, of her after-show fun had been with paid professionals. Once with Laurel, but she'd never talked about it or done it again because they'd broken up soon after.

"Being on stage and playing to an audience, it's powerful."

"In what way? How does it feel?"

Alex fell into the space beside Morgan, all thoughts of sex gone for the moment even if Morgan's curiosity was a turn-on.

"I remember the first time I really felt it. This energy I'd never experienced before. I was on stage with Solar Flare, we'd had a couple of top ten hits, and we were starting to get some traction with the media, TV shows were booking us every week to play, and we played out some mid-sized venues, that was when I first began to experience it."

"I need to investigate this band."

"Yes, you do." Alex's smile faded a little, her eyes misting over. "They were good times."

"We don't have to talk about it if you don't want to."

"I have spent a fortune talking about it with therapists, and life coaches and psychologists. I'm okay, but I don't need to go deep into it now."

"Alright, tell me about the best time."

"Wembley Stadium, that last night, before—" Alex closed her eyes and breathed deeply. She might be okay, but that didn't mean it didn't still affect her. Her fingers felt the warmth of a squeeze and she glanced down at Morgan's hand wrapped around her own. It was comforting, and welcome without being intrusive and suffocating. "That night it was something else. Us musicians rose up out of the stage hidden in the dry ice, and when we started to play, that crowd went wild, but when Lucy walked on, God, it was electric. This energy just consumed me. It builds and builds and takes over my body, like it's not even me playing."

"That must be magical."

Alex nodded. "I thought, after the accident and the band split up, I thought that was it, that I'd never experience it again. And then, months later, I was on a stage once more, just a small one, with no more than 300 people in the audience to watch a classical rendition of *A Christmas Carol*. I felt it," she said, laughing at the memory, "but there was a major difference this time. With the band, the euphoria used to make me relaxed and sleepy. I'd use up all of my energy on stage, it was high-energy. That was what saved me that night. I'd always strap in and sleep while everyone else would be so wired they'd party."

Euphoria

"It must have been—"

Alex pressed her finger to Morgan's lips.

Morgan understood, lifted Alex's hand, and kissed the palm. "Go on."

"I don't know if it's because classical is my calling, and the band was just a rebellious phase to annoy my mother, but when I come off of a stage now, my body is alive. Wired. It feels so sedate on stage that the adrenaline has nowhere to go. Now I guess, I understand how they all felt back then."

"And you can't control it?"

"I can control it or deal with it myself." She chuckled. "Unless I have no reason to and can unleash it on a willing partner. Which is much more fun."

Morgan fell onto her back, smiling at the touch of fingertips around the swell of her breast. "Consider me a willing participant."

"Yes, you are." This time it was Alex who leaned on her elbow. "I'll never hurt you. Or do anything you don't want to do. You know that, right? You just have to say—"

"Caesura," Morgan finished for her. "What does that even mean?"

Alex chuckled. "It's a musical term. It denotes a pause in a verse, where one might end a verse, and another begins."

"Okay, that makes sense. I like accelerando, and allegro…" Her smile turned into an embarrassed giggle, "But mostly, I just want the crescendo."

"To gradually increase," Alex splayed her fingers around Morgan's breast and squeezed rhythmically. and then her fingertips raced down the length of her torso. "Accelerando, to increase speed." When they reached the apex of her thighs, Alex lifted herself, making room to slide easily into the space between, enjoying the arching of Morgan's back when fingertips glided across her already throbbing clit. "Allegro, to play upbeat, briskly until…the highest point and—"

"Crescendo." Morgan sighed. "I want front-row seats every night." Morgan gasped, arms stretched up above her head, as she writhed to the touch. "I like to watch the euphoria take hold. I feel it a little bit too, different to you, but I like to watch you."

"I think that can be arranged."

Chapter Forty

Edinburgh

"I don't understand why we didn't leave earlier," Francine complained as the car cruised up the A47. Less than an hour into the journey, she already had a bottle of cava open and poured.

"Because even though I did refute the need for days off, it's still nice to get a lay-in now and then," Alex responded. "And anyway, I'm happy to drive and arrive a little later. With Mike at the wheel, it's comfortable and we have refreshments." She held up a glass of sparkling water, and caught Morgan looking away, lips pressed firmly together to stop herself from commenting. "Sit back and enjoy it."

"I guess so." Francine sighed, sipping from the flute.

"You'll be asleep in minute anyway," Alex added, and grinned when Morgan couldn't hide the smile any longer. "Have you been to Scotland, Morgan?"

"I went to Glasgow once." She pulled a face that intrigued Alex.

"There's a story there, isn't there?" Alex laughed.

"Hey, just remember I asked if there were any ghosts in the closet." Francine smiled casually at her.

"It wasn't that bad." Morgan reached for the cava and poured a small glass before topping it up with orange juice. "It was a date, of sorts. We met on an app, as you do." She shrugged. "She seemed nice enough, and I thought what the hell. I was young, stupid and adventurous, and looking for validation, so I got a train up—"

"Was she who she said she was?" Francine butted in.

Morgan nodded. "Yes, she was the person in the photos, she just happened to not mention that she had a boyfriend."

"That would be something you think most people would—" Alex was saying.

"Did you get back on the train and come home?" Francine interrupted before Alex could finish.

Blushing at the memory, Morgan shook her head. "No, she kind of didn't mention him at all at that point. I just assumed he was a roommate, or something because he didn't bother us. I slept with her in her bed, he had a room down the hall. It was only when I was leaving and wondering how I could make this work, that she said something about visiting me, and would it be okay if Rory came too."

Francine's eyes almost bugged out of her head. "What?"

"I know, I didn't understand at all. I just assumed he wanted to travel a bit, but I don't know. Something nudged at me to ask more about him, and she admitted he was her boyfriend. They were looking into open relationships, but Rory wasn't sure if he could deal with it, so I was kind of a test run, and he'd liked me and seen how happy I'd made her, so..."

"So, he was alright with it carrying on?" Alex chuckled.

"Yes, I guess he was. But it wasn't for me." Morgan giggled. "I'm not a sharing kind of person."

"No, me either. I'm an all-in kind of person," Alex said, holding her gaze until the sound of Francine snoring quietly broke the spell. "See, I told you she'd be asleep."

"Is she out for the count?"

Alex nodded. "Yes, that's it now. Once she sleeps, she sleeps."

"I can do that at work on night shifts, grab ten minutes here and there between patients, but I'm out of that sleep pattern now."

"I think she's on the go all day. Her brain must be on overload, so once the opportunity to sleep arrives, she switches off."

"I still can't believe we're halfway through already?"

Alex sighed. Winchester, Salisbury, Exeter, onto Gloucester, then Chester, and Carlisle. It had all been a success so far, and a blur. "Yes. It has flown by, and yet, it feels like we've been doing this for much longer."

"I was thinking that. It's a good thing, right?"

"I think so," Alex agreed. Then she grinned. "Exeter will never be the same again."

"Yes," Morgan said, remembering back. "Have you always been…kinky?"

"Kinky?" Alex chuckled. "Is that what I am?"

"Well, you've opened my eyes to a lot of things."

Alex narrowed her eyes at her. "I think there have been a few things you've certainly taken me by surprise with." She laughed. "Don't you dare blush, the things you do to me," she said wistfully.

"I'll have to remember that." Morgan chuckled, still blushing.

Alex turned more serious again. "What have you enjoyed most?"

Morgan fidgeted, the sense of arousal flooding her sex instantly. "God, this for a start, just the way you speak to me. So, confident and firm. I like when you demand more from me. When you put me on my knees or tie my hands."

"And that's kinky?"

"I think so." Morgan nodded. "Don't you?"

Alex shrugged. "I guess when you put it like that. I've never really considered it. I suppose over the years I've been introduced to things that I liked, and I just added them to my repertoire."

"Maybe we can look into extending that then."

Alex snorted. "Well, why not?"

Chapter Forty-One

Francine was still asleep, and Alex was nodding off, but not quite asleep. Morgan was reading her book. They'd hit pockets of traffic, and the journey was taking much longer than it should have, especially after a diversion had them miles off track.

Morgan was feeling hungry. Her tummy rumbled, and she wondered if they might stop somewhere to get something to eat. Just as she was about to ask Mike about it, the car lurched to the left and the brakes forced her forward. The seatbelt pressed against her chest as it did its job and stopped her from flying across the seats and landing on top of Francine.

All she heard was Alex scream, "No!"

"What the hell?" Francine shouted, waking from her peaceful sleep in an instant.

In that one moment, all hell broke loose as Francine stressed and Alex stared wide-eyed into nowhere. Twisting in her seat, Morgan reached for Alex's hand, but there was no response. She was breathing rapidly, her chest heaving and mouth gulping for air.

"Alex, it's okay. Can you hear me?" Morgan kept calm, even though she was worried herself. The window between Mike and themselves opened.

"There's been an accident in front. Everything's come to a stand-still," he said, his voice a little shaky at the obvious near miss.

Morgan could hear Mike and Francine discussing the near miss and what to do next, but her concern was on Alex. Reaching for her bag, she opened it quickly, unbuckled her seatbelt and, spreading Alex's legs apart, got down onto her knees into the space right in front of Alex.

"Alex, look at me," she said firmly, trying to get any response from her.

"What's wrong with her? This isn't normal." Francine now turned her attention on them.

"She's disassociating," Morgan answered calmly. She began to untie Alex's shoes and pull them from her feet, her socks following.

"What are you doing?" Francine looked at her, horrified. "Help her."

"I am helping her. She needs to be grounded, to feel the real world around her. Talk to her and pass me a glass of ice."

Looking confused but doing as she was asked, Francine filled a glass and passed it across.

"Alex, Alex, come on pal, you gotta snap out of it. You're worrying me," Francine was saying as Morgan pressed Alex's feet to the ground and rubbed the tops of them vigorously.

"Alex, you're safe. I need you to focus on the sounds. Hear my voice, listen to Francine. You're not there, you're not on that coach."

"You think she's on the bus?" Francine stared at her.

"She's not here, so yes, it's possible she's been triggered into a flashback with that jolt," Morgan answered, remembering the story from Alex's own lips. She picked out a piece of ice and slowly rubbed it against Alex's lips, around her face. "You feel that? Just breathe, in and out."

It took a moment, and like a switch had flicked, Alex's eyes focused and she was back in the car. At least somewhat; she was still dazed and not with it, but she was going to be okay.

"Hey, it's okay. You're okay." Morgan kept repeating the mantra, until finally, Alex showed signs of coming back fully.

Her voice shaking, Alex asked, "What…happened?"

"An accident, the car in front hit the one in front of that, everything came to a quick stop and Mike pulled the car out of the lane to avoid it all. That's why we swerved," Francine explained, grateful for Mike's quick thinking, because nobody could imagine the impact being hit would have caused.

Morgan opened her bag again and pulled out her stethoscope and a paper bag. She handed it to Alex. "Breathe into this."

"A paper bag?" Francine exclaimed. "That's all you got?"

Ignoring her, Morgan put the stethoscope into her ears and opened the buttons that covered Alex's chest. The pianist hissed as the cold steel touched her skin.

A good sign, Morgan hoped.

"Just keep breathing, okay?"

Alex nodded, the paper bag rustling as it scrunched and uncrunched with every breath she took. Her eyes, trained intently on Morgan, looked scared, but she said a quiet, "I'm okay."

"I think I'm the one with the medical degree." Morgan smiled, taking her wrist and counting her pulse.

"You do as you're told," Francine piped up, a warning tone Alex had heard before.

"I need some…some fresh air."

Morgan reached across and pressed the button that would buzz the window open, putting her face as close to Alex's as she dared. "Just breathe, okay."

Alex nodded.

"I'll see what's happening," Francine said. "Mike? Can we move yet?"

"It might be a while," he replied back.

"I need to get out," Alex insisted. "This feels too… I need to get out."

Morgan glanced out of the back window. Other motorists were climbing out of their cars and talking to each other, arms folded against chests, phones to ears. "If you do, people are going to be interested. A car like this, with blacked-out windows means someone potentially interesting, and you are that person. They've got phones, and you know it means your picture will be all over the news later, and the fact it's a crash on the motorway, and you're here—" Morgan was explaining when Francine chipped in.

"It'll be the very thing we've been trying to avoid."

Morgan nodded. "Yes, and if you have a further panic attack out there…" She reached back over Alex and pressed the window button up when someone wandered past and glanced in.

"Okay…" Alex managed. She smiled when she felt Morgan's fingertip rub against the back of her hand.

"I'm here. Francine's here. Nothing is going to happen to you that we can't deal with. Mike will have us out of here the moment it's safe to do so."

The sound of sirens approaching meant Alex tensed up. She grabbed Morgan's hand and squeezed. "I'm okay. I'm okay." She repeated it like a tune as the noise got louder and louder before passing them on the hard shoulder. "I'm okay." Her eyes closed, focused on just breathing.

"That's it. It's all okay," Morgan said again before turning to Francine. "Do we have anything to eat?"

"Eat?"

"Yes, food, lunch. I don't know about you, but I'm starving, and a sugar hit might be quite good for all of us right now." Morgan smiled at the P.A. "You did organise snacks, right?"

"Of course, I organised snacks," Francine replied indignantly, as Morgan noticed the crease of a smile appear on Alex's face. She looked amused by her friend's reaction to the idea she was incompetent in the snacks department.

"Well, what have we got?" Morgan pushed, wanting to keep Alex's attention on anything but the predicament they were in. "We might as well have a picnic while we sit here."

Francine huffed, but leaned over and opened the small cupboard door, pulling out what looked like a cool bag. She unzipped the top until it opened fully and revealed paper-wrapped items that Morgan hoped would be a sandwich.

"I ordered six subs, various fillings." She lifted the first and turned it over in her hand to read the label. "Chutney, cheddar and green leaves." Placing that one back down, she reached for another. "Maple bacon, brie and cranberry." She was about to take the next one out, but Alex held out her hand.

"I'll have that one, if nobody else minds."

Morgan shrugged, and Francine handed it over, glancing at Morgan hopefully. If Alex was hungry and eating, that was a good sign, wasn't it? She watched as Alex gingerly unwrapped the sandwich and nibbled at the corner.

"What else have you got in your magic box?" Morgan grinned, trying to keep everyone as calm as possible.

"Roasted pork with apple glaze and herb—"

Morgan thrust her hand out. "I'll take that." She smiled when Francine dropped it into her hand. "Any water?"

"I'll have the cheese then," Francine bemoaned and turned back to where the mini fridge housed bottles. "Sparkling or still?" she asked, already reaching for a sparkling to hand to Alex.

"Either, I'm not fussy."

Francine rolled her eyes at that. "Still then," she said, passing the cold bottle. "Ice?"

"No, thank you."

"Mike, you hungry?" Francine tapped the window and craned her neck around, holding out a wrapped sub for their driver. "Might as well eat something."

Chapter Forty-Two

They'd sat on the motorway for over three hours before finally a path was cleared, and slowly cars edged past the remains of several vehicles and a van that had all collided. The ambulances had long gone, and it was now just an investigation and clean-up operation, but Alex kept her eyes closed until they were well past and heading in the right direction for their next hotel.

Just outside of St Andrews, a picturesque building with climbing ivy and a grand entrance came into view. It looked just like the photo Morgan had seen on her phone earlier when she'd scoped out the next hotel on Google.

"Yep, we'll wing it tomorrow," Francine said into the phone. "It's a good job you guys took off early, so you didn't get caught up in it." She nodded at whatever Jessie was saying. "Alright, that sounds like a plan. I'll see you when we arrive, but everyone else can head off and enjoy the evening."

Morgan glanced across at Alex, who had been sleeping peacefully for the last thirty minutes or so. "Has the hold-up really messed everything up?"

"A little. I'll just have to shift everything around tomorrow," Francine said, continuing to stare at Morgan. "You know, I'm glad you were here earlier. If that had happened and it had been just me—" She shook her head. "I can manage a lot of things, but—anyway, thank you."

"You're welcome," Morgan answered, softening towards her. "It's really just about holding yourself calm. Talking her out of it."

"Yeah, all sounds so simple till you're faced with it. That day when I brought her to the hospital, I really thought she—it scared the shit out of me."

"Panic attacks often look and feel much scarier than they are."

Francine's attention turned to the sleeping form. "I just wish I could take it all away for her. How something from so long ago can still haunt her, it's just unfair."

Morgan nodded. "Yes, it really is."

They were greeted at the hotel by the manager, a large, exuberant man in his forties, wearing a kilt and with a beard that wouldn't have looked out of place in the trendy bars of London.

"Conner MacTavish," he said with a bold handshake that moved quickly between the three outstretched hands. "I'm the duty manager, and I'm looking forward to making your stay with us as comfortable and relaxed as possible."

"Thanks," Francine answered for them all. Alex was still a little groggy. "If you could get us up to our rooms, we'd be grateful. It's been a very exhausting day."

"Aye, I heard aboot the accident, very unfortunate turn of events. If you want to follow me." He grinned before turning on his heel and striding off to the left of the hotel entrance, along the front of the building.

"You go up. I'll organise luggage with Mike," Francine said to Morgan. "Get her to sleep it off, yeah. I need her fully focused by morning." She jutted her chin towards Alex.

"Sure, she'll be fine," Morgan assured, sliding her arm around Alex's waist. "You okay? You look a little sleepy still."

Alex eyed her. "I do feel tired. Did you roofie me?"

Morgan laughed. "I did not. I did however give you a light sedative to help you relax."

"Hm, I feel very relaxed."

"That's good." Morgan lowered her voice. "You can get into bed and relax further."

"I'm not sure…I'm up for that tonight."

"I meant sleep, sweetheart."

They tried to take notice of Conner as he explained the history of the building and how it had stood there for over 200 years, but he confused her when instead of walking inside, he climbed into a buggy out front.

"Hop in, it's a wee bit quicker than walking."

"Are we not staying in there?" Morgan pointed towards the building that looked exactly like a hotel in her mind.

"Och no, we've got something much more splendid for a star like Ms Montgomery." He turned a key, and the buggy kick-started into life and lurched forward. The sudden movement caught Alex by surprise, and she yelped, as her grasp on Morgan's arm tightened.

"It's okay, I've got you," Morgan said quietly as the little engine drove them down a pathway and around the side of the building. Green pasture surrounded by forestry came into view and both women were transfixed by the beauty of it all. Dusk wouldn't be too far away, and there was already a light mist hovering just above the ground. "It's beautiful."

"Yes, it is," Alex answered proudly.

They continued on and rode down a small incline where a lake, or giant pond, was glasslike at the bottom, a tiny island in the middle where birds were settled for the day, beaks tucked under wings. Just off to the side were three log cabin-style cottages.

"You cannae get any more private than these," Conner said as he pulled up outside and hopped out of the buggy, holding his hand out for Morgan, and then Alex to take. "I'll have your bags brought doon and send some supper. I'm sure you could all do with something hot and filling in ya stomachs, aye?"

"That would be lovely," Alex answered, stepping up the two stairs behind him. They waited as he unlocked the door and swung it open for them. Just as every other room they'd stayed in, this was opulent. Its rustic appeal though was something else. A huge log fire, the piano of course, a small kitchen area. "This is perfect."

He handed the key to Morgan, an old-fashioned proper key, not an electronic key card. "I'll leave ya to it. Just call up if you need anything. I'll send someone doon on the buggy."

"Take me to bed," Alex said the moment he was out of earshot.

"What about supper?" Morgan asked, dropping her bag onto the floor.

Alex yawned. "I need to sleep, I feel drained." She stepped up and stood toe to toe with Morgan. "And I need you beside me."

"What about Francine?"

"I'll call her, tell her to leave our bags outside and I'll speak to her in the morning."

"And she won't wonder what I'm doing that means I can't open the door and take the bags in?"

Alex's shoulders sagged. "You're right."

Without thinking, Morgan kissed her. A brief brush of lips. "I'll deal with Francine. You have a shower and get ready for bed, and then I'll come and join you."

"Do you promise?"

Morgan laughed. "I want to be with you too."

"Alright." Alex leaned in, and this time when they kissed, she made it clear how she felt, her tongue rolling and probing lazily until she couldn't breathe again. "I'll see you in bed then."

Morgan watched as she walked away towards the bedroom on the left. And again, a minute later when she came back out and went to the other room, where she must have decided it was the better option, because she didn't come back out again, and it wasn't that much longer before Morgan could hear the shower running.

A sharp knock on the door brought her attention back to the room and the plan she was supposed to be taking charge of. She opened the door, and a young man in a kilt appeared carrying two cases.

"I'll leave ya bags where?" he asked, and Morgan pointed to the room on the left.

"Thank you," she said after the second trip. She was about to fish out some money for a tip when Francine appeared in the doorway, already holding the £20 note out for him.

"Cheers," he said gleefully before heading off up the hill again in his little buggy.

"All settled?" Francine asked, peering around the room. "I'm next door if you need anything. Mike's on the end."

Morgan smiled. "Yes, all fine. She's taking a shower, and then she's planning to go to bed. I think the sedative will see her through the night."

"Good, and you? What do you plan to do?"

The question threw her for a second. "Oh, I think I'll probably read. Conner said he was sending supper down, so I'll eat and read and then probably get an early night, too. It's been exhausting."

"Yeah, it sure has." Francine took one last look around the room. "Okay, well, I'll get out of ya hair then. I've got plenty to keep me busy."

"Okay, good night."

With the door locked, and everything secure, Morgan poked her head around the bedroom door, expecting to find Alex already asleep, but that wasn't the case. She was in bed as expected, under the covers even, but sitting up against the pillows tapping into her phone.

"You're supposed to be resting," Morgan said, smiling at her as she opened the door and entered the room properly.

"I am. I'm just replying to a friend. She messaged the other day, and I hadn't had a chance till now."

"Oh, a friend?" Morgan teased. "Just a friend?"

"Yes, just a friend." Alex glanced up at her.

Coming over to the bed, Morgan perched on the edge. "So, do they have a name?"

Alex put the phone down and paused for a moment. "I'm sure she does."

"That sounds very cryptic and not at all transparent. I've told you about Zoe when she's texted me about Knight," Morgan said, feeling a little vulnerable.

Frowning, Alex considered that. "Yes, I guess it does sound odd. The thing is…" She grimaced. "I don't actually know her name. I don't know for sure she's a she either, but I think she is, and if that's the case, she's gay too."

"That makes no sense."

"I know." Alex smiled. Picking up the phone, she unlocked it and held it out for Morgan to read if she wanted to.

She didn't.

"I trust you, and I respect your privacy."

Alex locked the phone again and put it down on the bedside shelf. "Thank you."

Morgan waited a beat and when nothing further came, she asked, "So, are you going to explain?"

Alex chuckled. "It's silly really, but it was a wrong number weeks ago. Somehow, we just kept talking. I guess, I like it that I can be me. Anonymous. We haven't asked each other our names, and it's never come up. Randomly, we will message each other and see how we're doing."

"And that doesn't seem odd to you?"

"No, why would it? It was just a random wrong number."

"Single?" Morgan probed as she stood up and began to undress.

Alex watched the little show she was putting on. "Yes, although that was how we started talking. Her date had given her a wrong number, my number. She was texting to ask why she hadn't heard from them."

Unhooking her bra, Morgan turned to face her. "So, a gay single woman just happened to message your number, out of all the millions of numbers out there, another gay, single, famous woman whose number I assume isn't public?"

"Of course it isn't public, can you imagine?" Alex laughed before becoming more serious. "Leave those on," she demanded when Morgan went to remove her knickers.

"Why?"

"I like it."

"You're going to sleep, while I take a shower."

"But I'm not sleepy now." Alex pouted at Morgan as she neared the bed and reached out for her, fingertips gliding up the side of Morgan's thigh.

"I still need to shower." Morgan grinned, bending down to kiss her. "Unless that's another kink of yours."

"No, I think I can wait...but maybe put a clean pair back on?"

"You are incorrigible."

"And you are sexy and beautiful. Is it my fault if I can't keep my hands off of you?" Alex grinned at the retreating back. She picked up her phone again.

Alex: So, I was thinking. Should we not know each other's names by now?

Chapter Forty-Three

St Salvator's Chapel was exquisite. The college tower rose up above the main entrance as they walked inside. Francine led the way alongside two members of the chaplaincy and Jessie, the big bear guy Morgan had met previously. Sasha was talking with a woman from the university, and Morgan wandered along by herself at the back.

When they entered the huge hall, Morgan almost gasped at the beauty of it. It was unlike any of the other buildings they'd been in. Impressive was too small a word to describe it, but it felt bigger than it was. And cosy, it felt warm and tranquil.

She moved around the space unhindered as everyone else was too busy to stop and chat with her, which she was grateful for because she really had nothing interesting to say. She recognised faces now though, and nodded a hello as she carried on walking. Small talk didn't seem to go down too well with men who were working and trying to get things done on a schedule. Francine had already made a comment about it, so Morgan wasn't going to push her luck today.

The stage was in place already, the sound system going through soundchecks. It was noisy and echoey, as the 'one, two, one, two' testing repeated through various areas of the stage where mics were set up to aid the sound just enough without it being too much.

Morgan looked up at the piano and smiled to herself, imagining Alex sitting up there. As she turned to move, she noticed her. A blonde woman with short hair, quite pretty, lurking. That was the word Morgan thought of: lurking, like she wasn't supposed to be there, on the other side of the stage.

Edging closer, the woman hadn't noticed Morgan. For some reason, she gave Morgan creepy vibes, like she needed to be quiet and creep up on her. She wasn't doing anything, just standing at the back of the stage, watching everything.

Of course, she could work on the crew; maybe she was someone local drafted into help with the set-up, but she wasn't dressed like a roadie. They all wore a uniform of ripped loose-fitting jeans and t-shirts with pictures of rock bands on the front, both of which looked older than she was. This woman was wearing jeans, but expensive ones, and everything looked smart and new. Maybe she worked for the church.

That was an option, Morgan supposed, so why didn't Morgan feel at ease about her? She was too old to be a student, surely. Maybe a nosey local wanting to catch a glimpse of *Sasha*.

"Hello," Morgan said when she was just a few feet away.

The woman jumped back. "Oh, uh, hello."

She was English, which confused Morgan even more and seemed so out of place here.

"Do you work here?" Morgan asked, eyes scanning quickly for a tag around her neck like everyone else had to wear.

There wasn't one.

"Oh, no. I'm just…" She backed away. "I'm just visiting and thought I'd take a look around…" Her eyes furtively searched around her as though she were looking for an exit. "I didn't know what was going on."

That was a lie.

The building was closed off to visitors for three days. Yesterday to set up, today for the concert, and tomorrow in order to remove it all. Which meant the woman had sneaked in somehow.

Morgan was unsure what to do. There wasn't a security team as such yet. They didn't arrive until later when the doors opened and were provided by the venue. Right now, it was just Francine and the crew. Mike acted as a bodyguard of sorts when they were around the car, but he was still outside, and taking a break. Francine was busy.

"I don't think you're supposed to be in here," Morgan said firmly enough. Challenge the situation, that's what she would do at work. If she found someone wandering around A&E, she would stop them and press for answers.

The woman looked around again, still searching for an escape route, or checking nobody else had seen her?

It all felt off.

"I'm going anyway." She smiled, calmly turning away.

Morgan didn't move at first. Waiting to see if the woman changed her mind. When she was several feet ahead, Morgan followed.

The woman was almost at the door when Morgan spotted Jessie up ahead. She waved at him until she got his attention, and then pointed towards the woman.

His eyes narrowed as he shifted his gaze, understanding what she was telling him. He held a thumbs up and followed after her. And now, it was his problem. Morgan chuckled and headed back.

Alex took the stage and went through the quick sound check with the piano, instructing stagehands and technicians, while Morgan sat quietly next to Francine in a pew three rows back, just watching and enjoying the opportunity to study Alex this way.

"How she doing?" Francine asked when Alex stopped playing to speak to someone on the controls.

"I think she's fine, considering. Yesterday's panic attack was—" Morgan pulled a face.

Francine nodded. "Scary as fuck? Yeah, I've never seen her like that before."

"Hm."

Francine shook her head. "She rarely talks to me, just tells me occasionally when she's had one." She turned to face Morgan. "I was hoping it was all behind her. She hadn't had one for a while, or at least, she hadn't told me about it. It was my fault before. I set it off inadvertently, I didn't think and said something about a coach and—"

Morgan nodded. "I don't think we ever stop having the trauma, but I'm thinking maybe a new therapist could help some more?"

Rolling her eyes, Francine grimaced. "She won't do more therapy. I've tried with that; she just resolutely refuses."

Morgan nodded again. "I can understand that. It's difficult to keep opening up over and over." She knew from her own experiences, there came a time when you needed a break from it.

"Maybe she'd listen to you." Francine's raised brow insinuated something more than her words said.

"What makes you think that?"

Francine smirked. "She likes you."

"She likes you too," Morgan countered, feeling a little under pressure with the remark.

"Yeah, well, I'm not her type." Francine winked.

"And because I am, she will listen to me?" She glanced up at Alex, lost in the music. "I doubt it. She's pretty stubborn when she wants to be."

"Don't I know it." Francine grinned as the music changed pace, and Alex launched into something uplifting. "Just try, okay?"

"If a situation arises to bring it up, I'll do my best, but I'm here to make sure she doesn't physically hurt herself. And I'm hoping that I'll be getting paid to do absolutely nothing more moving forward."

"Yes, let's hope so," Francine replied. "Oh, I meant to give you these." She delved into her bag and pulled out an envelope. "Alex said you wanted them."

When Morgan took the envelope, Francine got up and walked away. Sliding her finger under the flap, Morgan eased the paper free and looked inside.

Two tickets for Taylor Swift.

"How's your friend?" Morgan asked.

Alex had her back against the pillows again as she rested before Nancy and Gert would arrive and transform them both. Morgan's head lay in her lap, Alex's fingers threading through dark locks. Morgan sighed contentedly at the ease of which they enjoyed each other's company like this.

"Which one?" Alex asked.

"The superstar American singer on tour," Morgan said. "Do you really know her?"

Alex smiled to herself. "I've met her. I wouldn't say that I know her, but my people know her people and the tickets were easy enough."

Morgan kissed the bare thigh closest to her lips. "Thank you." She lay there silently for a moment before adding, "And how's your other friend, the anonymous one?"

Alex chuckled. "I see it's hit a nerve."

"No, just making conversation," Morgan responded, lifting her head from where it rested to lay against Alex's chest.

"Well, I haven't heard from her, so I don't know." Alex ran a hand through Morgan's curls again. "How's your friend?"

"Zoe?"

"Yes, the cat sitter."

"She's okay. Still pestering for information about us." Morgan chuckled before adding, "I'm not jealous."

"About Zoe?"

"No, your friend. I'm not jealous, I'm curious, and I don't know but my gut is gurgling about it. Something doesn't feel right about not knowing who someone is, and I know that's ridiculous. I don't know her or what you've discussed, I just—"

"Feel off about it?"

"Yeah. Just be careful, there are a lot of weird people out there."

Alex wiggled down the bed and wrapped her arms around Morgan's shoulders. "Thank you for looking out for me."

Looking up at her, Morgan said, "I care about you."

"I care about you, too."

Chapter Forty-Four

"I am not cancelling," Alex said vehemently. The small dressing room felt very tense with all of the people currently standing in it, all looking very serious and concerned. Francine looked ready to kill. Morgan looked worried.

"It might be the sensible thing to do," Detective Siba said solemnly. He had actually been in the audience when he'd got the call about the mysterious threat.

"Is it? Or are we all just getting overexcited about a very bad joke?"

"But still," Siba tried again. "It's a decision that needs serious—"

"I'm not sure you have a choice," Francine said firmly. "We have to take this seriously."

"I'm not ignoring it, but I refuse to—"

"Sasha, it's a credible threat," said the officer in uniform who stood closest to her, a tall, thin man with a face that belied his years. He held the note up to make the point. "Everything goes boom!"

Morgan shuddered at the words on the note that had been found by one of the crew doing last-minute checks. It had been stuck to the side of a speaker.

Alex sighed. "There are 450 people out there who have paid ridiculous sums of money to hear me play. An entire crew who has worked tirelessly to make sure that happens, and who need to be paid."

"Do you think this has anything to do with that woman this morning?" Morgan mused.

All eyes turned towards her. "What woman?" Alex questioned.

"There was a woman. I didn't think to mention it because she seemed so ordinary, and she left the moment I challenged her. She said she was a tourist and just looking at the chapel, but I knew the building was closed to that. I had Jessie make sure she left, and she did."

"What did she look like?" Siba asked, the other officer standing to attention, pen at the ready.

"Attractive, short blonde hair, maybe 5'5" in height, slim, well dressed." Morgan rattled off a basic description of the woman. "I told Jessie and I assume he dealt with her."

The thin policeman asked Alex, "Does she sound familiar?"

Alex laughed. "Yes, I've probably met a hundred women who could fit that description."

"I'll need to speak to Jessie," Siba said, scribbling details down.

"This is crazy, a threat to kill you isn't to be laughed at," Francine said angrily. "We need to can—"

"I'm going on that stage," Alex said just as firmly, stepping towards Francine. "You can put extra security around, but I'm going to perform. And anyway, it wasn't a threat to kill me—"

"Will you speak to her?" Francine said to Morgan before pushing past her and leaving the room.

Morgan turned to Alex. "Is there anything anyone can say that will change your mind?"

Alex shook her head, determination written all over her face. "No, I won't be bullied by anyone."

"Right, then I suggest we prepare for a show," Morgan announced. "What do we need to do? It's too late in the day to hire extra security."

Mike stepped forward. "I can round up some of the crew. We can do walk arounds, guard doors, etcetera."

"Well, I can't say that I'm disappointed." Siba smiled. "I have a ticket, and my wife is a huge fan. But we'll make sure to have officers on the door, and we'll do another sweep of the grounds. Moving forward, I would suggest maybe hiring some more security."

"Yes, thank you, we'll look into that," Alex answered. "You can all go. I'd like a moment to calm myself."

One by one, everyone filed out, all except for Morgan. She closed the door behind them all and locked it. Turning back around slowly, she watched as Alex pulled a chair over and sat down.

"So, now everyone else has gone—" Morgan spoke quietly.

Alex stared up at her. "I'm concerned. I'm not going to deny it, but I can't live my life being afraid. Most likely it is a practical joke."

"True," Morgan said. "So, we've thirty minutes to get you focused and ready."

"Thank you, for supporting me."

Morgan softened her gaze, let her own fear dissipate a little. "What else am I going to do?"

Alex reached for her hand. "It's going to be fine."

When Sasha took the stage, she was almost blinded by the super trouper trained on her. The audience rose to their feet to clap, unaware of the threat she faced. Smiling, she gave a small wave as usual and addressed the audience.

"Hello, thank you for the welcome. As you probably all know already, I'm not one for talking too much, not when the music can say far more than I ever could. So, tonight, I'm going to sit right here and let the music take you on a journey, one I hope you will enjoy."

Another round of applause rang out.

Alex took her seat and began to play. With each note she hit, she moved further away from the goings on around her. Only one thought other than music was allowed to intrude into the peaceful, calm space she felt safe within: an image of Morgan, standing off to the side of the stage. Out of sight to everybody else, but here.

A focus point.

Her supporter.

Francine had queried it, her eyes narrowing at the idea of why Alex needed Morgan nearby, but Morgan had ended any suspicions instantly when she'd answered,

"If anything were to happen, I want to be able to get to her instantly, not dealing with climbing up onto a stage in this dress."

Morgan's warm eyes settled on her, her mouth curved into a supportive smile as she leaned against the wall and watched. In that moment, Alex was playing only for her.

By the end of the third movement, Alex closed her eyes and finally felt safe enough to allow the music to take her away from it all. She felt herself floating above the audience, looking down on herself as her fingers blurred and moved up and down the scales, hitting note after note perfectly until finally, she played the last one and her soul was thrust back into her body with the force of the eruption of sound.

Loud clapping and whoops from the audience erupted as they rose to their feet and applauded the musical genius in front of them, who had entertained them and brought something new to the chapel.

Standing, *Sasha* took her bow before leaving the stage and falling into Morgan's arms. "It's over."

"Not quite." Morgan smiled as a rousing encore was demanded from the enthusiastic crowd. "You'd better get back out there."

"Fine, one last—" She stared into Morgan's eyes. "This one is for you."

Morgan felt a rush of something heated. It melted her within, burned her skin and imprinted itself in the nerve endings that tingled around her body.

Reappearing on stage, Sasha breathed in the atmosphere, the excited crowd still applauding at the prospect of more. Like a chemical reaction the feeling rushed through her, electrifying her nerve endings.

"This is something unfinished, something I've been inspired to work on recently and well, I hope you like it. It's called 'Euphoria.'" She caught sight of Morgan, mouth gaping with surprise. She wanted to tell the world about her, make them understand with every note she played. These feelings that had escaped her for so long, that now rushed through her any time she thought about Morgan, feelings she knew only came because of Morgan.

The music rose and fell, hurried then slowed and ended with a crescendo of high excitable notes that had her almost jumping from the seat, and when she finished, the crowd jumped to their feet.

Allowing the breath to escape her body, she stood once again and bowed to her audience, before turning towards Morgan and grinning. She had to know, didn't she? She had to hear that and know how Alex felt.

And as she was about to bow once more, the sound erupted around her. Pop, crack, crack. The microphones amplified the sound around the hall. Alex didn't get a chance to think before Mike crashed into her, dragging her away and off the stage towards Morgan.

They didn't stop.

"Keep moving," he directed, leading them both away from the potential danger. Morgan ran, her doctor's bag bouncing against her leg and off the wall of the narrow corridor, until finally, they rounded a corner, and Alex's dressing room was right in front of them.

Mike pushed the door open and held it, ushering Alex and Morgan inside, before he slammed it shut and stood against it.

"What the hell was that?" Morgan said breathlessly as she almost collapsed against the vanity desk. She turned quickly and moved towards Alex. "Are you okay?"

Mike shook his head. "Dunno, but I wasn't taking any chances."

"Thank you," Alex said, touching his arm. She turned to Morgan. "I'm alright, I'm okay."

Keeping her hand from moving to check every part of her was the hardest thing Morgan ever did. "I want to check."

"I'm fine, I promise." Alex smiled and let her eyes do the talking. *I want you*, they said. *I need you*, they said. *I know it's hard*, they said.

A loud banging on the door made them both jump away from one another.

"Who is it?" Mike shouted, holding the door firmly closed with his weight as well as the locks that slid across and would be utterly useless if anyone really wanted to get in.

"Open the god damn door." The American accent was loud and clear.

"It's Francine," he said, looking to Alex for permission to let her in.

Alex nodded, and Mike slid the lock across and yanked the handle down quickly. The door opened and a harried-looking Francine pushed through it, followed by the police.

"You alright?" she asked, looking at Alex and then the others. "Is she hurt?" she asked Morgan, who shook her head.

"No, she's fine."

"I'm okay, just feeling a little shaken," Alex answered, stepping back towards Morgan, moving as close as she could get without being obvious. She needed her, needed to feel the warmth of her.

"Good, that's good." Francine exhaled, blowing out her cheeks. "It's fucking carnage out there."

"Is everyone alright?" Alex asked.

Siba stepped forward. "There was a bit of a stampede to get out, but nothing too serious, and my officers are dealing with an orderly situation now.

Morgan closed the space between herself and Alex. Her right hand, unable to not touch any longer, pressed against the small of Alex's back, allowing the heat between them to pass through more easily.

"Do we know what it was?" she asked Siba.

"We've got the chapel being searched now," Siba answered. "We don't think it was anyone firing a gun. I think it was just meant to scare you, but not harm you."

Alex finally slumped backwards against Morgan, not caring any longer what anyone might think. "It's okay. I've got you," Morgan whispered.

"Can we leave?" Francine asked Siba. "Or do we need to be here?"

"You can go, but I'd advise waiting until we've completely emptied the chapel and finished with the search both inside and out. Whatever this was, someone might still be around, wanting to enjoy the chaos," Siba warned.

"Why can't I just have a simple life?" Alex bemoaned, turning into Morgan's arms. She felt the heat of tears spring and wanted to bury her face and hide away from it all.

"Can we just have a minute?" Morgan asked, taking control of the situation. When nobody moved, she added, "Alone, please."

The room emptied out, all except for Francine, who stood there watching as each one left. When she turned, she found Morgan staring at her. Pointing to her own chest, she said, "Me?"

"Everyone, yes," Morgan demanded. "As her doctor, I'm asking for some space to treat my patient."

Francine glared at her, her gaze held by a determined Morgan Kelly.

"Fine, I'll be outside." Francine finally gave in and exited the room, closing the door behind her with a gentle click of the lock.

Turning her attention to Alex, Morgan pulled her close, wrapping her arms around the now-shaking shoulders and allowing Alex to let her emotions get the better of her. Fingertips grasped at her dress, the wetness of tears dripped down her bare chest, but she wouldn't let go, not now. Not when Alex needed her like this.

"It's alright, let it out."

For a few minutes they stood, clinging silently together until the sobbing subsided and the sniffing started. Morgan leaned back and smiled at the face in front of her. Mascara ran and blacked her eyes. Looking down, Morgan noticed the same stain against her chest.

"What do you want to do?" she asked Alex gently. She reached for a make-pad and some cleanser. Dribbling a little cleanser onto the pad, she wiped Alex's face.

Watery eyes stared back at her, the blue darker and more wounded than ever.

Shaking her head, Alex answered with a stuttering breath, "I don't know. I just need to get out of here."

"Then we'll get out of here," Morgan said resolutely. "I've got your back."

Alex smiled at that. It was sweet. "I know you have."

"Can I make a suggestion?"

Alex nodded.

"We go back to the hotel, cancel the rest of the tour and disappear somewhere."

The solution seemed so simple, and Alex actually chuckled. "We can't."

"We can, we can do anything we want to," Morgan insisted.

"Let's start with getting back to the hotel." Alex rubbed her cheek and smiled. "I just want to curl up with you and feel safe again."

A knock on the door was quickly followed by a policeman's head poking around. "They said you're a doctor?"

"Yes," Morgan answered.

"Aye, we've got a few people injured. Wondered if you could take a quick look before the ambulances get here."

Morgan turned to Alex, grabbing her bag in the process. "You'll be alright?"

"Yes, go. Help those people."

Chapter Forty-Five

Arriving back at the cabin, Alex was angry now. Their private space had needed to be searched. The hotel grounds were on lockdown, and despite Connor's assurance that everything was fine, she hated the fact that everyone was being inconvenienced because of this, because some idiot thought it was funny to try and scare her. And she was angrier still to admit that it had worked.

"The police are going to stand guard overnight, then we can organise some personal security in the morning and head back home first thing," Francine was saying while Morgan built a fire. The room felt chilly, and she needed something to do that got her out of the line of fire she could see coming.

"I'm not going home," Alex responded. "We're expected in Durham tomorrow. We're going to Durham."

Francine's face twisted into a grimace. "Someone just shot at you."

"That's an exaggeration. I wasn't shot at, at least not by anyone who could bloody well aim." Alex stared at her defiantly.

"Has there been any word on what it was that made that noise?" Morgan asked, on her knees, scrunching up balls of newspaper to shove in between the kindling.

Francine exhaled, pressing her lips together as she held back what she wanted to say. Instead, she turned to Morgan and answered, "I expect we'll be told when they find out. I've said you're not to be disturbed any further tonight, but they will want to speak to everyone in the morning, so I'm not sure we will even be allowed to move on. And for what it's worth, I think you're a fool if you do. This is serious, Alex."

"Do you not think I understand that, Fran? Morgan just spent an hour patching people up who were injured because of it."

Francine huffed out a breath again, this time more petulantly, and paced the room. "I'm just saying, and you know me, I'm all about the dollar and the legacy, but some things are more precious."

Alex flopped down onto the couch. "Let's just try and keep some perspective, get some sleep, and in the morning when we have more information, we can make a more informed decision."

"I've already got every newspaper and TV news bombarding me for information. I think sleep might have to take a back seat," Francine responded, before flopping down on the couch beside Alex, her head falling to the side to land against her friend's shoulder.

"Turn the bloody thing off," Alex said when Francine looked at her phone. "There's nothing you can tell them yet anyway."

"You do know me, right?" Francine said with a hint of seriousness despite the smile.

"Yes, do I need to have Morgan give you a sedative?" Alex chuckled.

Morgan turned at the sound of her name. The flames began to flicker, putting a soft glow over her face. "Hey, I'm not a drug dealer."

"You could earn a fortune if you were." Francine laughed more heartedly. "Imagine half the music industry would pay for that service."

"I imagine half the music industry already does." Alex chuckled.

A soft knock on the door interrupted them. "I told them no—"

"Just see who it is." Alex sighed. "It's probably the police, or Connor."

"I'll get it," Morgan said, standing and heading towards the door. She pulled the curtain back and sneaked a look past it. "It's the detective from earlier."

"Sorry," Siba said when Morgan opened the door. "I know it's late and you asked not to be disturbed but I wanted to fill you in before I head home."

Morgan stepped aside and made room for him to enter. He rubbed his hands together, enjoying the warmth of the fire, and Alex imagined a scene from a Christmas rom-com. All it needed was some snow to fall from his shoulders and a declaration of love.

She stood up and shook his hand. "Thank you, I think it would do us all good to know more so we deal with things properly."

"So, what are we dealing with here?" Francine asked, still on the couch, one leg crossed over the other as she glared in his direction.

"It would seem that someone hid a device under the stage. Firecrackers with a remote switch that could be activated from several hundred metres away."

"Firecrackers?" Morgan asked. "Like fireworks?"

"Yeah, a lot of noise, but basically harmless," Siba replied.

"Hardly harmless," Francine seethed. "That's not the point. Somehow, someone got close enough to plant this device. It could be a bomb next time."

"There won't be a next time," Alex argued. "We'll up security and make sure it doesn't happen again."

"Alex—"

"I'm not discussing it any further. The show goes on," Alex stated. When no further argument came from Francine, she turned and left the room.

"Well, I'll bid you all goodnight," Siba said. "I'll be in touch tomorrow about taking further statements. And I have two officers on the door until the morning."

"Thank you, Detective," Morgan said, showing him out. When the door was firmly closed, she turned to Francine. "So, I guess we're going to Durham."

"Hm, looks that way. I'll see you in the morning."

"Alright." Morgan opened the door again. "I'll speak to her, but I don't think anything I say will change her mind."

"No." Francine sighed. "I think you're right."

Opening the door to the bedroom, Morgan found it in darkness. Just the gentle waft of Alex's perfume in the air of silence. A gentle scent that instantly calmed her.

"Are you still awake?"

"Yes," came the response as the body beneath the covers shifted and an arm stretched out to hit the switch that would illuminate the area. Alex blinked at the sudden brightness.

"Francine's gone to head off the press," Morgan said, moving closer to the bed.

"I'll probably have to give her a raise after this." She sat up against the pillows, staring up at Morgan. "Not quite the night we were hoping for, huh?"

One knee on the bed, Morgan said, "No, it isn't, but I'm just glad that you're safe." She manoeuvred herself into the space next to Alex and snuggled in. "That was quite a scary night."

"Yes, funny isn't it? That a threat to my life doesn't cause a panic attack." Alex chuckled and kissed the top of Morgan's head. "I'm glad you're here though, that I don't have to do this on my own."

"You mean Francine wouldn't cuddle up with you?" Morgan joked with a smile that Alex couldn't see but knew was there.

"Again, I'd need to give her a pay rise."

Morgan twisted around. "Do you really think it's wise to go ahead with the tour?" Her face turned serious.

Alex considered her question before saying, "I don't know. But if I cancel, whoever is doing this wins, don't they?"

"I don't think they do. I think whoever it is, is someone deeply disturbed and potentially could do what they say they will, and I'm not ready to lose you like that." She glanced down before her eyes shot back up and stared into Alex's. "I'm not ready to lose you at all."

"Well, I've no intention of going anywhere." The intensity between them was always there, wasn't it? "Come here." Alex reached around Morgan's neck and pulled her closer, until their mouths almost met, lips brushing against each other. "I'm falling for you. You know that don't you?"

Morgan nodded. She did know that. It had been alluded to out loud, but not anything tangible, until now. The gap between them closed, and all that mattered in that moment was closeness. A need to be one. Slow and languid, there was no rush, not in this bubble they'd created. When it came to an end, Morgan sat up.

"You wrote me a song." They kissed again.

Breaking the kiss, Alex stared at her for a long time. Could it really be this easy, to fall for someone so deeply?

"I had to, I just feel it. When I'm with you, there's this…it's like I'm in a Disney movie and you're this Cinderella character, and with every move you make there's music."

Morgan's eyes widened with every word. "Nobody has ever…I can't explain what it feels like." She touched her chest. "In here, listening to something you composed because of me."

"I find every time I sit at the piano to write…all I feel, is you."

"Alex," Morgan said breathlessly.

Alex got serious. "So, if you want me to cancel—"

"No, I want you to do what you want to do. I just don't want you to feel forced into cancelling, that you have to do it because of some idealist notion that it's the right thing to do, and equally, I don't want you to feel forced into continuing because you feel like you should. This has to be something you decide."

"What I want to do right now is just switch off from it all and feel something real."

Morgan smirked. "I can help with that."

"Can you? How?"

Kicking the covers away, Morgan edged down the bed. "Why don't I show you?"

Chapter Forty-Six

Alex sighed at the question. She'd already spent an hour with the police giving pointless statements. She knew nothing that would help right now.

The early headlines had certainly been expansive. It was front page news on most of them, and the tabloids had gone to town, over-exaggerating and publishing pictures of people in white suits and booties checking out the scene. And of course, there was a picture of the bloody coach. Alex hadn't looked at any of them.

"I'm sorry, can you repeat the question?" she said, hoping he'd take the opportunity to change it. A press conference had been quickly assembled once it had become clear it wasn't going to be a story that disappeared.

A man in his thirties with a stubbled chin and thick-rimmed black glasses stood up again. "Yes, of course, I was asking if your new relationship had any bearing on this?"

Alex took a moment before she said, "I would imagine that whatever is happening or not in my private life, has no bearing on the mind of anyone who would do this."

"Do you have a message for those people who were injured last night?" a balding man in a ruffled suit asked.

"Obviously, I hope they're all okay. I am sure they feel quite shaken by it all. I have asked for the names of all of them and will be making sure they are all alright."

"Who do you think is behind it all? A jealous—" He was cut off.

"That's all for now. Thank you all for your concern. As you can see, and report, Sasha is perfectly fine," Francine interrupted.

"So, you're continuing the tour?" A woman this time, all smiling eyes and high cheekbones, quickly shouted out in hope of an answer.

"Absolutely," Alex said before standing and heading away from the lights and microphones. Cameras clicked away, flash bulbs blinding her as she moved through the small gathering and out of the room.

"Well, that went as good as we could expect," Francine said once they were out of earshot.

Alex frowned. "They do ask ridiculous questions."

"Of course, they want to catch you out."

"Of what?"

Francine shrugged. "Whatever they think will make a headline."

"Well, the incident should be enough." She sighed. "Let's just get going, shall we?"

"You sure this is what you want?"

Alex stopped and turned back to her. "You know it's what we have to do."

"I know, but still, there could be a way around it. I could talk to—"

"No, I want to finish this off and move forward with the plan. More now than ever." Her phone ringing in her pocket caught her attention, and she reached into her pocket for it, her face grimacing when she saw the caller ID. She held the phone up for Francine, and the American stepped back.

"I'll leave you to deal with the Tsarina."

Closing her eyes and composing herself, Alex watched Francine walk away, and then she answered the call.

"Mama."

"Alexandra, are you alright?" Her mother's voice sounded concerned, and she was reminded that despite her mother's standoffishness, she did love her. "I saw the news."

"Yes, Mama, I think it was just a prank, but you know how seriously everything gets taken."

"When they want rid of you, they find a way, Alexandra." By "they," she meant the KGB, the elusive men and women who would swoop in and remove the person they felt would damage the Empire.

"I don't think *they* are out to get me, Mama."

"Nobody ever does," her mother said dryly.

"Yes, Mama."

"And this new woman. She is very beautiful. Francine picked well; the press will eat her up."

"I—actually, she isn't a prop for the press. I like her."

Her mother was quiet for a moment before she asked, "Do you write music for her?"

The answer wasn't quite so simple. She had composed something, but it didn't feel done quite yet. There was so much more she could write, wanted to write. But to her mother, she simply said, "Yes."

"Hm, bring her to dinner when you get home. Stay safe, *umnitsa*."

Alex smiled at the term of endearment: a good girl, a clever girl.

Pulling her phone from her pocket, Morgan felt guilty at the missed calls and pressed the button that would call her mother.

"Morgan? Are you alright?" her mother's worried voice said quickly. "It's all over the news."

"I'm fine, Mum, there's nothing to worry about." She winced at the little lie and caught the raised brow from Alex and the warm smirk that accompanied it. It was a conversation not too dissimilar from her own earlier. Maybe they weren't too different, despite the age difference.

"Not a nice thing at all," her mum said sharply.

"No, it wasn't, and I'm sorry I didn't return your call sooner. It's been a little bit…hectic."

"Well, as long as you're alright." There was a silence before her mum whispered, "Is she there with you?"

"Uh huh."

Her mum chuckled. "And how's that going?"

"Surprisingly well, I suppose. But Mum, listen, I need to go. I have to call Zoe and check on Knight."

"Alright, call me when you can talk."

"Bye, Mum." Morgan smiled into the phone. "Love you."

"Love you too, bye darling."

She disconnected the call and turned to find Alex and Francine both looking at her. "What?"

"Nothing, it was sweet," Francine answered, fidgeting in her seat and readjusting the seatbelt across her chest.

"You don't tell your mother you love her?" Morgan asked.

Both women looked nonplussed.

"You've not met my mother," Alex finally said. "I'm not sure love is something she is able to admit to quite so easily."

"Yeah, she's a peach," Francine agreed before adding, "Mine's dead."

"Oh. I'm sorry about that," Morgan responded, feeling more than a little awkward.

"My mom was a hard ass. You might see that reflected in me." She winked. "But yes, we did tell each other we loved one another. In fact, it was the last thing we said to one another before she passed."

Morgan wondered how long she could keep them talking before they descended back into the stand-off from earlier. She could see it from both sides. Francine was scared, and she knew Morgan and Alex were too. If pushed though, she would side with Alex.

Alex was right. Nothing had actually happened that was a real threat. Yes, it was an issue that anyone had gotten close enough to leave a device. That opportunity had to be eliminated moving forward, but the device had been meant to scare, not wound.

"What do you think would happen if 'you' said I love you to the Tsarina?" Francine mused and smirked at the use of the nickname they had for Alex's mother.

Thinking about it a moment, Alex then said in a perfectly Russian accent, "Darling, why are you wasting air on words that mean so little without effort."

"Effort?" Morgan quizzed while Francine laughed heartedly.

"My mother believes that the only way to show love is through art, through dance, and through music, otherwise it is just language wasted on deaf ears. The only time she accepted love is when my music is for her." She thought about the piece she'd written for Morgan.

"Okay, she sounds scary."

"Uh huh." Francine grinned. "That's a word for it."

Chapter Forty-Seven

Durham

"We're here," Alex said, but Morgan only understood with lip reading. Pulling the buds from her ears, she switched off the music and thrust everything into her pocket. Francine was already out of the car and bossing everyone around.

"Everything alright?"

Alex smiled. "It will be." Her fingertips stroked Morgan's thigh, out of sight. "We've been instructed to wait in the car."

"Okay," Morgan answered, her hand moving to land on top of Alex's, fingers entwining. "What are we waiting for?"

"Apparently, I have a new security detail. His name is Mack, and he is organising everything with Francine." She jutted her chin towards the window and the two people in black suits standing guard. "Those two are on guard."

"Good," Morgan sighed. "It always worried me that you didn't really have anyone looking after you."

"I never needed looking after before." She sighed and sat back in her seat, head turned to face Morgan. "You look pretty."

"Do I?" Morgan laughed and fought the urge to blush.

"Hm, I'm very attracted to you, Morgan."

Now, she did blush. "I am quite aware, and the feeling is reciprocal."

"Yes, I know."

The car door opened before another word could be said, and a man slid in.

"Ms Montgomery, Mack Hudson, I'm in charge now," he said firmly, and Alex felt the urge to laugh. "I've set up a schedule. We will work to that moving forward. Where you go, I go. My team have already searched the hotel rooms and we've swapped suites from what was previously arranged, just in case. I'll be sending a team to the cathedral as soon as we have you settled in."

When he stopped speaking, he grinned at them both, something she was sure other people found charming and disarming. His confidence was certainly top of its game.

"I see," Alex said slowly. "Well, all of that sounds perfect, except for one thing, Mr Hudson."

"Oh, what's that?" He frowned. His face looked like his mind was running over everything trying to find what it was he'd missed.

"I don't do as I'm told. I pay the bills around here and that puts me in charge. So, in future you will ask me what my plans are before you go running off to decide what I will be doing. Do I make myself clear?"

"I'm not sure you understand the gravity—"

Her head tilted as she stared at him. "I understand all too well. Feel free to find employment elsewhere, Mr Hudson, if it's too difficult to discuss my plans with me."

He smiled, an element of embarrassment behind it. "I—" He inhaled and nodded. "Of course. You're the boss."

Reaching past Morgan to open the door, Alex said, "Yes, yes I am. Shall we go in?"

Morgan grinned at her, never more turned on in her life. "Yes, I think that's exactly what we should do."

Stepping out of the car, Alex waved at the small crowd behind a barricade twenty feet away. Morgan watched them, fascinated by the way some people would idolise someone they didn't know, how they would go out of their way to just meet them.

Alex moved towards the door, Mack by her side as she was introduced by Francine to the next manager and staff who would look after them for the following forty-eight hours.

As Morgan continued to stare, she caught a glimpse of someone familiar – not someone that she knew as such, but the blonde hair and the way her head tilted. It was her.

The woman from St Andrews.

Quickly, Morgan moved forward and took Alex's elbow. Leaning in, she said quietly, "She's here."

Alex frowned. "Who?"

"The woman I saw yesterday, at the chapel, she's—" She turned to point her out, but she was gone. "She was right there, I'm sure of it."

Staring at the group of fans, Alex waved again, and made it look as though she were just acknowledging them. "Maybe you think you saw her because we're all on alert."

"I know what I saw, Alex." Morgan glared, just as Francine caught wind of something up.

"What's going on with you two?"

Alex twisted around to face Francine. "Nothing, Morgan thought she saw the woman from yesterday."

An intense stare directed itself at Morgan. "The woman from the chapel?"

Morgan nodded. "I was sure it was her, but she's gone."

"I don't like this," Francine hissed. "Let's get inside."

"What woman?" Mack asked, overhearing the conversation.

Francine pushed Alex and Morgan forward. "I'll explain inside."

Chapter Forty-Eight

Press interviews had been switched to the hotel, something Alex wasn't comfortable with but had accepted as necessary for now. Mack wasn't taking any chances and didn't see the point in moving her around when they could have the press come to them, and it was a battle that Alex wasn't going to fight. A smaller room on the lower level had been acquired by Francine, the hotel manager only too happy to help.

"So..." The reporter scratched his head, and Alex understood how his hair had become so ruffled to begin with. "The incident in Scotland—"

Alex smiled before butting in. "A prank, obviously someone thought it would be funny. It wasn't of course, but we've moved past that."

"Oh, only from my conversations with the police up there. They seem to be taking it quite seriously."

"Well, they would. It's a place of importance, nobody wants to imagine that anyone could potentially cause real issues for them." Alex's smile remained relaxed. "But the idea that it was something aimed at me personally, and there have been no threats or communications to suggest an ongoing issue." A small white lie to omit the note they found wouldn't hurt, she supposed.

"Indeed." That seemed to halt him any further on that subject. "So, this new piece you've ended with recently, are we to expect a new album anytime soon?"

Alex grinned, hearing "Euphoria" play in her head, with images of Morgan tantalising her moving alongside every note. "Yes, you can expect one. I'm still in the process of composing but it's taken a while to feel so inspired and I'll be looking for the right team to produce and record it."

"Quite." He coughed and cleared his throat. "And rumours of a new love interest?"

"I am exploring that too, yes," she confirmed, an agreed statement to move the questions away from the Edinburgh event.

Now he grinned, imagining he had the scoop. "Well, that is wonderful to hear." He leaned forward. "Can we expect another appearance tonight?"

"Right now, I'd like for her to continue to enjoy not being part of the circus that is my life."

He smiled at that, but added, "She's younger than you, isn't she?"

"Is she? Would you ask me that if I were a man?" He didn't answer. "I didn't think so."

"I think that's enough for today. Thank you all for coming," Francine said, cutting off any further conversation regarding Morgan. "If those of you with booked interviews want to hang around, Sasha will get to you in due course. In the meantime, we'll take a little break, okay?"

Mumbles and grumbles echoed around the room as those not invited to stay longer got up and shuffled out of the room. Alex stretched out and then got up, her ankle now completely healed.

"I'm going to head into the bar for ten minutes and get a coffee," she said to Francine.

"Sure."

The bodyguard in a suit followed her, hanging back just enough that he wasn't quite so invasive, which she was at least grateful for. The bar wasn't that busy. A couple of journalists had snuck in and were ordering lunch, but mostly it was travellers and businesspeople going about their day.

"What can I get you?" asked the barman when she strolled up.

"I'm hoping a pot of tea," she asked with a smile.

"Of course, Breakfast or Earl Grey?"

There was no need to consider that question. "Breakfast, thank you. Can you put it on my room tab?"

"Absolutely, grab a seat and I'll bring it over."

She turned and looked for a vacant table. That was when she spotted her, at a table in the corner, staring over at her.

"For fuck's sake," Alex muttered under her breath as she took off and strode halfway across the room before the suit had a chance to catch up. "Laurel."

As though she had expected to see her, Laurel just smiled at her.

"Alex, how are you?"

She ignored the pleasantries. "Why are you here?"

"I wanted to see you." Laurel smiled up at her before noticing the man hovering. "Who's your friend?"

"None of your business," Alex said firmly. "I told you on the phone that I don't have anything more to say to you."

"I know, but you didn't really give me the chance to say what I wanted to say, and I was going to wait until you got back, but then you started flaunting this woman and I figured, 'act now Laurel, or you'll lose your chance.'" She chuckled. "Please, sit down, let's talk this through."

"Do you need assistance, Ms Montgomery?" the suit asked.

Alex turned to face him. "No, thank you, I can deal with this." Before she had the chance to speak again, the barmen arrived carrying a tray with a pot of tea, one China cup, a matching saucer and the accompanying sugar bowl and milk jug.

"I'll just set it down there," he said, assuming that Laurel must have been someone she was planning to sit with.

She barely had time to thank him before Laurel was pouring a cup. "Still no sugar?" she asked brightly, looking up at Alex. Her focus then moved over to a point in the room just behind Alex, the smile on her face changing to a scowl. "She doesn't need to be here."

Confused, Alex turned to find Morgan moving quickly towards them, wide-eyed concern across her features.

"Morgan, it's not what you—"

"That's her." Morgan pointed. "From St Andrews, that's the woman I saw."

Laurel held her hands up. "I confess, yes, I did sneak in. I was hoping to speak to you, but this one got in the way."

Alex rubbed her face. "Do you even hear how barmy that sounds?" Laurel was about to answer when Alex shushed her. "I don't care what you want to speak to me about. We are finished. We were finished the day you ended it and walked away. I'm okay with that. I don't want to hear from you again, Laurel, and I certainly don't want to see you. So, please, before you embarrass yourself further, leave." This time when she turned to the suit, she said, "Could you escort her out of the building?"

"You can't make me leave. I have a room. I'm a guest here." Laurel laughed.

"Just stay away from me, and if I find out you had anything to do with that prank with the firecrackers, so help me I'll—"

Morgan pulled her away. "Let's go, before you become a firecracker," she said, smiling and leaning in. "People are watching."

Alex glanced around quickly. Several pairs of eyes were staring in her direction.

"You've got a show to prepare for. Let's go," Morgan repeated, and this time, Alex allowed herself to be led away.

"I didn't get my tea," she moaned.

Morgan turned to the guy in the suit. "Can you bring the tea? Thank you so much."

Francine uncrossed her leg and stood up.

"I've talked with Philip, and he's adamant that unless she does something that can be construed as stalking or is found to be the guilty party in any act of aggression towards you, then there isn't much we can do. She's entitled to stay in any hotel. The fact you're staying there could be argued as merely a coincidence."

"So, she gets to follow me around and there's nothing I can do?"

"Isn't that what fans do?" Francine stopped mid-pour and smiled. "I didn't say there was *nothing* we could do." She topped the glass up and added an extra cube of ice. "Mack can put a couple of guys on her tail. Where she goes, they go, as discreet or not as you want it to be."

"Is that legal?"

"Technically…" Francine shrugged. "But her argument becomes theirs. They just happen to be where she is, just a coincidence."

"Hm, I don't like it but needs must, I suppose." She sighed. "It's all so bloody frustrating. Everything was going great, we're over halfway through, Goran loves me. And this is like a spanner in the works."

Francine sat down again. "I'm sure she'll get bored."

"Who the hell is she?" Morgan asked when it seemed as though everything else had been discussed.

"I'm going to leave that to you," Francine said and got up. "I'll be in my room if anyone needs me."

Morgan watched her leave. "She's an ex, right?"

"Yes," Alex answered. "We dated over a year ago, and she ended it."

"So, why is she back and following you around on tour?"

"Well, that's something you'd have to ask her. I personally do not care, I have no interest in her, Morgan," Alex stated concisely.

Morgan grinned. "I'm not worried about that. Like she'd be able to take you from me. I'm a doctor." She winked. "But seriously, are you not a little concerned about just how weird that is?"

"I guess, yes, but also, I know Laurel and she isn't—" She hesitated when Morgan's eyebrow rose. "She wasn't someone I would say would do anything untoward."

"Where does she live?"

"London, somewhere near Wimbledon."

Morgan nodded slowly. "And yet, she's been in Edinburgh, and now Durham, and for all we know she could have been at every other venue we've been to. That's stalking, isn't it?"

"What do you want me to do? Francine just explained there's nothing we can do with the police…" Alex crossed the room and stared out of the window.

"Don't get rid of Mack and his team, not just yet."

Alex sighed and rolled her eyes.

"I know it's not ideal, but Alex, you've got an anonymous friend texting you and an ex stalking you…how do you know they're not the same person?"

Alex turned slowly. That hadn't been something she had considered.

When Morgan left the room, she made a call.

"Mack."

"Ms Montgomery, is everything alright?"

She rolled her eyes. "Yes, all fine but I need you to do something for me, discreetly."

"Go on."

"I have a phone number. I'd like to know who's using it."

Chapter Forty-Nine

The show in Durham went off without a hitch. Mack and his team had everything under control. Bags were searched, tickets double-checked, and the only people allowed within twenty feet of Alex could be counted on one hand. Laurel didn't show.

On stage had been a strange sensation for Alex. A feeling of waiting for it, for the threat to come, but it never did. But with every minute she played, the fear dissipated, and the enjoyment returned, and thoughts of Morgan swam into her mind and swirled with the notes she played.

She could see Morgan in the wings, hidden from sight, smiling at her with an encouragement she had lacked in almost every relationship she'd tried to have previously. Women liked to date Alex, because they enjoyed everything else that brought with it, but Morgan was only interested in her. And when it came to the encore, once more Alex played the musical piece she'd written for Morgan, "Euphoria."

Coming off the stage, she walked with purpose, Mack at her side, Morgan behind along with Francine. They strode quickly down the hall until they came to her dressing room. The man on the door opened it and stepped aside.

Mack went in first, checked for any intruders and then beckoned them in.

"I'll be outside organising the car. How long do you need?" Mack asked.

Alex glanced at Morgan, her own euphoria pumping through her veins. There was no way she was waiting until they returned to the hotel room. Alex wanted her now.

"Thirty minutes," she said in answer, turning quickly to Francine. "You can all leave. I just want to decompress for a moment."

"Fine, I'll speak to Jessie about York. Then I'll head back to the hotel."

"Good." Alex smiled as they all filed out, and she followed behind, closing and locking the door behind them. "Take it off," she said without turning to face Morgan. The dress had been tempting her all night. From the minute Morgan had stepped out in it, she'd wanted to strip her of it.

She breathed in and out, trying to compose herself. Her breath hitched at the sound of the zip, and she smiled to herself knowing that Morgan would do exactly as she demanded.

"How naked do you want me?" Morgan asked, her voice low and sultry.

Alex turned slowly to find her standing in just her underwear. Matching of course, plum and black lace and silk. Her arms hung limply by her side, awaiting further instruction. She looked delicious.

"I think as you are, is just—" Alex stepped forward. "Perfect." Her eyes swept up and down the body she was enjoying so much lately; too much? Maybe, it would all end soon though, wouldn't it? "Turn around."

Morgan smirked before she twisted on her heel and turned her back on Alex. Unsure what her lover had planned, her skin pimpled in anticipation.

Alex moved in closer, breathing in Morgan's scent as her fingers touched flesh and slid easily around her to cup both lace-clad breasts in her palms. "Do you know what you do to me, Dr Morgan Kelly?"

"Hm, I think I have an idea." Morgan sighed, her head falling back to rest against Alex's shoulder.

"I need to be inside you. I want to feel your desire." Alex squeezed and caressed, enjoying the way Morgan's nipples swelled and hardened to her touch, pressing into her palms perfectly.

Morgan whimpered when Alex ran her thumbs across them, gently pinching and rolling each one between her fingertips, alternating the pressure with which she squeezed.

"I want to make you come," Alex whispered. "And you can choose how. But whatever way you choose, will be slow and deliberate. I want you to beg for release, Morgan. And then I want to take you back to the hotel, bend you over and fuck you senseless with your favourite toy. Can you handle that, Morgan?"

Alex squeezed her nipples a little harder.

"Yes," Morgan gasped. "Yes, please. I want…" She moaned, her hips beginning to thrust against the air. "Touch me."

"We have half an hour to fill," Alex said, suggesting that would be how long this would take.

"Please touch me," Morgan tried once more, knowing that every time she said please, she pleased Alex.

Releasing her nipples, Alex stepped back and admired the slender back, the silk-covered buttocks. She spanked her hard, surprising her with the movement. Morgan yelped, but pushed her backside out to enjoy the caress she knew would follow.

"Good." Alex rewarded her, stroking the softness of her flesh. With quick fingers, she unhooked the bra and pulled the straps down Morgan's arms, freeing her breasts of the lacy constraints. "Turn around," she commanded again.

Morgan didn't waste a second, spinning to face her, arms still hanging loosely by her side despite the desperate itch to use her fingers and deal with her building arousal.

She watched as Alex reached out, tenderly stroking the back of her fingers across her nipples again. "So excitable, aren't they?" Alex said with a smile. "Always so perky, and hard." She pinched them once more, hard enough that it made Morgan whimper, but not painfully, not cruelly. Just enough to throw Morgan from her thoughts, out of her head for a moment. "Would you like my mouth on them?"

"Yes," Morgan breathed the word out. "Yes, please."

Alex pinched them once more. "Maybe I will." She stepped back again and let her eyes scan downward, admiring the darkening wet patch becoming more evident on the front of Morgan's knickers. "You're so wet, aren't you?"

"Yes." Morgan nodded quickly, her breath quickening as she enjoyed being watched and admired. When Alex stepped in quickly, forcing her tongue into Morgan's mouth and her hand between her legs, Morgan gasped and released all of the air she'd held in her lungs.

Her legs parted of their own volition, the intruding fingers rubbing vigorously against her underwear, the friction against her clit so good, and yet, unbearable all at once. She wanted to come, she wanted to beg, but she wouldn't, not yet. That would be too easy, that would be disappointing to Alex. And that wouldn't get her what she wanted. She knew the game and understood the rules. She liked the rules.

As if reading her mind, the kissing stopped, lips brushing against one another. "Not yet, don't you dare." The fingers slowed, but Morgan felt her hips still thrust and jerk, trying too hard to betray her. "No," Alex warned. "Not yet."

"Please," Morgan whimpered.

"No, not yet," Alex insisted. "We still have more time."

"I can…twice, I can come twice," Morgan tried to bargain.

Alex dropped down to her knees. "I know, but I don't want that." She smiled up at her as she plucked Morgan's knickers between her fingers and dragged the silk slowly down her thighs. Breathing in the scent of her arousal made her own clit throb between her legs. "I want you in my mouth." She teased, blowing gently, and watched as Morgan twitched and jerked.

"Please," Morgan tried again. When the fingertip dragged slowly across the tip of her clit, Morgan cried out, "Please, I need—"

"There will be a punishment if you do," Alex warned.

Morgan's legs squeezed together.

"You want to be punished?" Alex asked, her hands firmly grasping Morgan's thighs and pushing them apart. "Is that what you want?"

"No, I—" Her head fell back, hands reaching behind to lean against the table, holding herself up as her knees weakened to the onslaught of teasing and cajoling Alex was torturing her with.

"Alex," Morgan cried out. "Please, I need—"

"Say it. Tell me what you need." Alex taunted her, a fingertip rubbing circles over the very tip of her clit, as lightly as possible.

"Come, make me come, please."

"That's better. Again," she demanded, her finger dipping lower to tease the entrance to Morgan's need. Dipping into the wetness and coating her fingers in readiness. "Tell me again, Morgan.

"Please, I'm begging, please, make me come, for god's sake Alex. I can't— I need—"

She didn't get the chance to finish before Alex pressed into her with her fingers, her mouth sucking Morgan's clit, until finally, Morgan was allowed to let go. She howled her orgasm, shuddering every wonderful, perfect, exquisite sensation out of her body and into the ether.

Chapter Fifty

"You're fucking?"

Alex had opened the door, ready to go find Mack and get back to the hotel where they could continue enjoying each other in more comfortable surroundings. Instead, she opened it to find Francine, face like thunder, arms rigid across her chest.

"In a church?" Francine glared at them both, disdain and disappointment in her voice.

It was posed as a question, but in reality, it was a statement. And one that hit hard instantly, like it was supposed to.

""It's a cathedral," Alex snarked back. "Not that it's anyone else's business—" she attempted to say before Francine interrupted.

"Oh, after that little performance…trust me, it's everyone else's business."

Morgan felt her cheeks heat, her mouth gape. "We—"

"Don't," Francine said, holding her finger up. "I don't want to hear it. I don't care. What you two do in your down time is your business, but this is work." She stepped in closer. "I can't protect you, either of you, if I don't know what I'm protecting."

The pair of them remained silent, like children scolded.

"Now, you both need to go out there and get into the car. There will be no mention of this." She waved her hand at the pair of them. "Not one word, I don't care who asks or what they ask. You avoid and evade until we have the chance to sit down and work this out."

"But…you wanted everyone to think this was happening. What does it matter if it is?" Morgan felt very confused along with the embarrassment.

"What does it matter? The idea was to create a vague possibility of you dating. Something you," she pointed at Alex, "told me to forget about because you didn't want her dragged through it, instead it's like Fifty Shades of Pink is being filmed."

Morgan's eyes widened.

"Oh, you thought because the door was closed that nobody would hear what you were doing?" Francine's sarcasm was on point. "Every member of staff who has access to anywhere within fifty feet of this room, heard that."

"Look, you're right, it probably wasn't the most sensible thing to do." Alex tried to calm the situation.

"Uh huh, ya think?" Francine shook her head. "I should have known better and just organised a playmate."

"What's that supposed to mean?" Alex responded indignantly.

"You think I didn't know this would happen?" Francine hissed. "But I thought you'd have the sense to remain discreet."

"What does any of that mean?" Morgan asked, only to be shushed by Francine.

"Now I need to prepare for the invasion of privacy that's going to potentially come hurtling in this direction, all because you two couldn't keep it in your pants until you got back to the hotel." Francine pointed a bony finger at Alex again. "Everything we planned is going perfectly. The last thing you need is a shitty headline." She waved her hand slowly across the imaginary headline. "Sasha's sex shocker in holy crypt." She clapped her hands together. "Bravo."

"This is my fault." Alex sighed. "You're right, okay, whatever happens, it's on me. I seduced her—"

"You did not," Morgan jumped in. "You make it sound like I'm some naïve girl who didn't understand what was happening."

Alex turned abruptly back to Morgan, thrusting out a hand to her. "I'm sorry, that's not what I meant at all. I just mean, this is on me. I know the game, and I should have considered that before getting you involved."

"So, you wouldn't have got involved had you thought more about it?" Morgan began to feel an anger brewing.

"No, I'm not saying that." Alex sighed. "Look, you and I will go back to the hotel and talk, and you and I," she turned to Francine, "will talk in the morning."

"Oh, you bet we will," Francine said, storming off just as Mack appeared at the door. His brow was raised, but he said nothing, turning to speak to his man who'd been guarding the door and could easily fill him in.

"I'm sorry," Morgan whispered.

Alex turned slowly. "What for?"

Red cheeks and the threat of tears faced her. "Because…well, I wasn't quiet, and—"

"Do you think I wanted you quiet?" Alex's eyes bore into her. "I should have had the sense to wait, that's what I meant, but I didn't. I let my euphoria and need for you overrule my head and—" She shook herself. "This is all on me." She leaned in and kissed her slowly. "All on me."

"It's not all on you. I really wish you would stop doing that," Morgan said.

"I'm trying to protect you."

"Then stop, stop treating me as though I've had no say in this, or that I've just followed along like a lost little sheep. I'm in this because I'm utterly attracted to you, and I don't care who knows it. I don't take my clothes off for you because you demand it and I'm just too weak to say no. I do it because right there and then, I want you to fuck me till I'm ruined, do you understand?"

Exhaling slowly, Alex nodded. "Yes, I understand. I'm sorry."

She went to walk away, but Alex grabbed her arm and pulled her back.

"Never apologise to me for enjoying what we do together. I want to play your body like a symphony. Every moan or gasp, every time you cry out, I like hearing it. I want to hear it. I don't ever want you to feel like you have to hold back because you're worried about headlines. And I will protect you from those when I can, not because I think you're weak, but because I know how this game works and they will eat you up. They will try and find every embarrassing photo of you, they will hunt down stories and find your ex-partners for any juicy titbit they can use to sell a story, all because you fell for me. I won't just let that happen, not without a fight."

"Well, I don't know how we get around that without you gagging me, or sound proofing every room we end up alone in, because I'm not going to stop you from sharing the euphoria with me." Morgan smiled.

"Gagging, huh?" Alex winked. "Now, there's a thought."

Chapter Fifty-One

The car ride back to the hotel had been silent. Francine sat with her head in her phone, typing frantic short messages and huffing with each send she pressed. Mack spent the short journey watching every car and pedestrian they passed. And Morgan stared absently out of the window, aware that this was not the time and place to try small talk.

When the car stopped outside of the hotel, Alex opened the door and got out.

"Ms Montgomery, will you please wait for me to do that?" Mack said, his patience wearing thin.

Alex rolled her eyes, and when Morgan stepped out, they all walked towards the hotel. The small gaggle of people waiting outside were all but ignored. A simple wave from Alex was all she could muster.

When they got to the suite, Mack said, "Alright, wait here and I'll—"

"Is this really necessary?" Alex sighed. "We're tired."

"Won't take a moment to quickly scan the room for any intruder," he said confidently.

"I'll be in my room," Francine said, continuing down the hallway without another glance in their direction.

"We've really pissed her off," Morgan said sadly.

Alex grabbed Morgan by the hand and pulled her into a tight hug.

"I'm so sorry. I never meant for any of this to happen." She nuzzled Morgan into her neck. "I should have been more—"

"We're both adults. Why shouldn't we be allowed to have this?"

"Because that's the transaction to fame and fortune. You can have it all, but they want your soul in return. They want every aspect of your private life. Francine is right, the wrong headline changes everything."

Mack returned and nodded once. "All clear. Have a good night."

"I'm surprised I'm not being requested to let him sleep in our bed with us," Alex moaned, pushing the door open and entering the suite.

Morgan stepped across the room to the bar and took two glasses out of the small cabinet. "It's unfair. We haven't done anything wrong." She bent down to the fridge and found the ice box, using silver tongs to drop one large ball of perfectly clear ice into each glass. She twisted around to face Alex. "What are the headlines going to say anyway, Sasha is happy?" she mocked before returning to the drinks. She poured a good glug of scotch into both glasses. "I mean, who is interested in this stuff anyway?"

Alex remained silent, letting her rant it out. When Morgan handed her the glass, she took it with an understanding smile, swirling the amber liquid around the ice before taking a swig and letting it burn its way down her throat. This wasn't the night she had planned, she thought as she sat down on the couch and patted the seat beside her.

"Morgan, sit down."

Huffing, Morgan did as she was asked and took the seat beside Alex, and after a second or two, she fell into her side and clung to her.

"You can drive yourself crazy trying to understand why, but you'll never work it out, not really. Acceptance is the only way you can really move ahead with things." Alex took another swig of the drink. "They're going to write about us whether we want them to or not. And this is why I was against doing this in the first place, the whole pretending business. It was naïve of Francine to think that you could just appear in the background and not be subjected to any questions. And I should have been braver and accepted that they will write what they want about me, about the band, the crash."

Morgan remained silent, the darkened room closing in around them both.

Morgan twisted and pulled her feet up and under herself, eventually saying, "What do you think they will write?"

Alex shrugged. "It's hard to say. I don't think it will be anything too bad, if anything. But I guess they'll probably mention how you're younger than me." She smirked. "They like me. I've mostly played the game and given them interviews when required to. And there's nothing about you that should give them anything to grab onto other than the fact that you're the woman in my bed."

"I need to speak to my mum," Morgan answered quietly.

"Yes, first thing, but right now it's almost one in the morning and we need to get some sleep before travelling to York tomorrow."

"Kind of spoiled our night, hasn't it?" Morgan said, sitting up. Sadness had settled in her eyes.

"Nothing can ruin this. Being with you is… I haven't felt this sense of calmness in a very long time. I came off stage feeling euphoric for a very different reason."

"Really?"

"Yes, knowing you were there. I felt euphoric about you."

Morgan's head tilted to one side as she considered that. "I think that might be the nicest thing anyone's ever said to me."

Leaning forward, Alex placed the glass in her hand onto the table, stood up and reached her hand out to Morgan. "Well, that is absolutely not good enough."

Morgan smiled. "I know." She took the hand and let herself be pulled to her feet. "But I wouldn't change it." She looked away quickly.

"What's wrong?"

Morgan turned back to her. "Nothing, I just…what Francine said, about organising your playmates, what did that mean?"

"Hm, you heard that." She tried to smile. "The thing is sometimes it's just been easier I suppose to…arrange for…" She ran a hand through her hair and pulled out the hair band. "I don't always have a girlfriend to—"

"You pay for it?" Morgan asked gently.

Alex nodded. "Francine organises it for me with a reputable escort service."

"Okay."

"It's not my finest hour."

Morgan shrugged. "It's fine. Probably a lot easier at times." She considered how often she was in need of some adult company but didn't have the time or inclination to meet someone and deal with the relationship side of things.

Alex nodded. "True, I'm not ashamed of it, but I'm not exactly proud of myself either."

"So…can I expect a raise?" Morgan grinned.

Alex laughed. "Maybe, but right now, let's get some sleep, so we're prepared in the morning."

"For the headlines?" Morgan asked.

Alex said, "For Francine."

Chapter Fifty-Two

"Well, so far, you've gotten lucky. Not a whiff of it in the headlines, that's not to say it won't be. It was pretty late last night; they may run with it tomorrow, though," Francine said, still pissed off at the pair of them. "Even the St Andrews mess has gone quiet."

"Okay," Alex answered. She sat as close to Morgan as she could physically get, one leg bent with her foot on the couch, the other knee leaning on Morgan's thigh. No longer hiding them.

Francine picked at a croissant, popping a piece into her mouth and chewing before she asked, "So, you gonna tell me when it started?"

Morgan had already decided that she wasn't going to be speaking unless spoken to, so she turned to Alex and waited for her to answer for them.

Alex pushed her tongue around her front teeth. "Winchester."

"Winchester?" Francine got loud again. "Are you fucking kidding me, the entire time? How many other public interactions have there been?"

"What do you want? A blow by blow of every time we've been intimate?" Alex asked. "We've been attracted to one another since the hospital visit. Neither of us thought it was something we could act upon, and then we were thrust together in this and things just…happened."

"Nothing in your life just happens, Alex. Breakfast arrives because someone cooks it and delivers it, your stage is set because a group of guys put it together, your world turns because I keep it spinning. This…" she waved her hand at the pair of them, "this didn't just happen. You didn't just slip and fall face first into her vagina. I put her there."

"What do you mean, you put her there?"

"How long have we worked together?" Francine asked her. "It's a lot of years and you forget how well I know you? I saw the way you looked at her at the hospital. I saw how easily you were convinced to bring her along. We didn't need a doctor on tour. We've got a list of medics to call on who wouldn't have cost more than five figures, but you needed something more, someone more. And I was right."

Alex frowned. "Right about what?"

Francine shook her head. "You lost your passion. Oh, you'd play the music and get by, but the excitement had gone from your eyes. I see that, I see you, Alex. And I saw it come back the moment you met her. The moment I suggested she come on the tour with us."

"That's ridiculous." Alex scoffed. "I didn't lose anything."

"Oh yeah, so why are we doing this tour and not bringing the Ivan thing forward? He's chomping at the bit to get you in the studio, and you keep finding excuses."

"Bullshit."

Francine stared at her.

"My father just died," Alex said incredulously.

"He did, yes, and you know how sorry I am about that, he was a good man."

Silence filled the space for a moment.

Francine held her hands up. "All I'm saying is, for the last year or more, you've been lost. You wanted out, and we came up with a plan to make that happen but in order for it to work, you needed to find something to inspire you." Francine turned to Morgan, but spoke to Alex. "Look at her. She's perfect. Beautiful but not overtly. Smart, kind, funny, challenging…she's your dream woman. And look at you, from the moment she entered your life you started composing upbeat music again, you get up, and do as you're told, all with a smile on your face. Because she inspires you."

"You used me," Morgan said quietly.

Francine turned back to her. "No, I gave you choices. I gave you both choices. Everything you did, you chose to do. I just gave you the opportunity to make a decision."

"What if I'd said no to the coming on this tour?"

Shrugging, Francine said, "We'd have gone on the tour, and I'd have needed to find another way to keep the plan on track. But you were never going to say no, not once I put the offer to you. Only an idiot would say no. The opportunity to spend three weeks with a celebrity you found attractive and earn six figures. Come on, even if this hadn't happened, it was still an experience most wouldn't turn down. My biggest issue was convincing your bosses, but even then, money talks, it always does."

"So, why are you angry with us that we did what you expected we'd do?" Morgan continued to question.

"I'm not angry that you found each other. I'm frustrated that you made such a public fucking announcement that could have scuppered everything." Picking at the croissant again, Francine said, "So, it's serious?"

Morgan looked at Alex again, waiting almost breathlessly for her response.

"We both appreciate that this is out of the ordinary, it's fast, and probably a little bit crazy, and I don't like to think too much about the future or put pressure on something before it's even really started—"

"I'm serious about it," Morgan couldn't stop herself from blurting.

"Of course you are, honey, she's the superstar millionaire musician, and you're the struggling medic with debt coming out of every orifice."

"Francine, enough!" Alex shouted. "Don't, just don't…you started this. This was your idea, so don't you dare get arsy when it doesn't go the way you planned."

"It's gone exactly as I planned," Francine said indignantly.

Morgan stood up abruptly. "I'm not interested in any of that." She fled to the bedroom, slamming the door behind her.

"Happy now?" Alex said, turning to Francine.

Francine pursed her lips. "I'm not here to make other people happy, only you."

"Then you had better understand real quick. Because you're right about one thing. She…" Alex pointed to the door that was closed, "makes me happier than anything and anyone I've known for the last decade, and you will not disrespect her for doing what you were prepared to let everyone else think she was doing and what you sneakily planned to happen between us. You do not get to judge her now." Alex got up from the couch. "Until I say otherwise, I want her treated like she's a fucking queen. Do you understand me?"

Francine grinned. "Whatever you say, buttercup."

The door slammed again when Alex followed Morgan.

"And that, is what they call passion. Welcome back, Alex."

Entering the bedroom, she found Morgan sitting on the bed cross-legged, phone to her ear and in mid-conversation. She was about to turn and leave when Morgan smiled and beckoned her over.

"That's the plan, Mum, yes."

Alex couldn't hear what Morgan's mother was saying, even after she climbed onto the bed behind Morgan and thrust a leg on either side of her, arms wrapping around her waist and her chin leaning on Morgan's shoulder.

"I know, I'm okay. I just wanted you to know that there might be things written about me in the paper." Something was said, and then, "Yes, I know that, no, she's...she's taking care of me, of course."

Alex chuckled and got Morgan's attention, pulling her fingers back and forth as a sign to give her the phone.

"Hang on, Mum." Morgan turned as best she could. "What?"

"Give me the phone."

"Why?"

Alex stared at her until finally Morgan sighed and handed over the phone.

"Hello, Mrs Kelly? This is Alex," she said calmly, trying not to laugh when Morgan's eyes widened.

"Oh my god, Sasha?" Mrs Kelly asked incredulously.

Alex giggled. "Yes, sorry, Sasha, but I'm Alex to my friends, and I do hope we are going to be friends, Mrs Kelly."

"Of course, why wouldn't we be?"

"Indeed, and I just wanted to reassure you that Morgan and I are enjoying the tour, and she's being taken care of completely, and I want you not to worry a minute longer."

"Well, that is good to hear. As you can imagine, we've been a little bit concerned about her."

"Absolutely, you should be very proud of her." As she spoke, she gazed at Morgan. "She's an amazing doctor and wonderful woman. I'm lucky to have her here."

"Of course, we've never doubted that at all." There was a pause before Mrs Kelly added, "Just don't hurt her, she's not used to this kind of thing."

"I'm not planning on that, much the opposite actually. I'll pass her back to you."

She handed the phone back to Morgan.

"Hi, Mum…" As Morgan continued to speak, Alex leaned forward and kissed her shoulder, moving her hair out of the way to kiss the sinews of her neck. "I need to go now, Mum… Hm hm, I'll call you in a few days, okay. Yep, okay…bye." Morgan disconnected the call and spun around. "That was mean."

"What?" Alex feigned innocence. "I don't know what you're talking…" Her words were cut short when Morgan pressed their lips together.

Pulling away, Morgan smiled at Alex. "That was a nice thing you said."

"I didn't say anything that wasn't true." Alex fell back, pulling Morgan with her. They wrapped their limbs around one another and rolled until they were on their side, facing one another.

"Maybe not, but still, it's nice to hear someone say it."

Alex tenderly pushed away a tendril of hair that threatened to fall over Morgan's eyes. "Do your parents not tell you they're proud of you?"

"Sometimes, I suppose they do, in their own way." Morgan fell backwards and sighed. "I am a capable woman; I don't need anyone else's validation anymore," she said, her neck turning so she could face Alex. "But I like it that I have yours."

"Oh, you definitely have mine. And I'm sorry about Francine. She got the sharp end of my tongue."

"As long as it's only ever the sharp end..." Morgan grinned. "Can we just stay like this?"

Alex caressed her face with a gentle palm. "I'd love to, but York beckons, and we need to vacate the rooms."

"Onwards then."

Chapter Fifty-Three

York

It was still frosty to say the least.

Francine sat back in her seat, head buried in her phone once more. Morgan turned enough that she could sprawl across the seat and slide her legs over Alex's lap and enjoy the teasing fingertips that swirled around her knee and inner thigh, rhythmically and unnoticed, as Alex continued to stare out of the window on their way to York.

Mack sat up front with Mike, his team going on ahead.

Neither reacted when Francine's phone rang. She answered it quickly with a brusque, "Hello…Yes, this is she."

Morgan rolled her eyes and put her face back into the magazine she was reading, using the opportunity to widen the space between her knees and subconsciously encourage further teasing higher up her thigh.

"Okay, are you sure?" Francine said, straightening up in her seat. "No, that's good. Yes, thank you for letting me know. Yes, I will pass that on. Okay. Goodbye."

Now, she had their attention as both Alex and Morgan turned towards her. Alex's fingers stilled instantly just as Morgan's legs clamped together, trapping her hand.

"That was Detective Siba," Francine said. "Apparently, the firecrackers and the note were the work of one of the choir boys who did it to get back at the choir master for berating him. He wanted to embarrass the school."

"Well, that's a relief," Alex said, squeezing Morgan's thigh.

"He said to say that the boy has completely owned up and apologises for scaring anyone."

"Right, so can we put all this behind us and stop talking about cancelling shows. We're over the hump now and—"

"I have a question," Morgan said, holding her hand up.

Alex and Francine looked at her and waited.

"Okay, so...who's Goran, and what is this plan you both keep going on about?"

"Let's get to the hotel, and I'll tell you everything." Alex smiled.

Room twelve was perfect as far as Morgan was concerned. More contemporary than the previous ones, it was light and airy, and on the ground floor with views over the gardens. The flowers were almost gone, and the grass was yellow in places, but still, even in the rain it was beautiful.

She wasted no time in placing her bag into the room. Only one bed. There was no pretence now of them having different rooms.

"This is amazing," she said as she strolled through the opening between the bedroom and the lounge. "I could live in something like this."

Alex smiled at her. "Good, you'll like my house then."

Morgan turned quickly. "Is that an invitation?"

"Well," Alex said, moving closer to her. "I thought once the tour was done, maybe..." She was right in front of Morgan now. "Maybe you'd like to come over. If you're not too busy with work, of course."

The mention of work made Morgan grimace comically. "God, I forgot about that." She laughed. "Is it bad that I haven't missed it one bit?"

"Nope, not bad at all, but maybe an inclination that you might prefer to do something else?"

"Maybe. I think the reality is I threw myself into it because I knew it would make my parents happy, but long term, I'm either going to burn out or..." She shrugged. "I dunno."

"It's never too late to make a change, Morgan. Try something else."

"I can definitely think of something else I'd rather be doing," she said, her cheeks blushing, "but I do believe that at some point, even that is going to even out. Anyway, stop distracting me, who's Goran?"

"Goran Ivanov," Alex finally said as she sat on the bed and swung her legs up. She was dressed in khaki combats and a baggy jumper over a white cotton shirt that looked as though it had seen better days, but Morgan knew was ridiculously expensive and made to look that way on purpose. Alex looked small and vulnerable as Morgan prepared to join her.

"Who is he?" Morgan asked.

"He's a multi-award-winning producer, hugely talented, and he wants to produce my next album."

"Okay," Morgan said, folding a jacket and holding it against herself. "So, some big wig in the music industry is rightly interested in working with you; what's the bigger picture?"

"Goran isn't known for his patience. He's a genius, but he's also someone who will only work with the best. He demands perfection. Commitment. Passion."

"And he wants to produce your next album?"

"Yes."

"So, why does Francine think you're scared to do it?"

Alex sighed. "Because she's right. I am scared. Working with him terrifies me."

"So, get another producer." Morgan flung the jacket onto the bed.

"Morgan," Alex got to her knees and shuffled down the bed, "if Ivanov produces my next work, it won't just be a hit. It will be a masterpiece. My mother will finally recognise me without the sly digs about popular music. It will be the kind of music that people six generations from now still talk about. It will make huge amounts of revenue—"

"So, all that's a win, right? It will catapult you into a fancier life."

"That's not why I'd be doing it," Alex stated, her eyes filling instantly with emotion. "That's not the life that I want. I exist in a world of transactions, of doing what I need to do to keep as low a profile as I can. Hiding you. Hiding me. In the shadows of life rather than in the sun. If I work with Ivanov and I get that album made—" She stopped talking, breathed in deeply and smiled. "Then I'm retiring and leaving all of this behind me."

Morgan stopped what she was doing and stared, dumbfounded. "You're—"

"I'm going to stop touring, stop the interviews, stop producing music for sale. I just want to merge into the background someplace where people forget all about me."

"But you love music and performing."

Alex smiled. "I won't stop enjoying music, but it will be nice to only play for me. To play because I want to, not because I have to." She reached for Morgan's hand. "I don't want to do this anymore. Living this life is…exhausting."

"But it won't be the same, will it? No audience, no euphoria." She smirked at Alex.

"I'm starting to realise that I have another supplier of that." Alex grinned at her, pulling her jumper up and over her head. "And in all honesty, I think I prefer it."

Morgan took a moment to digest those words. Was it so ridiculous to start imagining a life with this woman? This older, successful, talented, and beautiful woman.

Alex eyed her seriously. "You think you can handle that?" When Morgan's face became impassive, Alex laughed. "Being the source of my euphoria?"

"Well, I'll be too exhausted to even think about it," Morgan threw back, her fingers already unbuttoning the shirt Alex had revealed. "What with all the hours I'll be working while you're swanning around doing nothing."

"Maybe you should think about retiring too." She grinned when Morgan's fingers stopped on the third button. Alex took her hands and raised them to her mouth, kissing the backs of her fingers. "You could get set up in a small village surgery and work part-time."

"And be really flexible and have loads of spare time?"

"It's an idea." Morgan stepped back a pace and unbuttoned the rest of Alex's shirt, shrugging it off and dropping it to the ground. "I suddenly feel quite warm, Doctor. Maybe you could give me the once over?"

"Sure, why don't you take off all your clothes and lie back on the bed?"

"All of my clothes?" Alex hesitated, but the smirk couldn't hide her excitement.

"Yes, everything. I intend to do a full and very thorough examination."

"Well, in that case." Alex reached behind and unclipped her bra, dropping that to the floor, too, full breasts bouncing a little with the movement.

"Perfect," Morgan said before rushing out of the room. She found her medical bag. She didn't have a white coat, but the stethoscope around her neck would be enough for now. She could play Doctors; she was an expert in it. When she returned, she almost giggled at the speed with which Alex must have virtually ripped her clothes off in order to already be lying on the bed, was fast.

"It's a little cold in here now, don't you think, doctor?" Alex said when Morgan reappeared. Her nipples hard and erect quickly got Morgan's attention.

"Don't worry, it will soon heat up. Now, can you tell me, have you got any other symptoms that I should know about?"

Alex nodded, and bit her bottom lip. "Yes. I have this constant, throbbing ache."

"Really, that sounds torturous."

"It is, it's insistent. Do you think you could help with that?" Wide eyes stared up at Morgan and for a moment, anyone watching would think Alex was the younger of the two. All doe-eyed and innocent.

"Can you show me where this ache is?" Morgan asked, knowing already what the answer would be.

"Yes, it's right between my legs."

"I see." Morgan licked her lips and placed her palm on top of Alex's thigh. "Here?"

"A little higher."

Fingers glided several inches. "How about here?"

Parting her thighs a little, Alex said, "More central, at the top." She reached her hand down and took hold of Morgan's, bringing them closer, fingertips brushing against her lower lips. "More here."

"You say it's a constant, throbbing sensation?" Morgan asked, putting pressure against Alex's clitoris.

"God, yes, constant." She gasped, hips thrusting upward to meet the touch.

Morgan pressed again, moving slowly in circles. "And would you say that pressure eased the aching or made it worse?"

"Ease—definitely feels…better."

"Uh huh." Morgan moved her fingers away and lower, dipping into the heat of her lover and the wetness already abundant. She slid her fingers inside of her lover, and pressed up and back with curled fingers. "And how about now?"

"Hm hm, that helps."

Morgan moved her fingers back and forth, a come-hither motion that had Alex squirming and mewling. "I think the issue is a simple case of getting what you want." She smiled into the kiss. "Easily treatable, but a long-term condition."

Chapter Fifty-Four

Lincoln

The days were all rolling into one now they were on the last stages of the tour. York had been a success, as had every performance before it. Now, with their affair out in the open, at least with those who needed to know, Morgan was relaxed.

"There's been no panic attacks, and my ankle is fine," Alex said. "Go and enjoy the sights. I'll only be rehearsing and composing."

"Are you sure? I'd really love to go for a walk and check out the town. I might never come here again."

Alex grinned. "Of course, go and enjoy yourself."

"Okay, I have my phone if I'm needed." She bent down and kissed Alex on the top of the head while she ran the scales to loosen her joints.

Lincoln was a beautiful city full of old buildings and a lot of history. Morgan wandered the main street and perused the shop windows. She wanted to get something for Alex, something that was cute but fancy, and would remind her of Morgan when they were apart – which was bound to be the case often when all of this was over, and she went back to her real life and the hospital.

It was strange, she considered, how so much had happened in such a relatively small amount of time. Just a few days, not even a month, and her entire life felt as though it had twisted on an axis and something magical was happening.

She'd been in love before, and she recognised the signs instantly. She was falling for Alex, and the feelings were mutual. She grinned to herself as she stared in through the window of a clothes store at the silk scarf covered in musical notes.

She went inside and examined it. Not quite what she was looking for, but it was perfect. Silky soft as it slid between her fingers. Her imagination found an image of her wrists bound by it to a bed, Alex on top of her doing all manner of unspeakable things. The idea excited her, and she took the scarf to the till and paid the extortionate price. Tucking the wrapped package into her bag, she moved towards the door and as she was about to step out, she stopped. Right there in front of her was someone she hadn't expected to see.

Blonde hair, average height. The woman, no more than twenty feet away. Laurel. This was now beyond coincidence, wasn't it?

Morgan froze. Unable to take her eyes off of her, she watched as Laurel scrutinised her. No expression on her face, just a blank stare, hands limply hanging by her side.

Slowly, Morgan turned around and contemplated leaving through another exit, but there wasn't one. When she looked back, she half expected that Laurel would have vanished, but she hadn't. She was just stood there, still staring across the street at Morgan through the glass.

You have dealt with so much more than this, Morgan told herself. She reached for the door handle and opened it as calmly as she could and stepped outside into the bustling street.

"What do you want?" Morgan asked. She didn't need to shout. Laurel just continued to stare at her, or through her, Morgan wasn't sure, but she felt emboldened, even though she knew Alex would say it was stupid, Mack would agree, and god only knew what Francine would say.

Actually, she thought Francine would probably be the only one on her side, and maybe Nancy. Morgan stepped forward, one, then two, then three steps until they were barely ten feet away from one another. "Why are you doing this?"

There was no denial. As though coming out of a trance, Laurel's focus came to life, held in place by Morgan's slow approach.

"You have to go," she said, and Morgan felt a chill run down her spine.

There was something cold in her eyes, something not all there, as though she were in a different headspace to the rest of the world. It unnerved Morgan, and she'd seen a lot of people like this over the years, but not quite so personal as when the woman repeated her threat.

"You have to go. She's not yours. You have no business being in my place."

"I'm not going anywhere," Morgan responded as boldly as she could, but she'd stopped moving any closer.

"You will, you'll leave, just like all the rest. I just have to wait."

"I'm not going anywhere," Morgan repeated.

A siren blasted from somewhere, maybe the next street. It was close and loud and made Morgan jump a little. She turned in the direction it came from, and when she turned back, Laurel was gone.

She looked left, and then right. No sight of her.

Hurriedly, Morgan made her way back towards the cathedral. She needed to warn Alex.

Morgan could hear the sound of the piano playing the moment she opened the side door and flashed her ID card at the man currently guarding it. She breathed a sigh of relief. If Alex was playing, then she was fine.

Her heels click-clacked as she made her way quickly down the corridor and wound her way out into the area where the altar stood and where the choir would sing. The stage area, and where Alex currently sat on her stool at the piano, were in the centre of the N.W. and S.W. Transept. Her fingers glided across the keys, then she stopped momentarily to speak with Jessie.

Glancing around, Morgan found Mack standing to one side. His eyeline was already on her, eyes narrowing. She headed towards him.

"What's up?" he asked quickly.

Morgan looked sideways at Alex before she said, "Laurel, I saw her again. She spoke to me."

Mack straightened. "What did she say?"

The sense of relief to finally be able to relax hit Morgan, and she felt hot tears spring to her eyes, ready to cascade down her cheeks. "She said that I need to go. Th—that..." She felt her words stutter.

"It's okay, take your time," Mack reassured.

"Alex isn't mine, and that I...I've no business being...in her place." There was no stopping the tears once she'd got it all out. She hadn't even noticed that the music had ceased.

"What's going on?" Alex's voice cut through the air and Morgan turned, falling into her arms, trembling. "Hey, what's all this?" Alex held her close, one hand protectively around the back of Morgan's head, the other flat against her back.

"She's back," Morgan managed to say before Mack cut in.

"Laurel, Morgan saw her again."

"She said, I have to go, that you're...you're not mine." Morgan clung harder to Alex. "I was taking her place."

"Good god, what is wrong with her?"

"Look, we've got all the doors covered. She's not getting in. I'll check with the hotel to see if she's booked in."

"What about the police?" Alex asked. "Surely they must be able to do something now?"

"I'll inform them, and I'll insist on having some visibility tomorrow," Mack responded, already holding his phone. "Don't worry, we're going to keep you both safe."

"Come on, let's go back to the hotel." Alex stood back, taking Morgan's chin in her hand, staring deeply into her eyes. "Let's do that, shall we? Lock the door and it will be just you and me."

Morgan nodded and wiped her face on a tissue Mack held out for her. "Thanks. I feel like an idiot." She sniffed.

"No, I'm the idiot. I didn't consider for one moment that she would go after you." Alex took her hand. "I want this stopped," she said firmly to Mack. "It's one thing coming after me, but she doesn't get Morgan. That's not the transaction."

Chapter Fifty-Five

Morgan sat on the couch with her hand wrapped around a glass of scotch, gently sipping at it. Alex sat down beside her, the cushions shifting until she was comfortable.

They'd been back at the hotel for almost an hour. Alex had done her interviews and Francine had made sure that she had the rest of the evening and night to rest. Dinner was ordered.

"Are you alright now?" Alex asked when Morgan settled. She felt her nodding against her chest.

"Yes. I think Mack was right, it was the adrenaline. I went into the shop to—" She sat up suddenly. "I forgot all about that." She chuckled and got up, placing the glass on the table. Her bag was on the floor by the door, where she'd dropped it in her haste to sit down and leave everything outside.

"What did you forget?"

Bringing her bag back over to the couch, Morgan rifled through it as she said, "I got you something." She plonked back down where she'd been sitting before and held out the smaller package from inside. "It's not anything too exciting, but—"

"You bought me something, that in itself is exciting," Alex assured as Morgan handed it over.

"I hope you like it."

Alex unwrapped the paper and plucked the silk square up in her fingers. The fabric slid and opened up. "It's beautiful," Alex said, running her fingers down the edged seam.

"You like it?"

"Yes, thank you." Alex leaned in and kissed her gently. There was a reverence to it rather than the passionate need. Noticing the name on the tag, she said, "This must have cost—"

"You're worth it, and I can afford it."

"You can?" Alex smiled.

"Yes, I got this really cushy job that pays me a huge amount of money to pretty much sit around doing nothing."

"Sounds like a perfect gig?"

"It is. I'm kind of enjoying it too." Morgan grinned.

"Lots of perks?"

Morgan shrugged. "I guess so." She reached for the scarf and wrapped it around her wrist. "Does it suit me?"

"Looks perfect." Alex smirked. "Is it a gift for me, or you?"

"I was thinking both of us."

There was a knock at the door. A double *tap, tap*. Mack with dinner.

"Let's eat, I'm actually starving." Alex stood up and reached her hand down for Morgan, who took it and allowed herself to be pulled up, landing chest to chest with her lover. "I have a feeling we're going to need the calories."

"I have a feeling I'm going to need to go on a diet when I get home." Morgan grinned when the aroma hit her senses. "I don't think I've ever eaten this much."

"Is it too much?" Alex asked. "I've always skipped lunch and gone all out at dinner, but if you need something—"

"It's fine. I'm not complaining. When I'm on shift, I'm lucky if I manage to shove half a sandwich in before I'm needed to check on a patient. A banana in my pocket is generally my go-to. Sometimes, it will be someone's birthday and I might grab a cupcake."

"Sounds truly awful." Alex smiled. "How do you survive like that?"

Morgan shrugged. "I guess it becomes normal."

"Well, let's make the most of it then." She lifted the lid from the plate and pushed it across the table towards Morgan. "And then I was thinking we could go down and enjoy the spa?"

"Together?" Morgan asked, picking up her cutlery.

"Yes, I think it would do us both the world of good. I rarely get to enjoy the things hotels offer. Honestly, I don't know why Francine books them, it's a complete waste of money." She smiled. "But I do get to enjoy some semblance of privacy, so I suppose it's worth it."

"Don't fancy slumming it then?"

"I'm not above slumming it." She looked around the room. "But I guess I am a creature of comfort, and while I can afford it, I think I should just enjoy it."

"Well, I for one, would love to spend the rest of the evening getting wet with you." Morgan smirked.

Chapter Fifty-Six

The pool area was just as beautiful as the rest of the hotel. Lots of glass windows in the ceiling allowed sunlight in during the day but at almost 9 p.m., it gave the area a more relaxed feel. Loungers lined the entire wall of one side of the room, with others dotted between huge pot plants that allowed a minimal amount of privacy.

Morgan chose those as the position to dump their bag and towels. On the opposite side of the pool was a jacuzzi. Two women sat together with champagne flutes in hand, chatting and laughing quietly. The pool itself was empty except for one man powering back and forth, head down, goggles steaming up. He managed five lengths while they settled and peeled off their robes.

It was warm, and music played softly through the speakers. Some kind of spa-sounding vibe meant to relax and quiet the mind.

"This is lovely," Alex said.

"Isn't it?" Morgan agreed, dropping her robe to the lounger. "Coming in?" she beckoned, stepping backwards until she was on the edge of the pool. With a grin, she closed her eyes, pinched her nose, and took another step, disappearing as she dropped into the deep end. She reappeared a moment later, pushing her mane from her face, as one arm half pulled her up and rested along the edge. "It's so warm in here. Like a bath."

"Don't worry, I'm coming." Alex smiled at her. "But I'm walking in." She chuckled and made her way around the side of the pool slowly so as not to slip and injure her ankle again. The two women in the jacuzzi suddenly stopped talking as they realised who she was. She smiled at them but continued on until she reached the walk-in steps.

Morgan had swum over and was treading water, waiting.

"Gert is going to have a fit when she finds out I've been swimming and soaked my hair in chlorine," Alex said when she was close enough that she didn't need to shout. At the bottom step, she sunk down so only her head was above water and made her way over to Morgan.

Instantly, two long legs wrapped themselves around her waist. Arms followed around her neck with a kiss that heated every fibre of her being.

"I didn't realise swimming was quite so exciting."

Morgan grinned. "You know, I love that we don't have to hide us."

"Yes, though we still have to be careful not to upset Francine with any more public order offences."

"Like making out in a hotel pool." Morgan laughed at the look that covered Alex's face. "Okay, I promise to, what does she say? Keep it in my pants in public."

"Indeed." Alex tilted her head and kissed her again. "Once we're done and get home, it will be a little manic. I might not see you for a while, what with me being in the studio and you going back to work."

Morgan nodded and smiled sadly. "I know, but I think if we really want it to work then it's going to be the best test of our relationship. This isn't normal, what we have now is magical but not real life, and as much as we both hope it will be just as exciting, we should prepare for the distance to hit us hard."

"Hm, I already don't like it." Alex laughed. "But I've never been somebody who needs to live in someone else's pocket, and I kind of feel like you're the same. So, I think we will make it work."

"I'm not walking away."

"So, are we going to swim or just stay like this?" Alex asked, looking around them. The man who had been swimming had stopped at one end for a rest, ignoring them completely, but something else caught her eye. "For the love of—" She untangled herself from Morgan, her gaze fixed and steely on something behind them.

Morgan turned and set eyes on Laurel, standing by the lounger next to theirs.

"Alex," Morgan said, reaching out to grab at her lover's arm, but she slid from her grasp. "Leave it."

It was too late. Alex was already swimming back to the steps, and before Morgan could catch up, she was marching up them, water splashing everywhere. This time, she ignored the women in the jacuzzi and marched around the pool until she was within ten feet of Laurel.

"What the hell are you playing at?" she said, her voice echoing more loudly than intended. "You need to stop this. How dare you intimidate and threaten Morgan?"

"I don't know what you're talking about. I'm just enjoying a holiday and trying to relax by the pool," Laurel said, all doe-eyed and whimsical. "I'm not doing anything to you, Alex, or your precious girlfriend." Laurel's line of sight moved. "She's pretty." When she turned her attention back to Alex, she said, "How old is she?"

"I swear to god, if you ever come near me or Morgan again, I'll—"

"Alex," Morgan said from behind her. "Just walk away. She's not worth it."

Laurel's demeanour changed in an instant. From laid back and childlike innocence, she launched up from the lounger towards Morgan.

"Don't you speak about me like that," Laurel said, hands raised and ready to lash out. "I am worth it," she screamed and sprang forward.

She didn't get anywhere near Morgan. Alex stepped in between them, raising her hands, and shoved Laurel hard in the chest. "Back off, you do not touch her." And with one more almighty shove, Laurel was propelled backwards, fully clothed, into the pool. "I won't tell you again," Alex shouted at her as she leaned over the edge and glared down at Laurel, who was flapping about and screaming. "Stay away."

"That's assault," Laurel spluttered and sank under the water before popping back up again, righting herself enough to swim to the edge. "I'll have you arrested," she shrieked at Alex's back.

"Move," Morgan said quickly, pushing Alex towards their things. She swiped up their robes and handed one to Alex before grabbing their bags and hurriedly exiting the pool area. "We need to get out of here, right now."

Alex didn't say another word. She was getting good at doing as she was told.

Chapter Fifty-Seven

Francine strolled in like a woman on a mission.

"I thought the spa was supposed to relax you, not turn you into Rambo. What were you thinking, Alex?" she asked, looking back and forth between the pair of them. "And where the hell were you?" she said, turning to Mack.

He held his hands up. "We checked with the hotel, they had no one booked in under Laurel Canning. I searched further afield and found a room booking at another hotel. My guys went down to the spa, checked it all out, there was nothing there to concern us, so I posted a couple of guys outside. Somehow, she slipped past them. I can only apologise and say that we are working to make sure that doesn't happen again."

Francine shook her head. "Get out."

"I really think—" Mack tried to continue but was met with an ice-cold glare.

"I said, get out."

This time he didn't argue. When the door was closed, and it was just the three of them, Francine said, "So, the good news is, I had already made a complaint about her stalking you to the police. Coupled with the previous instances, it shouldn't be difficult for the police to prove that she's, at the very least, been intimidating you both."

"Okay, well that's—" Alex was about to add, good before Francine held up a finger forcing her to stop.

"There's nothing good about it. You pushed someone into the pool. The hotel is fuming. By law they don't require a lifeguard because they expect their guests to behave with decorum and not push each other into the pool fully clothed."

"Are we being thrown out?" Morgan asked in astonishment. She'd never been asked to leave anywhere before.

Francine tutted. "Don't be ridiculous. She's Sasha, not Ozzy Osbourne. However, I did have to explicitly agree that you would not leave the suite for the duration of your stay except to go to the cathedral and back."

"For god's sake, this is madness. The woman is stalking me, and I'm somehow the bad guy?"

"Nobody thinks you're the bad guy," Morgan said, wrapping her arms around Alex's shoulders.

"It feels like it." Alex reached up, wrapping her arms around Morgan's. "I'm livid."

"I've let a few more reliable websites and journalists know that there's a weird fan bothering you. Hopefully, that will head off any potential gossip should she try and sell the story."

"Thank you," Alex said, still annoyed.

"What I suggest we all do now is get a good night's sleep and ride out whatever happens tomorrow. I'm going to hope it all blows over." Francine picked up her bag and headed for the door. "And do not leave this room."

Morgan flopped down onto the bed and breathed a deep sigh. Staring up at the ceiling, she pondered the events of earlier. "How is she finding out where we are all the time?"

Alex was brushing her teeth in the adjoining bathroom. "Don't know," she said quickly before spitting and rinsing. She re-emerged wiping her face on a small towel. "I was thinking that. I trust everyone on the team. I can't see any of them risking their job, or future work for what basically is a nobody asking them for information."

"Yeah, that makes sense." She recalled Nancy saying how jobs like this didn't come around often, you grabbed them and hoped you'd earn a good rep and other tours would become available. "So, how's she doing it?"

"It's common knowledge where I'm touring, and fans find out where I'm staying all the time. There are plenty of fan groups that swap that kind of information. So, I guess it's just as possible that Laurel is a member of them and gets the same information. It's quite common for fans to book rooms in the same hotel, hoping they can get a better chance of meeting me."

"That's just obsessive," Morgan said, turning onto her side and resting her head in her hand.

"It is, but usually harmless. Mostly, they just want pictures and autographs and bragging rights to be able to say they spoke to me or saw me."

"Honestly, I think I will be glad when this tour is over."

"Me too." Alex smiled, climbing onto the bed. "In the meantime, we have three shows left after tomorrow night."

"When will you find out about Goran, and how quickly will you start working on the new album with him?"

"If he wants me."

"Of course he will." Morgan reached out and grabbed a handful of Alex's t-shirt, dragging her down to her level. "He's a fool if he doesn't."

"Well, I've already decided, whether he does or doesn't, I'm still going ahead with the plan. I have enough money to live a very nice life, and I already have everything I need. Now I've found you, I'm happier than I have been in a very long time."

"Really? You're not embarrassed?" Morgan asked.

Alex looked shocked. "No, why would you say that?"

Morgan shrugged. "Just…it was the comment about how old I was that set you to push her."

"There was a moment when we first met that I worried about it a little, I'm not going to lie, but the more we've spent time together, the more I realise we're…" She reached up and cupped Morgan's cheek. "I don't care about the age gap; I cared that she was mocking it. She was mocking you, and us, and I won't stand for it."

"I really like you." Morgan grinned before kissing her hard and firm. "Really like you."

Chapter Fifty-Eight

The phone ringing in the lounge was not an expected event. Alex dragged herself out of bed and lifted the receiver, mumbling, "Yes."

"Ms Montgomery, this is the hotel manager, Gareth. We have some gentlemen down in the lobby who would like to speak to you."

"What? Who?" Alex rubbed her face. It wasn't even 8 a.m. yet.

The voice on the phone went quiet as he whispered, "Ms Montgomery, it's the police, they want to speak to you following last night's…incident."

"Okay, send them up." She was about to put the phone down when she heard him speak again.

"I'm sorry, I did offer that, but they insist that you come down." He sounded awfully apologetic. "Also, they asked if Dr Kelly would come down too."

"They will have to wait. I'm not dressed yet."

"I'll let them know and ask them to wait in the bar area."

"Thank you, Gareth." She put the phone down and didn't move.

From behind her, she heard, "Everything alright?"

Twisting quickly, she tried a smile. "Yes, the police are downstairs. They want to speak to me and you about last night. No doubt finally they're going to arrest Laurel and put an end to this behaviour of hers.

"Good. Are they coming up? We should get dressed."

"No, we have to go downstairs. I don't know why."

"Alexandra Katerina Montgomery, I am arresting you on suspicion of common assault. You do not have to say anything…" The officer's words disappeared into the frenzy of other things being shouted.

"You are kidding me," Francine said as she watched the video that was now all over social media. A video that showed a bikini-clad Sasha, stalking around the pool to berate Laurel who was, to the rest of the world, minding her own business on a lounger, before the argument kicked up a gear and Alex pushed Laurel twice, the second time resulting in her being pushed into the pool. She turned it off and made a call.

"Phillip, we have a problem."

"You can't arrest her. She hasn't done anything wrong," Morgan was saying before another officer stepped up to her and said, "Dr Morgan Kelly, I am arresting you also on suspicion of common assault. You do not have to say anything, but it may harm your defence if you do not mention when questioned something which you later rely on in court. Anything you do say may be given in evidence." She was turned around, and handcuffs were produced and slapped around her wrists.

"Is that really necessary?" Francine complained once both of them were detained.

"Just doing our job, Ms?"

"Carlson, Francine Carlson, and I'll be taking this up with someone more senior. Where are you taking them?"

"Local nick, they'll be interviewed and then released or charged. Feel free to arrange a brief, otherwise one can be arranged for them," the first officer said before moving forward and taking Alex, followed by Morgan, out through the lobby of the hotel.

Guests gawped; some took photos on their phones, others just videoed the entire thing. Outside on the street, the press were already waiting. They'd had a tip-off, clearly. Cameras flashed, and questions were shouted out in the melee to get answers and a headline. Paparazzi grabbed shots of the pair of them being escorted out of the hotel and into a waiting police van.

It was less than two minutes before Francine's phone alerted her to the first uploads on social media.

"Shit," she mumbled and followed, Mack in tow. "This is your fault," she bellowed at him. "Get in the car."

In the back of the van, Morgan sat beside Alex on an uncomfortable bench surrounded by white metal grated doors. It was dark inside and noisy as the vehicle sped away, bumpy roads tossing them around.

"Don't say anything. Francine will get Philip, and he will sort this all out," Alex said. "Try not to worry."

"Worry? Alex, we've been arrested."

"But we haven't done anything wrong; self-defence isn't a crime."

Morgan turned her head and gave her the side eye.

"Are we going to be put into a cell?" Morgan asked, acutely aware of the seriousness of it all.

"Honestly, I don't know. I didn't think we'd be the ones being arrested. I'm going to kill Laurel."

"Don't even bloody joke about it. That woman has caused enough trouble," Morgan said, shifting herself as close to Alex as she could get. "We just have to tell the truth, and everything will be fine, right?"

"Yes, exactly. I'm sure Francine is already dealing with it."

It wasn't a long journey before the van stopped, almost knocking them off the bench as the brakes were applied.

"Maybe they don't like classical music," Morgan grumbled, just managing to stop herself from falling to the floor.

Alex couldn't stop herself from laughing. "Oh god, I hope so."

The back door was flung open and the same two officers helped them out. More photographers snapped away. With their hands cuffed there was nothing either of them could do to hide their faces. So, Alex raised her chin and stopped, giving them the image they wanted.

"What have you done, Sasha?" one called out.

"Defended myself against a stalker," she shouted back before being pushed away and into the police station.

"I thought you said say nothing," Morgan muttered.

Alex stared at the officers explaining to the duty sergeant who they were and why they were here. "To them, say nothing to them. Not until Philip gets here."

"Who is Philip?"

Alex exhaled. "My mother's lawyer. The family lawyer. The only man I'd trust in this situation."

Chapter Fifty-Nine

The media frenzy at the hotel when they all returned was bordering on ridiculous. Mike skirted around the back, but they were still greeted with several paparazzi willing to take the risk that this would be the move they made.

Mack had men in place already holding them back while Morgan, Alex and Francine vacated the car and ran for the entrance held open by Gareth.

"Welcome back," he said before wincing at the absurdity of it.

Alex thanked him anyway but didn't linger. They took a staff lift up and were back inside their suite by 4 p.m.

"I'm starving," Alex said. "Can you get something sent up for lunch? Soup, sandwiches, that kind of thing?" she asked Gareth as he was backing out of the room. "We missed breakfast."

"Absolutely, leave it with me." He smiled, turning and almost bumping into someone. "Oh, I am so sorry."

"No doubt, you did not see me," the distinctive voice floated in.

Alex stiffened.

Francine muttered an, "Oh fuck."

And Morgan frowned at the pair of them, confused by the reaction, until she looked back at the door, and a woman appeared. Tall, dark-haired but greying, elegance oozed from her as she all but floated into the room.

"Sasha." Her accent would have been the giveaway if it wasn't for the fact that she looked exactly how you'd expect Alex would look in twenty years-time.

"Mama. What are you doing here?"

"My child, did you think you would be arrested, all over the news, and I wouldn't hear about it?" The eyebrow arched as she turned towards Francine. "You just letting this ship run aground, Ms Carlson?"

"Mrs Montgomery," Francine said, very formally. "I think we both know I wouldn't be letting that happen, but—"

"And yet, here we are." The tone was flat and uninterested. Her head swivelled, and now it was Morgan's turn. "Ah, the accomplice, and the lover, I assume?"

"Mama, this is Dr Morgan Kelly." Alex stepped forward to introduce them. Morgan smiled nervously and held out a hand, the fingers of which were touched, barely.

"It's lovely to meet you," Morgan said.

The Tsarina breathed deeply. "We will see how lovely it is in a moment when my daughter explains the reason she is so desperately trying to denigrate herself in front of the world."

"That isn't what—" Morgan stopped speaking when Alex shook her head.

"Alexandra could speak from the age of twenty months, a child genius they called her. So, I think she can manage to speak for herself now, don't you, Dr Kelly?" She turned back to Alex. "Do you want to explain why our family is being dragged through the mire, Sasha?"

Francine poked Morgan, then nodded her head towards the door. Morgan silently shook her head. "No," she mouthed. Francine widened her eyes and pressed her lips together, the nod of her head to the door much more pronounced. Morgan's eyes narrowed, her mouth screwing up in annoyance. But Alex smiling and nodding at her meant she followed when Francine left the room.

Alex walked across the room to the bar, lifted the bottle of vodka from the shelf and poured two glasses over ice. She handed one to her mother, who raised a brow.

"Ice?"

"I like it cold," she answered. "We're not in Moscow, it's not minus fifteen outside, and I don't think now is the time to shake it and make cocktails."

Her mother smiled and then swallowed the glassful in one mouthful. "Not bad," she said, placing the glass down and then taking a seat on the couch, one leg crossing the other. "Sit, talk."

"I have a stalker," Alex said, taking a seat opposite her mother, "and if she was just bothering me, I'd handle it, but she's not. She went after Morgan, and that's not something I am prepared to let slide."

"This Morgan, she means that much to you? You barely know her."

"I know what I need to know, and I know that I want to know more," she said firmly. "Why are you here, Mama?"

"I can't visit my daughter, come to her recital and show my support when she's being dragged through the mud by an upstart trying to unsettle her when she needs to focus?" The Tsarina stood up, walked over to the bar, picked up the vodka, and brought it back to the table. "Goran won't wait forever. We cannot afford to allow this…Laurel? To create an issue."

"If my protecting Morgan is an issue for Goran, then so be it. I don't care about that. I won't risk the best thing that's happened to me in order to further my career."

"And are you now a criminal?"

Alex sighed and sat back. "Morgan wasn't charged. I, on the other hand, have been charged with common assault. I have to wait to see if the CPS will take it forward or not. Philip thinks the evidence is sound so, most likely, I will go to court and have to defend my name. Worst case is six months in prison—" Her mother gasped audibly. "But the likelihood is, as she wasn't injured and I didn't hit her with a fist, it will be a fine."

"So, a criminal." Her mother smirked, and Alex studied her.

"You don't seem to be bothered. I thought you'd be upset."

"You are more my daughter than you think you are."

"Am I? I always thought I was a disappointment."

Her mother chuckled. "Never. If I am hard on you, it's because I see so much potential, to be so much more." She poured another vodka. "I gave it all up for love, Sasha, and I never regretted a day of it. You, your brothers, your father, you all became my purpose. And how do you think that happened? That the authorities just shrugged and said, oh yes, you go elsewhere and be happy? No, I had to fight. I had to break the law, become a criminal, to get what I wanted."

Alex reached for the vodka she'd originally poured; she'd never heard her mother speak like this.

"If she brings you passion, and lights up your life then you must choose that path. But you must understand, it will come with a cost, Sasha."

"Doesn't everything? My life is an endless transaction."

"Greatness is often a lonely place. When I danced, there would be a room filled with all the best people, but on stage, it was just me. I chose not to be lonely. But I think sometimes lonely is where you are most comfortable, never letting any of us in."

Alex scoffed. "What? You push and push and push, my entire life, expectations, and other people's dreams. The only time I found my own path, people died."

"You blame yourself for the accident? No, you must never…this is not your fault. I pushed you, yes, of course. I gave you life, but God gave you the talent. Why waste it?" She shifted in her seat until she perched on the very edge, and then she reached out with her hands and took Alex's. "I pushed you to be the woman who could live in this world of men, and demand more from it. To become a great woman, who wouldn't shy away when her passion is so vigorous. You love your Morgan enough to risk prison, to risk Goran. That, my child, is passion." She looked at her watch. "And now, you go, and you put all of that into your music. You show the world what it means to Sasha to be in love."

Chapter Sixty

Ely

Ely, not ee-lie, but ee-lee, as Alex had had to tell Francine every time she said the word out loud.

"They could just spell things properly," Francine complained while Morgan tried not to laugh too loudly at the pair of them. The whole "ee-lee, ee-lie" debate had moved into various other places around the UK that made absolutely no sense. Morgan had to admit, on a fair few she might agree with the American.

"What is in Ely anyway?" Morgan asked. "I don't think I've been this way very much. Holidays in our house always ended up in Dorset, or abroad."

"There's a cathedral," Francine said dryly.

Alex smiled at the pair of them. "It's a beautiful town."

"With no decent hotels," Francine continued to grumble. Alex couldn't blame her, as she'd been busy these past few days fending off journalists. Alex was under strict instructions not to speak to the press. Regardless of what was said, they would have their day in court. Until then, Laurel could mouth off all she wanted. Evidence would speak for itself, Philip had instructed.

Checked into the Airbnb, unpacked, and lounging on the sofa by midday was perfect as far as Morgan was concerned. Alex was at the piano playing the piece that Morgan knew was for her. She smiled at that, even when Alex grumbled to herself, stopped and reworked something until she liked it and jotted down the new notes. If pressed, Morgan would have to agree that she probably wouldn't have noticed the changes that occurred regularly from each venue to the next that Alex played it, but there had been many. The more involved they became, the more they fell for one another, and the more emotion it evoked in her.

Alex played the piece from start to finish again and then closed the piano lid and sat up straight, swivelling on her stool to face Morgan.

"Did you want to go and do something?"

Morgan peered over the back of the couch. "Like what?"

Alex shrugged. "I don't know." She stood. "But it's my only day off until the tour ends, and I just thought it would be nice to do something."

"I'd love that," Morgan said, swinging her legs around to sit up properly. "Could we go into town and look around?" She slumped back into the soft sofa. "But what about Laurel?"

"What about her? She's not allowed anywhere near us." Alex held out a hand for Morgan to take and then pulled her to her feet. "Unless you'd rather—"

"No, I want to go out. I think we can manage one day without the need for you to ravish me." She smirked.

"Not that I'm counting, but I don't think I've actually ever been this intimate with anyone, almost every day for three weeks—" Alex admitted.

"Enjoy it while it lasts. But not now. Right now, I want to go for a nice walk, mooch around the shops, maybe stop for a coffee, and cake. I absolutely want cake."

Alex grinned. "Then that is what we shall do."

"Do you think the police will work it out that she's the cause of this mess?" Morgan said, unable to quite let the Laurel situation go.

"She can't bother us, Morgan."

Morgan stepped closer, brushing the back of her hand lightly against Alex's cheek. "I just want her gone, so we can relax and enjoy this."

"Then let's do that regardless. I'll call Mack and let him know we're heading out and if he insists on tagging along, that he's to do it from a distance."

"And we're not going anywhere near the cathedral until tomorrow. No work talk." Morgan grinned as Alex slipped from her grasp to find her phone.

"Yes, ma'am." Alex saluted while the phone rang. "Mack, we're going out."

"Alright, I'll be right there. Oh, and I got the information you asked about, the phone number. It comes back to a Sharon Ingles. She's a primary school teacher in Cumbria."

Alex felt a sense of relief. "Thank you, that puts my mind at ease greatly."

"No problem. I'll follow discreetly, enjoy the day."

Hair up, baseball cap on and a with long flowing black coat that reached right down to her booted feet, Alex walked arm in arm with Morgan up one side of the high street, stopping to look in shop windows they passed before reaching the end and crossing over to walk back.

"Fancy a coffee yet?" Morgan asked, checking over her shoulder just in case. She didn't trust that Laurel wouldn't ignore the law and just do what she wanted.

Alex noticed but said nothing, not giving Laurel any more power to come between them. "Mm, sounds good. I'm a little peckish, too."

"There was a nice little place about halfway up. We could try that. Maybe they'll have a sandwich or something?"

"I was thinking more along the lines of that huge cream cake." Alex laughed and pulled her closer. "I'm enjoying this."

Morgan met her stare and held it. "Me too." She leaned forward and chanced a quick kiss. "What you said earlier about it being not even three weeks, I feel so—" She smiled. "I know technically it's been longer. Your hospital visit was months ago, but it's like I've always known you."

"I know. It could be three months, three years, I just..." Alex breathed deeply. "I want this. When we get back, I really want *this*." She emphasised the last word. "Being able to just wander a high street and go for a coffee, and kiss, without being bothered by anyone." She was about to say something else when a raindrop hit her face, and then another. "Come on, we'll have to run, or we'll get drenched."

"Oh, I dunno, I quite like it when you're wet," Morgan teased before her hand was grabbed and she was pulled at speed along the street, both of them laughing like teenagers until finally the café appeared and Alex pushed the door open, and they both stumbled inside. "Grab that table. I'll get the drinks."

"And cake," Alex reminded with a grin before she turned and headed across the room to nab the only table still available. A moment later, Mack entered, looked around to ensure there were no potential issues and then stepped back outside, where he stood on guard in the rain. Alex couldn't decide between rolling her eyes or chuckling at the absurdity of it all. She couldn't wait for this part of her life to be over with.

Pulling her coat off, Alex hung it around the back of the chair before sitting down and taking off the hat. She looked around at the paintings hanging on the wall, art for sale. Most were drawings and paintings of the cathedral from various angles. Others were a more scenic landscape of the Fens. Turning back to the queue to see how much longer Morgan would be, she found a pair of eyes trained on her.

An older woman, her mother's age, she guessed. Half hidden behind a pair of glasses and a woolly hat. She smiled in that way people did when they recognised her but weren't going to make a big deal of it. Alex was grateful for that and smiled back. The woman raised a finger to her lips and made a shushing face before she picked up her cup and continued to drink.

Everyone else was too busy chatting, or just hadn't noticed her, or didn't know who she was, which happened more often than not. People don't expect a celebrity to be sitting in their local café.

Alex watched as Morgan paid with her card, then picked up the tray and casually made her way through, past the sticking-out chairs. She was smiling, looking happy, and Alex considered that it might be the most beautiful she'd ever looked. Her hair was haphazardly pulled into a ponytail of curls, little wayward ringlets snagging free and hanging around her face.

"They didn't have any cream cakes, so I got you a rather large slab of lemon meringue," Morgan said, feeling pleased with herself. She sat down, passed the plate across, and held up two forks. "I thought we could share."

"Share?" Alex said, her eyes sparkling with a playfulness that Morgan found enticing. "I suppose I could let you have that end piece."

Morgan thought for a moment before she leaned forward and whispered, "You could do that, and you could suffer the consequences."

"Hm, interesting point." Alex reached for the pot of tea and lifted the lid to stir the pot. "What kind of consequences?"

Picking up her mug of milky coffee, Morgan took a sip before she said, "I would have to consider how much of this body I'd want to share later."

"Hardly the same thing." Alex chuckled. "But I see your point." She pushed the plate to the centre of the table. "I was thinking about later and thought we could lounge on the sofa and watch a film. I'll get Francine to get us some popcorn and—"

"Hotdogs," Morgan insisted. "With mustard and onions. Can we have those?"

"I'm sure we can. What do you want to watch?" she asked, realising they didn't know many basic things about each other. "What kind of films do you like?"

"Comedy, romance, I don't mind really, anything that has a good story. You?"

"Spy thrillers, not horror though. I'm too much of a scaredy cat for that." Alex laughed and cut the side of her fork into the cake before she shovelled the mouthful onto the tines and held it up to feed Morgan.

Morgan leaned in, opened her mouth slowly and accepted the offering. "Mm, that's so good," she said halfway through as it melted in her mouth.

"We should get another slice for later," Alex suggested.

"I can get on board with that." Morgan smiled. "So, murder mysteries?"

"Hm?" Alex asked, her eyes locked on Morgan. "You look so beautiful. Did I tell you that?"

Subconsciously, Morgan reached for her hair and tried to smooth it down somewhat. "Thank you. I'm pretty sure I've looked better."

"Is there a limit on how often you can look beautiful to me?" Alex smiled and dug in for another mouthful, this time for herself. "And yes, murder sounds fun."

"What kind of music do you listen to? I assume you like music, of course."

"I like music," Morgan answered, grinning as she plunged her fork into the soft meringue. "I have a confession though." She sat back and watched Alex.

"You had no idea who I was?"

"Not quite. I'd heard of you, and knew why you were famous but… I'd never really listened to your music, not until after I got home that day from treating you at the hospital. I sat on the balcony with a glass of Ribena and let the smart speaker play your greatest hits, while I read all about you online."

"Oh, so you stalked me," Alex said playfully.

"Of course." Morgan winked. "I was hoping you'd call me, and I'd need to have reference points to continue the conversation."

"Hm, you were rather forward."

Morgan laughed loudly. "Uh huh, and in Winchester you hesitated because you didn't think I knew what I wanted."

"I wouldn't quite put it like that." Alex giggled. "I just…didn't want to take advantage."

"It's a good job I rectified that issue then, isn't it?" Morgan smirked, stealing the last bite.

Chapter Sixty-One

Canterbury

Francine was grinning as she scanned the media and socials she followed on Alex's behalf. "Tide is turning," she said gleefully, reaching for a coffee cup without looking.

"What do you mean?" Morgan asked.

Placing the tablet onto the table, Francine swigged her coffee, wincing when she realised it was cold. Then she shrugged and drank it anyway.

"The conversations happening online are now much less shocked at the fact Sasha would push someone into a pool, and more about how terrible it is that she was being pursued by lunatic intent on hurting her. There is now an outrage swing in our favour."

"That's good. People are starting to see Laurel for who she is. I knew it wouldn't be long before someone told the truth about her."

Alex sat quietly, half smiling at Morgan, while Francine picked up her tablet again.

"Quite," Francine said. "I mean, it's not like some well-meaning person wouldn't put a few well-meaning messages on a few boards and spread a little positivity."

"Ah, well, in that case, the well-meaning person should probably get a great big thank you." Morgan smiled at Alex.

Alex sat forward and poured more tea. "Yes, thank you."

"Just doing my job," Francine said without looking up.

"Well, you are appreciated, even if I don't say it often enough."

Francine glanced up at Alex. "I just wish it were enough to bring Goran back to the table. Still nothing from him. I've reached out but…"

Sipping her tea, Alex relaxed back into the seat. "I'm the happiest I've been in a long time. Whatever happens, I'm on the right path."

"Speaking of which." Morgan grinned. "You promised to spend an hour with me in town."

"I did. Add official tour guide to my repertoire, will you, Fran?"

"Just make sure you're back by three at the latest. Just because you can't talk about the gangster life choices, don't mean you get out of local press junket."

"I'll have her returned as planned," Morgan said, grabbing her jacket from the back of the couch.

Arm in arm, Morgan and Alex strolled the historic roads that interweaved the town centre, passing under overhanging timber buildings, and dodging tourists. It had started to rain, as the weather was almost obliged to do in autumn, no matter which part of the UK you were in.

People dashed into shops and cafés and pubs, and they followed, pushing open the door to the first shop they came to. When they stepped inside and shut the door behind them, they found they were the only people in the store. A scent of incense hit first, something musky and dense that sat heavily in the air.

Rows of wooden shelving filled the space with everything from books on the occult, black magic, and witchcraft. There were beautifully designed boxes of angel cards and tarot cards.

"This is interesting," Alex said, nudging Morgan when she spotted what looked like a voodoo doll. "Maybe I should get one and use it on Laurel."

"Don't tempt me," Morgan whispered. "Hey, look at these." She picked up a pair of candles shaped like a skull.

"There's a message for you." A voice out of nowhere spooked them both and they jumped, twisting around at the same time. A woman stood in the doorway behind a counter. She looked ordinary and not at all like one might assume given the type of shop it was if one was to think of things stereotypically. Smiling, she beckoned them over. "You've struggled with something recently. Something that is now lifting." She spoke to Alex before turning her head slowly to look at

Morgan. "And you are about to make a decision that will change your life forever."

"That sounds interesting." Morgan smiled politely.

"You're going to make a huge change in your life."

Alex was about to speak when the woman shook her head. "Not you. Your path is already being walked, you are where you're meant to be, but you." She turned back to Morgan. "There's a change coming, something big."

Morgan smiled politely. "I hope so."

"It's stopped raining," Alex said to Morgan before turning back to the woman, "Thank you."

She smiled and tilted her head slightly before watching then both walk towards the door. "She'll say yes," she said quickly, just as Morgan reached for the door.

Alex turned back. "Sorry?"

"She'll say yes. When you ask. The answer will be yes."

"Okay, thank you."

Stepping outside they both burst into giggles.

"Well, that was weird." Morgan laughed. "Come on, we've got to get back."

Chapter Sixty-Two

St Paul's- London

Princesses and Queens had walked these aisles and been watched and heard by the people of the day who had venerated them. Now, Alex stood on the stage and looked out at where her audience would sit and listen to her later that evening.

There had been something missing in her life for a long time, and her mother was right. Francine had been, too. It wasn't just love, it wasn't just music, it wasn't just anything; it was everything, it was the reason she existed at all. Passion. She'd lost it somewhere along the road between the accident all those years ago and where she was now.

She'd spent all those years trying to prove herself to everybody else when everyone else was just waiting for her to prove it to herself. She was Sasha, and her music had transcended everything else in her world for so long that when love was offered, it was she who had pushed it away. Not the Laurels of the world, or the Calistas; well, maybe that wasn't a bad thing. She chuckled to herself at that thought.

"You okay?" Francine asked. "Something funny?"

Alex stared down at her. "I was just thinking how lucky I was to have avoided a romance with Dr Urquhart."

"Alright, I'm not even going to ask why that thought is in your head." She climbed the stairs up to the stage. "But I'm glad you picked the right doctor."

"Where is Morgan?" They'd not seen each other all morning. Alex had left earlier than usual. The tour until now had been in reasonably small venues, but St Paul's was a different kettle of fish altogether. Over 1600 people would attend this recital.

Francine answered, "Entertaining her family at the hotel. They just arrived, and she said something about seeing her niece for the first time in—"

"Yes, Christie, she was very excited about it. I didn't realise it was that time already."

"Time flies when you're having fun." Francine smiled. Because Alex was having fun again. The joy when she played was obvious for all to see and hear. "I'll leave you to it. But hair and make-up in ten."

Alex nodded and started up with one of her newer compositions, loud and upbeat. Allegretto, allegro, vivace, and presto. Her hands flew across the keys, lifting her from the stool till she was almost upright as the music crashed into crescendo.

"Bravo." A figure she recognised walked towards the stage, clapping furiously. "Bravissima."

"Goran, what are you doing here?" She stood up and made her way down the steps. He was the last person she had expected to hear from.

"I came to see when are we working together, Alex? I give you time. I see the news, the passion. Oh, my, you push her hard into the pool, huh?" He chuckled. "I need to work with this, to create with this." His hand waved around her.

"You still want to work with me? After everything that's happened?"

"You go to court, you take the fine, pay her off, I don't care, we build a gangster reputation." He laughed again. "Come on, Alexandra, don't leave me hanging, begging. I'm a proud man."

"I'd be honoured, Goran, but I have a stipulation. I don't want to create just an album. I want to tell a story." She smiled and walked him up the steps of the stage towards her piano. "I want to create something that is more. I want it to flow, from the beginning, those first tentative movements towards something brighter, flowing into the veins of those who listen and bringing them along on a journey of love, lust, and something hot. Something that burns the soul and leaves the listener wanting it for themselves."

He grinned. "I think we can work together very well. And soon, okay? I want to embrace this passion, yes? We are going to create magic together."

The sound of people talking and footsteps running towards them made them both turn. A small child in a pink coat with long dark hair in bunches grinned at them as she ran, chased by Morgan.

"Christie, come back here, you little monkey," Morgan said, as she pretended to chase the little girl.

Christie ran straight up to Alex and flung herself at her legs, holding on for dear life as she moved around behind her, hiding from Morgan.

"Oh, hello." Alex laughed.

"You have a new fan." Goran grinned.

"Apparently, I do." Alex tried to twist around but the kid just moved with her.

"I'm sorry," Morgan said as she closed the gap. "She's a little bit overexcited."

"It's fine. Morgan, this is Goran. Goran, my girlfriend, Dr Morgan Kelly."

He held out a hand and shook hers when offered. "It's a pleasure." He looked over her shoulder at the small group of people working their way towards them. "Your family is here, so I will leave you. I have dinner plans before I am back here to witness the magic."

"Thank you, Goran, we'll speak later." Alex waved goodbye just as Morgan's family closed the space between them.

"*That* Goran?" Morgan asked urgently.

Alex nodded. "We're going to work together."

"That's awesome. I'm so excited for you." Morgan threw her arms around Alex's neck and kissed her. "Oh, sorry, Alex, this is my mum and dad, my brother Mason and his partner, Alison, and this is Leanne, Christie's mum, and obviously…you've met Christie." The little girl was bored now she wasn't being chased and slunk over to her mum to be picked up.

"Hi." Alex smiled at them all. "Why don't we all grab something to eat and get to know each other?"

"That sounds like a lovely idea," Morgan's mum said before adding, "I'm Steph, this is Gary."

Morgan's dad fiddled with the collar on his shirt before saying, "How do."

"Okay, people." Francine's loud voice cut through the air. "Table's booked and waiting for you all. You have two hours before your star needs to be back here. The rest of you are not required for another hour, so let's go."

She turned and led the way back down the long aisle with everyone following.

"All good?" Morgan asked.

Alex slid her arm around Morgan's waist as they walked slowly behind everyone else. "Yes, couldn't be happier. I'm excited. Tonight will be amazing, on stage and then…" She glanced at Morgan and smirked.

"The after-show party?" Morgan chuckled and kissed her cheek. "I'm looking forward to tonight's euphoria."

"Sweetheart, you have no idea what's coming your way."

"Is that so?" Morgan bit her lip. "I can't wait."

Epilogue

"And the award for Best Contemporary Classical Composition goes to…" The camera zoomed into the envelope, the famous fingers opening it, the paper being slid out of it and then, "Sasha, for 'Euphoria.'"

It took a moment for it to register; as the audience rose up applauding, Francine nudged her on one side, Goran on her other side leaned in to kiss her cheek. She looked as though she were in shock as she finally stood up and began to make her way towards the stage and the coveted award waiting for her. "Euphoria" blared out of the speakers.

Morgan and her team crowded around the small TV, and all watched, slapping her on the back and congratulating her like she had done something spectacular.

"Wow, your song," Pascal said. "Your song just won a gong."

It was common knowledge since the release of the album that it was dedicated to Morgan. Alex didn't shut up about it. Every interviewer would always ask, and she would happily tell them about the love of her life and the inspiration behind the music.

Morgan wiped a tear discreetly. Happy tears, of course.

A machine beeped, and one of the nurses touched her shoulder. "I'll see to it." Morgan smiled gratefully.

"Shh, she's gonna do her speech," someone else said, and the volume was turned up just a notch.

"Goodness, wow," Alex said as she looked around the auditorium and blinked a little at the bright lights. "Wow." She laughed and took a few deep breaths to compose herself. "Two days ago, I got on a plane and left behind the person who truly deserves to be here with me, accepting this honour. Dr Morgan Kelly, this is for you, and all of those working with you tonight, helping people and putting those in need first. You are my inspiration. You are the light in my life and calm in my storm and when I get home—" She grinned and stared straight into the camera. "When I get home, will you marry me?"

Morgan stood open-mouthed.

"Oh my god, did she just propose live on TV to the entire world?" Pascal said, with the biggest shocked grin any face could have.

"Morgan, what are you going to say?" another nurse asked. But Morgan was still flabbergasted. She watched the screen still as the camera followed Alex off to the side and away, with the next hosts appearing to announce the next winners.

"Dr Kelly, I need you in room four, patient's struggling to breathe," someone called out, and Morgan shook herself out of it. She was the duty doctor and needed to put her private life on hold.

"Coming," she called back, grabbing her stethoscope and tugging it around her neck.

The flight back home felt like the longest Alex had ever been on. Goran had stayed behind, enjoying every minute of their collaboration. Francine, however, was already planning.

"Well, at least the headlines will change from 'Sasha fined for pool push cat fight,'" she said from her pod in first class.

Alex smiled. "Can we never mention that again. I'm just glad that Philip convinced the judge to agree to an injunction to keep her away from us."

"But it was so much fun. Alexandra Montgomery, criminal." Francine chuckled. "Even your mother was impressed."

"Not as impressed as she was to listen to 'Euphoria' and be able to brag to all of her friends that I won a Grammy."

"You got what you wanted. Everything we planned."

"Not quite, I'm still working." Alex turned her head towards Francine. "But I wouldn't change it. You were right, I'd lost my passion."

"Don't worry, I'll take the plaudits at the wedding for getting you both together and creating the inspiration for the best classical music for a generation." She pulled her glasses off and turned to face Alex.

"Did you know before you went up on stage that you were going to propose?"

"Yes." Alex sipped her champagne, a gift from the airline. "I decided while they were reading the nominations, that if I won, I'd do it."

"Literally every headline is asking if she said yes."

Alex laughed. "Well, they're going to have to wait until I know."

"You think she will?"

Sipping the champagne again while she considered it, Alex said, "I am quietly confident. Otherwise, I wouldn't have asked. We've been living together for a year almost now. I know that we both want the happy ever after."

"You think she saw it?"

"I know her mother was watching, so even if Morgan missed it, her mother would have filled her in." She held up her phone. "I've already had several texts from Steph."

"I take it both families would be happy about it?"

"I don't care if they are or not. Morgan is the only person whose opinion I'm looking for."

Alex twisted in her seat, so she could see Francine more fully. "Remember when we were on the cathedral tour, and Morgan and I explored Canterbury?"

"Yes, and you both came back like drowned rats." Francine chuckled. "I remember. Gert was not happy."

"We did, and no, she wasn't." Alex laughed at the memory. "But before that rain shower, we escaped another one by quickly entering the nearest shop. I don't know what kind of shop you'd call it, it was all about the occult."

Francine's eyes widened. "Dear lord, imagine being snapped coming out of there. The headlines!"

Alex smiled. "It would have been a nightmare, but we didn't know until we'd stepped inside. Anyway, while we were nosing about waiting for it to stop raining the woman who ran the shop started talking to us...she told Morgan a big change was coming, then the rain stopped and we were about to leave when she said to me, 'She'll say yes. When you ask. The answer will be yes.' I didn't think any more about it until these past few weeks. I knew I wanted to ask her. I just hadn't worked out how, but in the back of my mind, I kept hearing the woman say, 'she will say yes.'"

"What a load of pipsqueak." Francine scoffed and opened another small bottle of champagne. "It all sounds romantic though, so make sure you remind her."

"I will." Alex laughed.

Alex pushed on her sunglasses, grabbed her bag, and after speaking with the air stewards who had looked after her, she followed Francine off the plane. They were given a ride to passport control and then baggage and then with everything loaded up onto a trolley, they had to walk through the area where hopefully Mike would be waiting for them. Francine took charge of the trolley, allowing Alex the opportunity to have both hands free to cover her face if there were too many photographers and flashbulbs.

As the doors slid open, she looked up and found a familiar face. Not Mike, but Morgan. Her face broke out into a huge smile when she saw the sign Morgan held in the air, everyone around them all watching and waiting for Alex to react.

She took off running. Reaching Morgan, she threw her arms around her neck and kissed her just as a huge cheer went up as those around them realised what was happening, and the small group of photographers started to snap away.

"Yes?" she asked.

Morgan nodded. "Yes, what was you expecting?"

Alex shrugged and held her face in her hands. "I missed you. I wasn't sure if you'd even seen it, or what you thought about it."

"Have to admit, was a little shocked, but Mrs Dodd's rectal collapse soon brought me back down to earth." Morgan grinned. "So, we gonna celebrate? Because I have the next seventy-two hours off, and I thought we could just stay naked."

"That's a plan I think I can definitely stick to."

"Excellent, because I have some euphoria of my own that's been building."

Alex reached for her hand. "I want to do so many obscene things to you later."

"I wasn't expecting anything less. You've got four lonely nights to make up for."

"I'll be at the car," Francine said, pushing the luggage past them. "Congratulations." She grinned.

Alex waved to the few people still looking at them. Leaning in and covering her mouth from any potential lip readers, she said, "Can you even begin to imagine how much euphoria I have building since winning…with nobody to help take care of that?"

"No pay rise for Francine then," Morgan teased. "Don't worry, I'm fully loaded on calories. I'm going to let you play me like a symphony and open a door to eternity."

"I love you," Alex said simply.

"I should hope so. I love everything about you and being with you, and I'm going to love being your wife." She squeezed Alex's hand. "Knight, however, said he expects to be asked."

Alex laughed at that. "I bet he does."

"Let's go home."

If you enjoyed Alex and Morgan's story, please consider leaving a review.

https://Mybook.to/EuphoriaCHS

You can sign up to Claire's Newsletter for all the news and upcoming book information:

https://bit.ly/EuphoriaCHS

You can follow Claire on social media.

Website:

www.itsclastevofficial.co.uk

Twitter: @Itsclastev

https://twitter.com/ClaStevOfficial

TikTok: @ItsClaStevofficial

https://www.tiktok.com/@itsclastevofficial

Instagram: @ItsClaStevofficial

https://www.instagram.com/itsclastevofficial

Facebook: https://www.facebook.com/groups/clairehightonstevenson

In the event that you found an issue with the book. If you think there is a typo, or a formatting issue etc, please message Claire: Claire@itsclastevofficial.co.uk

Printed in Great Britain
by Amazon